THE PUCK STOPS HERE

RACHAEL STEWART

Boldwood

First published in Great Britain in 2025 by Boldwood Books Ltd.

Copyright © Rachael Stewart, 2025

Cover Design by Lisa Horton

Cover Images: Lisa Horton

The moral right of Amy Andrews to be identified as the author of this work has been asserted in accordance with the Copyright, Designs and Patents Act 1988.

Every effort has been made to obtain the necessary permissions with reference to copyright material, both illustrative and quoted. We apologise for any omissions in this respect and will be pleased to make the appropriate acknowledgements in any future edition.

A CIP catalogue record for this book is available from the British Library.

Paperback ISBN 978-1-83633-172-8

Large Print ISBN 978-1-83633-173-5

Hardback ISBN 978-1-83633-171-1

Ebook ISBN 978-1-83633-174-2

Kindle ISBN 978-1-83633-175-9

Audio CD ISBN 978-1-83633-166-7

MP3 CD ISBN 978-1-83633-167-4

Digital audio download ISBN 978-1-83633-168-1

This book is printed on certified sustainable paper. Boldwood Books is dedicated to putting sustainability at the heart of our business. For more information please visit https://www.boldwoodbooks.com/about-us/sustainability/

Boldwood Books Ltd, 23 Bowerdean Street, London, SW6 3TN

www.boldwoodbooks.com

To Amy, Pippa and Clare,
My ride-or-die writer besties,
forever grateful for this project and for you.
Much love & prosecco!
xoxo

IN THE BEGINNING
CHICAGO, O'HARE AIRPORT, 21 DECEMBER

Astrid Sinclair merrily hummed along to Dean Martin's 'Let it Snow' as she sauntered through O'Hare airport... Okay, so sauntered didn't quite capture the shoulder-barging, bag-negotiating affair that was truly going on.

The place was rammed. Stuffed with grumpy passengers thanks to the DELAYED status littering the screens overhead. Caused by the – yes, you guessed it – snow.

So much snow, good old Dean would be proud.

And so was Astrid. Because it meant she wasn't going anywhere just yet. And every minute spent on US soil was another minute out of the UK where her mother, her mother's fresh squeeze, and an endless sea of questions about her daughter's *'latest failed relationship'* awaited.

And that was a topic-cum-man Astrid *never* wanted to explore again.

Especially when it was *that* time of the month, her PMDD – Premenstrual Dysphoric Disorder for those in want of a mouthful – choosing to visit right along with Santa.

So yup, she was more than happy to enjoy the sprinkling of

Christmas *this* side of the Atlantic for as long as humanly possible.

'Do you have to?'

'Excuse me?'

Some guy was giving her the evils. The woman next to him wasn't looking too chipper either. Though they *did* have two toddlers in tow and a screaming bairn strapped to said woman's bosom. Astrid winced. *Rather you than me.*

'The whole humming thing?' the guy said. 'It's a bit much...'

She backed away, zipping her lips with her fingers and tossing an imaginary key over her shoulder as she went. He probably thought she was bonkers, but she wasn't about to join in the frenzy. If her journalistic idol Gay Talese could make Frank Sinatra with a cold work for his creative juices, she could make a snow-crazed airport do the same for her. All she needed was a teeny tiny space to squeeze her butt and her laptop into and the words would flow.

But finding such a teeny tiny space in one of the country's busiest airports amidst the city's worst snowstorm in decades was proving to be as rare as unicorn poop – the stuff of pink magic.

'Miss?'

A woman burst through the heaving bodies, a bona fide puff of said *pink.*

Pink hair, pink lippy, pink clothes – pink!

Blinded, Astrid leapt back, taking out a crisp-looking guy in a suit who soon perked up when she gave him the dazzles – a smile she had perfected thanks to a lifetime of clutzy mishaps.

She waved him away as Ms Pink closed in once more...

'We have 10 per cent off at Just Desserts!'

She thrust out a fuchsia pink flyer in an equally pink talon-tipped hand.

'What's that?'

'A dessert bar just around the corner.' The woman smiled, her sparkling warmth as welcome as the DELAYED stamp on Astrid's flight. 'We do cocktails too!'

'Now you're talking...'

Astrid snapped up the flyer and scanned its contents, her eyes bugging out at the array of cocktail-themed cakes and cake-themed cocktails – *yum!*

'Doubt I'll get a seat though; every man and his wife must've set up camp in there.'

'You could be lucky,' the woman said with a wink, her bright pink hair too unicorn to ignore, and Astrid laughed.

'I'll check it out. Thank you.'

Ms Pink wasn't wrong. Round the corner, standing loud and pinky-proud in the middle of two thoroughfares, was Just Desserts. Not only that, but smack bang in the centre was her bright and shiny luck – a table, freshly cleaned and gleaming.

Gotcha!

Weaving like a bat-out-of-hell carry-on case losing its wheels, Astrid made a run for it. And all was going swimmingly until a waitress appeared in her path with what looked like a tray of chemistry experiments topped with candyfloss. *Holy shiiiiitttttttt.* Like a movie in slow-mo, Astrid took a giant leap for mankind – aka her beloved aviator jacket – and flew straight into the back of the chair she'd been aiming for. Crotch first!

'Fuckity-fuck!' she swore at the ground, face screwed up, eyes squeezed shut. When she eased them open it was to find three pairs of hands gripping the other chairs, the same pink leaflet scrunched in each.

She swiped her riotous mane out of her eyes and glanced around at her would-be table competition.

A sophisticated blonde with grey eyes as sharp as her clothes.

Another blonde, blue-eyed, softer in every way.

And an edgy-looking redhead, hazel eyes as electric as her hair.

They *all* wanted this table. And *bad*.

'If none of you are with anyone else,' the redhead said, 'we could share?'

Astrid was about to say, 'Thank fuck for that,' but she'd dropped the F-bomb twice already and she wasn't Hugh Grant enough to say it a third. Not among strangers at any rate.

Especially those close to her own twenty-six years and unlikely to understand the whole *Four Weddings and a Funeral* addiction. Her mother had started it, nurtured it over a gazillion rewatches, and now she couldn't shake it. Much like the PMDD, though the *FWAAF* hand-me-down brought giggles not gloom.

'I'm game.' Astrid threw down her bag and case. Coats were surrendered. Introductions were made.

The sophisticated blonde, Bella, was a posh New Yorker, a socialite through and through. Astrid's gran, *the* Lady Ashford, would totally dig her.

The doe-eyed blonde, Sienna, was from small-town Massachusetts.

And Paige, the redhead, was a fellow Brit.

'What can I getcha?'

Astrid glanced up at the waitress who'd appeared as if on cue and gazed longingly at the brightly lit bar with all the alcoholic beverages and all the sugary carbs... It was ten in the morning, but this was an airport. Normal rules didn't apply, right?

'Would you think me a terrible lush if I got a glass of prosecco?' Paige asked.

Astrid grinned. The redhead was her kind of woman.

'Oh God no.' Sienna heaved a sigh of relief. 'I hate flying and waiting around in airports even more. Let's get a bottle. I'll help you.'

Turned out the soft blonde was Astrid's kind of woman too.

'I'll have a glass,' Bella chimed in.

Make that both blondes.

Astrid glanced at the wall of clocks mounted above the bar, each displaying times from different capital cities around the world. 'It's five o'clock in Berlin.' She grinned at the waitress. 'Make it four.'

Because Astrid was settling in for the ride... work could wait a while.

* * *

Two bottles and two hours later...

Yup, that's right, two on both counts!

Funny how bubbles and bavardage could easily make one forget they were supposed to be doing a spot of typey-typey on the tappy-tappy thing still stowed away between one's feet.

But Astrid was too busy scrolling through Paige's business account on Insta, her friend's Virtual Assistant biz was crazy impressive. And entirely Paige's own doing too. 'I can't believe you have your own VA business. That's awesome.'

Her new bestie shrugged like it was nothing. 'Thanks.'

'So you don't have an office or anything?'

'Nope.' Red tendrils bounced, tickling at Astrid's nose they were sat that close together. 'I actually house sit for people so I move around a lot and the nature of my business means I can work from wherever I am. Have laptop, will travel.'

Astrid got that. She was a bit of a nomad herself, her work as a freelance journalist taking her all over the world in pursuit of her next big scoop.

'Is it why you're in the US? Work?'

'No. I was at a wedding in Chicago.'

'Oh, how lovely,' Sienna crooned. 'How was it?'

'You know. Pavlova dress. Drunken best man's speech. Smooshing cake into each other's faces. A handsy Uncle Chip.'

Ugh! Astrid swapped her phone for her drink – there'd been one too many *step*dads like Uncle Chip back in the day.

'I'd rather not talk about weddings,' Bella blurted.

'Not a fan?' Paige asked.

'Absolutely not.'

'Don't believe in love?'

'I did. And then six months ago I stood up in front of 400 guests to let them know that my groom wasn't coming.'

'Holy mother of...' Astrid spluttered over her drink, free hand launching out to grab Bella's forearm. 'You were jilted?'

'Yup. By text. The morning of...'

'By *text*? What kind of scumbag does that?'

'Who is he?' Sweet Sienna spat fire. 'Tell me! I'll bring you his head.'

Everyone laughed but beneath the joviality the sense of injustice burned deep... or was that just indigestion from the fizz and the sugar and the oh-so pretty candyfloss? Eek!

'He's not a bad person really, he just did a bad thing...'

And then Bella launched into a series of excuses while Astrid ground her teeth, because she'd heard it all before with Mum and her exes. They'd always had a reason to be a shit. Worse, they'd always managed to turn each one on Mum. Forever *her* fault, not theirs.

'Doesn't excuse him leaving you standing at the altar,' Sienna said.

'Via *text*,' Astrid stressed as her mind turned to her own *'failed relationship'* and how that had been very much *not* her fault. But her guilt was real. And she shuddered with reignited horror as the six-month-old memory clawed its way to the surface.

'Well!' she announced, recognising the kindred spirits around her and the safe space they had created. She could share her sordid little secret. Better still, her ex could get a verbal pasting by these ladies and make her feel a smidge vindicated. 'You can string mine up!'

'Were you jilted as well?' Sienna's big blue eyes rounded on her.

'No.' She took a courage-boosting gulp of fizz, then said, 'Unbeknownst to me, he'd already trotted up that aisle and merrily said "I do" to someone else.'

Bella – gorgeous, sophisticated, elegant, Bella – eyed her closely and Astrid withstood her scrutiny because it wasn't judgement she saw, but sympathy. 'So, he turned you into the other woman?'

'Too right he did.' Astrid's shoulders sagged, knowing that Bella got it, sensing they all got it. 'Made me feel like a piece of shit.'

Sienna shook her head, her honeyed locks doing a little dance of their own. 'Are you freaking kidding me? He was already married?'

'He's an artist too, all about creating the feels in people... Chase Miller can give you *the feels* alright. The kind you want F-all to do with. Believe me.'

'Chase Miller?' Bella repeated, as though recognising the name. But then of course she would. Bella was Upper Crust New York. Bella and 'her set' probably spent their weekends wandering the halls of art galleries as much as the shops along

Fifth Avenue. And Astrid wasn't being bitchy. No, she was distracting herself from the image of Chase's wife appearing at their hotel room door. Ashen and—

'What is *wrong* with these men?' Bella suddenly exclaimed, rocking Astrid's head back into the present. 'Doesn't marriage *mean* anything any more?'

'I don't think men get the concept of commitment,' Sienna murmured. 'Even the ones who seem to get it are just faking it.'

And now they were all looking at Sienna, knowing there was a story to tell.

'Sorry.' She gave a shaky laugh. 'That's a little dramatic, isn't it?'

'What happened?' Bella said.

'My ex kind of just... discarded me. It wasn't like some big, dramatic break-up. I didn't even get the chance to throw plates.' Sienna waved it off, but she wasn't fooling Astrid. She'd seen *that* style of break-up too many times with Mum, and they were the *worst*, the *most* unbearable. Because those were the ones that never made sense. Not to Mum. And not to her. The child in it all.

'I mean, we were just kids, but we were each other's firsts, you know? And I thought we were going to have a life together, but he hightailed it out of town without a backward glance. Like nothing we had mattered.'

Astrid downed her drink with a muttered curse. Men. *Bastard* men, and the shitty hand of pain they dealt.

'Can I bring you anyone's head?' Sienna asked Paige, who choked on a laugh.

The nervous titter had Astrid's Spidey-senses tingling. People only ever wanted to give away what they were comfortable with... when the really interesting stuff lay in the *un*comfortable.

And this definitely had Paige on edge.

'I broke up with my ex, Harvey,' she eventually admitted, 'after a brief, intense relationship and then he... posted naked pictures and video of me online. He'd taken them without my knowledge or consent.'

Every curse imaginable raced through Astrid's mind along with the billion-and-one hit pieces she wanted to release into the world about this man she knew nothing about but already wanted to ruin with every fibre of her being.

'Revenge porn?' Sienna hissed.

Paige nodded. 'I've never felt so degraded.' Her fiery-haired friend dropped her gaze to the table in humiliation – *humiliation*? – as she told them the whole sorry tale, from a dedicated law student with a bright future to a uni dropout with stunted career prospects, all because of a man!

Astrid shrivelled up inside. Ugh, men! She filled up everyone's glass, trying to get a handle on her emotions before she trusted herself to speak.

'They shouldn't be allowed to get away with it,' Sienna suddenly declared.

Now *that* Astrid wholeheartedly agreed with. 'Damn right they shouldn't!'

'Look, what if we...' Sienna did a quick sweep of the circle and leaned in, encouraging them all to do the same. 'I know this sounds crazy and I may be a little drunk.' And the little cutesy hiccoughed which caused them all to chuckle. 'What if we took it upon ourselves to exact some revenge?'

Astrid's eyes widened. Revenge! Was she serious?

And if so...

'I don't mean murdering them or anything.' Sienna waved a hand that Astrid had to duck. 'I mean, look, these guys have had everything go their way, right? They got to walk all over us. Or walk out on us. Why should they just get to live their best lives while we're picking up the remnants of ours? Why not have a little fun at their expense?'

'What kind of fun?' Bella asked warily.

'Nothing serious,' Sienna assured. 'Stuff that would inconvenience them. That we could have a laugh over. Like, signing them up to hundreds of mailing lists. Or putting a dead fish in their wheel hubs...'

Sienna kept reeling off ideas and Astrid stared at her in wonder, amazed that behind those big blue eyes hid such a mischievous mind. The woman was a genius!

'Some of those things would require us to get close,' Bella said.

'That's why we pick someone else's ex.'

'It's an excellent plan,' Astrid blurted. 'So good, I wish I'd thought of it. Who would you pick?'

'Harvey the horrible,' Sienna said, without hesitation. 'If he spends time regularly in the US, I'm sure I'll be able to figure out something. You?'

Well, if Sienna had Harvey taken care of then...

'I'd take your heartbreaker. Any guy who'd just walk out on a sweetheart like you deserves to be played a little.'

'And I'd take your cheating, married, bastard ex,' Bella announced, and Astrid wanted to giggle. In the two hours they had talked, watching Bella become a little unglued was fun in an adoring, newfound friend kind of a way.

'Which leaves you with Olly.' Bella looked at Paige. 'And that's perfect because he slunk back to England after the wedding. To his dad's place in Cornwall. How's your sitting schedule for the new year?'

And just like that Paige and Bella started talking deets. *Actual* deets!

They were *really* going to do this...

'Are we really going to do this?' Paige's hesitant voice over-rode Astrid's eager inner voice.

'Well, I sure as hell am,' she confirmed, the fire Chase had lit months ago now burning bright with the tales from her friends. And the fizz. And the fondant fancies. 'I don't know about you, but I'll sleep a little better knowing Horrible Harvey is getting his comeuppance.'

'Look, this only works if we all agree,' Sienna said, taking a more measured approach. 'Nobody should feel pressured into doing it if it doesn't sit right.'

'God, fuck, yes!' Astrid plopped a fondant fancy in whole to stifle her loose lips... though they were sinking a few men, not entire ships. 'The last thing I want to do,' she said over her mouthful, 'is browbeat my new co-conspirators.' She swallowed. 'Sorry, besties.'

'I do love a cream tea,' Paige said, and Astrid blinked. Cream tea? *Ah*, Cornwall, Cornish Cream Tea. Gotcha! 'I'd be safe there?'

'Definitely,' Bella rushed out. 'For all his commitment-phobe tendencies, he's a true gentleman. Painfully polite in that very English way. And I know he feels terribly guilty about the jilting. Which I'm perfectly okay exploiting to get you in there. I still have his number.'

'Oh yes,' Astrid said, her pulse picking up again. 'That's a great plan. You could text him now.' She glanced at the trusty clocks. 'It's six in the evening over there.'

They all looked at each other, still debating until Sienna declared it a case of 'kismet'... If Olly replied there and then, the plan was meant to be. If he didn't, they'd all had a laugh talking the talk without the walk.

So, Bella texted and no one moved.

Astrid wasn't sure anyone even breathed.

She felt like Hugh Grant stuck in the vanity cupboard while his mate *finally* got his end away in – yes, you guessed it – *FWAAF*. That was until an incoming text chimed sealing Olly's fate.

The trap was set. Karma was afoot!

And *that* needed toasting.

'To just desserts,' Astrid declared, raising a fresh glass of prosecco to her new besties as 'Last Christmas' rang out through the PA system, and they all clinked glasses.

'Now,' Paige said to Bella. 'Tell me more about Olly.'

'And while you're doing that' – Astrid turned to Sienna – 'you're coming with me. We have your heartbreaker to discuss... *and* I need the loo.'

'The perfect place to talk about him,' Sienna muttered as Astrid hauled her to her feet and made for the ladies. 'Aiden belongs in the toilet.'

She laughed. 'So his name's Aiden?'

'Yup. I told you he was a twin, right?'

'No?'

'An NHL player, too. Well, they both are...'

Astrid almost lost her footing. 'Are you kidding me?'

Sienna gave that cutesy hiccough. 'Aiden and Blake Carter, they play ice hockey for the New York Titans.'

'What the actual...' Astrid stopped in her tracks, jarring Sienna back. 'Aiden is *the* Aiden of the Titan Twins!'

Sienna wrinkled up her nose. 'Yeah, but he wasn't when we were together. He was just Aiden, my guy. Mom had died, Dad was a mess and heading for prison—'

'*Prison*?'

'He was in a car accident. It wasn't his fault but the authorities...' She took an unsteady breath. 'Anyway, Aiden was my everything, the one person I could depend on, and he promised me the world, said he'd take me with him. But *hello*, here I still am and he's...' She waved a hand skyward. 'I was just the lowly fool who believed him.'

'You're no fool.'

'And you're too kind.'

'Na-ah. He let you go; that makes *him* the fool in my book.'

She gave a lopsided smile. 'A fool you could break a little for me?'

Big blue eyes blinked up at her and Astrid stared back at the woman.

Sweet Jesus! Dealing with an unknown entity was one thing. But dealing with someone whose face she'd seen plastered on billboards and commercials – a sports hero adored by the masses! – was something else entirely.

Hell, he was right *there* hanging behind the counter of Just Desserts, his great big permatanned head and freaking white grin chowing down on a strawberry *sundae*. And no, she wasn't paying attention to the tightly clad abs sitting just behind said sundae... like what idiot believed you could get a bod like that with a dish like—

'Astrid?'

Blue eyes were still blinking, and she was still gawping!

She snapped her gob shut. Shock. That was all it was. Shock and the hit of reality now that she had a face to put to the man.

And of course, she could do this for Sienna. Sienna and her newfound friends. Because they'd made a pact that was bigger than one person, bigger than the four of them; it was about dishing out a little karma for all the wronged women of this world.

'Yes!' She hugged Sienna to her chest. 'Yes, I can do this.'

She bloody well *would* do this.

If she could bedazzle Mr Crisp amidst a frenzied airport, she could sure as shit bedazzle an ice hockey all-star chillaxed in his own environment.

'I take it by all the promotional stuff' – she hooked her arm in Sienna's and strode forth once more – 'he isn't media shy?'

Sienna gave a bark of a laugh. 'What do you think?'

'Perfect.' She grinned. 'Just perfect!'

Her job would give her a way in, all she had to do was come up with an angle.

'Now tell me all you can and don't skimp on the detail...'

'Do you think he's a boob man?'

Bella sprayed wine into her hand, narrowly missing Astrid's laptop propped open on the bed and the clothing strewn all around. 'Do I what?'

'You know, boobs!'

Astrid grabbed her own, thrusting them up in her cropped Metallica tee as she scrutinised her refection in the floor-to-ceiling mirrors lining one wall of the bedroom in her temporary abode, aka her uncle's New York City bolthole.

'You're asking the wrong woman.'

'Sienna didn't say. And I'm serious; in my experience, a man is normally one or the other.'

Bella frowned. 'One or the other?'

'You know, tits or arse.'

Bella choked on a laugh, but Astrid was pretty sure Paige would get it if she'd been able to join the Just Desserts group video call she'd left running on the off chance she'd wake up for it.

'If you say so...' Bella murmured, lowering her gaze to the

laptop and angling her head this way and that as she studied Research Exhibit C, a collage of Aiden Carter's ex-girlfriends.

Astrid joined her on the bed, did the same. Nope. It was no good. These ladies were giving nothing away. Maybe it was because most of them dressed like they were attending church. An uber glam, designer-gear-only church. A church for fashion-istas, if there ever was such a thing.

'Do we have to talk anatomy on his exes?' came Sienna's disembodied voice.

'Sissi, finally!' Astrid clicked on the video call and her little square joined the collage – how apt. 'You made it!'

'At the wrong time by the sound of it.'

'Sorry, babe.' Astrid gave her an apologetic smile. 'But if I'm gonna reel him in I need to nail my image; it's essential I get this right for Operation Heartbreak to work.'

'I know,' she grumbled. 'So long as you don't nail him.'

'Ha!' Bella said, hopping off the bed and reaching for the wine bottle. 'Can you imagine?'

'Absolutely not.' Astrid gave an exaggerated shudder. 'This is all about treating him mean, keeping him keen and then cutting him loose. No communication. Nada.'

'Cheers to that,' Bella said, upending the bottle and earning a dribble. 'Oh shit, we're out.'

Both Sienna and Astrid erupted on a laugh.

'What?' Bella asked, wide eyed.

'Did you just say shit?' Sienna said.

'Maybe.'

Astrid shook her head, affection filling her chest for the woman who was swiftly becoming a sister from another mister. She was so glad she was living in the same city for a spell, her uncle's apartment giving her the perfect base from which to work while infiltrating the Titans... And this was Bella's home turf. It also happened to be where a certain Chase Miller was launching a brand new art gallery. *He* was far too close for comfort, but thanks to Bella, comfort was the last thing he'd be experiencing any time soon.

'I fear we've corrupted you, B.'

'It was long overdue,' she declared, swinging the empty bottle. 'I was tired of being Miss Goody Two-Shoes anyway. Now, wine?'

'Please. There's plenty of choice in the kitchen.'

Bella swept from the room and Astrid lowered her gaze to the laptop. She frowned as Sissi gnawed on her bottom lip. 'Are you having second thoughts, love?'

'Not so much second thoughts...' She ran a hand through her blonde ponytail and tugged it over one shoulder. 'It's strange though, to think that in less than twenty-four hours you'll be in the same room as him.'

For you and me both, she wanted to say. The meeting had her feeling kind of squiffy too.

She had known so little about him when she'd made her promise. She'd been too high on alcohol, sugary treats, a frenzied snowbound airport and the buzz of a newfound friendship. She'd been bold and brave and desperate to play her part.

Then she'd googled him at the earliest opportunity. And Aiden Carter had become more than just a 2D sundae-eating, ice hockey all-star pin-up with a dodgy break-up against his name. He'd become a real person with a backstory, a family, a famed reputation... and a very selective dating history.

A history that suggested Astrid was going to have to do more than alter her look if she was going to win him over. She was going to have to undergo a personality transplant.

'There's still time to change your mind, Sissi. I can back out of the Titans meeting?'

'No.' She lifted her chin. 'It's been ten years and it's still there eating away at me. After everything we'd gone through together, everything we'd shared, everything that...' She broke off, her beautiful blue eyes awash with unshed tears and Astrid wanted to reach inside the screen and hug her.

'I know, honey, I know.'

'I just want him to feel what it's like. At least on some level. To be ghosted.'

'I'm going to do my best. My very very best. I promise.'

Because Astrid couldn't imagine it for herself. Ten years and to still have it cut so deep. As much as Chase had hurt her, broken her, she hoped to God she wouldn't still be stewing on it ten years from now. Though Bella was already helping with that.

'Your uncle has seriously good taste in wine,' said the woman herself returning with a fresh bottle.

'He can afford to.'

'Oh, to have a wealthy uncle with a New York City apartment to steal whenever you so wish,' Sienna said, 'and a decent wine collection too. It's the stuff of fantasies.'

'Wait until you see the view, Si,' Bella added.

'Hey, it can be your fantasy too,' Astrid said. 'You're more than welcome to come join me any time.'

'Chance would be a fine thing.'

Between waitressing and studying law, Astrid knew Sienna rarely had a moment to spare, but still...

'You work too hard.'

'Tell me something I don't know.'

That I'm not sure I can do this...

Could she admit that to her friend?

Bella topped up Astrid's glass and passed it to her, grey eyes narrowing as she did so. 'You look pensive. What's wrong?'

Trust Bella to notice. The girl didn't miss a trick.

Astrid blew her unruly waves out of her eyes and thought about how best to say it. 'I'm no Kate Hudson, ladies.'

'No Kate Hudson?' Bella picked up her own glass and flopped down beside her. 'I don't get it... You mean, because she's blonde and most of his exes are blonde?'

'No, not really. Well, not quite.' She gave Sienna a sheepish glance. She didn't want to worry her, or worse, let her down. But at the same time, she needed to get it off her chest. 'I was meaning more in the whole *How to Lose a Guy in Ten Days* sense. The facade...'

'I'm lost,' Bella said, chugging some wine then squinting at the drink. 'Maybe we should have sorted your image before consuming so much wine.'

'She means the film where Hudson's character has to date a guy and scare him off,' Sienna explained. 'Though you're in role reversal.'

'Ha!' Astrid huffed into her glass as she took a nerve-soothing swig. 'I'm no Matthew McConaughey either.'

Bella snorted. 'I don't know, maybe there's a slight resemblance. The twinkly eyes, the dimples, the cheeky streak...'

Astrid gave her a playful shove. 'Hey!'

'If it walks like a duck, swims like a duck...' Sienna said.

'Quacks like a duck,' Bella added.

'Yeah, yeah, I'm the duck, I get it.'

Hell, they were probably right. She had to be cheeky to get access to the people she had over the years, but it still begged the question – could she do *this*?

'I think it would have made more sense for you to take on Aiden, B. You're naturally more his type.'

'Na-ah, one man is enough, and I've got Chase for you. He's driving me crazy enough. Besides, I don't have the right assets to gain access to the Titans like you do.'

'Assets?' She cocked a brow. 'Are we back on the boobs now because—'

'Enough with the boobs!' both girls chorused with a laugh.

'I'm talking about your way in,' Bella said. 'Your job and your skills and your angle!'

Her angle...

She opened up Research Exhibit B. The man who had given the Titans Media and PR team enough cause to bite her hand off when she'd pitched her idea of a profile piece to them.

And no, it wasn't Aiden Carter filling her screen. It was his brother, Blake. The other half of the Titan Twins. Identical in the basics – blue eyes, dark hair, a sensual mouth and jaw of steel. Infamous swoon-worthy dimples too.

But there the similarity ended.

Where Aiden was golden – bronzed skin, clean shaven, carefully groomed, affable Prince Charming in every way – Blake was the total opposite. Dark and brooding, zero tan, all the stubble, and as guarded as Fort Knox... so freaking intriguing that she was salivating, her creative juices overflowing with a need to pick apart what made him tick, what drove that dangerous glint in his eye...

And her brain wasn't the only thing enjoying an extra juicy charge.

Why did she have to dig the bad boy every time?

Hadn't Chase taught her anything?

'He's something,' Bella murmured, leaning in.

From Blake's official headshot for the team, to an action shot mid-play, to an action shot mid-brawl taken outside a New York bar just last week, he was 'something' all over.

It was the brawl that had given her a way in, inspiring an article her heart, soul, and career were now invested in. A feature piece that would deliver the truth on the twins. The past, the present and the glory of these men. Two of the greatest hockey players the world had ever seen.

The aim as the Titans saw it: to turn the tide on Blake's rapidly deteriorating reputation and save his position on the team.

The aim as Astrid saw it: to save one brother's career if he so deserved, while dishing up just desserts on the other.

It had been perfect. It *was* perfect. And it was going to be another great step in her career too. *Vanity Fair* great if she got it right. Which she would. Her professional ability wasn't up for debate. The karma however...

'He's a bit...' Words failed Bella.

'Fierce?' Astrid suggested.

'Uh-huh.'

'Huge?' she added.

'Uh-huh.'

Astrid sipped on her wine as she lost herself in Blake's brooding gaze. 'Hot.'

Bella's head snapped around. 'I was going to say rakish.'

'This is almost as bad as talking about your anatomy,' Sienna said, sipping her own drink and grimacing. 'Next time we do this, can you sneak one of your uncle's bottles my way? This stuff is...' She pulled another face. 'Insufficient.'

'Sorry, babe,' Astrid said, making a mental note to do just that.

'What for? My cheap plonk or having the hots for my ex?'

'That's just it, Aiden's too clean cut for me, but Blake...' Her tummy gave a flutter. 'I don't know.' Only she did know. He was right up her street.

'He terrifies me,' Bella said. 'Are you sure about this?'

'You're meant to be encouraging me, not putting me off.'

'But... look at him.'

Astrid shrugged. 'He doesn't scare me.'

He appealed to her and that was worse. When would her body learn that bad boys were no good? The clue was right there in the name.

'But you were supposed to be getting close to Aiden, not Mr Hard-Ass.'

'*Mr Hard-Ass* is how I got in the door. The team are so well guarded during the season and without the threat of expulsion hanging over Blake, they'd never have agreed to let me shadow them. Besides, he's all bark and no bite. Tell her, Sissi.'

They both looked to Sienna who appeared ever more on edge, her hand twisting through her ponytail. 'The guy I knew won't hurt you; the opposition on the ice, that's another matter.'

'But that fight he got into,' Bella said, pointing one French-manicured nail at the pub scene, 'wasn't on the ice.'

'Rumour has it he was defending a teammate,' Astrid said.

She'd investigated it. Along with everything else she could find in the public domain, info spanning their entire career. Though very little of it had come directly from them. Most of it was hearsay. People with an axe to grind. Old coaches with nothing but praise. Old classmates more interested in getting their name in print than the truth.

And she craved the truth from the horse's mouth.

As did so many other journos, and here she was, *this close* to getting it.

'Do you buy that?' Bella leaned in closer, scanning the text beneath the picture. 'No one's corroborated the story.'

'Because the team will be telling them to keep quiet, paying off people if need be,' Sienna said, the law student in her shining through. 'Hoping it'll all blow over.'

'And I'll find out the truth when I get in there and start asking questions.'

Bella's eyes bugged at her. 'You're going to ask him about the fight?'

'Of course. I'm going to ask *all* the questions.'

'You really want to rattle that snake?'

Astrid shimmied her shoulders. 'I'm all for a bit of rattling.'

Bella squinted at her. 'Are you talking sexy time now, or...'

Astrid laughed. 'And you think *I* have a one-track mind...'

'But you know you're going in there to get Aiden, right?'

'While doing my job. Absolutely.'

'It's the doing both simultaneously that worries me.'

'It's only what you're doing with Chase and working at the gallery.'

'But Chase is a single entity, this is... he doesn't come with a Blake.'

'Bella's right,' Sienna said. 'You don't have to do this. If it's too messy or you're worried about how it'll go down, I'd rather you didn't.'

'Ladies, if you'd seen half the shit I've dealt with in the past, you wouldn't be concerned for a second. The job I can do standing on my head, it's luring Aiden that's the challenge. And we're only talking a bit of mild messing with his ego, nothing career ending. For him or me!'

'I still don't get why you couldn't catch his eye in a VIP club or something,' Bella said, her nails drumming nervously against her glass. 'I could have got you access to one of those.'

'Because from what I can tell the guy doesn't do clubs. He doesn't do parties. He's not Blake.'

'After a game then, just strategically thrown yourself at him, broke a heel and feigned a twisted ankle. Given him no choice but to notice you without having to hang around with...' She nodded to the screen.

'And then what? How could I make him stick around? The

women he's dated, they all had a reason to be on his arm in some way. For a sponsorship deal, an advert, a staged event... work always put them in his path and my job will do the same for me. The more time I get in his life, the more I can mess with it.'

'In that case' – Bella plucked an outfit off the bed and shoved it at her – 'go get this on, because *this* is the one!'

Astrid frowned down at the sedate black skirt suit. 'Really?'

'Quit it with the doubts!'

'Says you!' But she grinned. 'You know, I think wine turns you into a bossy devil.'

Mortified, Bella gawped at her glass. 'Oh, God, do you think?'

'Don't oh God me, B. I love it. You're a *classy* bossy devil.'

And she was going to have to channel some of that classiness if she was going to lure one brother in while writing an expo involving the extremely distracting and disturbing other...

'And don't forget Paige's contribution to the outfit.' Bella grabbed the black-rimmed specs that had arrived in the post that week and handed them to her. 'I think she's suggesting you go in for the whole Clark Kent vibe.'

'You know glasses make a shit disguise, right?'

'It's not about a disguise, it's about getting into character.'

She eyed them with a shrug. 'Well, if it's good enough for Superman...'

'*And* good old Delia with some of those bedroom scenes.' Bella tapped the *very* racy book she had bought for Astrid on the bedside table – a copy of one Bella had been gifted by said Delia at the airport last month. 'Though perhaps it's best not to think of those while...'

She twirled a finger at the guy on the screen.

'Hell, no!' Astrid blurted. Blake and bedroom equalled bad bad bad. 'Justice, here I come... right after I finish this wine!'

2

Blake was fucked.

Royally. Proverbially. Every which way, fucked.

The second he entered the general manager's office and saw the trio stationed behind the desk – Coach, the GM and the pretty PR chick – he'd known.

No one smiled. No one spoke. He took a seat.

To his left, the big screen playing the NHL Network had been muted. To his right, the glass gave a bird's-eye view of the practice rink, and to his rear was the door. The exit through which he wanted to bolt.

He'd never been great at taking a beating lying down – physically or verbally.

Even when he'd earned it.

'You're out of lives, Carter.'

Blake eyed the GM, his clean-shaven face, designer suit and perfect hair irritating the crap out of him. The guy was money through and through. Daddy's money to be precise.

'With respect, Walker...'

Coach winced. PR chick sucked in a breath. And the GM

cocked an unimpressed brow. But Blake couldn't care less. He wasn't about to address the GM with some ass-kissing title. Not when the man had yet to earn it. He'd been gifted the role by his billionaire father, the Titans owner, a year ago. And so far he'd failed to demonstrate any passion for the sport; it was all about him and his appeal to the masses. Not the team.

'With respect,' Blake repeated through his teeth, 'it wasn't me being stretchered off the ice.'

Coach's eyes shot daggers across the table, screaming at him to shut the hell up as Blake's head advised the same. Problem was his mouth liked getting him into trouble and his fists were too quick to follow. But then he'd never been great with words. Doing was more his style.

Just like dear old Dad...

Though Blake didn't prey on the innocent, the weak, the vulnerable, like the old man had.

'And what about the brawl that came after the game?' the PR chick, Stella, clarified, her blue eyes narrowing as she glanced at the tablet in her hand. 'The one you got into outside McGinty's?'

She glanced back up, tucking her smooth blonde bob behind her ear as she pinned him with her cool gaze. A fortnight ago, that gaze had been on fire for him. Today however...

'Someone takes a swing for me, I'm going to swing right back.'

'Even when you're taking a detrimental swing at the Titans every time you do it?'

Blake ground his teeth. 'The guy took a detrimental swing at the Titans first.'

Or more specifically, his teammate Danny and his husband, Ross. Coming out in this business took serious courage. And witnessing the abuse...

Danny and Ross had seen fit to ignore it and walk away, but

Blake had seen red. Truth was he could take people flinging shit at him, but when it was about his family or his buddies, and when it was as vile as...

He clenched his fists, shooting down the memory and the anger it evoked.

'You're not in the playground any more,' Coach said.

'The problem is a lot of people seem to like taking a swing for you,' the GM spoke over him.

Blake shrugged. 'Comes with the territory.'

'For you, a lot more than most. Your fiery nature is a problem,' Stella said, a hint of colour in her cheeks now. Was her head back in the club, recalling what he'd done to her up against the alley wall, what she'd done to him in turn? She hadn't been complaining about 'his nature' then. 'Twenty years ago, it wouldn't have been an issue, you'd be our enforcer, and we'd make no bones about it, but now... the rules are changing.'

'The rules *have* changed,' the GM added.

And officially, he was right. But unofficially, everyone knew it paid to be a hard ass both on and off the ice. And intimidating the opposition was as much a psychological mind game as it was a physical play.

If people feared dancing with you *before* the puck dropped, the advantage was yours for the taking.

'When your behaviour has you in the box more than you're out of it, something's gotta give,' the GM said. '*You've* got to give.'

Blake frowned. What the hell was the schmuck on about? Give? Like, back down? Wave the white flag? Skate out of the brawl, not in? Was he *crazy*? He was nicknamed Fury for a reason...

'You want to stay on the team, you need to change.'

Stay on the team...?

Blake's gut rolled, his skin shrinking until it felt too small for his body. He scanned the trio across the table. Were they serious? Did they not realise his team needed him like this? That this was what he was good at?

Sure, he had skills. Gone were the days where enforcers got a full-time position on the team. But still...

'Coach?' He settled his sights on the man for back-up because if anyone was going to give it, it was him. 'Come on, Fury isn't just a name, it's who I am for the sake of our team.'

'The doc thinks you would benefit from seeing Lisa.'

Not what he wanted Coach to say. And Lisa? Who the hell was—

Wait.

'The *shrink*?'

'Lisa is a sports psychologist,' Stella said smoothly, 'she'll help you get—'

'I don't need no shrink.'

Sports psychologist or not, Lisa was most definitely a shrink.

And hell, he wanted no one poking around up top. His demons were just that. His. No one else's business but his own.

'Your brother seems to think it might help.'

'*Aiden*? Aiden said that? When?'

They had to be kidding him. Aiden was his teammate, his brother both on and off the ice. What the fuck was he playing at? Talking about him behind his back. Feeding this drama. This crazy ass idea.

'I wouldn't look so angry about it,' Stella said in that same smooth tone that was beginning to grate. 'He's trying to do you favour and dig you out of the hole you've found yourself in. You'd do well to take a leaf out of his book.'

Words he'd heard on repeat his entire bloody life. He hadn't listened then, he wasn't about to now.

'I don't need my brother digging me out of anything. As for

taking a leaf, we work because we're yin and yang. He's Ice. I'm Fury. It's what our fans love. It's what the team needs. And it's what the franchise has exploited well enough up until now so I fail to see the problem.'

'*That* we can't exploit.' She pointed to the TV where a replay of last week's match against the Rangers was underway, overlaid by a static shot of him outside McGinty's – the bar he and his buddies favoured when they wanted to avoid the puck bunny circuit.

A bar he wouldn't be able to return to any time soon thanks to this shot that had gone viral.

Even in the dim light being cast by the pub window, his side profile was easily recognisable. The aggression on his face too as he pinned the scumbag to the wall by the scruff of his judgemental neck. The guy had deserved it, running his mouth off like that.

And he'd drawn the first punch, not Blake.

Though saying as much wasn't going to help him now. Nor was the suspicion that the guy had set him up. He'd been *looking* for him to do just this.

If you'd been more like Aiden, you'd have taken a second and realised it in the moment too...

Rolling his head on his shoulders, he stretched out his fingers and took a breath. 'Look, I know—'

'This isn't open to debate, Carter,' the GM cut in. 'From now on, we say jump, you say how high.'

Blake's eyes snapped to his, the fire reigniting – how *not* to help.

The GM shrank back in his seat, eyes lowering as he cleared his throat and adjusted his tie.

'What we're saying is,' Coach hurried out, drawing Blake's laser-focused gaze his way, 'go and see Lisa. Talk. Work out what's going on up there and calm it down out there.' He pointed from Blake's head to the glass. 'You know you're good, Blake. You and your brother, you're our all-stars. The best pair of forwards the Titans have ever seen, but that temper, it needs reining in before it costs you everything. You *and* your brother.'

Blake stiffened. *Low blow, Coach.*

'And while you go about fixing your behaviour, we'll go about fixing your image,' Stella added.

'Fixing my image?' he sneered. 'And how do you plan on doing that, because as we've already established, I'm not my brother. I'm not about to whore myself to the sponsors and pose shirtless with some lousy energy drink to keep the media happy and the dogs at bay.'

That was Aiden's bag. Being the face of whatever paid to top up his brother's nest egg and Blake wasn't about to judge him for it. But he wasn't about to join him either. Never in a million years.

Aiden was the pretty boy. Blake was... how had Stella put it just the other night, the diamond in the rough. He preferred asshole. Blunt and honest. Why try to dress it up?

'The sooner people see you in a different light, the sooner the league will ease off,' Stella said, looking past him to the door and waving someone in.

It had to be Aiden, coming to join the force against him. He turned, ready to give him a piece of his mind and – and lost his tongue.

'Welcome, Astrid,' Stacey said, giving a name to the dark-haired voice-stealing woman stepping in.

Who was *this*? And how soon could he get acquainted? Because *this* was the kind of woman he wouldn't mind going one on one with. Dressed in a black skirt suit that flaunted every curve, a hell of a lotta leg, and stilettos that made a man think of only one thing... It was her sleek no-nonsense ponytail and black-rimmed glasses that told him she was here for business and not the fun he had racing through his mind.

Though her don't-mess-with-me vibe instantly made him wanna do just that.

Her eyes found his and a bolt shot through him. *Holy mother of...*

It was working its way through her too if the subtle parting of her pink lips was anything to go by.

'I'm so glad you could make it,' Stella said, calling those eyes back to her and he found himself craving their return.

'Astrid?' He pushed out of his chair to welcome her properly. The name suited her. Especially her eyes – the colour of rich honey, cosmic and divine – as they gave him the quick once-over before dashing back to Stella, slashes of pink appearing in her creamy cheeks.

'Thank you for coming in, Astrid,' the GM said, his voice much more obliging now and Blake couldn't blame the guy. He was pleased, too. She was a welcome distraction, her presence exhilarating for all the right reasons.

'Thank you for having me,' she said, her eyes darting to Blake once more, her words taking on a whole new meaning as he grinned.

'You must be Aiden, or...'

She wet her bottom lip, the quickest flick of her tongue as he stepped forward. Was she nervous? Or was it mutual appreciation?

'I can be whoever you want—'

'No,' came his brother's self-assured drawl. 'I'm Aiden.'

'Dammit, bro!' He looked over her head to take in his twin's untimely arrival. 'Give a guy a chance.'

Because if she liked him, she'd sure as shit like A. *Everyone* liked A.

She gave a laugh, the colour deepening in her cheeks as she turned from him to his brother, tucking her notebook to her chest so that she could offer out her hand. And why the hell should he get the handshake first?

'It's a pleasure to meet you.'

She did the rounds, from Aiden to Coach, to the GM, Stella and then... as her hand slipped inside Blake's, her notebook started to drop in the other and she dipped as he did, his hand saving it from hitting the deck.

'Thank you,' she murmured, straightening back up, her hand still in his, warm and welcoming, her eyes too, and something inside him took off. Was that... *butterflies*?

He didn't do butterflies unless he was pre-game and even then, they were promptly quashed before they cost him the ice. But these were hot, and frenzied, and growing by the second.

'It's good to meet you, Blake.'

'You too.'

God, was that his voice? Gruff. Weak. *Fuck, get a grip!*

He could sense Aiden's cocked brow, his observant brother not missing a beat, and he promptly released her hand and tucked his own into his pocket as it thrummed to a tune he didn't recognise. The tune of her touch.

God, he needed a drink. *The tune of her touch,* what kind of nonsense was that?

The day had taken its toll if a simple handshake from a woman had him losing his head. So much for wanting to get better acquainted. He needed his own space, stat.

'I'll leave you to whatever this is,' he said, making for the door.

'Not so fast, Blake,' the GM said, interlacing his fingers on the desk and stopping him in his tracks.

'What now?'

He flicked her a look as she tensed. *Don't worry, I'll come back for you,* he wanted to say. She was probably a marketing rep if she was here to talk with Aiden. And he was more than happy to leave them to get the job done and then, when he had his head on straight, he could seek her out for a reintroduction. Minus an audience.

'Astrid is here to see you. You *and* your brother.'

'She's *what*?'

'Why don't we all take a seat and Stella can explain?' Coach said, gesturing to the vacant chairs opposite. Three. Why hadn't he noticed there was an extra chair today?

And why was he seemingly the only one surprised at her presence?

'Someone wanna tell me what's going on?'

He slipped her the side eye as he took his seat once again, positioning her between him and his brother and feeling every nerve prickle to life, awareness of her proximity and a rising sense of unease a confusing cocktail in his bloodstream.

'Astrid here is an award-winning journalist,' Stella said.

'A journalist, you say.' Yeah, he could see that. The inquisitive gaze behind the glasses. The notepad and pen at the ready. The way she already had him wanting to get up close and personal. 'Good for you. Though I fail to see what this has to do with me.'

'It has everything to do with you since you're the reason she's here,' Stella explained. 'Her feature articles demand quite the attention. Her words have the power to transform people's views in a mere page or two. The way she breaks down an individual and pieces them back together in a way that the public can understand and indeed empathise with really is quite something.'

'Thank you,' Astrid said, her smile seeing off another of his brain cells.

Aiden was smiling too.

Hell, everyone was smiling bar him.

Hang on. They couldn't be saying what he thought they were saying.

'No offence, but I wouldn't know,' he said warily. 'I don't have much time for reading.'

'Astrid wrote the profile piece on Marcus Tanner last year,' Stella continued. 'Used his life story to turn what was hatred and fear into something akin to reverence. It was impressive to say the least.'

Blake huffed. Marcus 'Mad Dog' Tanner was a headcase who played for the NFL. He couldn't care less what the glorified ball thrower did with his time, or what people thought of him. But that wasn't the point, was it? They were talking about him. Blake. *He* was Mad Dog Marcus in this context.

Well, fuck that.

'So, you can imagine how pleased we were when Astrid approached us with the idea of a profile piece on the Titan Twins,' Stella said, confirming his fears, suffocating him from the outside in as the idea took a vice-like grip around his throat. 'A deep dive into your past, to paint a rosier present. It's the perfect solution to our current predicament.'

Christ, was that how she'd pitched it? Astrid. All to gain access and drill him for the thrill of her readership. Because she didn't know him from Adam, she had no reason to save his ass, only promote her own.

'And a way for you to secure your future with the Titans,' the GM added. 'She'll become your shadow for the next few weeks, longer if need be. Until she gets what she needs to write the article that *we* need.'

Blake was shaking his head. 'Now isn't the time to have some hot chick poking around. We're supposed to have our head in the game, not...' He flicked her a look and wished he hadn't. Damn, she really was hot. And fuck, he was scraping the barrel for excuses not to go along with this. To give away anything but admitting the truth. He didn't want to talk.

'A shame you didn't think that way when you got into that fight,' Stella said. 'You're lucky charges weren't pressed, because then we'd be having a very different conversation.'

He'd heard those words once before. A very *very* long time ago, and he had no interest in revisiting that day... not in his head and certainly not in any '*deep dive*' chat with Foxy the Hot Reporter.

'Indeed. But everyone loves an underdog,' the GM said, his smile smug. 'They just need reminding that's you.'

'An *underdog*?'

'Why not? An article about the legendary Titan Twins, their journey from the streets to stardom, ought to do it.'

'We weren't on the streets,' he heard himself say as an icy shiver ran down his spine.

'I was speaking metaphorically. It'll be down to Stella's team and of course, Astrid, to come up with the right angle.'

'Sure, I have plenty of ideas, but...' Astrid glanced his way, her tender tone abrasive as it raked along the open wound. 'I wouldn't go with anything that made you uncomfortable. I'll involve you every step of the way. Make sure you're happy before we go to print.'

'Happy?' he choked out. 'You'll be lucky to get that far, because I ain't talking.'

'You don't have a choice,' the GM said. 'This is how you fix a train wreck of a season PR-wise and if you're lucky, still get to start when we hit the playoffs. Because we will get to the playoffs; whether you're a part of them remains to be seen.'

'Are you *fucking* serious?'

The entire room tensed. Apart from the GM who was holding his own remarkably well. Probably because of the desk between them. And he paid the bills.

'If we have to trade you, Blake, we will. Before the NHL takes the choice out of our hands and renders you worthless.'

'But it won't come to that because you're going to play nice with Astrid. You and' – Stella looked to Aiden, her smile imploring him to assist – 'your brother.'

'And while you're doing that off the ice,' Coach said, readjusting his Titans' training jacket, 'we can get our heads back in the game and focus on what we should've been all along, wiping the ice with the opposition.'

Stella grimaced. 'How about we just call it *winning*? Wiping the ice with the opposition one too many times is why we're in this position in the first place.'

Coach suppressed an eye roll. 'Winning it is.'

Blake stared at them in disbelief. Could they hear themselves? He looked to Aiden. Please *God*, let his brother have the good sense to tell them all where to go. The team couldn't afford to piss them both off. They didn't need this distraction. Hell, *he* didn't.

His brother held his gaze before turning to Astrid. 'You have our word, anything you need, you only have to ask. Isn't that right, Blake?'

Anything? Was the man crazy? Because any profile piece would mean digging into their childhood. Their father. Their misery.

And now everyone was looking at him.

'Fuck this.'

He shoved out of his seat and walked. He could already hear Aiden smoothing over his exit. Playing nice. And he punched the wall with a growl, not breaking stride.

Over his dead body was he going to let a journo into his life.

And he'd thought talking to a shrink would be bad...

Talking to a woman with a licence to publish his demons to the world...

Not gonna happen. Not now. Not ever.

3

Astrid watched Blake go, clutching the notepad to her chest like it might somehow save her from the guilt clawing its way up her throat.

Man, she felt bad.

Really bad.

If she'd learned anything since the post-airport hangover had lifted, it was that she was rubbish at deception. And she hated lying, period.

But you're not lying, not right this second.

You're doing your job.

'He'll come around.' Aiden stepped into her field of vision. She hadn't realised she'd stood when Blake had risen, and now his brother was standing too, blocking her view of Blake's rear as the door rebounded off the wall.

'You reckon?' she said, her eyes narrowing on her true target. The man she wanted to break, not the man she had unintentionally broken by getting him caught up in her scheme.

Caught up in it? You made him the centre of it.

Though *technically* he was already broken, the question was why.

Sienna had given her titbits of their past. Of an unhappy childhood with an abusive drunk for a father and a mother too terrified to speak out. Their home under constant threat of foreclosure and a society that shunned them. But she was hungry for *their* story, *their* version. And was that fair? Not to this guy, but to his brother?

'I'll talk to him.'

She suppressed a frown, wishing she could smother the inner wrangling as easily. 'Thank you.'

'Hey, don't let him scare you,' he said, misreading her reaction. 'Underneath the tough exterior, he's really just a pussycat.'

'A pussycat?' She gave a hitched laugh. 'If you say so.'

'Scout's honour.'

She cocked her head. 'Were you actually in the scouts?'

'We both were for a time, then it became all about the game. Is that going in the article?'

'Probably.'

He grinned, flashing the infamous Carter dimples – she half expected his teeth to give a cartoon twinkle too. 'Everyone loves a scout, right.'

'Right.'

She held his gaze and she realised he wasn't kidding. He was so desperate for the world to see his brother in a new light, a better light, not for his own sake, but for Blake's. Ever the protective brother.

If Sienna wasn't in her head, she'd truly think him Prince Charming with the golden aura. Blake on the other hand...

The images on her laptop had nothing on his presence in real life.

And the way he'd made her feel...

She could breathe fully now he wasn't in the room. Breathe and strategise as her brain turned over at a more regular pace. Free of all that fire and passion, his blue eyes as rakish as Bella had said, and utterly brazen as they'd devoured her on the spot.

Devoured you? What about you *licking your lips?*

She swallowed down the memory and focused on golden boy. He was far more contained, measured... Not too warm, not too cold. Just right.

And hell, now she sounded like goldilocks testing out her breakfast.

Though cold was the only way to go when dishing out someone's just desserts. And her smile in return felt just that.

'Think you can make him into a talkative one?' She adjusted her glasses as she adjusted her attitude, dialling up the warmth as she sought to build a connection with the *right* brother. 'It's hard to write a profile piece on the Titan Twins if one half is refusing to speak to me.'

'Don't take it personally.' His grin lifted to one side. 'He doesn't like talking to anyone.'

'And what about you, do *you* like talking?'

'If it pulls his reputation back from the brink, I'm game.'

She lifted her chin, ignored the way his impassioned response warmed her through. He was *not* good. He was bad. Very *very* bad.

Even if his words made it clear that he was doing this against his will too. That it was all about saving his brother's skin. That he cared about his brother. That he loved his brother.

Where had that kind of passion been when Sienna had poured her heart out to him?

'Good.'

'I can't promise it won't be like pulling teeth though.'

'I have my ways,' she said, balancing flirtation with professionalism as she remembered their audience.

He gave a choked laugh, his broad frame rumbling with the move. 'I'm sure you do.'

'If Blake gives you any trouble, you come to me.' Preston Walker came up alongside them. Every bit the rich and entitled general manager she'd read about in her research on the team. 'I'll make sure he toes the line.'

'I'm sure that won't be necessary,' she said smoothly.

'You say that now, but knowing Blake like I do, you'll be needing backup.'

'That's what I'm here for,' Aiden assured them both. 'You can rest easy, boss. I've got this.'

'I'm sure you have, but just in case, I'll send my details over so that you can contact me. Any time. Day or night. Anything I can do, just call. Perhaps you'd be interested in a similar article at a management level? I'll happily clear my schedule for you if you—'

'I prefer to work on one article at a time,' she hurried out, lying through her teeth. She always had more than one article on the go. She was a freelance journalist; it *paid* to have multiple pieces on the go, but it was clear the GM was interested in more than the story she would write, the way his grey eyes now dipped to her chest sealing that suspicion. Awks!

'The offer is always open.'

'Thank you.'

'In the meantime, keep that ID handy.' He gestured to the card on a lanyard around her neck and she wondered whether it was an excuse to continue dipping south. 'It gives you access to all areas within the arena.'

'I will.'

'And speaking of the arena, why don't I give you a tour?' Aiden suggested. 'When we're not playing away, we practically live here so it'll be good for you to know your way around.'

'That would be great!' She set her dazzles on him – some alone time already. Perfect! 'If it's no trouble?'

'Not at all, shall we?'

He gestured for her to precede him out. Ever the Prince Charming. She wanted to roll her eyes over the act. The smooth appearance, the warmth in his smile, the blue eyes that made one think of the beach on a bright summer's day...

Instead, she walked ahead, swaying her hips to draw his gaze... even if she cursed the pinch of her heels as she did so. Give her trainers any day of the week. But Aiden liked his women with class. Class and skyscraper heels according to his track record, so she would suffer the same in the name of karma.

'So, what's it like?' she said as he came up alongside her in the corridor. 'Working with your brother, *living* with your bother?'

'You've been doing your research.'

'What journalist would I be if I hadn't gleaned all I could beforehand?'

His eyes slid to hers. 'Maybe it would be useful for you to tell me what you think you know and then I can tell you if you're hot or cold.'

'That sounds too much like a game...'

'I live for games so it works for me.'

He stepped ahead of her, pushing through a door that led into a stairwell and holding it open for her.

'As much as I love a good game too,' she said, passing him by, 'I prefer to get into specifics. That way it's less open to interpretation and my article will ring true.'

'Makes sense, I suppose.'

Though he didn't sound happy about it.

They walked past a group of young players not much older than school age, all of whom gave her a sweeping once-over as the middle one let out a low whistle.

'Who's the hot chick, Ice?'

Hot chick? Her inner goddess and karma queen preened, hoping Aiden saw it too.

'Behave, Eddie,' he told the kid before addressing her. 'You'll have to excuse the rookies, they don't get out much, do you, boys?'

'I'd get out more if she is,' one of them said.

'I'd stay in more if you are,' she rebuked before Aiden could intervene again, setting off a string of laughter and a deep-throated chuckle from the man himself.

'That was probably a bit cruel, wasn't it?' She adjusted her glasses as they carried on down the stairs.

'You're kidding, right? The sooner they learn to get their head out of their pants the better. I swear Blake and I weren't that cocky at their age.'

'You sure about that?' She couldn't believe it, not for a second. 'I thought all lads around that age were bubbling pots of testosterone.'

He huffed. 'Blake maybe. Me, not so much.'

'Why do you think that is?'

He shrugged. 'More important things to be doing with my time than hitting on the next hot thing I see. If your head's down there, it's not up here, and if it's not up here, you're not playing with your all.'

'Is that why you haven't had a relationship that lasted longer than a few months?'

She sensed the tension feed through his limbs, saw the tightness around his mouth and the stilted step he took. 'I fail to see how that's relevant to your article?'

No, it was relevant to Sissi's heartbreak. Relevant to the fact that he'd left her alone in their small town, her mother dead, her father as good as... Her entire life in tatters because he'd found a new one. A more exciting one.

'I think understanding how focused you are on the game helps people sympathise with your life choices.'

'And you think my sex life demands sympathy?'

'I wasn't referring to your sex life.'

'No?'

'I was referring to love, Mr Carter.'

'Love?'

'Yes, you know, the kind that sees you married, setting up home, maybe adding a few kids into the mix...'

The kind of future he'd once promised Sienna.

Or had those dreams died with the boy who'd left Ashbury Falls?

Or had he been lying all along? Leading her on?

'Those idealistic wants are for people who have yet to see life for what it really is.'

'And what's that?'

'One big game. The only way to win is to keep it in your control.'

And hell, didn't she know that. Didn't she agree with him wholeheartedly. Not that she was about to admit as much. Because *she* hadn't fooled someone else into thinking it was all possible.

'And how does one go about that?'

'By keeping your emotions in check. Always.'

The severity in his voice dried up her mouth. The charming

affable man had been replaced by the renowned Ice King. And *this* was the man she was going to mess with.

She adjusted her glasses, aware it was becoming something of a habit, and paused on the bottom step.

'You, Mr Carter...' The warmth of righteousness flowed through her veins as she tilted her head and gave him a coy smile. 'Just get more and more fascinating.'

He blinked. Blinked again. Shocked at what he'd admitted or shocked at her response, she wasn't sure. And then he grinned.

'If that means you can spin it into a positive for the masses, I'm good with it.'

'I'm sure I can do *something* with it.'

She stepped forward with him and – whoops! The ground disappeared beneath her heel. One minute she was upright and smiling, the next she was in his arms, one hot arm locked around her, one hot chest acting as a bumper. Oof!

So much for being all classy and elegant.

It got you in his arms though... Now, work it baby!

'Are you okay?'

She nodded as she found her feet, stroking a karma-led hand up his shoulder.

'I am.' She blinked up at him, purposefully breathy and grateful. 'Thanks to you.'

'Glad I could be of service.'

His eyes were glazing over, his pupils flaring... Was he – was he about to *kiss* her? *Already*?

'Astrid?'

'Yes?' she whispered, heady on success – an early leap in the Ice King takedown!

'Could you get off my toe please?'

'Huh!' Her eyes flared wide as she registered the spongy

surface beneath her heel. His foot, not the ground. Shit! She leapt back. 'Sorry!'

'Hey, it's fine, but I need these bad boys in one piece, they pay the bills.'

His smile was full of good humour, but she was *dying*. Like kill her now and forget she ever existed, *dying*.

She pressed her fist to her lips. 'Are you *sure* you're okay?'

Though the devil in her figured he deserved a little impaling...

'I dice with blades every day of the week; I can handle one lethal heel. Now come on, the rookies are due on the ice for drills, you can see them in action.'

She followed him through the double doors ahead, his soft, 'And there she is...' making her frown.

'She?'

He gestured to the ice, the pride in his gaze unmistakable. Oh, right, the rink.

She blinked as her eyes adjusted to the bright white surface gleaming in the overhead lights. At its heart was the red and blue crest of the Titans, a fist punching through ice. Ha! Much like her karma mission.

'You been to a game before?'

She dampened her smile. 'Can't say I have.'

He tutted. 'You don't know what you're missing.'

And then he was in his element, taking her through every detail of the rink. From the players' benches to the penalty boxes, to the viewing galleries and the four-sided Jumbotron currently switched off... And as he went through every detail, and she meant *every* detail, the rookies spilled onto the ice, their red and blue kits a blur as they swept around.

Music started to pump through the overhead sound system and Aiden smiled. 'We don't like to train in the quiet.'

'Why is that?'

'I don't know. I guess the beat helps you to push out whatever's going on off the ice and focus on the puck and your team and whatever Coach has to say. It also makes it less of a shock come game day when the whole place reverberates with noise...'

'It sounds intense.'

'It is. You'll have to come see it for yourself. We play the New York Knights in a couple of weeks, and nothing beats a game between local rivals.'

'I'd love that.'

'I'm sure the boss will see you get a seat in the luxury box.'

'I'd rather stay in the thick of it, soak up the atmosphere.'

His eyes sparked. 'I'll see you get tickets. You could bring a friend.'

'Thanks.' She was about to say an extra ticket wouldn't be necessary; she was so used to travelling that she rarely stuck around long enough to form a friendship. But now she had Bella. Would she come?

'Once you understand our passion for the game, you'll understand us.'

A passion that left no room for love, he'd all but told her.

And if she was honest, she understood it, even as she hated him for misleading Sienna, making her believe he was in it for the long haul when he wasn't. At least Chase had never made out he wanted more... no, he'd just been a lying, cheating scumbag with a wife. A poor broken woman who she'd had a hand in breaking.

Not your fault, came the voices of her girlfriends.

'I'll let you into a secret...' Aiden said, leaning in close. 'It's better than sex.'

'You've obviously not been having sex with the right person,' she murmured, refusing to dwell on how great sex could be with the wrong one too, and he chuckled.

'Come on, you're shivering, we should get you out of here.'

She was? She *was*. 'It's okay, I'd like to watch them for a bit.'

'Maybe you ought to dress for the rink next time you're here.'

He was right. Why hadn't she thought about that when the girls had been dressing her up for seduction rather than work?

'Sorry, rookie error.'

And now her teeth were chattering, and she knew the past was as much to blame as her present environment.

'Ha! Don't let the rookies hear you say that. They'll take it as an insult and roast you more.'

'Duly noted.'

He shrugged out of his training jacket.

'Wait, what are you doing?' Alarm had her thrusting her hand out as she spied his intent. 'No, I can't.'

'You can and you will.' She stopped fighting as his warmth enveloped her, his scent too – fresh and clean, and all man. 'Better?' He cocked a brow over those bright blue eyes.

'Much.' She swallowed, hating his thoughtful gesture even as it warmed her. 'Thank you.'

She looked away from his far-too-charming self to take in the players on the ice. Just because he was thoughtful now, didn't mean he wasn't an arse back then. An arse deserving of being taken down a peg or two.

She concentrated on the rookies, most of whom were huge enough *before* they donned their protective gear that saw them looking twice as big and twice as menacing and found herself readily captivated. They were as graceful as they were fierce. The way they moved over the ice, backwards, forwards, pivoted, passed the puck, they made it look easy. The clutz in her envied them that ability.

'Do you skate?'

She gave a choked laugh. 'God, no.'

She felt his intense scrutiny and flicked him a look. 'What?'

'Just the way you're watching, it's almost like you wished you were out there too.'

The man was astute as well as charming... *Oh Sissi, I can so see how you fell for this one.*

'Do you?' he pressed.

'You saw me almost faceplant in my heels; can you imagine what I'd be like on a thin blade of metal?'

'Have you ever tried?'

'My nickname was Twinkle Toes back in school, and I don't mean it in a good way.'

'Twinkle Toes?'

His eyes sparkled and she looked away, biting her cheek. This was hardly the stuff to convince him she was date material. But now she'd said it...

'I was forever falling over my own feet.'

He gave a low chuckle. 'You know what they say, practice makes perfect.'

'Not if most of that practice is spent on my bum.'

Unless... She turned to look up at him. 'Are you offering up your time to teach me, because in that case, I'd be a fool to say no.'

'Great. Blake and I—'

'Blake? You're volunteering him too?'

'Anything to help get a glowing article in our name.'

'Bribery?' She tried not to let her panic set into her smile, because the idea of being in the care of his brother on the ice... that had a whole other fire lighting up within.

'I prefer to call it a healthy exchange of skills.'

'You know I'm getting paid to write this.'

'See it as the icing on the cake then. Besides...' He gave her a lopsided grin. 'Anyone that looks at the ice like you do deserves to be at home on it.'

Fuuuck. He was being sweet again. Sweet and considerate and making her question everything!

'You ready to move on?' he asked.

'Sure.'

If only she could move her thoughts on as easily... Aiden was the baddie, she was the goodie, and Blake was a distraction she needed to keep in a professional box.

* * *

'What's got you so riled?'

Blake grunted as he chest-pressed the barbell, racked it with a clang, and sat up.

'Who says I'm riled?' He fixed his glare on Larsson, their Swedish goalie and resident tattooed giant. Even Blake looked small next to him. The guy's blond Viking man-bun as mean-looking as the rest of him – making him great in nets, not so great in an alley after dark.

Larsson gave a low rumble. *Shiitt.* Was that a laugh?

'You grunt more than me today.'

Blake dragged his mouth back into a half smile. 'Is that so?'

'The gym was full before you came in.' Larsson jutted his chin before executing a heavily loaded skater squat. 'Now look at it.'

Blake rocked his head side to side, grabbed his water bottle off the floor and took a long slug. Larsson had a point. There'd been at least eight other guys hard at it when he'd arrived, five of them rookies, all of them gone. Not that he'd noticed them leave.

With the music playing full blast, he'd been locked in his

own head, moving through the equipment with no thought to anyone or anything save for the ongoing battle in his head. The GM, Stella, Aiden, Astrid, the article from hell.

'You saying we cleared the joint?'

'I'm saying you did. No one cares what I'm doing. This is my setup, my space; they stay away and leave me to it.'

'You saying they couldn't do the same for me?'

'*I'm saying* you didn't give them a choice; the bad energy coming off you is hard to ignore.'

'You ignored it.'

Larsson cracked a grin, a move as rare as his laugh and flashing the gap in his top front teeth courtesy of a biscuit to the face last season. 'Because I can crush you like a fly.'

'Alright, Big Man.'

Blake shook his head with his own low rumble-cum-laugh and fisted his towel. Scrubbed the sweat from his face. Poor bastards. He hadn't meant to mess with the room. His only thought had been: bar bad, gym good. That throwing alcohol on what was already a combustible mix could backfire spectacularly. Life lesson #1 handed down by dear old Dad.

So, he'd done an about-turn in the parking lot, hoping exercise would put out the fire.

But it was still there, the heat in his veins, the pulsating panic... the realisation that he had no choice but to do what they asked. To delve into his past, the one thing he'd spent a lifetime running from. Ashbury Falls. His father. His fists.

Now they wanted him to face it all. Not just face it but talk about it. Put the truth into the hands of the public who'd been more than happy to share the gossip that had spewed out of Ashbury Falls with his success. His and his brother's.

And it was one thing for it to come from everyone else, another for it to come from them. Unfiltered. Honest. 'Fuck.'

'I didn't say it was a bad thing.' Larsson's blue eyes danced in the overhead lights, his neck tattoo straining as he hoisted the barbell onto his shoulders. 'Suits me fine. The quiet. The space. Less rookies and their silly talk. But if you want to talk, get whatever it is off your chest, I will listen.'

Blake blinked. Had the Big Man just offered to lend him an ear? 'What is it with everyone wanting to listen to my problems today?'

'Someone once said to me, the more you talk about it now, the less you'll have to apologise for later.'

Blake gave another rumble. 'I can't believe you just said that to me.'

'I think it makes sense, no?'

The words chased around Blake's head: talk, be honest, let it out...

He ran a finger through the collar of his compression tee, struggling to breathe as the memories tumbled free, one after the other, his past fighting through the wall he'd erected long ago. He didn't want to revisit those days because, sheer misery.

'I think' – he got to his feet, tearing the tee over his head and cherishing the chill of the aircon against his sweat-drenched skin – 'you talk too much.'

Words he never thought he'd hear himself say about Edvin *fucking* Larsson.

'And you talk too little, Pretty Boy.'

Blake shook his head and crossed the room. 'Bite me, Big Man.'

He exited the gym on Larsson's chortle, straight into something soft and warm and yelping like a pup.

'Blake!'

He frowned down at the woman rebounding off his chest. 'Astrid, what are you...?'

Her eyes collided with his, two slashes of pink riding high in her cheeks. 'You're sweaty!'

Laughter fizzed its way through the fire in his veins. 'I am.'

Her honeyed eyes flitted down. 'And *naked*.'

If her voice reached any higher the dogs would come running...

'Not quite, sweetheart, but that can be arranged.'

She swallowed, the tiniest squeak just audible over the heavy metal bassline pounding through the gym wall.

'You're funny.'

'I was being serious, and did you just... did you just *squeak*?'

'No, of course not.' She scrunched up her face and hugged her notepad tight against her chest, so tight that her cleavage heaved above the neckline and he had to fight to keep his eyes up. The way her babies were shifting... she was struggling to breathe. Something he could relate to. Roll with even.

'If you want to drop the pen and paper, I can give you something more engaging to tangle with.'

Her lips parted as she drew in a shallow breath. 'I don't think that's...'

The words faltered as her gaze fell to his right pec, to his tattoo. Slowly, her hand lifted towards the ink. '*Est suae quisque fortunae.*'

His chest twitched in response, anticipating her touch. But just before her fingers met his skin, she stopped, curling them into a tight fist.

Shame.

'It's Latin,' he said. 'It means—'

'Every man is the architect of his own fortune.'

Of course Foxy Journo would know what it meant...

'Yes.'

She wet her lips, her inquisitive gaze lifting to his. 'Which explains the compass too.'

'Yes.'

'And the eagle...?'

It took him a second to steady his pulse, another to fight the urge that wanted to respond to the appreciation cutting through her curiosity.

Was this her trying to detract from the heat? Trying to change the subject? Or was this a cunning ruse to get him to spill something personal? Well, fuck that!

'Fortune favours the brave and the bold.'

Blake stiffened at the sound of his brother's voice, turning to see him approach with Harry their latest recruit by his side.

'And those who escape the trappings of their past to reach for a better future,' Aiden added, more than willing to give up all the detail.

'It's my tattoo, bro,' he threw at him. 'You think you can leave me to explain it?'

Not that he'd been about to...

'Tell me I'm wrong.'

Both Astrid and Harry watched the exchange with interest and Blake was done being interesting. 'I'm going to shower.'

He moved off and his brother stepped in his path.

'I figured we could take Astrid for a drink, get acquainted on a more casual level before she—'

'Be my guest. I have better things to be doing with my time.'

He pushed past him on a mission to get clear of the scene that had changed so swiftly. From desire to despair – the chill of his past too ready to take over.

'Blake...'

'Maybe it's best to let him cool off,' Astrid interjected, her soothing tone trailing after him. 'You and I can go for a drink though. It's been a day.'

Great. Now he was the cause of 'the day' and his brother was taking Foxy out for some one-on-one time.

You were the one who said, "be my guest"!

Didn't mean he had to like it though.

Didn't mean he was jealous.

Didn't mean he wasn't as messed up as everyone said.

He stalked through the locker room, stripping as he went, every player present parting like the sea did for Moses. He hit the shower and slammed it to cold.

Let Aiden do the talking; it's safer that way.

She'd only hate you if she knew you.

The real you.

He scrubbed at his chest, his nails raking over the tattoo she had taken such time over and its meaning... his brother's apt description...

'Tell me that I'm wrong.'

No, his brother wasn't wrong. The eagle was about him, the compass was about him, the words too. It was all about breaking free of the past, the pain and his mistakes... the problem was, he still felt as chained to them as ever.

And here he was, hiding out in the locker room like he had as a teen, anything to avoid going home. To avoid the drunken onslaught, the fighting and the shouting...

The noise that never ceased.

Until he'd made it cease.

His gut rolled and he pressed his palms into the cold tiles, willing the memory away. The police, the blood, the—

'You alright, Blake?'

It was Harry, the young rookie Aiden had been with in the hallway. The lad looked nervous as hell as he stood in the doorway. Not too dissimilar to the boy he'd once been in these same four walls. Green, freshly drafted, trying to find his place in a team of peers and idols alike.

Took some balls for the lad to come and ask, and he took pity on him. Gave a smile.

'Aye, I'm alright, Harry.'

Or at least he would be once he put himself back in the driving seat of his own destiny...

'Every man is the architect of his own fortune.'

Time to start acting like it.

4

'You have to excuse my brother.'

Aiden set a glass of prosecco down beside her glasses on the table and slid into the cosy pub booth across from her, his knee grazing hers as he took a slug of cold beer straight from the bottle. She eyed his thirst-quenching drink, the condensation around the neck, the light layer of foam just visible through the glass and resisted the urge to smack her lips.

She really wanted a beer. It didn't need to be a fancy IPA, just any old beer would do. But Aiden's ladies were classy. Classy meant lady-like drinks, straight posture, crossed legs and a demure smile. Check, check, check, and—

'You did ask for a prosecco, right?'

'Hmm?' She refocused on his face, the puzzled crease to his brow. 'Oh yes, of course, thanks.' She grabbed her glass, almost knocking it over in her eagerness. 'Prosecco is the answer to everything.'

Or it had been *before* she'd had a few too many in a snowy airport and felt the aftereffects for days...

He turned his head, giving her the side eye as he took another slug and her mouth watered. 'You sure about that?'

'Yes. Absolutely.' She dragged her eyes back to his and took a dainty sip from her glass. 'Now, what were you saying about your brother?'

'He really is a good man underneath all the...'

'Grumpiness?'

'I was going to say something more profane,' he said with a laugh. 'But yes, that works.'

'Why do you think he's so opposed to doing the article?'

'I think every man has skeletons in their closet, things they'd rather keep that way, and my brother is no exception.'

'I meant what I said in the meeting, though. I won't print anything you're not comfortable with.'

'And what if you don't have a choice?'

'I don't follow.'

'If this article is to do what the franchise hopes it will, those skeletons are precisely what you'll need.'

Interesting...

'And what about your skeletons? Are you worried about those too?'

Would Sienna be one? One of many? Because she couldn't believe the sudden tension in his frame was all about his brother.

'I thought this drink was about us getting *casually* acquainted.'

She forced a smile. 'You're right. Sorry. It's hard turning off the journalist in me.'

'What about turning her on?'

'Wow!' She laughed into her glass. 'Smooth, real smooth.'

He grinned. 'Got you to switch off though, didn't I?'

She shook her head, her laughter still rolling as she scanned their surroundings. She didn't want to like him. She didn't want to enjoy his company. She wanted to stay in control of every emotion, but then, so did he. Mr Life Is One Big Game.

'You know, when you'd suggested going to a bar, I hadn't expected one quite so laidback.'

'You call a pub with a VIP member-only policy, laidback?'

'If you forget that bit, yes.'

She'd expected a chic, upscale wine bar – not a classic pub brimming with charm and a crackling fire too. Despite being early evening, midweek, the place was already bustling. The steady hum of laughter and conversation blended seamlessly with the soft background music while the comforting scent of home-cooked meals and freshly poured ale filled the air. Her nose twitched; she could so scoff a steak and ale pie!

'You don't like it?'

'No, I love it! It's my kind of place.' Her jeans and trainers would fit right in here. *She* fit right in. 'I'm just surprised it's yours.'

But only because of the women in Research Exhibit C. He was a hockey player at the end of the day, not some city slick billionaire...

He gave her a lopsided grin. 'I'm full of surprises.'

'Is that so?' She followed what felt like a flirtatious lead and took a *seductive* sip of her fizz – the girls would be proud! 'Care to share another?'

He held her gaze, his eyes sparkling with whatever he was thinking. 'I prefer to make you work for it.'

Game on, baby. She licked her lips, her knee lightly kissing his as she crossed and uncrossed her legs. 'And just how—'

Her phone started to ring with an incoming call, the unmistakable beat of Tay Tay spearing the moment so spectacularly.

One of the girls was ringing...

She eyed her handbag on the bench beside her and lifted a finger. 'Hold that thought.' She peeked inside. Winced. *Sissi*. Oh God. She muted it and shoved it back, propped her elbow on the table and leaned in, chin on her hand. 'Sorry. Now where were we...?'

'It's okay if you need to take it.'

'Oh no, it's fine.'

'Your face said otherwise.'

Because she'd been freaking out at her double-dealing. Panicking that he'd gain telepathic skills and work it out, too.

The phone started to ring again, and she slapped her hand over the bag.

'Honestly, take the call. It must be important for them to ring twice.'

Maybe it *was* important. Maybe Sissi was in trouble. Maybe Paige or Bella...

'Are you sure?'

'Totally.'

'It's a bit loud in here, I'll just...'

She gestured to the entrance and slid out of the booth, taking her phone out of her bag as she went. She checked the screen with a curse. The Just Desserts WhatsApp group had been blowing up all afternoon; no wonder Sissi had resorted to ringing.

JUST DESSERTS WHATSAPP GROUP. 13.45 EST.

SISSI

How is it going? xx

Are you home? x

Astrid??

BELLA

She's probably still with him x

SISSI

You think? It's been hours!

PAIGE

Keep your knickers on, love. I'm sure it's a good sign

SISSI

Shall I call her?

BELLA

I'm sure she'll call you when she's free x

SISSI

I'll just give her a quick call …

PAIGE

What are you so worried about? Thought you said he wasn't a serial killer…

BELLA

No but Blake might be…

PAIGE

Not helping, B!

SISSI

She's not answering

She pushed through the doors into the foyer and dialled Sissi back, finger to one ear, phone to the other. A blast of icy wind and a flurry of sleet followed a customer inside and she shuddered, turning toward the wall for shelter. *Brrr.* What she wouldn't give to be in her shark onesie right about now…

'Astrid!' came Sissi's panicked voice.

'Hey love, I'm so sorry. I've only just seen your messages.'

'Are you okay?!'

'Everything's fine. I would've called sooner but I'm still tied up with *you-know-who*.'

'You *are*?'

'He's taken me for a drink.'

'*Already*? Wow, you don't waste time, do you? Not that you should. It's good – excellent – *great* that he's taken you out already.'

'It's not what you're thinking.'

Though it might be given chance...

'No?'

She screwed her face up, the conflict in her friend reaching down the phone and giving her a guilt-laden slap. It was one thing to *want* Astrid to break Aiden, another to sit by knowing she had to get close to do it. Like, *close* close. 'It's more of an apologetic drink than a *date* date.'

'Apologetic? Why on earth...'

'He's doing it to make up for Blake's behaviour.'

'Why, what did his brother do?'

Good question. What *did* he do?

He was rude. Dismissive. Arrogant. Pissed off. And yet...

Dammit nipples, stand down.

'Astrid? What's wrong?'

'Nothing.'

'You just swore.'

'I did?' *Brilliant*, now he had her uttering things unaware too. 'It's nothing I can't handle...'

Are you telling yourself that or Sissi?

'You sure?'

'He made it clear he didn't want me around, that's all.'

'Oh dear.'

'And he's a *real* force of nature up close...' Her mind teased

her with his half-naked image – that chest, those abs, the ink...
'You know he has a tattoo on his chest?'

'That doesn't surprise me...'

'No, but when it's right there, pressed up against your face
and—'

'*What*?'

TMI, Astrid!

'I walked into him.'

'And he was *naked*?'

'*Half* naked,' she quickly corrected, clutching an arm around
her middle as the disloyal little flutters in her abdomen warmed
and trebled. 'He was coming out of the gym.'

'And you just... walked into him?'

'I think technically he walked into me.'

'Must have been some collision.'

She nipped her lip.

'And where was Aiden?'

'Around.'

'Astrid, are you getting distracted?'

'Of course not! I'm here with Aiden having a drink. One
hundred per cent focused. Or at least I was until *you* distracted
me.'

'I was worried. We hadn't heard from you all day and... I don't
know. How does he look? No, don't tell me. I don't need to know.'

'He doesn't look as perfect as he does in all the photos.'

And that was the truth. All those images had been enhanced
by the magic wand of creative advertising. A touch of smoothing
here, a bit of blending there... though the chiselled strength, the
carefully applied permatan, the silvery glimmer of a scar to one
cheek, the easy grin and eyes so like his brother's. She shivered.
Yeah, he was *awful* to look at. *Not.*

'Good. It would be just like him to age like a fine wine. And what about the plan? If Blake isn't being all that receptive...'

'Doesn't matter. The GM's given them no choice but to give me what I need for as long as I need it.'

'Excellent. And Aiden... do you... was he... do you think...?'

The line fell silent as her friend left the question hanging: *Do you think he likes you?*

'He gave me a tour of the arena,' Astrid said with a strained smile. 'And now he's taking me out for a drink, so I guess that's a good sign.'

'How come Blake didn't join you if he's the one that owes the apology?'

'Like I said, he's not a happy boy...'

'Maybe that's not a bad thing, if it gives you more time alone with Aiden. He'd do anything to help his brother and if that means wining and dining you then so be it.'

'Are you saying he only wants me for my article, Sissi?' she teased.

The door opened, sending another waft of ice-cold air her way.

'Ha, no way. You're hot!' Sissi declared, sounding much more resolute now. 'Go knock him dead, hun!'

She grinned, Sissi's turnaround giving Astrid the oomph she needed to go back to the table and do exactly that.

'I will, Sissi, and don't—'

'Hey Foxy.'

She jolted at the voice behind her, heat shooting through her rigid spine – the oh God, cocky burr, the scent on the draught. All spicy, earthy, male. *Oh no.* She spun to find Blake filling the doorway. Dressed in top to toe black, even his eyes looked black in the gold light of the entryway.

'If you're gonna hang out here talking, you ought to dress for it.'

And before she could say another word, he was shrugging off his fur-lined aviator jacket and wrapping it around her shoulders, his warmth and scent making her nostrils flare and her body melt.

'Astrid?' Sissi's voice came down the line, muffled by the whirring in her ears. 'What's going on? Who's there?'

What had Blake heard? What had she said this side of the convo? What the hell did she do now?

Slowly she lowered the phone and blindly cut the call, her heart in her mouth as she tried to read his face. The intensity of his gaze. But then he always looked intense.

Did he look *intensely* suspicious though?

'You didn't need to give me your coat.'

What was it with the Carter boys and their dashing gestures?

'Your lips say otherwise.'

'My lips?'

He nodded, his hooded gaze settling on her mouth. 'Or are they supposed to look blue?'

'They are?' She lifted her fingers to the flesh now tingling with his attention, his look as tangible as any caress. *Dammit*, he might as well have kissed her!

'Not any more.'

He gave a satisfied smile but didn't move away, didn't lift his gaze either. As his coat warmed her from the outside, his gaze burned her up from the inside.

'You're very hot.'

And *oh my God*, where had that come from? She squeaked and swallowed in one.

'I mean temperature hot! This!' She gripped the lapels of his jacket together, squeezing her eyes shut and opening them again. 'What I mean is, I'm now hot, thanks to you.'

He gave a deep, panty-melting rumble. 'I think your hotness has nothing to do with me and everything to do with you. But we can debate that later. Back at my place, if you're game.'

Not what she was expecting after her totally uncool behaviour.

And *not* something she could ever say yes to in a million years. Because the offer wouldn't help her get payback, or get her article written, it would land her in a whole heap of hot trouble. And hell, she shouldn't be getting high on it.

It was an absolute no. Never gonna happen. No.

'Don't you live with your brother?'

Hardly the put down of the century, Astrid!

'We have separate wings, and we don't like to share.'

Share?

Gulp.

Where was her sanity when she needed it? Evaporating with her freaking ovaries!

'I don't think me coming back to yours for what you have in mind would be wise... do you?'

He ran his teeth over his bottom lip, his dark stubble shifting and flashing those too-damn-sexy dimples.

'No, probably not, but then, if you know anything about me, you'll know I'm all about the unwise,' he murmured. 'The more unwise the better... And Astrid?'

She could do nothing but nod as he leaned in close.

'I'm onto you.'

Her breath snatched from her lungs – *shit!*

'I don't know what you mean.'

'Oh, I think you do... Now, why don't you go back to your phone call...'

'My what?' And that's when she realised her phone was ringing, Tay Tay's tune muffled beneath his jacket.

'I'll go keep my brother sweet. We can pick this up later.'

'There's nothing to pick up. There's nothing to tell. There's nothing—'

His grin cut her off. He couldn't know. He couldn't have worked it out. He couldn't have heard enough to...

'Don't keep Sissi waiting.'

Shit. Shit. *Shit.*

* * *

'What's her deal do you reckon?'

Blake sat opposite his brother, but his eyes were trained on her through the glass to the foyer. He couldn't make out her features, but she still wore his jacket and *damn*, did it suit her.

'What do you mean? She's a journalist doing her job.'

'What kind of a journalist rocks up to an ice rink in the depths of a New York winter looking like she's about to do a televised interview with the president?'

Aiden shrugged. 'One that wants to make a good impression with the powers that be.'

'Her track record does that for her.'

'It does? You been reading up on her?'

'I did a google, yeah.' He toyed with the glasses she'd left on the table... so she obviously didn't need them all the time. He'd kind of missed them on her.

'And?'

His brother's prompt snapped him back to his senses. 'She's impressive. She writes some decent stuff. Still doesn't explain the killer heels and the kick-ass suit.'

Aiden gave a laugh as he slugged his beer. 'You know what your problem is?'

'What?'

'You've got the hots for her.'

Blake huffed. 'Tell me you don't.'

Aiden followed his gaze to the glass. 'She's attractive. Any man would have to be blind not to see that.'

'Attractive or not, she'll be sick as a dog if she keeps rocking up to the arena dressed like that.'

'Play nice, Blake.'

'I'm here, ain't I?'

'You are... but I know that look.'

'I have no idea what you're talking about, bro.'

'Let her do her job and humanise you to the masses.'

'Humanise me?' He choked on the beer he'd just chugged.

'Yeah.'

'Did you forget the article is about you as much as me?'

'I'm not the one in need of an image overhaul.'

Blake gave him the once-over. 'You sure about that?'

Aiden punched him in the arm. 'For once in your life, can you be serious?'

'I am being serious. I don't want to do it.'

'You don't have a choice; did you not hear them this afternoon? The NHL want you out, bro, and then it won't be up to the Titans any more, you won't be worth trading, you'll be hanging up your skates for good.'

The idea chilled him to the bone.

He was nothing without the game.

A no one.

'Would it really be so bad to let her in, tell her your truth? Let the world see that you do have a heart. Get to the man beneath the mask. The boy behind the goon.'

'For fuck's sake.' Blake rolled his eyes. 'How many more ways do you wanna put it?'

'I'll put it every which way until you realise it's about saving your ass.'

'Worried what you'll be without me on the ice to save yours?'

'I can save my own, thanks.'

'You wouldn't have an ass to save if it wasn't for me.'

'You wanna bet?'

Aiden was grinning now. So was Blake. The camaraderie much easier to deal with than reality. 'You know she's gonna wanna know all about dear old Dad.'

Aiden's smile shrivelled. 'You only have to give her enough, you don't need to tell her everything; she doesn't need to know about that night.'

Blake ground his teeth as the memories threatened to take hold. 'Do you not worry that one day the story will surface? That a police officer will talk, or a neighbour?'

'The neighbours were used to the yelling, and they didn't see jack shit.'

'But Dad... the money he could make if he were to offer it up.'

'He wouldn't dare. If it weren't for us, he'd be living on the streets now.'

His brother was right. It didn't take the edge off though. His blood still ran cold, goosebumps prickling across his skin as he scratched that same itch upon his chest. He let his eyes drift to Astrid beyond the glass, let the miraculous warmth she triggered soothe away the chill and push all thought of his father out...

'So, you wanna tell her to change her getup?' he said. 'Or shall I?'

'The Mother Teresa act is all yours, buddy. But just so you know, she wore my jacket first.'

'She what?'

Aiden gave him a shit-eating grin. 'She was shivering at the rink...'

'Bloody hell, do you reckon she did it on purpose? Some kind of test to see if she could coax out some chivalry?'

'Who knows.' Aiden swigged his beer. 'Bet you're impressed with her outfit choice now though.'

Blake gave a tight chuckle. 'The cunning minx...'

Aiden laughed. 'I'm not so sure. She seems fairly genuine to me.'

He frowned at his brother. 'What makes you say that?'

'Stuff she said.'

'Like?'

'Like the fact she was nicknamed Twinkle Toes when she was younger because she's clumsy as fuck.'

'Twinkle Toes!' Blake spluttered over his beer. 'How on earth did you get onto that?'

'She fell on those killer heels you're obsessing over.'

'And let me guess, you saved her?'

'Like her knight in shining armour, buddy.'

'Ha! Pull the other one.'

'I'm serious about the name though – Twinkle Toes. No devious piece of skirt goes about sharing something as blush-inducing as that.'

'And was she?'

'What?'

'Blushing.'

'Like a beacon.'

Blake's mouth twisted up into a smile. 'Twinkle Toes... I like it.'

'So, we're agreed then?'

'Agreed?'

'To play nice with the reporter.'

'Define "nice"?'

'Give her what she needs and – no, Blake, not that.'

'What? I didn't say a word.'

'You didn't have to.'

'Are you telling me she's off limits, because you know how that's going to go down?'

His brother's eyes were laughing even as he ground his jaw. 'I mean it, Blake.'

'So do I.' Because telling him 'No' only poured gasoline on the fire already simmering for her. 'Scared of a little competition, bro?'

'There's no competition.'

'If you say so...' But Blake didn't believe it. His brother was no saint when it came to the opposite sex and someone like Astrid, as *hot* as Astrid, as *real*... was catnip.

'Is this a private stare down or can anyone join in?' A nervous laugh accompanied her sudden presence at the table and slowly Blake released his brother's gaze to meet hers.

He rubbed his jaw, more for something to do that didn't involve hauling her into his lap, caveman style, and staking his claim up front. 'Hey Twinkle Toes, good of you to join us.'

Her eyes shot to Aiden's, wide, horrified. 'You told him!'

Aiden kicked him beneath the table, the move fierce and invisible from above. 'Why would you tell her that?'

'If she's hanging out with us for the foreseeable, she might as well know we share everything.'

Her eyes shot back to his, her cheeks flushing crimson as her mouth opened but no words came.

'You're such a jerk,' Aiden threw at him and Blake grinned, their face-off resuming as readily as his next breath.

'Takes one to know one.'

'Oh my God, you're like children!'

Their heads snapped to her, voices dropping low as they said as one, 'We can assure you we're not.'

5

Fuckity fuckity fuck...

Two pairs of identical blue eyes blazed up at her.

Well, you did question their manliness.

And there was no mistaking the man in them now.

She'd wanted to chop off her own tongue as soon as she'd said it. Watching the brothers in a standoff and somehow knowing she'd been the cause sent a fire up her like none other.

And *then* Blake had purposefully contradicted his earlier taunt – *we don't like to share* – but clearly that only applied to women. And seriously, right now, she'd share.

And that said more about her than them.

Get with the karma, Astrid!

'I say it as I see it, and right now, you two' – she waved her phone between them, cocking a hip with as much confidence as she could muster – 'are behaving like you're yea high.'

'She's not wrong,' Aiden said, his eyes softening with good humour.

'She's not entirely right either,' Blake said, his eyes still blazing as his grin made a return. 'You want to put that judge-mental ass down and I'll go get you that drink I owe you.'

Why, dear God, did his commanding air shoot an illicit thrill straight through her? What was *wrong* with her?

'You don't owe me—'

'Oh, I do, my brother here says it so it must be true.' He rose up, towering over her with his broad frame, alluring mouth, dizzying blue eyes and her objection died with the fanny flutters. *Fucking fanny flutters!*

Oh, how she'd missed those babies, but now wasn't the time... he wasn't the guy. Delia's book could deliver on those in the fictional world later. Bella had promised!

But her body wasn't getting the message. Worse, he knew it too. The arrogance in his gaze, the cocksure twist to his mouth as he stepped around her and she watched him go. Helpless. Drowning in a sea of lust. Could one expire from such a thing? She certainly felt about ready to combust.

And what about Sissi and his whole *'I'm onto you'*? Had he really put two and two together, realised who she was talking to, mentioned it to his brother even... and how the hell could she find that out without giving the game away herself?

'Told you he was a pussycat,' Aiden said wryly, calling her attention back to him as he swigged his beer. 'I'd like to say he softens the more you get to know him but...'

She gave a wavering smile, unable to trust her voice or meet his eye as she shrugged off his brother's jacket. Its style making her long for the comforting familiarity of her own aviator jacket that she'd swapped out for the fancy cashmere coat her grand-parents had bought her for Christmas. Granny would be so pleased to see her wearing it, not so pleased with the reason *why* she was wearing it. It was aviator out, cashmere in for Aiden.

Though for Blake...

Quit thinking of Blake!

She slammed her butt down and grabbed her prosecco, downing it in two.

'Yeah' – he eyed her empty glass – 'he has that effect on people.'

She let out a nervous laugh. 'I'm surprised you're not an alcoholic – *oh God!*'

As soon as the words were out, she wanted to clamp a hand over her lips. How could she say something so foolish, so careless, when his father...?

'I'm so sorry.'

Aiden's silence echoed louder than the chatter all around and she floundered for something to say. She was a prized reporter, famed for getting on people's good side. But these guys, these twins... they were quickly becoming her kryptonite. She couldn't keep her head in their company. And that was a problem. A great big career jeopardising problem.

People wouldn't want to work with her again if word got out that she was a rambling unprofessional mess.

'That was thoughtless of me. I shouldn't have said it.'

He attempted a smile. 'I think I implied it first.'

She swallowed. 'You were teasing.'

'And you weren't?'

He was being kind, giving her an out. Why, oh *why* did he have to be so nice?

'Of course. But still...'

He leaned back into the worn leather seat. 'Might as well get it out the way now. Yes, our father was a drunk. A mean drunk. And it had nothing to do with Blake, nothing to do with anyone else but himself and his own weakness.'

'It's a horrible affliction.'

'One that affects more people than we'll ever know because most won't admit to it. My father being one.'

'That had to be tough growing up.'

He rubbed at his jaw. Unlike his brother, he lacked the stubble to run his hands over, but the move was identical. 'Tough doesn't come close. And my brother suffered more than most.'

'How so?' she couldn't stop herself from asking, wanting to know it all. For her article, for karma, for her.

He shifted in his seat, his eyes drifting to the bar and her back prickled – Blake was on the move. 'And *that* is a question for another day.'

'Sure, but... I'm sorry anyway.'

'Apology accepted.'

'Woah,' Blake drawled, planting two bottles of beer and a prosecco on the table. 'He's got you apologising now too, what gives?'

She gave a flustered, 'Nothing.'

And Aiden didn't contradict her.

'In that case, shift over so I can get in; my ass ain't gonna perch all that easy.'

What? She glanced up. He wanted to sit on *her* side?

Though to be fair, they were big guys – it made sense for her to be the one to share. But still... she swallowed, scooting over slowly, and he joined her. No such worries on his part as his thigh came up against hers, his biceps too, her body thriving on every connected millimetre as her heart raced.

'So...' He slid her drink over and she reached for it on impulse. 'Sissi alright?'

Her hand faltered, her galloping heart with it. 'Huh?'

'Sissi?' Aiden probed.

'Her friend. She was on the phone to her when I arrived; seemed like it was a fairly intense convo.'

'She's – she's fine.' Astrid wet her lips, tucking an errant curl behind her ear. *Her* friend, he'd said. No suggestion of a connection to them. And Sissi didn't have to be short for Sienna. And even if it was, there had to be a million Siennas in the world. 'Or she will be soon. Thanks for asking.'

'Glad to hear it.' He settled back in the booth, and she took a drink to settle her nerves. Another to fill the silence that suddenly felt strained. Though it was entirely possible that the tension remained wholly within her, sparked by him stepping in on her phone call and magnified by the very real body heat closing in on her.

What had he meant by *I'm onto you* if he hadn't been referring to Sissi?

She could hardly ask him with Aiden sat right there. But she could hardly go home with him either. No, no, no.

'You want to know what I think would be fun?'

'No,' her and Aiden blurted in unison and Blake chuckled.

'Tough, I'm going to tell you anyway. I think if this little firecracker is going to spend her days quizzing us on our life story, we should get to do a little quizzing of our own.'

'Little *firecracker*?' she shot at him.

'Sorry, would you prefer Twinkle Toes?'

'I'd prefer Astrid; it's my name after all.'

'And it does suit you, but we're all about monikers in this business. It's an occupational hazard. He's the Ice King, I'm Fury, and you' – he dialled up the intensity of his gaze as it swept over her – 'are definitely a firecracker. It's in your eyes. And that smile... when you choose to give it like you mean it.'

Fuck fuck fuck, there went her heart and her foo foo and her brain.

And she couldn't escape, hemmed in by his body as much as his gaze.

'Seems like a fair trade to me,' Aiden said.

Fair? She sipped her prosecco while fighting the urge to climb the wall to her left.

Just chill, it's not like they're gonna press you on Sissi and a certain pact you made...

'What do you want to know?'

'You're English, right?' Blake said.

'Half English. Half Scottish. Brought up in the Cotswolds.'

'Sisters, brothers?'

'Neither.'

'Mother, father?'

'Mother. The latter I haven't seen since I was seven.'

'No?' Blake was quick to pick up on that one. 'You don't seem all that sad about it?'

'My life improved greatly the day I stopped depending on him to make it better.'

Something akin to admiration shone in his gaze. 'Sounds like we have that in common.'

'So it would seem. Next.'

She didn't hesitate. She was brave and in her comfort zone because she could talk about her childhood in spades. She'd found peace with her father, or lack thereof, long ago.

Blake looked at Aiden who tipped his bottle, granting him full rein. Either he wasn't interested, or he wasn't concerned about his brother's line of questioning. She hoped it was the latter because the former would be an issue, his disinterest the polar opposite of what she was trying to achieve.

She upped her game, slipping off her suit jacket so that her semi-sheer blouse came into play and giving Aiden her best angle while focusing her gaze on Blake.

'A mommy's girl then?'

Bah, she laughed at his suggestion. 'No. I wouldn't say I'm a mummy's girl. I love her. She's an incredible woman to have gone through all she has and raise me to be the *wonderful* person I am, but a mummy's girl, no siree. We're nothing alike.'

Unless you counted how they looked, their movie fetish and blasted PMDD. And she wasn't about to talk about that.

She sipped her prosecco and Blake's eyes dipped to her chest. So swift she could have imagined it. Only she hadn't. But what about Aiden...?

'What's she like?' Blake pressed.

'My mother?' Astrid glanced at his brother to see if he was as invested in her as Blake.

He gave her a smile – was that gentle encouragement, a dose of sympathy for the grilling, or something else?

'She's an old romantic,' Astrid said, looking back at Blake. 'A free spirit too. She gives love as freely as breathing and doesn't think the rules apply to her.'

'The rules?'

'The generally accepted social norms. What you should and shouldn't say, how to dress, how to be. She's quite... unique.'

'Good for her.'

'My grandparents wouldn't agree. As Lord and Lady Ashford—'

'Lord and Lady Ashford?' Blake cocked a brow.

'What? Surprised I come from such good stock?'

'Not at all,' Aiden was quick to say.

'You make it sound like we're talking about horses,' Blake said over him.

'We have those too,' she said. 'But now you're making me digress.'

His eyes danced. 'My apologies, my lady, do continue.'

She pursed her lips on her laughter. So, Blake was capable of being playful. Who knew!

'My grandparents hoped my mother would follow in their footsteps and be another darling of society, someone to show off to their friends, to be proud of... Instead, they found themselves with a high school dropout, pregnant at eighteen, a father unwilling to come forward, and they made no bones about expressing their disappointment.'

'Parents can be assholes,' Blake muttered around his bottle.

'They're actually not that bad beneath all the airs and graces.'

'Spoken like a woman with a very forgiving nature.'

She laughed off Blake's remark. He wouldn't be saying that if he knew the path that had brought her to this point. Forgiveness couldn't be further from the truth. As for her grandparents, life had moved on... as had their high expectations.

'I actually adore them. They came to terms with the fact they couldn't change Mum a long time ago. As for me, I hardly fit their idealistic view of what a woman should be...' *Careful Astrid, a lady is right up Aiden's street.* 'I chose the wrong profession and don't spend enough time in the UK,' she quickly added. 'But it hasn't stopped them loving me. Loving us both. Thankfully my uncle is the perfect heir to the title and more than willing to dance to society's tune and give them what they need to show off to their friends.'

The brothers laughed.

'Heir to the title,' Blake mimicked. 'God, the English are weird.'

'I'll drink to that,' Aiden said.

'Hey!' She jabbed Aiden's calf with her toe but it was the shove to Blake's thigh that shot sparks through her body. *Daft move, Astrid!*

She glanced at Blake, praying he couldn't tell, though she got the impression the man missed nothing where she was concerned. And right now, he was loving every inch of her, the hint of bra through her blouse, her nipples like projectile missiles... *Bugger, wrong brother!*

Though he was very much the right one according to her body.

She averted her gaze. 'You can't help tradition when it's been around far longer than we have. It deserves some respect.'

'There's respect,' Aiden said, 'and then there's being governed by the constraints and expectations set down by a society that has no relevance in today's world.'

'And now you sound like my mother.'

'We love her already,' Blake said.

A phone started to ring and Aiden shifted, pulling the chiming device out of his pocket. 'One sec... Hey Harry,' he said into the phone. 'What's up? ...Now?' Aiden glanced at Blake, eyes narrowing. 'You're sure it can't wait? ...Okay, I'm on my way.'

He hung up, eyed the phone for a second before looking at his brother. 'I'm needed back at the rink.'

'You best go then.'

He didn't budge.

'It's okay, bro,' Blake said. 'I can take care of Astrid, make sure she gets home safe.'

'I'm quite capable of getting myself home safe, thank you very much.'

A, she wasn't a woman in need of a man to protect her.

And b, with her body in its heightened state, she needed free of Blake pronto.

She'd call him out on his whole *'I'm onto you'* when she wasn't so *into* him!

'Of course you are,' he replied. 'I'm just assuring my overly concerned brother that you're safe being left in my hands.'

'Why wouldn't I be safe?'

Oh, heaven help her... as if she didn't already know.

The brothers sized each other up, some silent message passing between them.

'Yes, why wouldn't she be safe?' Blake pushed and Aiden shook his head, got to his feet and shrugged on his jacket.

'It's been lovely to meet you, Astrid.'

'It was lovely to meet you too.' She gave him her trusty dazzles, swallowing the rising flutters and the nerves. 'I'll see you at the rink Tuesday, if not before.'

'Tuesday?' Blake said.

'That's the plan. I'm hoping to catch your training session and then Cheryl has our one-to-ones scheduled in, back to back.'

Cheryl was their publicist, the woman who should have had the situation all in hand long ago. Not that she was about to discredit the woman openly; she could totally see what a challenge Blake would be. And how butting heads over this could have led to her losing her job, too.

Far safer for an outsider, aka Astrid, to come in and threaten the status quo.

'So soon?' Blake said.

'The sooner the better,' she replied, keeping her focus on Aiden. On the plan and the job and not the distracting man beside her. 'It will give me a better understanding of you both and from that, I'll be able to work out where to head next. I promise not to make it too gruelling.'

Blake cursed and Aiden smiled, all charm and cooperation. 'Makes sense to me.'

'I guess it does,' his brother conceded.

'You know it does. I'll see you at home later, bro.'

'Sure.'

They watched him leave, her eyes drifting back to Blake and then she saw it, the mischievous spark in his eye.

'What did you do?'

'I don't know what you mean.'

She dared to lean closer. 'You have that look in your eye.'

'You say that like you know my full array of "looks" and I assure you, you don't...' He leaned closer too. 'Though I'm more than happy to run you through a couple more.'

How did he turn everything into a come on?

Perhaps because you want it to be a come on?

Ignore. Ignore. Ignore.

'It's the same look you had in your eye when you were verbally sparring with your brother earlier.'

'Ah... that look.'

'So?'

'So?'

'What did you do?'

'I *may* have coaxed one of our rookies into sending out an SOS that only my brother as the captain of the team can respond to.'

She lost her breath. 'And why would you do that?'

'Because I get me a firecracker all to myself.'

'You... you orchestrated our alone time?' She struggled to pull air into her lungs as Blake's glittering gaze held hers. She could feel his heat and his interest and *good God*, she wanted to shift on over and put the connection to the test. But she couldn't, she wouldn't, which meant...

'It's probably time I got home too.'

He straightened up. 'You still have your drink to finish.'

'Not any more.' She threw the last of it back and got to her feet, pulling on her suit jacket and picking up her coat. 'Thanks for the drink.'

'Wait up, let me sort us a cab.'

'There's no need, I only live a few blocks away.'

'Even better, we can walk and talk.'

'You know for a guy that wouldn't talk,' she said, shrugging on her coat, 'you really are turning into quite the chatter box.'

'When the company is worthy of it' – he got to his feet, his eyes locked on hers and setting off butterflies – 'I can be very engaging.'

She pressed her lips together, trying to trap the rising heat inside as she grabbed her bag. 'So long as you keep that in mind for Tuesday.'

'Sure thing, Twinkle Toes.'

And why oh why did her age-old, utterly humiliating pet name make her sizzle when he said it?

She started to flee...

'Hey, are you forgetting something?'

'Huh?'

He plucked her glasses off the table and handed them to her. 'Can't have you leaving these behind, can we?'

Bugger. She'd taken them off the second they'd steamed up indoors and forgotten all about them. She gave a tight smile. 'Thank you.'

'After you...' he urged.

She walked ahead of him, trying to think up a reason for him not to walk her home and coming up blank. Every reason just sounded petty, or worse, ungrateful. It wasn't that she didn't feel safe with him, she just... she wasn't safe from herself. She couldn't trust herself not to do something completely unwise and karma-ending.

They stepped out into the night and the icy wind slapped her in the face. *Hello wake-up call!*

'I really need to get a job in the sun,' she grumbled.

'And yet you chose an *ice* hockey team to get up close and personal with.'

'I know, what was I thinking?' She was only marginally teasing.

'Don't look at me, I've no idea. And this morning, I would've told you to go to hell.'

'You pretty much *did* tell me to go to hell.'

He shoved his hands into his jacket pockets and bowed his head to the cold. 'Yeah, I'm sorry for that.'

'You *are*?'

'You're just doing your job, and I really want to keep doing mine, so...'

'Is this you calling a truce?'

He sent her a look. Open and vulnerable and hell, if Blake dark and brooding was sexy as fuck, seeing him vulnerable and bowing down was something else. Especially with the way his cheeks had pinked up with the chill, his eyes ever bright.

'It's me saying I'm sorry I was a jackass, and yes, I'm agreeing to give you what you need for your article. I can't promise it'll come easily but I'll try.'

'That's...' She wet her lips. *Crushing my resolve. Making me like you more. Making me want to explore this connection more.* 'That's great to hear.'

Ugh, that sounded so hollow.

'The more you give me up front, the sooner I can be done and out of your hair.'

His eyes burned into her. 'You say that like it's a good thing...'

'Well, isn't it?'

Their breaths curled through the frosty air. She'd said it for his benefit; he was the one so anti this whole thing...

'I guess,' he said eventually, turning away and walking on.

It took her another second to move, her body delayed by her

brain that wanted to pick apart the moment. Understand him. Understand *this*.

Then she saw the electronic billboard up ahead roll around and Aiden filled the screen, his grin lighting up the pavement with his bottled tan of choice in hand...

'I know we agreed to keep tonight light and about me,' she said, head shifting into work gear, where it should be, 'but can I ask you something?'

His mouth twisted. 'Depends on what it is.'

'How come your brother is everywhere, and you're not? I assume the sponsorship deals come your way too...'

He looked up at the flashy advert, a wry smile on his lips. 'Aiden's image carries more appeal.'

'There must be plenty of brands out there wanting to lean into your bad boy rep.'

He flicked her a look that had the heat creeping into her cheeks. Thank God it was cold and her upturned collar hid half of her face. Next time she'd wear a scarf too!

'Some.'

'But you don't do it.'

'No.'

'Why is that?'

He shrugged. 'Just not my scene.'

She *knew* there was more to that answer. She also knew he wasn't about to give it.

'I'm going to need one for the article, if that's okay?'

'What? A picture?'

'Yes.'

'I said I'd give you what you need, didn't I?'

'You did.' She gave him a small smile. 'Thank you.'

He nodded, taking a few more strides. 'So your mom... she sounds like a pretty cool lady?'

She smiled. 'Yeah, she is. *Too* cool.'

'How can someone be too cool?'

'Someone who trusts too readily, loves too readily...'

'Gets burned many times over?'

'Yup. You'd think she'd learn but no, Mum's all too willing to give people the benefit of the doubt. Men especially. I used to wonder whether she was in love with the idea of falling in love, rather than the men themselves.'

'There've been a few then?'

'Oh yeah, my mother seemed to make it her mission in life to find us a replacement for my father. The sooner they could move in the better, too.'

'That can't have been easy for you growing up.'

She shrugged. 'It kind of went in cycles.'

'Cycles?'

'A happy few weeks, maybe a few months if I was lucky, of her falling head over heels. And then the misery of her falling apart when they inevitably walked away.'

'What happened with your father? How come you don't see him?'

She hesitated, worrying over what she was saying and realising she needn't. What her father had put her through, put her mother through, it was child's play compared to his past. Not that he'd told her any of it himself yet. But if she shared, maybe he would. Eventually.

'He was a friend of my grandfather's, a married man who gave a lot of this' – she chatted with her fingers – 'sweet talked his way in, promised her the world and got her pregnant. To this day, my grandparents don't know he's my father, and we don't want them to know. They'll only blame themselves.'

'Jesus, she was so young. How long were they together before you...?'

'A year. No laws were broken, only hearts. Well, one heart. He doesn't have one.'

'Shit.' Blake shook his head. 'And he was in your life for seven years, but no one knew...?'

She shrugged. 'In my life is probably an overstatement. He was around, at family functions and he'd visit for the odd weekend under the pretence of travelling with *work*. It's amazing how easily one can hide a second family when they have the money, the means and the motivation.'

'What changed?'

'His wife found out. Not about me, but about Mum. And things spiralled from there... It wasn't a fun alternate reality for him any more.'

'A *fun* alternate reality?'

'Oh yeah, that's exactly what Mum was. Twenty years his wife's junior with a child who was so desperate to make him stay longer I doted on his every word. Made him feel like super dad. Then one day his wife turned up on the doorstep and Mum hid me in my room, but I could hear everything. She was a screaming mess...'

And it was Chase's wife Astrid now saw when she reimagined that scene. Knowing she'd done the same thing to another woman. Didn't matter that she hadn't known, she'd still done it.

'Mum finally saw him for the man that he was, a heartless liar who didn't have the balls to sort his life out. So she ended it. For a time, he pretended to care about me, to want to see me but it was just a ruse to see Mum. And when he realised it was over, he stopped calling and she gave up making excuses for him. She realised it was far healthier for me not to know him at all, than to know the douchebag that he truly was.'

'And he let you go, just like that?'

'You missed my point; he didn't want me. He wanted her. She

was young and beautiful. A total ego boost and a break from the mundane – a wife, three children, and a dog.'

His curse was lost on the wind now lashing sleet at their faces and making further conversation impossible as they walked the rest of the way.

'Well, this is me...' She paused beneath the covered entryway to her uncle's building, and he gave a low whistle.

'Nice place.'

'It's my uncle's.'

'Is he home?'

'No. He splits most of his time between Barbados and the UK.'

'Lucky man. Any chance you're going to invite me in for a nightcap?'

'If I thought you were asking for just a drink, maybe.'

'Who says I'm not?'

'Your eyes.'

He flashed a dimple with a lopsided grin. 'I can see I'm going to have to watch what they do around you.'

She laughed. 'You're incorrigible.'

'So they say.'

'Goodnight, Fury.' She turned to walk away and paused, looking back over her shoulder. Could she ask him? Dare she?

'Blake...?'

His eyes lit up. 'Yes?'

'What did you mean, earlier?'

He frowned. 'Earlier? You'll have to be a little more specific.'

'When you said you were onto me. What did you mean?'

He paused for a beat and she held her breath. Maybe she shouldn't have asked him. Maybe she should've let it go and hoped that he would too. Maybe—

'I meant...'

He stepped forward, the devilish glint in his gaze stealing all thought, save one – *you definitely shouldn't have asked!*

'...you dress like you're all about business – the hair, the suit, the shoes.'

His gaze swept over her, more effective than any central heating.

'But really, you're all about the fire. The fire, the fun, and the—'

'If you say fornication...'

He chuckled low and slow. 'That too.'

She shook her head, suppressed a dizzied laugh of her own. 'You don't know me.'

'No. And you don't know me either. But I'm enjoying unravelling the mystery of you.'

'There's no mystery,' she was quick to say. Too quick.

'I'll be the judge of that. Goodnight, Twinkle Toes.' He leaned in and swept a kiss to her cheek, his stubble tantalisingly rough. 'Sweet dreams.'

And then he was gone, leaving her on a cloud of his aftershave and pheromones... and God, did she just *sigh*?

She shook her head and stomped into the foyer, stomped into the lift, stomped into her uncle's apartment, right up to her bed and face planted.

She. Was. Doomed!

* * *

Blake let himself into his apartment and tossed his wallet onto the console table. Catching his reflection in the mirror above, he shook his head. What the hell was that goofy smile about?

'Didn't trust herself alone with you, huh?'

Aiden appeared in the hallway, a glass of water in hand.

'What can I say?' He shucked his jacket. 'The girl's got it bad.'

His brother shook his head, but Blake wasn't interested in being humbled by his big bro. Grin still fixed, he swept past him into the open-plan living space. The glittering New York cityscape through the floor-to-ceiling glass greeted him, perfectly set off by the dark room with its black leather furnishings, dark wood and polished concrete floors, accent lighting set to low. Sometimes he still had to pinch himself that this was how they lived now.

'Ever the humble one, aren't you?' Aiden said, following him into the room as he set the sound system going. The dulcet tone of Tracy Chapman's 'Fast Car' hitting the spot.

'You're just pissed you had to leave early.'

'Yeah, about that...'

Blake headed to the bar and poured himself a bourbon. 'What about it?'

'Got something you wanna tell me?'

'No, don't think I do.'

Aiden sipped his water. 'So that's how you want to play it?'

'Play it?'

'Astrid?'

Blake threw back his drink. 'You want me to play nice with her, I'm playing nice. And now I'm off to bed.'

Aiden watched him go, muttering under his breath, 'Playing dirty more like.'

'I heard that...'

'You were supposed to.'

And Blake just chuckled, Chapman's lyrics about being someone with nothing to prove melding with his determination to show the world exactly that...

6

The next day Astrid woke determined to push Blake out and pull Aiden in.

She had a few days before she was due at the rink to interview the twins. A few days where she could do something karma-orientated, something without the distraction of Blake...

But what?

Caffeined up, a run under her belt, and in the zone, she pulled up the Titans schedule on her laptop. The team rarely had more than a day or two between games, and they were out of state tomorrow for two.

Today was her best bet and hot off the back of last night's antics, she even had a way in.

Picking up her phone, she sent a message to Aiden.

ASTRID

> Sorry you had to dash last night, how about dinner for two on me tonight?

Dinner for two made clear she meant *just* them. And *on her* meant she was paying so he wouldn't suggest extending the invite to Blake. She hoped.

AIDEN

Now there's an offer I can't refuse...

She smiled. A swift response; that had to be a good sign.

AIDEN

Just tell me when and where

A quick google and a few clicks later she had a table booked in one of the most exclusive and most romantic venues in Manhattan. She sent him the details, wondering whether he'd baulk at her choice.

AIDEN

Fancy! See you there.

Her smile grew. She opened up WhatsApp:

JUST DESSERTS WHATSAPP GROUP 09.10 EST.

ASTRID

Guess who has dinner with a certain Aiden Carter tonight... how long is too long to be late for a dinner date?

BELLA

Haha! Fabulous! That was quick!

ASTRID

What can I say I'm freaking irresistible!

BELLA

😂 😂 😂

ASTRID

I won't ask why you're laughing...

BELLA

🐻

And as much as Astrid would love to think that Aiden's eagerness was all about her 'irresistibility', she knew it had more to do with sibling rivalry, their egos, and his desire to keep her sweet for the article. All of which she was more than happy to exploit in the name of karma.

PAIGE

Love it! Timewise, it all depends on whether you message him to let him know you're going to be late... 😈

SISSI

Ten years? Xx

Astrid gave a soft huff. *I feel ya, honey.*
And tonight, Sissi would get a little of her own back...

* * *

Astrid had never been purposefully late for anyone in her life, and it was harder than she'd envisaged. Every minute dragged and though she tried to use the time productively, working through her research for the article, she spent more time watching the clock than reading.

At fifteen minutes past her reservation time her phone went ping.

AIDEN

I'm here, where are you?

She was right across the street in a cosy little bar, head half hidden by a cap. She'd seen him arrive. Seen him take up a seat at their table. Seen him order what looked like a club soda, peruse the menu for a spell before resorting to his phone.

AIDEN

We did say 7 p.m.?

Her fingers twitched to reply. *Not yet,* she could hear the girls urge.

At twenty-five minutes past, a waitress approached his table. He waved her away and messaged again.

AIDEN

Is everything okay?

He looked out the window, his frown obvious even from this distance. Just a few more minutes...

She eased out of her booth and headed to the ladies, firing off a message as she went.

ASTRID

Sorry! I got caught up with work – in the zone!
Be with you shortly!

Take that with your passion and no time for love spiel, matey! A taste of your own medicine, right back atcha!

Buzzing on her teeny tiny victory, she snapped a shot of the convo and sent it to the girls. Then she stripped her cap, shook out her hair, topped up her makeup, and left the bar, pausing when her phone went ping ping ping ping.

She checked the screen...

JUST DESSERTS WHATSAPP GROUP. 19.43 EST.

BELLA

Karma 1, Aiden 0

> **SISSI**
>
> love love LOVE!
>
> Even better, have you seen this? https://www.tiktok.com/@puckbun2468/video/12732637?q=AidenCarterDateless
>
> I'm dying over here! 😂😂
>
> **BELLA**
>
> Oh my God, that is gold!!! 😂😂 😂😂 😂😂

Astrid clicked the link and her screen filled with a clip of Aiden, sat alone at the table, Celine Dion's rendition of 'All by Myself' playing out as a superimposed girl with bunny ears gave a rundown of the scene... an ice hockey all-star all bummed at being stood up. Stood up in *real* time.

OMG!

> **SISSI**
>
> Did you plan this?

> **ASTRID**
>
> Hell no!

> **BELLA**
>
> But it's genius. One thing to be stood up.
> Another to have the world know it too.

> **ASTRID**
>
> Yeah, but what do I do now? If I rock up, they might snap me next?

> **BELLA**
>
> Would it matter?

> **ASTRID**
>
> I guess not. But then they'll know he was only left waiting...

BELLA

Do you think anyone will care? That video is out there now, there's no pulling it back.

SISSI

It's made my day!! 😄 🙏

And if it had made Sissi's day, it had totally made Astrid's too!

Pocketing her phone, she looked up to see the waitress once more at his side and took the opportunity to get across the road unseen.

Now to be suitably apologetic and not laud her lateness...

As she entered the restaurant, his gaze landed on her and he stood, his grin coming easy. *Too* easy. Did *anything* shake this guy?

She hurried up to him, engaging the dazzles. 'I'm so sorry I'm late.'

She set her coat and bag on the chair and without debating it, leaned in to give him a kiss on the cheek. *All* the dazzles. 'You must have thought you'd been stood up.'

His brow crinkled. 'No, why would I think that?'

Because any guy with a normal sized ego would...

'Ha!' She gave a wave of her hand. 'Why indeed!'

'Can I get you a drink?' the waitress asked, her eyes sparkling with curiosity as she gave Astrid the once-over.

'I'll have what he's having.'

'I'm on the soda today, game tomorrow.'

'Suits me fine.'

She smiled and sat as he did. 'Have you chosen what you fancy?'

'Yeah...' Though he was distracted by his phone as it remained lit on the table, a flurry of notifications rolling in. Did he know? Had he seen the video? The lines in his brow deepened with each passing second...

'Everything okay?'

'Huh?' He glanced up at her. 'Oh yeah sure.'

The waitress placed her drink down. 'Are you ready to order?'

'I am,' he said, his stomach giving a growl as if on cue.

'You order first,' she said, having no idea what she fancied as she stared unseeing at the menu; she was too hyped to fancy anything.

'I'll have the chicken fusion, but easy on the spice.'

'Not a fan?' Astrid asked.

'*It's* not a fan of me.'

'An allergy?' the waitress asked.

'More a mild aversion.'

Astrid was taking notes...

'I'll have the same. But *all* the spice. I like it hot.'

She held Aiden's gaze as she said it, keeping his focus as the waitress took their menus away.

'So...' he said, placing his phone aside. 'Work kept you away, hey?'

She gave a sanguine smile. 'I knew you'd understand, what with your passion for the game and all.'

His eyes sharpened, a flicker of amusement dancing around his mouth... or was that a slight prickle in his ego? 'Can I ask what you were working on?'

'What do you think? Or rather, *who* do you think?'

'Anything you want to talk about?'

'So much, but...' It was far easier to flirt over small talk. 'Let's save it for the interviews and keep tonight light.'

His phone started to ring, and he cut if off, only to have it start up again and he smothered a curse.

'Is something up?'

'It seems a video of me is going viral.'

'It is? Is that a good thing or a bad thing?'

'I don't know yet.'

'What kind of video?'

'I don't know that either.'

She glanced at the screen, saw Cheryl's name flashing up. 'If your publicist is after you, you should probably go and deal with it.'

'Would you mind?'

'I kept you waiting for almost an hour, I think you can step out and deal with this while I wait.'

He was on his feet before she'd finished. 'Thanks.'

She pressed her lips together. *Here we go...*

He stepped outside the restaurant and she watched him through the glass. Watched as he took the call. Watched as his frown deepened. Watched as he lowered the device to view what must be the video...

Take that, heartbreaker!

His eyes widened and flicked to her, but she was quicker to look away, sipping her drink. Nonchalant. Nothing to see here. Nothing at all. She suppressed a giggle as her own phone started to ping, and she picked it up.

BELLA

I don't believe it!

SISSI

I know 😅

ASTRID

Believe what?

BELLA

Look at the comments... 🙈

The *comments*?!

Astrid turned the volume down and opened up the video beneath the table. *My God, how many views?*

She clicked on the comments and her mouth fell open. *You've got to be kidding me.*

The man was getting an outpouring of *love*!

He wasn't a bloody laughingstock.

He was a god!

This could not be happening.

She scrolled and scrolled, the love ever swelling and making her stomach roll.

His ego was meant to take a bashing, not receive a public stroking!

She glanced out the window, saw his shock turn to smugness as he too saw what she did. What Cheryl must do as well. That the Ice King being stood up was apparently the best PR move ever! And she'd bloody orchestrated it!

No-no-no-no-no...

ASTRID

Sissi, what do you know about Aiden's spice aversion?

SISSI

He ate a chilli dog once, the trots for days. Why?

ASTRID

Stay tuned...

Aiden was still outside when the food arrived. It was a waiter this time. The waitress was probably too busy giving Aiden puppy-dog eyes through the glass...

'I have one chicken easy on the spice,' he said, 'and one all in.'

'Easy on the spice, please.' She beamed up at him, her smile growing as he set both dishes down and she could see they looked identical. 'Thank you so much.'

Aiden returned to the table, his grin too wide to ignore.

'I take it things are okay then?'

'Better than okay!'

Christ, he looked smugger than ever as he took up his cutlery.

'And this looks delicious.'

He tucked in with gusto and slowly she took up her cutlery, her insides smiling with glee. *That's right, buddy, eat up!*

Thirty minutes later and sporting a shiny grimace on his once smug face, he was doing the clenched butt walk into an awaiting taxi, his apology hurried and harried and music to Astrid's ears as she snapped a surreptitious clip and sent it to her girls.

ASTRID

[image] Karma is an arse on fire 🔥 🔥 🔥

SISSI

OMG! 😂 😂 😂 I fluffing love you!

ASTRID

Love you too babe 💋 Nite nite! xx

7

The morning of the interviews, Astrid was buzzing.

This time she knew what to expect and couldn't be blind-sided by her body's reaction to Blake. There was no man on this planet worthy of losing one's head over.

Never had been, never would be. That first day had been a blip. A mind-bending, tummy turning, foo foo fluttering blip. All because she couldn't engage her head for her hormones.

And speaking of losing one's head, the heels had to go. As much as they were supposed to make a man lose theirs, she valued hers too much to risk another tumble. Today, she was dressing for her and ensuring her confidence and her control came with.

She'd stuck with the no-nonsense ponytail, kept her makeup on point but opted for layers – *all* the layers. A cami, white shirt, checkered blue waistcoat and matching blazer paired with her favourite jeans and trainers. The sophisticated rebel and her in every way.

She snapped a selfie and sent it to the karma crew:

JUST DESSERTS WHATSAPP GROUP. 08.15 EST.

ASTRID

[image]

Suited and booted and ready to kick some hockey butt! 🐱

BELLA

Loving the waistcoat! x

SISSI

Wow, that is some outfit 😄

PAIGE

Hot stuff! I *almost* feel sorry for him xx

ASTRID

Cheers my loves 💋

BELLA

PS Finished Book One yet?

Astrid pulled a face. Yes, she may have used Delia's book to distract herself from the hotness that was Blake over the last few nights... and had the dreams to match.

ASTRID

Nearly 😅

She slotted her phone away, shook out her hands, shrugged on her long cashmere coat and looked in the mirror.

She was Astrid Sinclair, Journalist of the Year twice over, capable of winning anyone over, from the most meretricious of models to the most sullen of celebs. She would get to the truth.

And if she could extract a little karma vindication while she was at it, all the better.

Striding for the door, she snatched Paige's glasses off the console table. *These* she would keep. More as a lucky charm than a necessary accessory and a way to take the girls with her.

Her phone pinged again and swapping the glasses for the device in her bag, she checked the screen expecting Bella, only...

AIDEN

> Bring something you can skate in. I'll take you out later.

What?!

ASTRID

> Today?

AIDEN

> If you're going to put me through my paces, it's only fair I put you through yours 🛼

ASTRID

> Funny

AIDEN

> I'm serious.

Her fingers hovered over the phone. *Her? Freaking* Twinkle Toes, on *ice*?!

She could pretend she had some place else to be. But to bail on extra time with the Ice King, especially after their eventful dinner date... she couldn't risk giving the wrong impression. A *disinterested* impression.

ASTRID

> You're on!

She did an about-turn as her phone started to ring – *bleeding Nora*, she was popular this morning. Then she saw who it was and swiftly answered, 'Hey Mum.'

'Darling, are you okay? You didn't text this morning.'

Bugger. She'd been so distracted by the twins she hadn't sent her daily greeting.

'Sorry...' She put the phone in the crook of her neck as she slid open her wardrobe. 'All's good.'

'How's the new article going? Are those ice hockey players really as huge as they appear on the TV?'

She laughed. 'It's going, and yes.'

'And the dating pool?'

'Mum!'

'What, darling? You're working in a male-dominated environment, you can't blame a mother for hoping her daughter might meet her match.'

'I'm working,' she said, shoving her exercise gear into a bag. 'Not hunting down a husband!'

'Well, you know, I was working when I met John and—'

'Yeah yeah, I know, and John's a wonder.'

A wonder that he's still around after a few months, Astrid couldn't help thinking.

'He *is* a wonder.'

Astrid was being sarcastic, her mother wasn't.

'And I'm not giving up hope that one day you'll bring someone home. I really thought that Chase—'

'*Mum!* We had this conversation at Christmas.'

She'd only mentioned Chase to get her mother to quit nagging and it had backfired spectacularly because months down the line she was still bringing him up. She would quit if she knew the full horror of *that* relationship, but there was no way Astrid was going to tell her. Far better to let her think her daughter had 'self-sabotaged' yet another relationship...

'And we'll have it forever more because I'm worried about you. I'm worried that it's my fault you—'

'It's *not* your fault!' She zipped the bag closed and straightened. 'You don't need to worry about me. And I don't need a man to make me happy.'

'What about a woman then, because I'm—'

'Mum!'

'Okay, okay, I'm shutting up. I'm just glad you're alive.'

And tomorrow, Astrid would make doubly sure she messaged *before* her mother could ring if this was how it would go.

* * *

Blake sensed her enter the rink. He couldn't see her yet, but her presence rippled down the ice, the guys shifting in their stance, heads turning...

Everyone knew who she was and why she was here. Not that they cared about the latter. She was new and she was hot and the team's WhatsApp group had blown up with surreptitious pics and lewd banter from the off.

He tightened his grip on the stick. Bunch of damn hornballs, every last one of them.

Even Danny had stirred the pot.

Not Blake though. He wasn't getting involved. And Aiden had been noticeably quiet too.

He eyed his brother now as they ran through their drills, weaving through the cones and passing the puck down the ice in flawless rhythm. Matching Ice's burst of speed, he sent the puck into the crease, and his brother tipped it in with precision. He broke away, his gaze flicking to the edge of the rink, and there she was, Coach at her side.

'Distracted?' Aiden said, spraying ice as he came up to him.

'I could ask you the same.'

'I'm not the one with the sloppy stick work.'

'No, just the sloppy footwork.'

Blake could've said something a whole lot worse considering the amount of time his brother had spent in the can these last few days. But there was a line to their banter, and he wasn't about to cross it. Though the smirk on his brother's face as he rejoined the line up almost made him reconsider.

Blake set his jaw and caught him up. *Just tune her out, tune the hornballs out, get it done and—*

A low wolf whistle cut through the noise. *For the love of...!*

He broke rank, seeking out the culprit and cutting across Vincent as he did so.

'What the fuck, Fury?'

'Chill, Pidg.'

V's eyes flashed beneath his helmet. 'Who the hell you calling Pigeon?'

'You really want to cause a fight in training, bro?' Aiden swooshed up, shoulder barging Blake back into the drill.

'Wasn't top of my list for the day, no.'

Though V deserved a beating. He was the guy who'd kicked off the Astrid chatter in the group that morning, and had upped his game since she'd walked in, doing his damnedest to impress. But then they were all behaving like preening princesses...

'I told you having a hot chick around was bad for the game,' Blake grumbled.

'Bad for the game or bad for you?'

His brother had a point. He never let anyone outside the rink get inside his head while on it. It had been his safe space since he could skate. A way to block out reality and focus on the game. Nothing else mattered but the puck.

'It doesn't have to be as painful as you're making it out to be.'

'What?' He frowned at his brother. 'Having her watch our every move?'

'No. The interview. I assume that's why you got out of bed the wrong side this morning.'

'Whatever, buddy.'

'Don't whatever me. You've been pissy ever since you woke up. Or are you still stewing over the fact that she took me to dinner instead of you?'

'Yeah right, is that the same dinner that gave you the explosive shits?'

Banter line, be damned.

Aiden didn't answer as Astrid's laughter tinkled down the rink. It wasn't like she could hear them across the distance, but his brother was as red as his sweater as he glanced her way and Blake followed suit.

It was Coach who had her laughing, Coach who was *never* funny. Go figure.

Blake couldn't see her properly through the glass and the reflection off the ice, just a flash of her camel coat and dark hair, but he could see enough of Coach to know the man was grinning from ear to ear.

'Hey Coach!' he hollered. 'You gonna train us today or stand there gassing?'

The cosy twosome turned his way, and damn if he didn't pull a Bambi. Nothing to do with her attention and everything to do with a sideswipe from a vengeful V. Honest.

'Jackass!' Blake swiftly righted his stride, the team's laughter carrying his insult down the ice.

'Yeah, you sure told him,' Aiden teased, sweeping past him to join Coach at the boards. 'Good to see you, Astrid.'

'Good to see you too.' She beamed at his brother. 'I hope you're feeling better; I was worried about you after...'

'Yeah, I'm all good,' his brother blustered as Blake skated by.

'Except when you eat spice, Ice,' he couldn't resist saying as he gave Astrid a brief nod of acknowledgement, fearing if he paused any longer, he'd be on his ass.

'Wait,' V said, coming up behind Blake. 'Did you just say the reason Ice almost got caught short against the Hawks was down to a spicy dish?'

Oh dear...

'Yup,' said Harry, sweeping past. 'I heard that too.'

'Get outta here!' V chuckled low and slow. 'Ice is afraid of spice!'

'Say that again, V,' Aiden ground out, 'and I swear I'll...'

* * *

Astrid didn't know whether to laugh or beg for Coach's forgiveness as the phrase took on a life of its own, spreading through the players and making Aiden growl...

'Ice is afraid of spice.'

It was kinda catchy...

'I'm so sorry, Coach,' she said.

'You ain't got nothing to be sorry for; these lot on the other hand, between the catcalling and the banter...' Coach turned to the ice. 'Knock it off, Titans, or you'll be doing suicides until you puke!'

A groan echoed around the arena and she laughed. 'It's okay, Coach. I can take it.'

'But I can't. It's a question of respect. Give them an inch and they'll take a mile. You'll wanna keep that in mind while you're with us.'

She gave a salute. 'Gotcha.'

He pushed away from the boards and blew his whistle. 'Right, suicides!'

'But Coach, you said—'

'I didn't say anything about puking this time!'

He sent her a wink and she grinned back. He was fun. *This* was fun.

Setting her bag down on the bench, she chose to stand, keen to get as close to the action as possible. Watching them was hypnotic. As was the sound. The blades cutting through ice, the thwack of the puck, the background music too... Thrash metal seemed to be the tune of choice, and she could more than cope with that.

She pulled out her notepad and pencil while Coach issued orders, matching faces to names to jersey numbers, her lips twitching up every time a guy swept past and threw her a silent acknowledgement. A nod. A cheeky wink. A grin.

The only one not giving her any more attention was Blake.

Strange. Considering everything he'd said to her, everything he'd hinted at...

What was his problem?

Aiden did another sweep by, caught where she was looking and shook his head. 'Don't worry about him, he's just rattled about this afternoon.'

She didn't have time to respond, he was gone in a flash. The speed with which they zipped around was exhilarating – and, if she was honest, a little terrifying.

The thought of being out there herself later...

Now she sat as her knees gave a wobble and forced her attention on the *entire* team, rather than a certain giant who clearly wasn't in the mood to talk.

But the more Blake avoided her eye, the more she found herself seeking him out...

* * *

'Ice, you're wanted!'

Blake looked up to see the assistant coach lean into the locker room and through the gap in the door, a glimpse of brunette. Astrid.

'Coming.' His brother slammed his locker shut and shrugged on his sweater, his eyes meeting Blake's. 'You alright?'

What his brother really meant was, *You're not gonna run, are you?*

'Sure.'

'You want to do this together because—'

'Don't you trust me, bro?'

'That's not what I meant.'

He sensed every ear in the room tune into their conversation – ten pairs and counting.

'Butter her up for me, yeah.' He turned away and tugged open his locker, eyeing his reflection in the mirror on the door and flicking at his hair like it was the most important thing in the world.

'It's rude to keep a lady waiting,' he muttered, his twin senses telling him his brother hadn't shifted. 'You taught me that.'

That earned a few sniggers and had his brother moving.

'Don't do anything I wouldn't do,' he called after him. 'Or if you do' – his eyes caught Astrid's as Aiden yanked open the door – 'make sure you don't get caught.'

Then he slammed his locker shut and moved in the opposite direction, to the gym. He suddenly had boundless energy and there was only one way to kill it off – one way that wouldn't land him in more trouble at any rate.

Then, he'd be ready for her and whatever she had to throw at him.

And in the meantime, he wouldn't be thinking of her and
Aiden and whatever they were throwing around together.

Wishful thinking, much?

8

Cheryl had sorted them a small room in the private exec suite on the upper floor. Close to the GM's office but far enough away from the hustle and bustle of the public areas and the player facilities to remain undisturbed.

She took off her coat and Aiden reached for it. 'Here, I'll put it in the closet.'

'The closet?'

'These rooms have everything you need to ensure you don't have to leave once you're in. Don't want to risk missing any of the action.'

He nodded to the glass doors that led out to a private balcony and an undisturbed view of the rink.

'The rest room is through here too.'

He disappeared off and she twirled on the spot, taking in the small but flashy space. A wood-panelled wall brandishing the Titans logo backed a fully stocked bar complete with stools, while a giant flatscreen filled another, and the other was covered in team paraphernalia lit by the Titan colours – red, blue and white.

'Drink?' he asked, coming back into the room.

'A club soda would be great, thanks.'

She dropped her bag on the coffee table that stretched down the middle of the room, flanked by two cosy sofas, and started pulling out her things – notepad, pencil, mobile...

'You happy to do it here?' she asked. 'Or would you prefer the stools?'

'Here is good.'

She sat as he did, accepting the drink he offered out to her. 'Thank you. Do you mind if I record our conversation?'

She gestured to her phone on the table and he followed her gaze, the bob of his throat the only indication he was in any way ill at ease.

'I promise I won't use anything you ask me not to, I just find it saves me having to stop all the time so my notes can catch up.'

He gave a weak smile. 'I'm surprised you bother with pen and paper these days.'

'Force of habit. I like having something in my hand to twiddle with.'

His eyes fired. 'There are so many things I could say to that.'

'I'm sure there are...' She bit her lip, karma at war with the professional. 'But then I'd have to accuse you of stalling.'

'Never. Though before we get started, I will say, it's good to see you looking more prepared for the rink today; my brother was worried you'd catch your death.'

'Blake was worried?'

Don't get all giddy about it!

'Sure. And he has a point. We wouldn't want you getting ill while you're following us about. And let's face it, the sneakers are a much safer bet.'

She wagged her toes. 'No more having to save me from these twinkle toes, hey?'

'Not that I minded breaking your fall.'

'You like coming to my rescue, Ice?'

'You think I make a good knight in shining armour, Sinclair?'

Absolutely not. Steel shot through her spine with the honest answer she couldn't give. Because no knight would have bailed on Sissi like he had.

He made a good flirt though. A flirt who was skilled at turning questions back on her and avoiding a straight answer. Well, two could play at that game.

'Do you often spend your time rescuing damsels in distress?'

'Is that a question for the article?'

'Maybe.'

'Depends on the woman who needs rescuing.'

Sienna! she wanted to scream, but again, she knew she couldn't.

'Your mother, perhaps?'

He stiffened in his seat, the smile leaving his eyes, his lips...

'Straight in there like a true reporter.'

'You're not the only one who's good at their job.' She softened it with a smile. 'You gave me a lead and I took it. Though we can park that conversation for later if it suits and talk about other women who might have played a role in your life.'

Like Sienna... because if *he* mentioned her, then Astrid could too.

'My mother is the most important woman in my life. And like I told you yesterday, my father was a brute. A drunk. A nasty piece of work who took out his inferiority complex on everyone else.'

The Ice King reigned supreme as he let rip on his past. Eyes cold, jaw set, his voice devoid of any emotion.

'But you know all that already so what you're really asking is: was it so bad that we had to rescue her from it?'

'Yes.' Because karma pact aside, her article demanded that she understand this.

'You want to know if he beat her? If he beat us? If we played hardball with our very first contract to ensure it wasn't just us being gifted an escape, but our mother too? Yes. Yes. Yes. And too right we did.'

She swallowed, admiration swelling, even as she realised that the contract to which he referred was the one that saw him walking away from Ashbury Falls. Walking away from dear sweet Sissi.

'That was quite the risk, negotiating like that?'

He shrugged. 'By that point, we had several colleges vying to recruit us; we used the competition to secure a deal to take her with us. To start a new life, free of him and it got Blake – well, it got Blake away.'

He'd hesitated... she felt like he'd been about to say something else. Admit something else. But what?

'You say that like Blake needed it more than you – did he?'

He stared back at her, eyes revealing nothing. 'We *all* needed to get away.'

That didn't really answer her question... She scribbled a note to pick it up later.

'All you need to know,' he said, rubbing the back of his neck, 'is that my father was poison, he killed everything he touched. After he lost his job, it was unbearable. Mom became this tiny, broken woman. Quiet as a mouse most days. Unless she was at the rink, watching us play...' He gave the smallest of smiles. 'Then she was so full of life, fierce, amazing and everything we wanted her to be at home.'

'That must have been heartbreaking to witness. And the pressure you must have felt at such a young age to make her life better, to make your own life better...'

Astrid ached for the boy-cum-man he'd been. But to leave without explaining it to Sienna... Not to have answered her calls. Given her some closure. After all the promises he'd given her.

'Do you see your father now?'

'Not if I can help it.'

'So, you do see him?'

'He'll rock up every now and then, when he wants something.'

'Like?'

'Tickets to a game, an introduction to someone, money...'

'Do you give it to him?'

'That depends.'

'On?'

'How much trouble he's likely to cause if I don't. Sometimes it's easier, and quieter to give him what he needs and move him on. Though I draw the line at introductions. I don't want anyone in my life tainted by breathing the same air as him.'

His eyes flashed, the first sign of a simmering anger just below the surface and then it was gone. Like it had never been there at all.

'Where does he live now?'

'Around.'

Deliberately evasive.

'Do you know where?'

'Why? You planning on talking to him too?'

'I like to speak to as many sources as possible, especially if they're mentioned.'

He raised a brow. 'A reporter who likes to fact check...'

'That's a good thing, is it not?'

He nodded slowly. 'I suppose.'

And speaking of people cropping up in the article...

'Do you think your mother might talk to me?'

'I don't want her brought into this. She's been through enough and I don't want her having to revisit the past. She's a different woman now.'

'She's the woman you glimpsed at your games as a kid...?'

His smile made a return. 'She is.'

If only he'd had the same protective instinct over Sissi, the woman he'd promised to love and protect too...

'Do you have any regrets about that time? About leaving Ashbury Falls?'

A cloud came over him, a flicker of something and then, 'No.'

'No?'

It hadn't looked like a 'no'. There was something he wasn't saying. Something he didn't want to tell her or something he didn't want to admit... even to himself.

Which was it? And what was it?

Could it be...

'What about friends? Maybe a childhood sweetheart you—'

'It was the right thing to do,' he cut in, stone cold, the pulse in his jaw working overtime. 'For Mom. For Blake.'

'For you?' she had to press, and he gave a delayed nod, his jaw tight.

She wasn't convinced. Not the journalist in her, or the woman that knew of the supposed love he'd once shared with Sissi. The man she was getting to know – the loyal brother, loving son, conscientious team player – he wouldn't lie about those feelings back then and he wouldn't forget them now.

If he had no regrets, if he was over Sissi, he wouldn't have shot her down at the mere suggestion of a childhood sweetheart. And that was worth exploring every chance she got.

'Do you always do that?'

'What?'

'Put yourself last?'

He huffed. 'I'm the eldest.'

'You're twins.'

He gave a one-sided grin, flashing that dimple...

'I was born minutes before him and I don't let him forget it.'

'I bet you don't.'

'And one of us needed to become the man of the family,' he said, seriously. 'Take control of the situation and get us out of it.'

'And that had to be you?'

'When you grow up with a man like our father, it shapes you in some way. For me, I craved stability and control. A future no longer threatened by the unknown, my brother and mother safe from his reach and on a better path. Family is a motivation like no other.'

'Of course it is,' she agreed, but she couldn't forget that he'd promised Sissi *she* was his family too. Promised her the exact same future and then taken it away.

'Leaving Ashbury Falls was a clean break for us all, it was what we needed, and we haven't looked back.'

But she was going to make him look back, and she was going make him see Sienna if it killed her...

* * *

'You're doing it again.'

Blake didn't slow, his punches landing hard and fast against the bag. He didn't have the patience for Larsson's comments today.

'What is it this time?'

He shifted his stance, went at it again and Larsson chuckled, his big frame locked in a hands-free squat.

'You got it bad.'

Blake grabbed the punch bag as it swung back at him. 'Got what bad?'

'Foxy has you all...' Larsson shook his huge hands either side of his head. '*Tokig*. Crazy.'

Foxy. Dammit. He'd said it out loud once, maybe twice, and now they were all calling her it.

'Her name's Astrid.'

Larsson's blue eyes danced. '*Real* bad.'

'Do you want to take this up in the ring?'

Because Blake couldn't care that the guy at a towering six foot seven, had four inches on him and umpteen pounds, he was ready to go. At something, anything...

'I'm not that stupid.' Larsson dropped the barbell and brushed off his hands. 'We have a game tomorrow.'

They did. And hell, Blake's head was elsewhere. Currently in a room upstairs with his brother and a certain pair of overly inquisitive, mind-bending, honeyed eyes.

He wasn't sure what disturbed him more – the line of questioning or his brother being alone with her – but one thing was painfully clear, he wanted her.

He wanted to be better than his brother to get her, too.

And he'd never been better than his brother. Not ever.

9

Aiden was easy to talk to. If not for Sissi, she'd go as far as to say he was a pleasure. Astrid could see why he was so well regarded in the sport and beyond. Why his exes – aside from the all-important Sissi – never had a bad word to say about him, too.

None of it fuelled her karma quest, but all of it made great fodder for her article.

'A model player, a model pupil.' She reflected on what he'd said about his schooldays. 'And you still found the time to save your brother from flunking out, too.'

'That's not what I said.'

She smiled. 'Okay you said you forced him to study with you when it was clear he'd rather be out with his mates.'

'Even the best hockey players need to make the grade for the best scholarships.'

She nodded. 'And did he?'

'He got into college, didn't he?'

That didn't answer her question...

'I thought deals were often spun for the sake of the sport rather than academia.'

His eyes narrowed. 'I don't appreciate the insinuation, Astrid. He got in because he deserved to get in period. He studied hard and he trained harder.'

'Because of you.'

'Because he wanted it as much as me.'

She wet her lips. Either he was being modest about it, or there was more to the deal than he was willing to share. She made a note to do more digging and moved on.

'What about role models? Was there someone who stood out for you back then?'

He nodded. 'Grady Marshall. He's a legend. A veteran of the game. When we first joined the Redstone Devils, he took Blake and me under his wing, helped us settle into the game, taught us not to be such cocky little shits.'

She pursed her lips. 'And that worked you think?'

'For me, I'd say so. Blake... well, you've met him, what do you think?'

Even his name kickstarted a simmering heat down low and she cleared her throat, checking her notes...

'Aside from your home life, what other challenges did you face early on?'

'It's a competitive sport and we were from a tiny town with no real resources. It was an hour's drive to get us to the rink, and our mom worked long hours; she had to bust a gut to get us to all our training sessions.'

'Would you say you owe part of your success to her?'

'One hundred per cent. Most kids probably want to get away from their folks. Not us. We loved taking her with us. And we were so freaking useless, we needed her. She made sure we ate, slept and studied, when all we wanted to do was train twenty-four-seven. Now she lives in Brooklyn, and we see her as much as we can. Try to return the favour so to speak.'

'Brooklyn. Nice.'

'It is nice. It's a traditional brownstone on a tree-lined street right next to the park. It's everything she always wanted for us growing up; now we get to give it to her.'

'You pay her rent?'

He shrugged. 'Sure we do. She helps out in a local school and at the homeless shelter too. She has freedom and the financial stability to do the things she always wanted to do.'

'Thanks to you both.'

It caught in her chest, the acknowledgement of all he and his brother had done for their mother, and what the woman in turn was doing for others. It was good, it was kind, it was giving back. Didn't make him good, kind and giving to Sissi though. But the more she listened, the more she was struggling to reconcile her karma mission with the man before her.

'And what's it like playing with your brother? Have you ever been tempted to split up, play for different teams?'

'Playing with my brother means the world to me. We're a pair. We always have been. On the ice, off the ice. I'm a stronger and better player because of him.'

'I imagine he feels the same.'

'He does, whether he'll admit it though...'

'I'll make sure I ask.' She adjusted her glasses and scanned her notes for her next question. 'What do you think of the NHL's shift away from permitting violence in the game?'

'It's a good thing. Too many guys are getting into bad scrapes, too many are ending up with injuries that see them in an early grave. It doesn't make it any less tough, any less aggressive, any less thrilling. Just safer.'

'Have you had any major injuries?'

'No.'

'Setbacks?'

He shifted position. 'The first time we bombed out of the playoffs, I wasn't prepared for it. I like to win, and unfortunately, in any sport, at any level, no matter how hard you work, you can't always win.'

'And that's important to you?'

He gave a laugh. 'Isn't it to everyone?'

'Some more than most.'

'Yeah, well, we live and breathe competition. We want to win, and for a long time, it felt like the only metric to judge my career by. I still struggle with it but I'm learning to dust off the losses.'

'How so?'

'I don't look back. Not ever. You can't change what's in the past. You learn from your mistakes, and you move on.'

And is that how he'd moved on from Sissi? Classed her as a mistake? Dusted her off? She spied her pencil bending in her grip and forced her fingers to relax.

'Is that a motto you apply to your personal life too?'

'Why not? It works.'

Why not indeed...

'What's been your toughest challenge to date?'

'Easy. The physical exertion. It's gruelling. The training schedule, the games... the pressure never lets up.'

She took up her water as she feigned an understanding nod. 'Not leaving Ashbury Falls behind? The people you must've—'

'I told you I don't look back.'

'Right, you did.' Too quickly. Too forcefully. And that was the bit she wanted to unpick... 'So how do you deal with the pressure?'

'I keep focused on my goal. Get better. Be the best.'

'It must take its toll mentally.'

'There's pressure in every job.'

'But not every job comes with the added pressure of being a

public figurehead and with all your sponsorship deals, you're more than just the face of the Titans; how do you cope with that?'

'I tune it out. It's just fuzz. I'm here to play the game and make our fans proud.'

Gah. He was so good at this, every answer so noble and agreeable.

'What about all those sponsorship deals? Do you truly believe in the products you promote?'

'I wouldn't put my name to anything I didn't.'

'So the aftershave, the bottled tan, the strawberry *sundaes...?*'

'You've seen that one?'

She gave a sceptical hum as she raised her brows at his chiselled torso.

'Everything can be enjoyed in moderation, Astrid.'

'You're seriously telling me you eat them?'

'Off season, absolutely. And don't knock it until you try it.'

She had tried it, right along with a stack of fondant fancies and candied cocktails! Now focus...

'What's your proudest moment to date?'

'That's a hard one. Getting recruited into our college team was the validation of a lifelong dream. But lifting the Stanley Cup for the first time, there's no rush like it.'

His eyes shone with the memory alone.

'Do you think you'll get to do it again this year?'

'You better believe it.'

'And what if you don't?'

He looked taken aback by the question. 'Like I said, I won't dwell on it.'

Her eyes tightened. *Like you didn't dwell on Sissi. Only you did, I'm sure of it...*

'Would you say hockey has changed you as a person over the years?'

Made you selfish. Made you all about your career and your family. Given you the ability to push out the girl whose heart you broke? Or is she still in there?

'Man, everything changes you over the years, right? I mean, I'm ten years older than when I got picked for a college team. Back then, I felt like I had everything to prove. Now, I want to make guys like Grady Marshall proud. They had faith in us when they didn't need to. It's my job to pay that forward.'

'What about future goals? You're twenty-eight now; are there any milestones or achievements you're still striving for?'

'I'm never going to stop wanting to win the Stanley Cup. I made that promise to myself a long time ago – that nothing would come between me and the ultimate win.'

'And after the game, when you can't play any more? How do you see your life then? Do you intend to stay involved in the hockey world or pursue something else?'

He leaned forward, resting his elbows on his knees as he looked at his hands.

'Hockey changed my life. My whole family's life. I want to work on bringing our sport to more kids. Whether that's investment in rinks, clubs, training or working with schools to expand their sports programmes. I want to give back to the game that's given us so much.'

It was so noble, and so sincere, and so maddeningly infuriating because she wanted him to be the egotistical prick she'd had him painted as from the outset. She *needed* him to be that guy to continue to deliver on the karma he so deserved. She *needed* Sissi.

'What about your life outside the game?'

'Are you hitting on my love life again?'

'I was thinking more hobbies, interests... but if you want to go there, I'm listening.'

His eyes sparkled. The charm making a return. 'I'll find hobbies when I retire.'

'And a woman?'

'Not on the agenda.'

'Now or ever?'

'Who knows.'

Deliberately vague.

'You've been seen with enough women on your arm in the past.'

'I date, I'm not a monk.'

'Anyone serious?'

'So you really are going there?'

'It's important that any profile piece gives a balanced view of its subject.'

He studied her steadily, then, 'No, nobody serious.'

'But there was?' Because she swore she could see Sissi in his eyes, the past, the regret...

'Nobody that needs bringing into this,' he ground out. 'Next question.'

She hesitated. The desire to call him out on it, to name Sienna and put him on the spot burned inside her, begging to be voiced. But how could she do that without letting slip what she already knew and how she knew it. Unless she could get Blake to name Sienna... now *that* had potential.

Then there could be no stopping her.

In the meantime...

'So if there's no serious relationship, and you don't have any hobbies to distract you, how do you balance your personal life with the professional?'

'What's balance?'

She shook her head with a twisted smile. Time to wrap it up.

'I reckon we're pretty much done for today, but how about some rapid-fire questions to finish?'

'Go for it.'

'Favourite place to compete?'

'Easy. Home ice. With our fans in the stadium, it's like truly coming home.'

And as far from Ashbury Falls as he could get, she sensed.

'If you weren't a professional athlete, what career would you have pursued?'

'I thought you said these were rapid-fire?'

'They are. The trick is not to over think it.'

He smiled. 'Yeah, okay. As a boy, I wanted to be a builder. I liked working with my hands. I would sit in the yard for hours nailing shit together. I could be happy with that.'

'Good answer.'

'I didn't know I was being judged with every question.'

Always.

'Don't worry, if there was a scoring system at play your answers would be considered top shelf.'

Top shelf and restricted to what he was comfortable with off-loading. She recalled Paige's edgy laugh at the airport, her friend's delay before she'd spilled the beans on Horrible Harvey... Aiden clearly didn't trust her with Sissi yet, but she'd get there.

'You throwing hockey lingo at me?'

'Trying.'

He laughed and her own smile grew against her will.

'Got any more? Seems I've found my groove.'

She checked her sheet. 'Okay, final question, what's one thing about you that your fans might be surprised to know?'

His grin widened. 'You really want to know?'

'Not me, your fans... well, maybe me too.' She eased closer, genuinely intrigued.

'I love a bit of Amy Winehouse. I warm up to "Rehab" every day.'

She shoved her glasses into her hair and gawped. 'You don't!'

'Hey, what's wrong with that?'

'You really do?'

'I really do.'

The idea of him warming up with the deeply soulful Winehouse fuelling his moves was bloody hilarious! She choked on her own laughter, grabbed her water, throwing it back for a swig only to completely miss her mouth. She yelped and shot to her feet, the dampness over her crotch spreading before her eyes.

He chuckled. 'Let me go grab you a towel.'

For fuck's sake. 'They have those in there too?' she called after him, slamming the glass down and flicking the droplets from her hand.

'I told you' – he reappeared with a fluffy white towel – 'once you're in, you have no need to leave. I'd offer to help but...'

'I've got it, thanks.' She snatched it from him, cheeks ablaze as she imagined just how he might assist. 'I'm such a clutz.'

'It's actually kind of sweet,' he surprised her by saying as he buried his hands into his pockets – was he imaging it too?! 'When you're used to girls being so polished and careful, being around one that's...'

She looked up, towel frozen mid-swipe. 'That's...?'

He shrugged. 'Real. Genuine. It's nice.'

Genuine? Her!

Oh God, now she felt like the biggest fraud ever. Who was the true baddie in this setup?

'Thanks,' she squeaked out. 'I think.'

He kept his gaze locked on hers. 'You got everything you need?'

'Need?'

'Yeah.' He nodded at her discarded notepad on the sofa.

'Oh yeah, for now. Loads to work with.'

She nodded vigorously, rubbed vigorously too. Until she realised *how* vigorous her hand was moving and just *where* she was rubbing. And now he was looking at her invigorated crotch too. Shit. Shit. Shit. She was on fire and not in a good way.

'You want me to send my brother up?'

She gulped on thin air. 'Please.' He started to turn away. 'And Aiden...'

He paused, meeting her gaze, and she forced herself to at least appear serene and grateful. 'Thank you. You've given me so much of you and I appreciate it.'

He returned her smile. 'Happy to give you more, any time.'

'I'll take you up on that.'

'Make sure you do.'

She wanted to fist bump the air and shove it through her chest in one. The conflict, a total mind-fuck. Good vs bad. Karma vs article. Who the real man was.

She waited for him to leave then quit the recording on her phone and raced to the rest room, cursing when she saw the state of herself in the mirror.

Red cheeks. Eyes overbright. Hair already in disarray. As for her jeans... she looked like she'd wet herself. No, no, no.

Blake was going to show up any minute and... this!

Desperate, she spun on the spot. Spied the hand drier. Thank heavens for small mercies. Shrugging out of her suit jacket, she hooked it on the open door and propped her leg up on the vanity unit. If she could just tilt her hips high enough to activate the blower, she could... nope! The damn thing wouldn't respond.

She thrust higher. Nothing. Fanned her hand beneath the sensors. Power at last. Thank the—

'Need a hand with that?'

She froze mid-thrust. *Oh good God, no!*

'I've heard of a shower head offering up the perfect stimulation, but a hand drier?'

She squeezed her eyes shut. 'Blake...'

It came out like a curse uttered between her teeth but the only person she was truly cursing was her Twinkle Toe self.

10

It had to be the oddest sight Blake had ever seen.

And the most evocative.

He didn't know whether to laugh or...

No, he shut that thought down before it could take hold, because those hips, that ass, those curves – *dammit*, the damage was done.

She dropped her foot to the floor and spun to face him. 'I was – I didn't – it was... Oh, for fuck's sake!' She threw her hands out, eyes wild, hair askew. 'I spilled my water. I was just drying off my jeans. I wasn't doing whatever you're suggesting!'

He had to grit his teeth against the almighty laugh that wanted to erupt along with the words, *More's the pity*.

'Whatever you say, Twinkle Toes. I'll be right out here when you're done.'

Because everything he wanted to do would only make her wetter... and he needed to ditch those thoughts, stat!

He strode up to the glass, putting as much distance between them as possible, and focused on the Zamboni gliding across the ice. Its steady back-and-forth hypnotic as Luke, the caretaker, erased all trace of their training, leaving behind a surface so pristine it practically dared him to lace up and carve right through it.

'Drink?'

He turned to find her at the bar. Jeans now dry, sleeves rolled up, her glossy dark hair pulled back, save for one stray curl that seemed forever on the loose. He wondered if it had a mind of its own or whether she left it free to tease... a taunt his fingers were more than happy to respond to as they tingled within his fists.

He'd never met a woman capable of evoking such a reaction by look alone.

And today's choice of clothing – the white shirt, the chequered waistcoat, the jeans and trainers – did it for him big time. Had that been her plan all along? Had the skirt and heels failed another of her tests and she was mixing it up? Aiming to seduce the man, win the story...

Had his brother liked it too?

He'd bet his life he had.

'Blake?' She swept the curl behind her ear. 'It's going to be difficult to interview you if you've stopped talking to me altogether.'

He thrust his hands into his pockets. 'I'll take a beer.'

'Don't you have a game tomorrow?'

'And?'

She hesitated, mouth opening and then closing as she turned away to pull open the fridge. She bent down to peruse the bottles, and he tore his gaze away before he broke a tooth.

'Any beer in particular?'

Don't look. Don't look. 'You choose.'

'Do you want to take a seat and I'll be with you in a sec?'

He pulled out the stool beside him and promptly sat. Like a schoolboy caught doing something he shouldn't. And what the hell was that about?

'I might as well join you; it's not often you get to enjoy a free beer after— Oh...'

He caught her frown. 'What's up?'

'I thought we might sit on the sofa, it's cosier.' She coloured. 'More relaxing.' She got redder. 'What I mean is, it worked well for your brother.'

And she promptly shut her mouth, eyes wild once more.

I bet it did, honey.

He started to move, and she hurried forward.

'No, no, stay there, it's— *oof!*'

She collided with the coffee table, her body lunging forward as her hands complete with beers soared north and the rest of her fell south. He dived into her path, grabbing her around the waist and she landed against him hard.

'I'm so sorry,' she blurted.

'I'm not.' His body was on fire with the heat of hers, loving every second.

She blinked up at him, beers still skyward, body still imprinted.

'I thought you were making shit up when you told my brother you were called Twinkle Toes.' He gave a low chuckle. 'Now I know it's for real.'

'If you'd seen the amount of superglue my mum went through when I was a kid, you wouldn't question it.'

He set her back on her feet, his body grumbling at the loss of hers. 'Okay?'

'Yeah, thank you,' she said, handing him a bottle. 'And I'm happy to sit on the stools if you'd prefer it?'

'Even if it worked better with my brother on the sofa?' he teased and her brows hit the heavens.

'Blake!'

'What?'

'I'm going to pretend I never saw that glint in your eye!'

She moved to the sofa and promptly swapped her bottle for her phone, all business. *The sofa it is then...*

'I recorded your brother, are you happy for me to do the same?'

He paused mid-step. 'Record it?'

'My notes are good but they're not as good as replaying the actual thing.'

He gave a slow nod. 'But it's just for you, yeah?'

'Of course.'

He breathed a little easier. 'Okay.'

He settled into the sofa and took a swig of beer as she set her phone back on the coffee table and perched beside him. Far enough away not to touch, but not so far, he couldn't catch her perfume. Subtle. Tropical. Deeply appealing.

'You good to dive right in?'

'Are we still talking about the interview?'

She pursed her lips, her pointed stare enough to see him shifting in his seat.

'Okay. Okay, yes, I'm good.'

She took up her notepad and pushed her glasses up her nose. 'So, tell me about your school life?'

He gave a bemused snort. 'School?'

She flicked him look. 'Sure.'

'What about it?'

'Did you enjoy it?'

'I enjoyed aspects.'

'Like?'

'I enjoyed seeing my buddies. I enjoyed sport. I enjoyed playing hockey as much as playing hooky. You don't seem surprised by that? Has my brother been telling tales already?'

'More reaffirming what I'd already read about you, that academia wasn't really your vibe. That it was questionable whether you would get the grades required for college.'

'Wow, you don't pull your punches.'

'I didn't think you'd need me to.'

Ordinarily he didn't. But then ordinarily he didn't care what the other person thought. Astrid however...

'I don't.'

'He said he had to make you study with him?'

'That's fair.'

'Because you'd rather be out with your buddies?'

Not quite how it was. It wasn't the homework he was avoiding, but the home.

'Something like that.'

'It can't have been easy though.'

She cocked her head, her posture softening. Had she read his freaking mind?

'Your school lacked resources, and your home life was hardly conducive to study time. That would have been tough for any kid.'

Her honeyed eyes were full of compassion and it sent his skin crawling on the inside. He didn't need compassion over his past. And he certainly didn't want it.

'Aiden tell you that too?'

'He told me enough.'

'Did he tell you he used to haul our books to the rink with us? Wouldn't let Mom bring us back until I got through whatever work I needed to get done.'

She gave a small smile. 'Crafty.'

'Devious, more like.' Though he grinned as he said it.

'He's very protective of you, isn't he? You and your mother.'

He huffed. 'You worked that out already? He was born minutes before me, yet he always plays the big brother card.'

'Must be frustrating?'

He jerked. 'Frustrating?'

'Suffocating then?'

He frowned. 'Not really.'

'You don't ever feel... patronised?'

'Woah, step those twinkly toes back, honey. If I felt patronised or belittled by my bro, he'd know about it, believe me. He does it because he cares. He feels responsible for us even though he shouldn't. And it wasn't like I gave him any choice in the matter. One of us had to become the man and get us the hell out of there, and it couldn't have been me.'

'Why?'

And there it was, the question he didn't want to answer.

The question he *couldn't* answer.

'Why couldn't you have stepped up to the plate when your family needed you, Blake?'

He opened his mouth, but nothing would come out. His head was elsewhere. Trapped in the past and a moment he'd spent a decade trying to forget.

* * *

Fuck fuck fuck.

Astrid wanted to shrink into the sofa. But this was her job. To get to the truth.

Liar, you were trying to twist Aiden into the baddie of the piece and Blake refused to let you. And now you've backed him into a corner. Hit on something he doesn't want to spill.

But then, didn't that make it something the reporter in her *wanted* him to spill?

'Have you ever done something monumentally stupid?' he said into the strained silence, his voice distant and unrecognisable as Blake 'the Fury' Carter. 'Something that threatened every dream you ever had, and know that if you had your time over, you'd do the exact same thing again?'

No, she was pretty sure she hadn't. But her mother had. Because that 'thing' for her mother had been to fall in love with her father. And her mother had told her enough times over that she wouldn't change it, not for the world, because it had given her Astrid.

Though looking into Blake's bleak gaze, she had a feeling whatever his demon was, it didn't have the love of a child at the end of it.

'I can't say I have.'

'And there I was thinking you might pretend the opposite just to make me feel better about what I'm about to tell you.'

'Would it really make it any easier?'

'I guess not.'

He took a swig of beer and grimaced as he swallowed, rubbing at his chest.

'It's okay, Blake,' she assured him, his vulnerability making her own chest ache. 'Whatever it is, you can trust me with it. I promise.'

And she meant it with her all.

He gave a small nod, his eyes probing hers. 'What did Aiden tell you about our father?'

'He told me that he was mean. Abusive to you all. That he' – she swallowed, gripped her pencil upon her notepad as she read – 'that he beat you.'

She wet her lips, her scribbled note urging her to add, 'He also implied it was worse for you than it was for him.'

He gave a harsh laugh. 'And that's my brother being kind. *Too* kind as usual. Which is him all over once you scratch beneath the surface, forever making excuses for me.'

Not what her karma-conscience needed to hear. 'How do you mean?'

'*I* was the one who made it worse for me. *I* was the one who couldn't keep a lid on my anger. *I* was the one who reacted to Dad's physical abuse with more of the same and almost robbed us all of the chance to escape.'

She frowned, her gut giving the smallest of rolls. 'I don't...'

'No, he won't have told you that, will he?' He threw back more beer. 'My brother has the most amazing ability to just shut it down, you know. Keep his cool no matter what.' He clenched and unclenched his empty fist in his lap, a rhythmic pulse that she sensed he wasn't even aware of. 'God, I envied him for that. Still do.'

'It doesn't make you any less of a man. Any less—'

'You don't understand,' he interjected, his eyes colliding with hers. 'We were so close to getting away, the contracts were being drawn up and everything was on track. But that night...'

'What night?' she pressed as his voice trailed off, his eyes too as they landed on her phone, and he gave a rapid head shake.

'I told you I wouldn't share anything you're not happy with.' She paused the recording. 'And I meant it.'

His blue eyes lifted to hers, the fear and the torment swirling in his depths, a sea of pain that she could feel herself drowning in as she held his gaze and waited.

'We were late getting home from the rink. Mom had dropped Aiden with... with a friend and Dad was steaming. Going on about dinner not being on the table. And I don't know what was different about that night but Mom just... she snapped, told him he knew where the oven was.' He gave an unsettling laugh, his eyes glazing over as he stared at the beer in his hand. 'She was fierce and I loved her for it... then I saw him flip, the back of his hand sweeping through the air, and my only thought was to get to him first.'

'You can't blame yourself for that.' She pressed against her pencil with her thumb until it hurt, desperately trying to contain her own emotion while absorbing his. 'You were defending your mother.'

Sweat beaded across his brow as he gave a slow nod. 'But I couldn't stop. I was so mad. Years of watching him beat down on her, on us, and now he was down, and I wasn't letting him get back up. I guess a part of me was terrified of what he'd do. We'd never fought back before. In my head I kept thinking if he gets back up, we're dead.'

'My God, Blake.' It was a whisper, one she wasn't even sure he heard.

'When I was certain he was down for good, I grabbed Mom. She'd been screaming before, but she'd stopped. She was silently sobbing, rocking, her eyes pinned on his body. She couldn't look at me. I called for an ambulance and told her we needed to go, get out of there but she was all scrunched up, frozen in place. I was carrying her out the front door when the police sirens came. The neighbours had called the cops.'

'The *cops*?'

He nodded. 'Aiden rocked up just as they were hauling me in.'

'But your father was the one...'

'He was still out cold. I was the one with blood on my hands. He hadn't struck Mom because I got there first.'

'It was self-defence.'

'Our word against his.'

'But...'

'I was already on their radar. The entire gang I hung around with were. They were itching to convict me of something, and I'd just handed them the perfect charge.'

'But you weren't charged?'

She would have unearthed it if he had been.

'No.'

'Neither was your father.'

Because she'd found nothing on him too.

'No.'

'Why didn't your mother report him?'

'Because my father was a controlling, manipulative, bastard. He always managed to make her feel like it was her fault...'

'Yeah,' she said quietly, 'I know the kind.'

Her father had been one such man...

'Let me guess, your dad?'

She nodded, unsurprised that he'd worked it out for himself. 'I was young when he stopped coming around, but I remember the arguments towards the end. When he gave up promising to leave his wife. When he'd make out Mum was too needy, too demanding, that she didn't understand that he had responsibilities, a family...' She gave a soft scoff. 'He seemed to forget it went both ways, that we existed, that *I* existed.'

'Asshole.'

'I'll drink to that.'

She clinked her bottle to his, let him take a quiet sip before asking, 'How did you get off? With the police...'

'Aiden and a guy called Grady Marshall from the Redstone Devils stepped in and saved the day. They swung a deal. Got me the hell out of there and they didn't stop until Ashbury Falls was firmly in the rearview mirror. That's why it had to be Aiden who stepped up...'

His eyes shone with gratitude. Gratitude, love and age-old shame.

'He saved my ass, my brother. He could've gone to college without me, taken Mom and gone, but he fought to keep the deal for us both. Told the Devils he wouldn't come without me and that meant getting me off that charge. A conviction would have ruined any chance at college for the foreseeable future. He risked his hockey career to save mine. And we joke about it, you know. Him being nothing without me and vice versa. But it's only ever true one way around. Deep down we both know that.'

'I don't know, Blake. Everything I've read about you both, the way you play on the ice together, part of your magic is that you're so in tune. Always knowing where the other is, what they'll do... Yes, your brother helped get you out of a bad situation, a situation that *wasn't* your fault—'

'It was my fault. I should've used *this* before acting.' He tapped his temple with his beer bottle. 'Just like Aiden would have. I should've shut it down. Instead, I lost it, and I was no better than him.'

'No better than *who*? Your father.'

He nodded, his Adam's apple shifting uncomfortably, and she couldn't take it any more. She reached out, her palm soft against the taut muscle of his thigh. 'You fought back, you didn't instigate it. You weren't the one beating on your mother because your dinner wasn't on the table. You are *nothing* like your father.'

He eyed her hand, and she pulled back. 'Sorry I—'

He stopped her retreat, his fingers folding around hers. 'Thank you for saying that.'

'I'm not just saying it, it's true.'

He gave the smallest shake of his head. 'I've waited a lifetime to hear those words.'

'Don't just hear them, *believe* them, Blake.' She clung to his gaze while the heat of his palm around hers had her pulse racing, her head spinning, but she was determined to have him hear her. 'You must—'

'You barely know me.'

'I know enough. I know your team admire you, respect you. I know your brother loves you and would do anything for you. And I know you feel the same about him and your mother. I know that on the ice, it's the combined skill of you both that makes you the best. I know that you give off this gruff exterior but beneath it all, you're just as vulnerable as the rest of us.'

She leaned in with every word, her eyes telling him as much as her words, and he reached out. Made her breath hitch as he stroked a loose strand of hair behind her ear.

'And you think you know all this after knowing me for less than a week?'

'It's my job to read people. It's what I'm good at.'

'No one's ever called me vulnerable before.'

His hand hovered beneath her chin, his eyes drawing her ever closer as they dipped to her lips. She felt them part under his gaze, felt the space between them shrink with every breath they took...

'Astrid?' Blake said softly, their noses almost brushing.

'Yes?' she breathed.

Bam! The door flew open. 'Sorry, I forgot—'

'Aiden!' Astrid gasped, launching to her feet. 'What are you— why are you...?'

'Jeez, bro, ever heard of knocking?' Blake said, easing back in his seat.

'I wasn't aware I needed to. *Did* I need to?'

'Of course not,' she blurted on a laugh, nudging Blake's foot. 'Tell him, Blake.'

Blake looked at her, a question in his gaze she had no desire to answer.

Especially in front of his brother.

'I forgot to give you these,' Aiden said, his eyes flitting between them.

'These?' she squeaked, wiping her palms on her jeans as she took the cards he was holding out.

'Your tickets for our home game in a couple of weeks. I'll get an electronic version sent over too but nothing beats the real thing in your hand. You might want to save them as a memento when we win.'

'Oh wow, great, thanks.'

Then sound it, Astrid!

'They're rink side. You said you wanted to be in the thick of it... you can't get any closer to the action than the glass seats.'

Though the way his eyes were still assessing them, he clearly sensed there'd been enough 'action' going on prior to his interruption and heat flooded her cheeks anew. 'Unless you've changed your mind and would prefer to be up here with the execs, I can—'

'No no, these are perfect. Thank you!' She leapt forward and planted a smacker on his cheek, gave him the tightest hug too... only registering the OTT action when he froze in her hold. What on *earth* was she doing?

There was gratitude and then there was *gratitude.*

She shot back, fanned her flushed face with the tickets and held her smile. 'Really great!'

It was only a hug and a kiss to the cheek. Nothing incriminating. Nothing like the kind of kiss she'd wanted to plant on his brother moments before...

'You're welcome.' He cleared his throat and raked a hand through his hair. 'I'll let you get back to it.'

He fled, the door swinging closed behind him, and Blake filled the abrupt silence with laughter.

'It's not funny.'

'Oh, it is.'

And she didn't know what had him so amused. The fact that his brother had walked in on them, her reaction to him walking in, or that she'd squeezed the air out of his brother's lungs while slamming a kiss on his gobsmacked jaw.

She wasn't about to ask him to clarify though.

'Shall we get back to the interview?'

'Fire away, Twinkle Toes. I'm all yours.'

Her heart skipped a beat. *He means to question, idiot, not to jump.*

She returned to the sofa and perched on its edge, a *safe* distance away. But her thoughts were a mess. How could she press Blake to expose Sienna's role in Aiden's life knowing what she knew now? The man blamed himself enough. If he believed he'd also stolen his brother's chance at love…

It would be like rubbing salt in an open wound. She'd have to find another way or try another day. As for Aiden and his just desserts, her tummy squirmed. She'd unpick that later. For now, she had an interview to continue…

'How about we move onto some questions just for fun?'

'What kind of *fun*?'

And the suggestion that lit his gaze was all kinds of wrong yet all kinds of right to her all-too-willing libido.

'The kind your fans would love to hear about.'

His eyes danced. 'Sounds good.'

She adjusted her glasses and using her notepad and pencil as a shield, she began, 'If you weren't a professional hockey player, what would you be?'

'Definitely something physical.'

For fuck's sake! Her eyes launched to his as her clit pulsed.

'Like?' she said tightly.

'Something skilful.'

She grabbed her beer.

'Where I get to use my hands.'

She took a swig.

'A lot.'

And choked.

'You okay there? You want me to pat it better?'

No. No, she did not.

But yes, yes, she did.

This was going to be a *long* afternoon...

An extremely long and flustered afternoon.

11

'You're late.'

Blake hadn't meant to sound surly with his brother, but he'd been through hell and back in a day, every emotion imaginable making itself known and now they were all rolling inside him and he couldn't shut it down.

He'd barely touched his dinner which was stupid considering they had a game tomorrow and instead of hitting the sack, he'd stayed up, cracked open a beer and replayed the entire interview, over and over again.

He'd spilled his guts. Confessed his deepest darkest secret to a woman he'd only just met... a woman he hardly knew. Though it didn't feel like that. Not with all that they had shared. Her as much as him.

And here he was now, feeling yet another emotion that he didn't want to acknowledge. Jealousy.

All over a woman who should mean nothing to him. But there was something about her. The candid way she'd opened up from day one, the way her eyes always gave her away –

vulnerability, compassion, desire – all raw and unfiltered and equally effective at drawing him out.

He'd been putty in her hands.

And he hated being putty in anyone's hands.

'Who are you? Our mother?' Aiden joined him in the kitchen, pulling a ready prepped meal out of the fridge and sticking it in the microwave to warm up. He leaned back against the counter and pinned Blake with his stare. 'What gives?'

'It's not like you the night before a game – especially when we're playing away against a team like the Kings.'

He cocked a brow. 'You were worried about me?'

'I worry this chick has got you acting out of character, yeah.'

'Got *me* acting out of character? Don't you mean you?'

Blake sipped the beer he'd been nursing all evening. It was warm, funky, flat. Though he couldn't blame it for the face he pulled. 'No.'

'I don't know, bro, you're looking a little green around the edges.'

He gave a tight laugh. 'Whatever.'

'You're not going to ask where I've been?'

'I know where you've been.'

'You do?'

'I think the entire team know that you've been teaching Twinkle Toes to skate.'

Aiden pressed his lips together, blue eyes bright in the low hanging aluminium light that stretched along the breakfast bar. 'And you still say you're not green?'

'No.' He shoved the bottle away and stood.

'Not going to ask me how she was?'

'No.' He was already moving off.

'She really is true to her name,' he called after him. 'Spent more time in my arms than on the ice.'

'Not listening.'

'She'll get there though, just needs a lot of one-to-one attention from the best...'

'Night, bro.'

His brother's soft laugh worked its way through him, provoking every green nerve. He *was* jealous. So jealous. And that bothered him more than he'd care to admit.

Because he'd never been jealous of his brother. He'd coveted his cool. His ability to shut down every emotion and focus. But he'd never been jealous of him. Until now.

And over a girl, of all things.

Hell, he needed his head examining.

Or a good game to thrash it out of him.

Tomorrow's face-off couldn't come soon enough.

* * *

'Do you like hockey, Astrid?'

'I can't say I know hockey enough to like it or dislike it.'

Astrid stripped her clothes as she listened to the replay of her interview with Blake, catching up on all he had said after Aiden's interruption and realising it had mostly been him asking, her talking – some journalist!

But she'd been lured in by his bad boy blues and his recounted truth. Listening and sharing because he'd done the same. And she was as caught up in his voice now as she had been then. Only vaguely aware of the candle-lit room – the scent of soothing spice on the air, the steam rising from the bath she was pouring, the soft music playing in the adjoining bedroom – as everything about her stayed attuned to him.

'Hockey saved me from the worst in my life, what saved you?'

'Me?'

'I had hockey, you had...?'

'Books. Games. Whichever worked best...'

'What kind of books?'

'Fact or fiction, I wasn't fussy. The written word always fascinated me.'

'And games?'

She recalled how he'd cocked a brow with that one.

'Console games. A bit of role-play action and adventure, one vs one... Sometimes it was easier to lose myself being someone else when Mum was going through a particularly bad spell.'

'Because of your father?'

'No, not always...'

She heard the way her voice faltered in the recording and her heart did a little flutter now as she listened to herself admit, *'Mum has PMDD.'*

'What's that?'

She stared at her phone on the side of the bath, shocked she'd said it. Shocked even more that she'd sat and explained it. How it dictated her mother's moods and affected her childhood growing up.

She'd stopped before confessing that it had become a part of her too as she'd got older, driving her into the deepest, darkest of places. Though she'd never been as bad as Mum, probably because she'd developed well-ingrained coping strategies by that point. Plus, she had Mum.

But she had days, days where she'd rather hide under the duvet. And those days she'd drag herself out of bed and run. Or throw herself into a beastly hot yoga session. Ring Mum for a mindless chat. Lose herself in a gaming session when reading wouldn't cut it. Anything to get outside her own head. And it worked.

The day it didn't, then she'd worry.

'*That must have been hard. Her a single parent and you an only child.*'

'*It was. After Dad, the men who came and went... they never stuck around through the worst of it. Never took the time to understand it – hell, we barely understand it, but we have to live with it...*'

She shook her head at her brutal honesty and picked up her glass of red. Taking it to the bath, she turned off the taps and slid beneath the water. A sigh escaping as the warmth cocooned her, soothing every bump and bruise already making itself known after her session with Aiden. Not one blackened spot was his fault. He was a great teacher, an attentive one. A great brother and son too. A hero?

Gah. How could she seek karma on a man who at the age of eighteen, became the head of his family, desperate to save them, so desperate he'd run and blocked his past from view. And Sissi with it.

She sipped her wine, hoping it would ease the chill so deeply rooted with the tale Blake had shared. Of Aiden's control. Blake's loss of it.

She hadn't been Bambi on the ice because of her twinkle toes, she'd been useless because her head had been elsewhere. Going over the interview, the interview that hadn't been an interview at all, it had been a conversation. Because every other question, he'd brought it back to her, had her sharing things she hadn't shared with anyone before.

She closed her eyes and his own shone back at her, sparkling with compassion and understanding as his voice filled her ears:

'*Distraction is a powerful thing.*'

'*Far better than any medication.*'

'*Too true.*'

'*And you're distracting me from my questions, from giving me more of you.*'

'*Not intentionally.*'

'*No?*'

'*No. I find myself intrigued by you. I want to know about you. I want to know everything there is to know about Astrid Sinclair. The woman, the daughter, the foxy reporter...*'

A breathless laugh. '*And how's that going?*'

'*The more I know, the more I want to know...*'

She'd never had a man look at her like he had then, like he could see inside her soul to all the fractured pieces she kept hidden and wanted more. More and more. Until he had it all and then what? Would he try to piece her back together, healed and whole?

'*I can assure you, Blake, you're far more interesting than me.*'

'*Spoken like someone who doesn't value who they are enough and is too used to focusing on everyone else but themself. Am I right?*'

'*Perhaps... It's a career hazard.*'

'*A hazard I'm more than willing to tease you out of...*'

His voice caressed her through the phone, and she sank beneath the bubbles with a groan. Maybe listening to his voice, all low and sincere and vibrating through her speakers, while she lay naked in the tub, wasn't the best of ideas.

She wanted him. More than any man she'd ever met. More than Chase...

Fuck, Chase!

The man who had driven her to this point... his wife's face at the hotel room door. All that hate. She eased back up the bath and reached for her phone, quit the recording and fired off a text to Bella, needing to be grounded by her friend and their plan. Not her neglected libido – or her heart – that could be calling this all wrong.

ASTRID

Wanna come to a hockey game in a couple of weeks?

BELLA

You're joking right?

ASTRID

No, I've got a spare ticket. Promises to be 'intense'... Aiden's words.

BELLA

I think I'd rather cut off my right arm, unless... do you need me to come with you?

She paused. What she really wanted to say was, 'Yes, damn right I do. Because someone has to help me make sense of Aiden and keep my cakehole off Blake!' but her friend was in the thick of it with Chase, all on her own and all for Astrid's sake. The least she could do was cope the same.

ASTRID

Of course not. I can go rogue for the night

BELLA

Go rogue? Heaven, help him/them!

ASTRID

BELLA

Things going well then?

She pondered another white lie, a bending of the truth, but she didn't have it in her. She loved these women like sisters, and they had her back. Plus, a problem shared...

> The article's coming along nicely, but I'm not gonna lie, I'm not sure I have what it takes to deliver tit-for-tat on Aiden... 😕

Her phone started to ring with an incoming video call, Bella's chic avatar coming up in a circle. She should have known her friend would ring. She eyed the bubbles floating on the surface of the water and happy she wasn't about to flash her friend, she swiped the call to answer.

'Woah, are you in the bath?'

'Yeah, but you can't see anything, look...' She did a quick sweep with her phone, laughing when she brought it back to her face and found Bella squinting. 'Sorry, babe.'

Bella gave her a flushed smile. 'Don't be. I'm almost used to you now.'

'Only almost?'

She laughed. 'So, what's going on?'

Astrid chewed her cheek.

'Honey?'

'I think we might have called this wrong, called Aiden wrong...'

'How do you mean?'

'I'm just not sure he's... he's a bad guy.'

Bella frowned. 'He left Sienna high and dry, what more do you need to know?'

'But it was ten years ago, and the more I uncover about that time the more I question whether he deserves this now. He had good reasons for leaving, B.'

'Like what?'

'I can't... I can't say. It's complicated. But it's all linked in with his brother and—'

'Are you sure this hasn't got more to do with said brother and how you feel about—?'

'No. Absolutely not. Not really. No.'

Bella brows twerked with Astrid's response.

'What I'm trying to say is that Aiden was only eighteen when he left, barely a man himself and he had some serious shit going on.'

'Didn't we all, but we weren't taking it out on others and ghosting people who cared about us and deserved better.'

'No, but...' Astrid stopped; she couldn't tell Bella about the fight, she couldn't tell anyone. She'd promised Blake.

'Did any of those reasons stop him from answering one of her calls? From being there for her when she needed him the most? When her father got sent to prison and she had no one?'

Bella made a very good point. There'd been nothing to stop Aiden being a friend on the other end of the line... unless...

'No, but I wonder if it was a self-preservation thing. I've got a feeling Sienna isn't the only one feeling the mark of their relationship ten years on.'

Bella jerked back. 'Seriously?'

'I don't know anything for certain.'

'And you can't go telling Si something like that unless you *know* know. She's been through enough misplaced hope.'

'I know, you're right.'

'I'm always right.'

Astrid chuckled. 'Does Chase know this yet?'

Bella coloured a little. 'He's a slow learner, but he'll get there.'

'How are things going in Chase land and the gallery?'

Astrid eased back into the bubbles and let Bella recant her endeavours so far, enjoying the twinkle in her friend's eye and happy that she was happy. Or at least, happier than the jilted bride she'd been at the airport a month ago...

Perhaps knowing that Olly was getting his comeuppance in Cornwall had put that twinkle there or Bella's own karma mission. Either way, Astrid was glad of it.

She just needed to get her own twinkly toes back on track now... *twinkly toes, urgh!*

Those Carter men had a lot to answer for. One more than the other. No prizes for guessing which...

12

'What do you think about inviting her to Sunday dinner?'

Blake yanked out his earbuds and stared at his brother like he'd just suggested they take up figure skating. 'What?'

'Astrid?'

'I know who you meant, I just—'

He lowered his voice as he registered the late hour and his teammates snoozing up and down the plane. Their flight out of LA had been delayed and they were all cranky as fuck. Not least because they'd lost in sudden death to the Kings the night before and they were all desperate to get home. Hence why he was plugged in, music blaring, eager to block out the world and everyone in it.

And now his brother was throwing him *this* curve ball.

'Have you been sniffin' the Zamboni fumes?'

'Why?'

'Because whenever we manage to sort a Sunday roast, Mom is with us. And last I checked we weren't letting her anywhere near Mom. Or are you saying we cook up a roast just for her? That's some special kind of ass-licking, bro.'

'No, no ass-licking. As for Mom meeting her, that's how I felt before we knew her, but I don't know, she seems nice. I think Mom would like her. And I think it will look good for you – sorry, *us* – if she saw us in our natural environment.'

Blake twisted in his seat so he could give his bro the full weight of his stare. 'Are you trying to sound like David Attenborough?'

His brother gave a low laugh. 'Look, she's going to be hanging out with us at the rink...'

'Our home away from home.'

'But I figure it makes sense for her to see us in our actual home, doing normal stuff.'

'Like feeding Mom a roast?'

'Well let's face it, Mom does the feeding, we just provide the setting.'

'But you know Mom prefers her kitchen.'

'Good point. So how about dinner at ours and Sunday roast at Mom's? That way she gets to witness the lot.'

'Now you want to do *two* dinners?'

'Do you have any better ideas?'

'One family dinner. And let's take her out for it.'

'That's hardly showing her our "softer" side. And you know the GM is hot on her being our shadow. This will keep him sweet too. Why are you so averse to it anyway? I thought you liked her.'

'I do, but when have we ever introduced Mom to a girl?'

'She's not a girl, she's a journalist writing about us.'

'And you think Mom, *I'm-desperate-for-a-wedding-and-grand-babies*, is going to see the difference?'

Aiden shrugged. 'I don't know, but we should do it. Two dinners. I'll message her.'

'Who?'

'Astrid.'

'Don't you think you should check with Mom first?'

'Like she's gonna say no.'

He was already unlocking his phone and Blake covered it with his hand.

'You really want to wake her up with a *dinner* invite?'

He checked his watch. 'You're right, it'll be two in the morning for her. I'll do it first thing.'

Blake shook his head. 'Where's the fire?'

'No fire. But it'll be something to look forward to.'

Oh. My. *God*. His brother had lost his mind. Either that or... he actually did *like* her. Had feelings for her, *liked* her.

And that green thing inside him twisted and grew – all because of her.

Pucking Twinkle Toes.

* * *

Astrid pulled the pot of freshly brewed coffee out of her uncle's machine and sloshed it into her pint-size mug as Blake's interview played through her phone...

'What are your hobbies or interests outside of hockey?'

'Do women count?'

'Funny.'

'I'm not being funny.'

'So you admit to being something of a player then?'

'I admit nothing.'

'You're maddening, you know that, right?'

'Always.'

Astrid felt the ridiculous grin on her lips, the rampant butterflies in her stomach, and promptly smothered both. He's *not* amusing. He's *not* fun. He's a nightmare!

A woman's worst nightmare. Much like his brother.

But at least Blake was honest about it. Kind of. Aiden on the other hand had promised Sienna the world and lied through his teeth.

Only you're finding him quite likeable too...

'Traitor,' she muttered, pausing the recording and adding milk and two sugars to her coffee. She stirred it vigorously as she took it to the table before the window where her work was all spread out.

She hadn't seen the twins in two days, but she'd lived and breathed them – focusing on the article because that was far easier than focusing on the confusing mess of her feelings towards them.

Today, she had interviews lined up at the arena with Coach, Stella, and the equipment manager Ezra. She had other people to contact and book in, too.

She checked her list of potential sources, their mother and father right up top. She understood the twins' need to protect their mother and she'd respect that. But their father... if ever there was a villain to the piece. She had to try and speak to him. Though the man was proving difficult to trace. Sissi had said he'd not been seen in Ashbury Falls for months now, the house they'd lived in standing very much empty. Empty but well-tended to by an agency.

Astrid had done some digging and discovered that Aiden had bought it last year. Which was odd in itself. Why buy a house you had no intention of returning to? As far as she could tell he hadn't been back since taking ownership. And she doubted Blake had any intention of doing so. Their mother had to be glad to see the back of it, too. So why buy something that held so much misery for them all?

Her gaze drifted to the early morning frost hovering over Central Park. It looked as cold as she now felt.

Had Aiden bought it for their father?

Their old man was well known for his financial troubles. Would Aiden have bailed him out? Hated the man while gifting him a roof over his head? And if so, didn't that make the Ice King ever more likeable?

Bugger. She snatched up her mug. Every step forward in her article seemed to be one step back on the karma path...

Why couldn't he be a Grade A jerk? The 2D guy with the Hollywood smile splashed all over O'Hare airport, arrogant and unfeeling, self-absorbed and selfish.

Perhaps because he'd never been that man at all.

And where did that leave her and the grand karma plan?

If she could just get him onto the subject of Sissi, unpick that thread to his tale and get her friend some kind of closure...

Her phone buzzed with an incoming text and she glanced at the screen.

> MUM
>
> Good morning, darling. Hope you have a glorious day! All is sunny this side of the pond xoxo

She smiled and was about to pick it up when another message dropped in...

> AIDEN
>
> How are you fixed on Tuesday night?

She snatched up the phone. Blinked. And blinked again.

Tuesday night? She checked the Titans game schedule – clear.

Was he... was he asking her on a date? After the disaster of the last one?

Whatever the case, it's an opportunity to dig for Sissi and the article; get on it!

ASTRID

Good morning to you too! Why do you ask?

AIDEN

Sorry, morning! Just in diary mode and getting organised. Blake and I would like to invite you to ours for dinner.

Blake and I... Her mouth fell open. Her, Aiden, and Blake. In their pad. Just the three of them...

AIDEN

We don't bite.

Heat rushed through her core as his text conjured up an image worthy of Delia's book. *Holy mother of... Down, nips!*

She blew out a breath and typed: *I'm free and that sounds...*

How did it sound? Lovely. Productive. Cosy. Intimate. No. No. No. *Definitely* no.

AIDEN

I promise.

Sweet Jesus, the man was persistent.

ASTRID

I'm free and that sounds great.

AIDEN

Good. I'll send you the address.

ASTRID

No need. I already have it.

AIDEN

Of course you do 😉

A wink? What was that about? A tease? A cheeky slap at the journalist in her? A flirt? And if it was a flirt, how would Blake feel about it after their near-miss kiss?

ASTRID

What can I bring?

AIDEN

Just you. Any allergies?

Only to men who can't treat a woman right...

ASTRID

No, I'm as easy they come.

There. Delicately flirtatious. A bit of easy banter. And much easier to manage when the other brother wasn't on the scene. Though he would be come Tuesday when she got to see inside their home. *OMG.*

AIDEN

...

The typing icon appeared and disappeared. She frowned, drumming her nails on her laptop. Could the guy not take a flirtatious prompt? Had she scared him off?

No way. Snatching up her phone, she went to type something else, but in buzzed:

AIDEN

Blake will be pleased.

She wound her neck in. Okaaaay, not *quite* the response she was expecting...

> **ASTRID**
>
> Why? Is he cooking?

> **AIDEN**
>
> Haha! No chance! See you Tuesday if not before!

> **ASTRID**
>
> Great

And it *was* great. The twins were doing as they'd promised, welcoming her into their life, facilitating the story she needed to write and unwittingly giving her the opportunity to dig deeper with Aiden. Great. Great. Great.

Buoying herself up, she opened the Just Desserts WhatsApp group and the message from Sissi that she had left hanging late last night because she hadn't known what to say...

JUST DESSERTS WHATSAPP GROUP. 22.03 EST.

> **SISSI**
>
> What's next in Operation Heartbreak?

> **ASTRID**
>
> I've been invited into the lion's den... Aiden's cooking dinner!

> **PAIGE**
>
> 😮

> **SISSI**
>
> Be careful, Aiden can be pretty charming when he wants to be.

No shit, Sherlock.

ASTRID

Well, technically he's cooking for Blake and me,
but it beats a meet up at the rink.

PAIGE

Blake is going to be there?!

Hmm, yup. How to manage that one? As far as the girls knew,
it was karma-as-usual. As for herself, she'd need to make doubly
sure she kept Blake at arm's length. There could be no getting
carried away on hormones, pheromones, whatevermones…

ASTRID

I'm sure there will be opportunities to get up
close and personal with the right twin…

PAIGE

So long as you remember which one that is!

Eek!

ASTRID

😏 Have you been speaking to Bella?

PAIGE

She may have mentioned you have something
of a bad boy addiction…

Astrid winced. Affliction more like. And Bella wasn't wrong.

ASTRID

I have it all under control 😏

Now she just had to make it so…

* * *

'Dinner Tuesday, sorted.'

Aiden placed his phone down on the breakfast bar and stretched his arms above his head, his naked torso flexing.

'Jesus, put it away, bro. Some of us are trying to eat their breakfast...'

'You first.'

Blake glanced down at his semi-naked self and shrugged. He wasn't the one flexing it. He also wasn't the one looking pretty smug with himself.

Did his brother really have a thing for her? They'd never gone head-to-head over a woman before, and he wasn't thrilled about doing so now. Especially when that girl held the public reformation of his character in her dainty and distracting hands. Hands that had given him a surprising hit of comfort when he'd dredged up his past for her to dissect.

'What's got you in a mood now?'

Blake chewed over his cereal before answering, half expecting it to get stuck in his throat.

'Are you sure this is a good idea? Bringing her here.' He looked around their very masculine, very high-end pad. 'It's hardly going to make people sympathise with us.'

'We're not looking for sympathy, we're looking to inspire kids like us to reach for better things... it's why we got these, remember?'

He threw a thumb over his shoulder, pointing to the tattooed Latin script they shared at the base of their spine: *Ad meliora*. Towards better things. A simple phrase that had meant as much at eighteen as it did now.

'We can also show her we're not a pair of hockey neanderthals incapable of keeping their house straight. I mean, have you *seen* how half the team live?'

He grunted. 'But we never bring women back here.'

'And we're not bringing one back now.'

Blake cocked a brow.

'Like I said about introducing her to Mom, this is different. This is business. You know that as well as I do... don't you?'

Was that his brother's way of asking if he'd crossed the line in that exec suite? He hadn't quizzed him on it since. He'd asked how it had gone and left it at that. Was it possible his brother was wholly focused on the article rather than the woman writing it...?

And all his jealously was misplaced?

And that it was all about him being a charity case? The little brother in need of rescuing as ever.

'Whatever you say, bro. It's my ass that needs saving, right?' He spooned up more cereal, though he was swiftly losing his appetite. 'And what about Sunday lunch at Mom's?'

'I figured it was best inviting her in person on Tuesday, that way we can lay down some ground rules and see how she reacts to having her journalistic strings cut. Make a call on it then.'

He nodded as he got to his feet and shoved his bowl aside. There was only one way to rid himself of the ants now having a party in his gut.

'Where are you going?'

'To the gym.'

'What about your bowl?'

Blake paused.

'Not neanderthals, remember?'

His mouth hitched up. 'Speak for yourself...'

13

'You talk very highly of the twins,' Astrid said to Stella who'd taken Ezra's place behind Coach's desk.

They had a big function underway in the exec suites today and Coach had kindly offered up his space as a base. It was a 'busy' room, the rapid pace of the hockey world everywhere you looked. From the whiteboard marked up with game formations, to the posters, team schedules, books, trophies, hockey gear, to the screens showing the current NHL standings, player stats, and latest news, it was a hive of activity.

'Of course,' Stella said with a smile. 'And I hope you will too.'

Astrid nodded. 'I get the impression this isn't just business for you, that you have a real passion for the sport.'

The woman had talked nonstop about hockey and the twins from the moment she'd walked in, her eyes alive with a genuine excitement for it all.

'Oh yes, I've been hockey mad since I was a girl. It's in my blood. My father is the coach for the Michigan Warriors.'

Much like the Titans, the Warriors led the pack when it came to the NHL standings. 'You didn't fancy working for them too?'

'Heavens no, you can have a little too much father and daughter time, you know?'

No, Astrid didn't, but she nodded anyway.

'I'm going to be honest with you,' Stella said, her eyes suddenly narrowing, 'when your request first came across my desk, I was a little suspicious...'

The hairs on Astrid's neck prickled. 'Suspicious?'

'Sure. You haven't worked in the world of ice hockey before and you don't come across as a fan, and it all begged the question, why? Why hockey? Why us? Why the twins?'

Astrid resisted the urge to wriggle in her seat.

'I guess what I'm really trying to say is, I was concerned the well-meaning pitch was a front for something else.'

Gulp. 'Like what?'

'Something more' – Stella licked her lips – 'destructive.'

Astrid frowned. 'I meant it when I said I won't print anything you and the twins don't sign off on.'

'Oh, I know.' Stella waved a nonchalant hand. 'Though these things have a habit of getting leaked... but I'm not worried about that. Not any more. Not with you. I like you. I think the twins like you. And I did my due diligence before I let you in the door. You're one hell of a writer, fair and just, and your articles shine. I trust you to make our boys shine too.'

Astrid felt her chest puff up at all the praise, suppressing the nervous wriggle that continued to writhe. She took a sip of water. 'Thank you.'

'But make no mistake, Ms Sinclair, ruin them and I'll ruin you.'

Astrid choked on the water, her eyes popping.

'Sorry.' Stella gave a tiny laugh. 'My dad calls it my Rottweiler streak. It comes out when I need it.'

'No apology necessary,' Astrid assured her, admiration

swelling despite the threat of being potential dog fodder. 'It's good to know you care about them that much.'

'I do. Both professionally and personally. It's hard not to.'

Astrid placed her glass down and took up her notepad. Every question was crossed off save for the last.

'So to round off the interview, do you have any last words to sum them up?'

She smiled. 'Well Aiden's Aiden. I mean, look at the guy. All charm and professionalism. A true figurehead for the franchise. He keeps the team in line and leads by example both on and off the ice.'

'And Blake?'

'Bad boy rep aside, that man's passion outshines the rest. Whether it's making game-changing plays or mentoring our younger players, he's an all-round all-star.'

No hesitation. No publicity spiel. Just her honest truth and it tallied with everything Astrid had heard that day, with Coach, with Ezra... It had been one thing to hear the respect Coach had for them, another to hear it from Ezra. She knew some guys could be real arseholes to those 'lower down the ranks' but the twins were anything but.

And now she was in conversation with Stella, a woman who would sooner claw her eyes out than let her print a bad word in their name.

'Do you think it's Blake's passion that gets him into trouble?'

'Are we talking on or off the rink now?'

'That depends, are we talking about sport in both cases?'

Stella pursed her lips, her blue eyes sparkling as she leaned in close...

'Between you and me, and off the record?'

Astrid cleared her throat, feeling distinctly uncomfortable as she paused her recording. 'Okay.'

'Blake has a way with women, you know. Well, they both do. Though I can't speak from personal experience when it comes to his brother...'

'But you can with Blake?' And why did that stick in her throat so much? Stella was an attractive woman. Blake was an attractive man. It shouldn't be a surprise.

But from a professional standpoint... *Like you have any right to judge her, almost-kissy-wissy-karma-seeking-hypocrite!*

'Don't get me wrong though, it never means anything more than what it is, a bit of fun, you know. He's honest about it. Brutally so. And I respect that.'

And how the hell was the woman spinning this into a positive?

'Isn't it a conflict of interest, sleeping with a player?'

'Not the way he does it. No strings, just fun. No one can get hurt, right?'

Her tummy twisted. 'Right... well, I think that's us done.'

She closed her notebook and popped her phone on top, all too keen to get out of there and give herself a slap.

'Already?'

'I think you've given me plenty to work with.'

'Are you sure? I can knock up a few more quotes for you, give you some extra juice to work with...'

'It's fine but thank you.'

'No problem.' She rose to her feet, her smile relentless. 'If you're done for the day, how about we hit a bar? We can debrief over a drink or two – my treat.'

Astrid made a show of checking her watch. 'I'd love to, but I promised I'd meet a friend this evening.'

'Another time then?'

A rap on the door came to her rescue and Coach popped his head in. 'Can I just grab my jacket?'

'Of course,' Astrid said, 'we're all done here.'

'Everything going okay?' He directed the question at Stella.

'I think so.' She beamed at Astrid. 'I believe we have an understanding, don't we?'

Astrid matched her smile. The woman was fierce, and to be fair, everything Astrid would be in her position. 'We sure do. Thank you so much for your time today. Both of you.' She dropped her stuff into her bag and pulled on her coat. 'I'll leave you to enjoy the rest of your evening.'

'Good night,' Coach said.

'And don't be shy, Astrid,' Stella called after her. 'Let's grab that drink sometime.'

'Sure thing.'

She stepped out into the hallway, trying to get her bearings. The place was a maze, but she knew there was a back way out somewhere around here. She just had to find it. And she wasn't going to risk asking Stella to point her in the right direction in case she insisted on accompanying her out and giving her anything more 'off the record'.

Her phone pinged with a message as she moved off and she pulled it out, her heart doing a traitorous jig when it caught Blake's name...

> **BLAKE**
>
> Aiden says you're coming for dinner Tuesday.
> Heads up, he cooks like he's feeding the whole bench and the reserves!

She couldn't stop the gentle curve to her lips as she replied:

> **ASTRID**
>
> Consider me warned. Does he have a favourite tipple?

Aiden had said no need to bring anything, but she never went to dinner empty-handed. Not even to Mum's. And here she was going to theirs and she was... she was excited. Nervous but excited. And as conflicted as ever.

She passed by a wall of press shots, pausing over one of Blake. It had to be a few years old. He was grinning just like his brother beside him but the sense of caged masculinity gave her pause. The way his eyes suggested he was only a moment away from pouncing. Or bolting.

Was that what it had been like living with a father like his? Always knowing that you had to be ready to react, to run...?

She felt her heart contract, her eyes drifting to Aiden, same grin but his *looked* easy. Natural. Affable. But now she knew what that grin hid, and she felt for him. Felt for them both. And the more people told her, the more she liked.

Giving herself a long-overdue shake, she strode forth, straight into the locker room where the players' shirts were hung over their seats. The Carters' were front and centre. She automatically stepped up to them, her hand reaching for number 44 – Blake...

'Lost, Twinkle Toes?' an oh-so familiar voice asked into the quiet, the deep rumble setting her soul on fire.

She closed her eyes, took a breath and turned, preparing herself for Blake. But *nothing* could have prepared her for Blake, semi-naked and dripping wet, a team-embroidered towel slung low around his hips...

Holy mother of... Delia!

'Bloody hell, Blake!' she blurted, pressing a hand to her chest as though it could physically suppress the surging heat within. 'You scared the life out of me! I thought – I wasn't – why are you—'

* * *

'Well, well, Twinkle Toes has a twinkle mouth.' He stepped towards her, as amused by her eyes twitching south as he was by her floundering lips. 'Are you lost?'

'Am I what?' she blurted, cheeks as red as the heart of the Titans logo on the floor beneath them. 'No.'

'So, you regularly pay a visit to the men's locker room then?'

'I...' She nipped her lip, eyes still twitching. 'I just finished up with Stella and... I didn't want to disturb the function going on out there and I thought there was a back way...'

'Riiiight, so you weren't hoping to cop an eyeful?'

She was copping one all right and by the way she just licked her lips, she was enjoying the show.

'Of course not.' She lifted her chin, forcing her eyes up with it. 'I thought you players were having a rest day.'

'We are.'

'And yet, you're here?'

He shrugged. 'Needed to work last night's loss out of my system.'

'How?'

'How what?'

'How do you do that?'

Foxy the Reporter was back in the room, straight on with the questioning.

'I work out. In the gym, on the ice... in the bedroom.'

He threw the last in to throw her off; he wasn't in the mood for the deep and personal today. In the mood for her though, always.

But instead of backing up, she let her gaze drift to his arms. 'Right-handed?'

'Huh?'

Her eyes twinkled. 'It would explain why your biceps are bigger on the right.'

She gestured to said arm and he laughed – amused, surprised, ever more enraptured. 'You know one night in my bed, and you wouldn't tease about it.'

He gripped the knot in his towel, forcing his bicep to flex.

Two can play at that game, baby...

She took a shallow breath. 'You sound pretty sure about that.'

'That's because I am sure.'

And man, he wanted to stride across the room and prove it to her. Right here, right now. Brother's judgement, public opinion, the article, be damned.

'Why don't you hang back on Tuesday, and we can put it to the test?'

'I'm sure your brother would love that.'

'I'm more concerned about what you'd love.'

She swallowed, her delicate throat bobbing and teasing him with the desire to lean in and give her just a taste... but a taste wouldn't be enough. Not for him. And he was pretty sure it wouldn't be for her either.

'Was it his idea that I come over?'

'Yes.'

'But you were happy to go along with it?'

He... what was he? Beneath the frenetic pulse beating through his veins at the idea of having her in his home, so very close to the bed he wanted her in, he was wary.

And he didn't like it.

'He's the grown-up in this relationship.'

He strode past her and set his phone down – funny that he'd been messaging her when she'd only been across the hall. Maybe he'd been attuned to her presence before he'd set eyes on her. Maybe that was why he hadn't been able to get her out of his head in the gym, in the shower...

He started to pull his stuff from the locker. 'I do what he says. Most of the time.'

'Why do you do that?'

'Because he tends to be right.'

'I didn't mean, why do you do what he says, I mean, why do you put yourself down?'

He snapped around. 'I'm not.'

'No?'

'No.' He swallowed the tightness in his chest. 'If you don't want an eyeful, you best turn your back.' He took the towel in both hands and her eyes flared. 'Or you can leave. Your choice.'

He thought she'd hurry off. He'd *hoped* she'd hurry off. He had no desire to explore the path she wanted to venture down.

Instead, she turned to face the wall. 'Don't you have a gym in your building?'

He hesitated. Was he really going to strip with her just a few yards away?

Oh, fuck it. He dropped the towel and set about his business, trying to tune her out. But his body had other ideas, hyper aware of her perfume on the air, the subtle sound of her breath... *down, dude, down.*

'Of course we have our own gym in our suite.'

'So why come here to use this one?'

'I knew it would be deserted and sometimes, that's all I want. To be in my own head, in my own space.'

'Even though the traffic is hell?'

'Funny thing about being in a blacked-out 4x4, you're anonymous and everyone gets out of your way. Just the way I like it.'

He zipped up his jeans, relieved to be contained, even if it was uncomfortable as fuck. 'You can turn around now.'

She did so slowly, her eyes alighting on his chest as he picked up his tee.

'If you like your own space so much,' she said as he pulled it over his head, her words hitching with her breath and he fought back a grin. 'Why do you still live with your brother?'

And just like that the grin died. 'Do you ever quit with the interviewing?'

He yanked his shirt into position, the action as aggressive as his question.

'Sorry, I didn't mean it to sound like that. I was genuinely curious... personally not professionally.'

'So the journalist in you isn't getting all hot under the collar right now?'

'No, that's just me.' And then she blushed. 'Funny Blake. Very funny.'

'Why are you so interested in my living arrangements, if not for the article?'

'Because you're twenty-eight, you have the money to go your separate ways and yet you choose to live together? Even though you've just said you'd rather sit through traffic and come here to work out than exercise in the home you share with your brother.'

'There's more equipment here.'

'And you live together because?'

He shrugged. 'We live in one of the most expensive cities in the world, rent in Manhattan is extortionate, even for someone with our success it makes good financial sense to share the rent. Especially when we also rent a place in Brooklyn for Mom.'

And hell, he was quoting Aiden now. He knew it even as he said it. But it was better than acknowledging the truth. He was scared to go it alone. Scared what he'd do without his brother reining him in.

'So it has nothing to do with your brother keeping an eye on you?'

He stalled, shrugging on his jacket. 'You think I'm that bad that I need babysitting twenty-four-seven?'

And how the hell had she got inside his head so easily?

'No. I don't. I'm asking if you do.'

He shook his head on a choked laugh. 'Wow.'

She's got you sussed though, hasn't she? That's why you're freaking out.

'I'm asking if you think your brother does too.'

He scooped up his keys and his bag and headed for the exit, unsurprised when she fell into step beside him. 'You'd have to ask him that.'

'But in your opinion?'

'My brother has spent his life looking out for me, and he'll carry on looking out for me, it's what he does.'

'Would you say you're co-dependent?'

'Jesus, Astrid, I thought you said you weren't interviewing me?'

'I'm not.'

He stilled so that he could look down into her eyes. Spot the lie. But her own were wide. Open and honest. 'So this is you caring about me?'

'Yes.'

He almost said nothing, but then he considered what she was asking and, 'I have no idea whether what we have is some weird, twisted co-dependent relationship. I know I wouldn't be here now if it wasn't for him. And you already know what he's risked to save my skin. So hell yeah, maybe I do have an unhealthy need to have him around and vice versa. I guess you'll get a taste of what it's like for real on Tuesday. You can judge our living arrangement all you like.'

'I'm not judging you.'

'If you say so.'

He pushed through the back exit to their private parking lot and nodded to security standing guard as they let him through.

'I'm really not, Blake,' she said, hurrying to keep pace with him. 'I just feel like you have this carefully curated life that has been driven by your brother and you're too scared to step outside of it and reach for your own dreams. And I wouldn't be surprised if he's the same. Compromising on his own to make sure they fit around you.'

'You don't know what you're talking about. We're hockey players, the game is our life; our dream is one and the same.'

'But at some point, you'll have to move on from the game and then what?'

He stared back at her. 'Then whatever, Astrid, we'll deal with it.'

'We'll...?'

'What?'

'You said "we'll" rather than "I'll".'

'So?'

She didn't answer. She didn't have to. He'd given away enough.

'Do you ever think about getting married, having a family of your own?'

He laughed. 'Seriously? You can't tell me that's not an interview question.'

'It wasn't.'

'No? Have you asked Aiden about it?'

'I did. But not in the interview.'

'So it just came out in conversation?'

'Yes.'

Could she not see how that only incriminated her further?

'Just as curious about his love life as you are mine, hey? So either you want to get us both into bed and you're not fussy which, or you're lying about this not being an interview.'

He paused beside his car, effectively positioning her between him and the great big hunk of metal.

'Which is it to be?'

* * *

Astrid blinked up at Blake's blue eyes glittering above her and tried to take a breath, only there was no air without his invigorating scent, his heat...

'Are you always so suspicious?' It came out as a whisper, her body on fire with his looming large over her. 'Can't I just care?'

'In my experience, people only care when there's something in it for them. So either you want the story...' He stroked the hair from her face and her head lifted with the motion, her lips parting of their own accord. 'Or you want me.'

'This isn't a good idea, Blake.'

That's hardly a rejection, Astrid. Think of Sissi. Think of the twin you're supposed to get. Do this and you've screwed it all!

He leaned closer, his mouth a dizzying few inches away and oh, how she wanted to close that gap. Wanted to kiss him and let the heat consume her. Consume them.

'You sure about that? Because I think this feels *very* good, don't you?'

She shook her head, the tip of her nose brushing against the tip of his. 'Blake...'

It was breathless, a question and a plea.

'Tell me you want it, Astrid, and I'll give it to you.'

She closed her eyes, tried to block out temptation, but it was no use... He was offering himself to her, a kiss that would lead to his bed... a night she would never forget.

And then his words pierced the lustful haze. *People only care when there's something in it for them.*

'No!' She pressed her palm into the solid wall of his chest, her eyes flaring open. 'You're playing dirty.'

He eased back, his head cocking to the side. 'Oh, I can get dirtier.'

'Stop it, Blake. I know what you're doing.'

'I was seducing you...'

'No. You're pushing me away. Making this about sex and need. Because you don't want to believe that I care. Is that what makes it safe for you? Relationships? Women?'

He clenched his jaw, the fire in his eyes turning frosty. 'I guess you have your answer.'

'My answer?'

'Marriage. Kids. A family of my own.'

In the depths of his gaze were the echoes of his past and a fear for the future. A man who didn't dare hope for any of it.

'You can have it all if—'

'How can you say that when you know the truth about me? You know what I did? You know why I left Ashbury Falls? I am my father's son, Astrid. I can *never* have what he had because I will never destroy it like he did.'

And then he strode away, rounding the car to reach for the driver's door.

Oh my God, no! She couldn't let him leave, not like this.

'Blake please—'

'Get in.'

She did a double take. 'What?'

'I said get in.'

'But...?'

'I assume you're heading back into the city, I'll drive you.'

It had to be an hour's drive with the traffic at this time of night; it would be quicker via the sub, but...

'You coming?' He rose out of his seat to eye her over the roof.

Pulling open the door before he could change his mind, she slid inside and buckled up.

Neither said a word as he pulled out of the parking lot. Astrid's head was racing, so many questions and assurances wanting to erupt but she wasn't sure where to start, and she certainly didn't want to put the guy any further on edge. Not when he was driving, but...

'Your turn.'

She shot him a look. 'My turn?'

Her heart went pitter patter with the windscreen wipers, the snow falling as thick and fast as her sudden dread.

'Sure. I just told you outright that I don't do serious when it comes to relationships. What about you? You hardly had the greatest upbringing with your father...'

'No but my mother did a great job, thank you very much.' Her hackles were up, a reaction born of a childhood where people judged her, judged her mother, judged her absentee father without ever taking the time to truly understand it. Not to mention her pulse that couldn't settle with him mere inches away, his body heat and scent a constant attack on her weakened defences.

'I didn't say she didn't. My mother did a great job too, my father just made it impossible for her to make it great as a whole. You can't tell me you didn't look at your friends and wish you had it different back then.'

Oh, she'd wished alright. She'd wished for a father to come to her school productions, a parents' evening or two, anything to show a real interest...

'You can't control how other people behave.'

'No, so you just stop depending on them. I have been listening you know...'

They shared a look so loaded with meaning that she didn't breathe for a beat. And then she realised that this man who she'd known for little more than a week likely knew her better than those she'd known her entire life.

'So tell me, Astrid, after all you've been through, do you crave a white wedding and babies and love ever after?'

'*Jesus*, Blake...' she laughed out, distinctly uncomfortable.

Because deep down, underneath the scars, she did want all of that. She just didn't think it would happen for her. Like with her mum, men would never stick through the worst and so she chose not to hope for it. Planned for the opposite.

He leaned closer. 'I'm asking because, and I quote, "I care".'

'Don't do that.'

'Do what?'

'Take the piss out of me.'

'I'm not.'

'Liar.'

'So it's okay for you to say it but when I say it...'

He had her there. Dammit. The man was infuriating.

'Seems to me, you can give it, but you can't take it.'

'Right. Fine. No, I don't see love and marriage in my future. No kids. I don't trust anyone to be in it for the long haul and I wouldn't put a child through the same upheaval I went through.'

She waited for him to say something, anything, but nothing came. His silence worse than any spoken judgement.

'Are you not going to say something?'

The passing streetlights cast shadows over his face, making it impossible to read.

'What do you want me to say?'

'I don't know. Something. Anything.'

'I don't think you'll like what I have to say.'

'Why don't you try me?'

'Because we'll only end up back where we were in the parking lot.'

She frowned. 'I don't know what you mean.'

'Can't you see, Astrid, you're not looking for love, I don't expect love, the future is the future, but the now... we could have so much fun in the now.'

She swallowed. Fun? Oh, how she wanted that.

Wanted it but couldn't. Not with him.

And not because of karma, or work, she realised. But because she had a sneaking suspicion that this man had the power to make her want so much more.

'I have an article to write.'

'But when you don't...?' He sent her a look.

When I don't, your brother is the one I'm supposed to be leaving for dust... not you.

'I'll be heading back to the UK.'

She looked away and prayed he'd drop it. *Pleaded* that he'd drop it. Because what she really wanted to say was, yes, yes, yes!

When it was a no, no, no!

In fact, if all went according to the original plan, she was the last person on earth he'd want to see again.

And that left her feeling even shittier than before.

14

Tuesday, aka dinner date day, came around all too quickly for Astrid who was still reeling from her last dose of Blake.

And she didn't mean the semi-naked dose.

She meant the way he'd burrowed into her soul and made her realise too much about herself. Too much about her true desires for the future and the path she had carved out for herself. She needed to get back to being the woman she'd been a fortnight ago. Determined to do right by her friends and the article.

When it came to Blake, her head needed to be in the driving seat.

Not her foo foo, and certainly not her heart.

She was just about to step into the shower when her phone rang, Tay Tay's tune telling her it was the girls. They probably wanted to wish her luck...

She could ignore it.

She probably *should* ignore it.

She hardly had a spine of steel right now, but if anyone could talk her back on the straight and narrow it was them.

Pulling on her robe, she picked up the phone and returned to the bedroom. Only Sissi was on the call but seeing her friend's face in the bubble had her heart twisting. She swiped to answer before she could chicken out.

'Hey babe, you good?'

'Better for seeing your beautiful face.' Sissi smiled. 'I'm so sorry I'm only just checking in now. Between studying, work, and my ex going AWOL on his daughter, I'm spent. Not to mention Horrible Harvey is a hard nut to get access to, let alone crack. I'm in a world of chaos here.'

Sienna *looked* like chaos. The dark shadows under her big blues ran deep. Her blonde hair fell from her ponytail in tiny wisps. Her apron from the diner was covered in what looked like coffee *and* ketchup, and her pale cheeks were streaked with something.

'We'll help you with Harvey, you know that right?'

'Na-ah, this is my responsibility. I'll get it done.'

Oh, how to feel even worse...

She tried to smile, to be all, *Yeah, I'm on it*, but the words stuck in her throat and Sissi frowned. 'What's wrong?'

'*Nothing.*' Too quick.

'Astrid, I haven't known you all that long, but I *know* you. And something's up... what is it? Is it Aiden? Is it Blake?'

Astrid buried her head in her hand with a groan. *Try all of the above.*

'Okay, now you're worrying me.'

She flicked her head up. 'It's nothing for you to worry about, it's just...' *I'm not sure Aiden deserves to be messed with and I'm terrified of my growing feelings for Blake.*

'It's *just...*?'

'Aiden... he's not... he's actually...'

'Oh my God, you've fallen for his charm, haven't you? I knew this would happen.' She threw a hand at the screen. 'I warned you...'

'It's not like that, not quite,' she hurried to say. But what was it like?

'I don't even know why I'm surprised.' Sissi shook her head. 'He managed to fool me and I trusted no one until he came along.'

'What he did to you was wrong, honey, I'm not questioning that. I'm just questioning whether he deserves to be punished for something he didn't have a say in.'

'Didn't have a say in? He had every say!'

'But you know what his father was like, what his home life was like...'

'His life was always that way; it didn't stop him making all those promises and then walking away without so much as a backward glance.'

'What if he'd had no choice?'

'There's always a choice when it comes to answering the phone, but he ghosted me, like I meant nothing, and I deserved better than that.'

'You did, honey, you did.'

'And there's nothing he could say now that would make me feel any different so I don't understand how you can.'

'He should've answered the phone, he should've been there for you, especially when your dad was sent down but...'

Sissi's eyes welled up and Astrid bit her lip, her friend's obvious pain making her hesitate. She wanted to tell her about the fight, about the police and Blake, but she couldn't. Not without betraying Blake's confidence and she wouldn't do that.

'I think he felt that if they stayed, their father would ruin their lives for good.'

'And what about *my* life?' her friend choked out with a sudden fire in her eyes. 'What about our baby's life?'

What! Astrid jerked alert.

'Sissi? Did you just... were you *pregnant*?' Her gut rolled, her mind with it. Never had Sienna mentioned a baby, a pregnancy... at sixteen! 'When he *left* you?'

'He didn't know. I tried to tell him but...' she whispered, eyes blinking back the tears that insisted on falling anyway. 'Sorry. I shouldn't have – I never talk about it. I...'

'Honey, it's okay, you can talk to me. God, I wish I was with you...'

Sissi gave her a tremulous smile. 'Me too.'

'You don't have to talk, but...'

Sissi looked away, her eyes turning distant as Astrid absorbed the magnitude of what she was saying. Of how terrified and lost and all alone she truly had been. Astrid's mother had only been a couple of years older but at least she'd had Granny and Grandpa. She'd had support. She'd had love.

Sissi had had no one.

'I found out after he'd left...' she said softly, her tearful gaze returning to the screen. 'Everything was such a mess. I didn't know what I was doing, how I was going to cope, how I was going to tell Dad... I just needed him, Aiden. I knew that if I spoke to him, he would make it all okay, that I wouldn't be alone. But he wouldn't answer the phone. I called and called. I wasn't begging for him to come back to me, I was begging for him to just be *there*. For me and our child.'

'Oh my God, Sissi...'

'And then... I lost the baby,' she whispered. 'I wasn't taking care of myself, I was so broken over Aiden, then my dad was involved in that car accident; he was going to prison. My whole world was falling apart, and I... I miscarried.'

Astrid pulled her robe close, shivering with the weight of it – what her friend had gone through all alone, her loss and her continued pain. 'I'm so sorry, honey.'

'It was my fault. If only I'd looked after myself properly. If only I'd—'

'No! No, you can't see it that way. You can't blame yourself.'

'But I do. I blame myself and I blame him. For all his broken promises and for not being there when I needed him the most.'

'Yeah...' Astrid nodded, she got it now, truly got it. How Aiden had swanned on with his life while poor Sissi... a miscarriage. She couldn't bear it. 'I'll make him pay, love, I promise.'

And the sooner the better... for her own heart's sake, too.

* * *

'She's here,' Aiden said, tossing Blake the remote for the sound system. 'Why don't you put some decent music on and I'll get the door?'

He tossed it straight back. 'Why don't *you* put something decent on and *I'll* get the door?'

He moved before his brother could object, though it appeared Aiden was too busy laughing. 'You've got it bad, bro.'

'I ain't got nothing bad.'

Though he did check his reflection in the hallway mirror, mussing up his hair and smoothing down his black tee. He didn't like this, not one bit. Bringing a girl here. No matter what his brother said to the contrary. As for her turning him down...

Whatever. He tugged open the door. *You win some, you lose— lose your effing mind!*

It was the knee-high boots that did it. Heels for days. Or was it the sweet glimpse of thigh disappearing into a black dress that left little to the imagination? Or the glossy dark waves tumbling free, framing the plunging V of her neckline and electrifying his palms as well as his eyeballs...?

'Hi,' she said, and his head shot up.

Honey-coloured eyes, dramatically enhanced by shadow and liner, sparkled back at him. Blood-red lips curved into a slow, knowing smile. And her perfume, warm and rich, hit him like a one-two punch.

'Hi.' Hell, was that even his voice?

'Can I come in?'

Yeah, Blake, move!

'You'll have to excuse my bro.' Aiden came up behind him. 'I think he's still at the rink reliving today's training session. Can I take your coat?'

'Thank you,' she said, her eyes warm as she turned her focus on his brother. 'I bought you this to say thank you for cooking, Blake mentioned you enjoy a Scottish whisky every now and then?'

Aiden took it from her with a grin. 'Wow, that's a decent bottle too.'

'My grandfather is something of a whisky connoisseur.'

Blake closed the door, refusing to acknowledge the way she cosied up to Aiden, and the way they were now walking and talking intently as his brother led the way.

It meant nothing. She had an article to write. This was a business exchange. No green-eyed monster necessary, but...

But nothing, you're letting her rejection rule your head.

Not to mention the fact that she looked... *Stop looking!*

But those boots – how the hell was *she*, clumsy as fuck *Twinkle Toes*, walking in *them*? He'd bet his life she had a pair of sneakers in her bag.

'Can I get you a drink, Twinkle Toes?'

He waited for her to bite over the use of her pet name, his grin at the ready.

'I'd love one,' she threw over her shoulder. All smiles, no snark, go figure. 'Thank you.'

'What would you like?'

'What are you having?'

He'd like to say 'you'... In fact, he was pretty sure his eyes were doing just that as they entered the living area and she turned to face him, her cheeks pinking up under his gaze.

'A beer.'

Her eyes fired with something, the same something he'd seen that day she'd interviewed him and he'd requested the same.

'You know before I met you, I thought all you guys were angels the night before a game.'

He gave an abrupt laugh. 'Do I *look* like an angel?'

Her eyes dipped over him, their fire becoming a full-on blaze. *That* was desire. He was convinced of it. So why in the hell had she rejected him? Why in the hell was she cosying up to his bro, fawning over him like a bear with honey – one sexy, curvy, smokin' hot bear? And holy fuck, why had his head gone there? A bloody bear!

'Behave, Blake, and get the woman a drink,' his brother called from the kitchen. 'And she's right, you shouldn't be drinking, not that you'll be told.'

'Where would the fun be in that?' he muttered, heading to the bar. 'What will it be? Wine, prosecco, champagne... a beer with me?'

She wet her lips. *Jesus*, don't look. 'I'll have a white wine, please.'

He set about making the drinks while she wandered deeper

into their domain, the masculine monochrome setting off her feminine appeal... and those come-fuck-me boots. Brutal.

'Shit.' Chilled wine spilled over the glass as he overfilled it.

'All okay over there?'

'Absolutely,' he said, flicking the droplets off his hand behind his back. *Nothing to see here.* Hell, his brother was right, he did have it bad. All for the good in her.

Those caring eyes jazzed up to the nines, the compassion mixed up in the seductive sizzle... Maybe she meant it. Maybe she truly did care. And it was the possibility of her caring that was steadily undoing him. That and the green-eyed monster.

Not the boots.

Though he liked them. A lot.

* * *

So this was the lion's den?

She set her bag down on the luxurious leather sofa and drifted up to the panoramic glass. Astrid thought her uncle's place was impressive, but this... her gut took a wobble, and she palmed the glass, not trusting her toes in these heels when her knees were knocking.

From here, even Central Park looked small. A tiny rectangle bordered by the bustling city all around. The Hudson River on one side, Harlem on the other. People impossible to make out this high up but their mark in every structure, every flickering light... and how inconsequential it made her feel. A tiny fleck in the world's canvas.

'Impressive, isn't it?'

She jumped as he came up beside her.

'Sorry, I didn't mean to startle you.' He handed over her wine and she took it, careful to keep her fingers to herself. And careful not to look too closely at him either. She'd already seen enough. Black was definitely Blake's colour. Even if it was no colour at all.

'I was thinking how small it makes you feel, how insignificant...'

He gave a bemused laugh. 'We chose it for the total opposite.'

'How so?'

He pocketed his free hand, rolling his shoulders back as he turned to face the glass with her. 'The second we stepped into this living space our eyes were drawn to Manhattan sprawling out beneath us. It was like that moment in *Titanic*, when DiCaprio—'

'Wait! You've watched *Titanic*?'

'We've watched a lot of movies with our mother over the years, don't judge me.'

Oh my God, the idea of it. Blake with his mum. Popcorn. Tears. *Stop the imagery, stop the feelings, just stop, Astrid.*

But how could she when everything this man did had her going all gooey on the inside? And he kept surprising her, again and again.

'I'm not. Or I am. But it's all good. Believe me.'

He huffed into his beer. 'If I showed you a photo of our home back in Ashbury, you'd understand. To have come from that to this... we signed the lease that very first visit and have lived here ever since. Three years and counting...'

His voice trailed away. He wasn't boasting, he was comparing his old life to his new one. But there was something in his tone... A bittersweet twang, a dissatisfaction, a want?

'Do you still feel the same about the place?'

He shrugged. 'Driving aside, it's convenient. It works for us. No complaints.'

'It's home?'

'What is home?' He sent her a guarded look. 'Fucked if I know. Hungry?'

He gestured to the dining table where Aiden was serving up and she knew he was calling an end to the topic. She might have pressed further if it weren't for the timely reminder of the man she had dressed to get...

Karma-mode, engage!

Then her eyes dipped to the steaming plates of pasta and bugged out. 'Woah, that's some portion.'

'Welcome to the life of a hockey player,' Aiden said.

'You're the ones playing! I'm going to have to run the long loop of the park to work this off and then some.'

'Entirely unnecessary, though don't feel pressured into eating it all.'

She wouldn't – *couldn't* – but... 'It smells delicious.'

'It's simple but satisfying. The right kind of carb, heavy on the protein with the chicken, and you get a good dose of vitamins from the greens too.'

'Amazing,' she said, taking a seat and scooping some salad onto her plate, setting her dazzles on the right twin. 'I'm guessing you like to cook?'

'I like knowing what goes into my food...' He caught her eye, a very subtle blush marring his cheekbones and she knew he was remembering spice-gate. As was she, preening in her teeny-tiny victory. 'So you could say it's a passion born of necessity.'

'My bro is also a bit of a control freak, if you hadn't figured that out already.'

Her eyes snapped to Blake's. Was that a light tease or a full-on jibe?

But Aiden was grinning. 'Too right I am, and I'm happy to own it.'

Blake's smile twisted. 'Oh to be so comfortable in one's own skin...'

'You're not?' she couldn't help blurting.

'I'm working on it,' he replied.

'We're all working on it, bro,' Aiden said carefully, lowering his fork. 'Nobody's perfect.'

'Some of us are closer to it than others.' He raised his beer to his brother. 'And this meal is damn near perfect too. Thanks, buddy.'

'No problem.'

But Aiden was on edge now, his posture, his eyes... She glanced between the brothers.

'Something not to your liking, Astrid?' Aiden asked and she wanted to say *this*, whatever this was between them. But what did she know about siblings and rivalry and what was normal.

And she shouldn't care.

Tonight she had come for one thing and one thing only...

'Not at all, this really is delicious.' She filled her mouth, gave an appreciative hum. 'You're a good cook. I'm surprised you have the time to spend in the kitchen, what with all the hockey.'

'I make time. Between our mom and me, all our meals for the week are portioned out and labelled up. It helps us to keep on track and ensure a healthy diet around our schedule.'

'That's impressive; I barely know what I'm going to eat from one meal to the next let alone day to day. Does it ever get boring?'

'Does it taste boring?'

'No.' She smiled. 'Not at all.'

'There you go then.' He grinned back. 'I'm glad you like it.' And then his eyes dipped. Was that... was he checking her out?

She bloody hoped so! She leaned in. 'Would you say you're quite regimented in your routine?'

He pulled his eyes up and leaned back, sipped his water. 'We make time for fun, don't we, Blake?'

'Always.'

She looked at the man himself but he was too busy locked in some silent exchange with his brother.

'Some of us more than most.'

Was that another dig? It sure felt like one, especially with that brooding look in his eye.

Aiden cleared his throat. 'Why don't you tell us what got you into journalism, Astrid?'

And now Aiden was using her to get the focus off him.

'Was it something you always wanted to do?'

'Err, yeah, I guess it was.' She glanced between the brothers but they only had eyes for her now. Two sets of blazing blues. Intent and... *ohmigod*. She grabbed her wine, took a soothing chug. 'I was always a big reader and I love people. They fascinate me. What motivates them, how they feel, how they behave...'

Much like you two are fascinating me right now...

'I don't know whether to be flattered or scared,' Aiden murmured.

'Flattered, definitely flattered,' she reassured him with a smile she hoped would lure him back in.

'Who's the most interesting person you've met?' Aiden asked.

'Aside from us, of course,' Blake added.

'Easy. Kate Middleton,' she told Aiden. 'But I'm biased. She's British. She's classy. She's everything I would love to portray and never could, not with these feet...'

'Why would you want to do that?'

It was Blake who asked, forcing her to address him. 'Have you seen the woman?'

'I have and I'm looking at you right now, and I know who I'd choose.'

Her heart hit her tonsils, her eyes hot with the heat of his.

'Now you're just trying to sweeten me up when there really is no need. The article is shaping up nicely. Everyone who knows you both talks very highly of you.'

'Speaking of everyone who knows us,' Aiden said, pulling her focus back to him – thank heavens. 'We wondered whether you'd like to join us one Sunday for a roast at Mom's.'

Her mouth fell open. 'But I thought you said—'

'I said I didn't want you interviewing her, but she's a big part of our life, and we see no harm in you spending time with us all together. What she chooses to tell you is up to her. How does that sound?'

'I can't remember the last time I had a Sunday dinner... do people still do that?'

'We do when we're not playing and it's always with Mom. What do you say, you up for it?'

'Yes!' she blurted, head and heart racing. Because yes, it would be great to have that insight for the article. 'Thank you!'

But being invited into their mum's home, seeing the twins with their beloved mom... you'd have to be an ice queen not to melt!

And she couldn't afford to. Not for karma, and not for Blake.

15

Astrid's voice had gone up an octave or two. Her smile was too wide, her eyes too startled... could his brother not see it?

Maybe they were pushing their lives on her too much. Hell, the woman probably knew more about them than they knew about themselves by now. But he wasn't about to draw attention to her discomfort by asking her outright. Instead, he finished up his main meal in silence, letting Aiden, the king of schmoozing, do his thing.

And normally he'd tune it out. Not tonight though. Not when it was Astrid offering up more of her life...

Her career, her mother, her grandparents and their ancient family home in the English countryside with its freezing cold halls and hounds that she adored. How much happier she'd been running around its grounds with them than playing the shivering lady indoors. He found himself smiling as he imagined her doing just that...

'I'd like a dog.'

Both Aiden and Astrid shot a surprised look his way. Had they forgotten he existed?

'You would?' his brother asked.

'Not now, while we're away so much of the time, but yeah, in the future.'

Astrid smiled, a teasing twinkle in her eye. 'I can see you with a dog.'

'If you're thinking of a Chihuahua, you can stop it right now.'

She laughed. 'How did you guess?'

'You had that look in your eye.'

He loved that he could read her. Loved that it made her blush too.

'Just think of all the extra ladies you could attract if you had a cute little handbag dog...' she murmured.

Aiden chuckled. 'It would soften your image quite nicely, bro.'

'I thought my image was being softened quite nicely by Astrid's article.'

'Is it, Astrid?'

'Well, yes, but an added dose of cuteness wouldn't go amiss. Maybe we ought to get one for the photoshoot we have lined up.'

Aiden laughed harder. 'Oh yes, that's a great idea!'

'You've booked it in?' Blake said over him.

'Oh yeah, sorry buddy, I forgot to say. Between the powers that be and Astrid, they've lined us up a photoshoot week after next.'

'Great.' *Not.* 'Where?'

'Good question. Where do you think would work best?' Aiden asked her.

She caught her lip in her teeth, her eyes drifting to the living area...

'Oh no you don't,' Blake said, reading her mind. 'The rink makes more sense. We're players, it's who we are.'

'Yes, but everyone sees that side of you all the time. This would give them an insight into another side of you.'

The side they were now showing her, but... a photographer? Pictures that would then be pushed to the world... lauding their riches... 'I don't like it.'

'I think we take Astrid's steer on this, bro.'

'I wouldn't want you to be uncomfortable, but for the purposes of this article, this is what the readers will want to see.'

'I just hope you know what you're doing.'

'I do,' she assured him with a smile. 'And Fin, the photographer, is a friend of mine. You can trust him.'

'We trust you,' Aiden said and Astrid's smile gave the smallest quiver. What was that about? 'And if you trust him that's good enough for us.'

Aiden's phone started to ring, and Blake frowned at its unexpected presence on the table, the high volume ringtone too. 'Expecting someone?'

His brother ignored him as he checked the screen. 'Sorry, I just need to get this.'

He rose from the table and headed to the window, his voice too low to hear.

'Well, that's me done,' Astrid said, easing back in her seat and pulling his focus back to her. 'I can't eat another bite.'

'Don't let Aiden hear that, he's made his chocolate protein pudding for dessert.'

'Dessert?' Her eyes popped. 'I'm so full!'

'You'll want to make room for this, it's good. *Seriously* good.'

'Okay so that'll be a half marathon I'm running tomorrow then.'

And what he'd pay to see her do that, to do it with her too.

Aiden came back to the table. 'Really sorry, but I've got to go.'

'Now?' both Blake and Astrid blurted.

'Coach needs me to swing by his place.'

'At this time?' Blake said as Astrid shot to her feet.

'I best get off too then.'

Woah woah woah, they were both bailing? Was this some cunning ruse to get off together?

'Oh no, you stay,' his brother said.

Not together then...

'Dessert is in the fridge and Blake's more than capable of serving it up.'

She looked at Blake like his brother had just suggested he serve *her* up.

'Yeah, I can take care of that...'

Her throat bobbed.

'How late will you be?'

'No idea, but you guys have fun, yeah?' And was that a wink? 'It was lovely to see you, Astrid. Thank you for the whisky.'

He leaned in to give her a peck to the cheek, so chaste she almost fell over as he swept away and Blake watched him go, a perplexed smile glued to his face.

The moment the front door clicked shut, Astrid rounded on him, eyes burning. 'Right, what did you do this time?'

'I didn't do anything.'

'Don't lie to me.'

'I'm not,' he insisted, a laugh choking out of him. How was he supposed to think straight, let alone speak straight when she was looming over him like some hip-popping vixen? The outfit gave her a dominatrix vibe that his body was all too willing to respond to.

'You didn't ask Coach to call him away? Just like you asked Harry...'

'No! Regardless of what you might think' – he shifted in his seat, wishing his jeans were more forgiving – 'I don't lie. Well, I kind of lied earlier, but that was different.'

Her brows arched, her golden eyes shooting sparks. That's when it hit him – she wasn't wearing glasses tonight. She must switch to contacts when she dressed to go out-out... or go looking to score.

'When?'

'When I said *Titanic* was my mom's choice of movie. I chose it.'

If ever it was possible to watch a person melt, she just did. 'You're serious?'

'As serious as mustard on my hotdog.'

'That's not a saying.'

'It is now.'

He turned in his seat, lounging back in front of her and making the most of the view... a view he wanted to understand better.

'But now he *is* gone...' he murmured as her eyes hesitated over him, dipping low and staying low. 'Are you going to be honest with me, Twinkle Toes?'

Her eyes shot back up, her cheeks warming. 'What about?'

'Who you're wearing this for – him, or me?'

'*What?*'

'If I was a betting man, I'd say you were looking to score. So, him, or me? Or do you have a predilection for a threesome with twins?'

She choked on thin air. 'Hell no!'

'And now the lady does protest too much.'

'Doth.'

'Doth what?'

'It's "doth protest" not "does".'

'You say tomahto, I say tomayto.'

She shook her head, her hair shimmering all the way down to that deep alluring V...

'Who's to say I don't dress like this for dinner normally?'

'I do.'

Her eyes gleamed in the low light, her cheeks hollowing. Was she biting them?

'Tell me I'm wrong.'

'For someone who strikes me as open-minded about a lot of things, you seem to be very opinionated when it comes to how I dress. Why is that?'

'I don't know. You seem to spark a lot of opinions in me.'

She surprised him with a laugh. 'And what's that supposed to mean?'

'Damned if I know. It's a new one on me too.'

And it wasn't something he wanted to ponder too deeply. It ran along the same lines of caring too deeply and he wasn't about to go there. He pushed himself to standing and tore his gaze away. 'I'll get that pudding.'

'I'll help you clear up first.'

Not neanderthals remember, came his brother's voice in his head.

'No, you won't, I'll take care of it later. You take your drink into the living area, and I'll bring them through.'

* * *

Astrid knew she was in trouble. The kind of trouble Delia would probably relish in the fictional world, but this wasn't fiction. This was real.

Real feelings. Real desires. Real hurt.

Blake's. Sissi's. Hers. Even Aiden's.

She should have insisted on leaving with the latter... shoulda, woulda, coulda!

Too late now, Beverley Knight!

And she was pretty convinced that Aiden wasn't into her. Or maybe it was that Blake was so very obviously interested that it made his brother appear apathetic by comparison. Not to mention her body's own preference on the matter.

She tried to ease back into the sofa, but it was too cosy. The fire flickering in the seamless opening that ran along one wall cast a warm, golden glow over the deeply masculine room. The soft ambient music filtering through the surround sound system, building on the intimate vibe.

'Here we go, one Carter special.'

Awareness rippled through her as a chocolate-filled ramekin appeared over her shoulder.

'Thank you,' she murmured, taking it from him.

'You're welcome.'

He walked around to slide in beside her and her mouth watered, salivating over his proximity and not the rich-looking chocolate she was determined to stare at.

He gave a low chuckle. 'You look ravenous again.'

'Ha!' It burst from her chest, the heat in her cheeks as serious as the burn in the rest of her body as she avoided his eye *and* his lips which were sure to taste even better than the pudding. 'What can I say, I'm a chocolate addict.'

She scooped some up and shoved it in.

Her eyes slammed closed as her tastebuds exploded, her blissful murmur impossible to contain.

What kind of lethal combination was this?

'That good, hey?'

'*Seriously* good!' She scooped up another, eager to fill her mouth with more of the tasty goodness. The safe tasty goodness. Though her eyes wouldn't be told, they were drawn to him on repeat. The way he was lounging back, his big strong thighs spread, biceps flexing as he spooned the pudding into his equally tasty mouth. The glimpse of tongue as he opened up, the way his lips shifted around it, the way his throat bobbed as he... *fuck.*

'What was that?'

Her eyes snapped to his. 'What?'

'Did you just squeak?'

'No!'

'You just made a noise like a mouse. You did it the other day too.'

'I really did not.'

'You really did.' His mouth curved into that irresistibly sexy grin of his. 'Don't worry, I'm pretty sure I squeaked the first time I tried Aiden's pudding too.'

He leaned forward, his knee grazing hers as he set his empty pot down. Heat fizzed up her leg and she clamped her thighs together, shovelled in more pudding. Kept going until there was none left to distract her. Damn.

'You should go into advertising...' His gravel-like tone rasped along her skin as his eyes raked over her. 'You're making me want to go grab another.'

She gave an edgy laugh. 'Ha, as if! Much better to leave that to the Aidens of this world.'

'Yeah, it does take a certain kind of individual...'

She sobered as she remembered how she'd asked him about it on the street that first day, how she'd been so sure there'd been more to his reasons for not doing the same.

'I know you said it's not your scene, but you have the looks, the style, the whole package...'

He huffed. 'Like hell I do, and I won't fake it. Aiden's the man that people should idolise and want to emulate. Not me.'

He pushed himself to standing, his self-deprecation no longer a surprise, but the ache it triggered in her chest. That was new.

'Can I get you another drink – more wine?'

'No. Thank you.' Absolutely not, her inhibitions were already running low, and it was high time she left. But what he'd said... it bothered her. The way he put himself down while bigging his brother up. It had been there all through dinner too, driving the banter.

'Coffee? We have decaf?'

She wet her lips, her 'time to go' spiel sticking in her throat.

'A water would be great, thanks.'

She watched him go and took a breath. One that still caught the dredges of his aftershave and the air that felt too hot and heavy to go down easy. She wished she'd worn layers so she could at least remove one; even her legs felt clammy in her boots.

She weighed up a quick exit against stripping them off, and unzipped the leather before she could talk herself out of it. Slipping her feet out, she flexed her toes. Better. Much better. Then she dug inside her bag for her phone and messaged her mother:

ASTRID

Mum, do I squeak?

'One water,' he said, reappearing beside her.

She set her phone down and took the drink, her pulse hitching as his eyes flicked to her legs, their heat rendering her 'thank you' inaudible as he twisted the cap off a fresh beer and took a long, deep slug.

Had she driven him to that?

Her brow furrowed. She hoped not. Especially with Aiden's words ringing in her ears – *she's right, you shouldn't be drinking.*

'Are you sure you should be having that?'

He shook his head, his smile wry. 'Don't you start.'

'I'm not, I'm just saying...' She wriggled into the sofa as she chose her next words with care. 'If I was playing a big game tomorrow, I'm not sure my nerves could take it.'

'I have it because of my nerves.' He dropped down beside her, caught her expression. 'Shocked you, haven't I?'

'No. Well, maybe just a little...'

'Yeah, well, don't tell anyone. I ain't proud of it. Fury doesn't get nervous. Not ever.'

'Only... you do?'

He gave her a twisted grin. 'You wouldn't believe what goes on in this head of mine the night before a game.'

'Something tells me it might be similar to what I have going on up here every time I stare at a blank page.'

His eyes narrowed. 'A fear of getting it wrong? Of not being good enough?'

'*Total* imposter syndrome.'

'And how do you deal with it?'

'It depends.' She leaned into the sofa, curling her legs up underneath her. 'Sometimes all it takes is exercise or an outing with some friends, anything to silence the negativity and shift my focus. But there are times...' She licked her lips, surprised at what she was about to say but knowing that she wanted to. That she wasn't scared to. That he wouldn't judge her or ridicule her like some men had. 'There's always a week every month when it gets harder, virtually impossible.'

'A week a month?' He frowned and then his brows eased as her meaning hit home. 'You have it too, don't you? What your mother has? The PMD?'

'The PMDD, yeah.'

And it was about to hit any day and there wasn't a damn thing she could do about it. But she'd deal with it, just like she always dealt with it.

'I did wonder, when you were telling me. I wanted to ask but...'

She gave a small smile, warmth blooming in her chest. 'You didn't want to pry? Even though I was doing just that with you.'

He shrugged. 'It's your job.'

But this wasn't. This conversation now. It was something else entirely.

'Is it really bad?' he asked.

'It is what it is. Its own kind of hell. But better to know what it is, than to think you're going crazy like my mum once did. Things weren't so well talked about back then, for years she battled it without knowing it or understanding it. So I'm actually quite lucky really. And I know to hide away because the pressure of sharing the worst of you with someone only makes the anxiety worse. *And* I don't even know why I'm telling you all of this. I'm sorry.'

'Don't be sorry. I'm sorry. I can't begin to imagine what it must be like to be at the mercy of your hormones one month to the next.'

'I've learned to live with it, and Mum and I do our best to watch out for each other, even across the miles.'

Though if she was honest, Mum had needed her less and less over the past few months. Ever since John had arrived on the scene... When he was gone though, Astrid would be ready and waiting to pick up the pieces and be her rock once more.

'You're very close with her?'

'We have our moments but yeah, she gets me. She's also very good at reminding me of all I've achieved, when I can't see it. She helps me focus on the positives and push past the negatives so that I still get words on the page.'

His eyes wavered over her face, the compassion in his depths unravelling something deep within her. Something unrecognisable, deeply rooted...

'It's what *you* need to do too,' she said, needing the sensation within to stop before it grew out of her control. 'Focus on the positives, big yourself up...'

He gave a tight laugh. 'I don't think anyone has ever dared tell Fury to big himself up before.'

'No, but I'm telling Blake Carter to do it.' She grew serious, determined. 'It's like I told you, you give this front, but underneath it all, you're just as vulnerable as the rest of us. And you deserve some ego-boosting too. You've earned all those accolades you seem to be ignoring.'

He gave a small smile, his eyes falling to the bottle that no longer touched his lips as often. 'It doesn't matter where I come in the player rankings, how many assists, or how many goals I score, the doubts are always there, eating away at every achievement. And you can't show weakness. Not in this game. The first sign and you're out.'

'That's harsh.'

'That's hockey. And the older I get, the worse it is. You have rookies coming in all the time and they play faster, harder, and you compare yourself to them all. And then there's Aiden, there's *always* Aiden.'

'You know what your problem is?' she said softly.

He shook his head and she reached out, wrapped her hand around the beer bottle and eased it from his fingers.

'You gonna tell me I should know better,' he said, his voice gruff, eyes stormy. 'With a father like mine...'

'No. I'm going to tell you to quit being so hard on yourself.

You've spent your life in your brother's shadow. You've spent your life looking up to him, idolising him, letting him take the lead rather than trusting yourself with it. I don't think you've ever taken the time to truly appreciate what you've achieved. Or questioned what you want going forward.'

'I'm where I am because of him.'

'No, you got here because you were just as skilled, just as strong, and if you were to speak to anyone on your team, like I have, you would see that you are his equal. That you are someone to be admired and adored on his own merit. And if you were to tell yourself this the night before a game, instead of drinking this, you might find those screaming doubts become whispers that eventually die out.'

He gave a choked laugh. 'Quite the poet, aren't you?'

'Not according to my old English teacher.'

'And how do you suggest I silence that voice in my head when burning calories through exercise is totally ill-advised the night before a game?'

Her eyes drifted over the room, looking for inspiration – both twins had made it clear they lacked hobbies – but if she wasn't much mistaken there was a games console tucked into the wall.

'Who's the player between you and your brother?'

He smirked, his eyes dark and teasing. 'I thought we'd already covered that conversation in the interview, but if you want to bring up sex as a—'

She barked out a laugh, killing the idea before Delia's book could take hold. 'I meant the games console!'

'Pity.'

She purposefully ignored him. 'I told you it was one of my coping strategies way back when. Maybe it could work for you too.'

He glanced at the console. 'It's mine.'

'Play it much?'

'Sometimes.'

'Favourite game?'

He gave her a funny look. 'This is where I'm supposed to say something cool, isn't it?'

'Says the guy who's already confessed to watching *Titanic* by choice...'

He chuckled. 'I'm pretty retro in my tastes.'

'*How* retro?'

'Like *Street Fighter* retro.'

Now she grinned. 'Favourite character?'

'Easy. Ryu.'

'Too obvious.'

'Alright then, Twinkle Toes, who's yours... no wait, let me guess. Chun-Li.'

'Every time.'

'I'm sure we're playing into gender stereotypes here.'

'Nonsense, she's a kick-ass character and has earned her right at the top. She'll wipe the floor with Ryu any day of the week so long as these babies are at the helm.' She fluttered her fingers at him.

'You're on.'

He was already rising up.

'What? You want to play *now*?'

He paused, cocked his sexy head her way. 'I thought you were teaching me other distraction techniques... unless you want to go down the bedroom route because I'm totally up for that too.'

Her phone buzzed with a text and she picked it up.

MUM

Haha! Are you talking about your foodgasm?

My what?

'Everything okay?'

She looked up to find Blake hovering over her, a games controller in his outstretched hand.

If she'd been blushing before, she was a beacon now. 'Nope. All good.'

She threw her phone aside and grabbed it off him. 'Prepare to get annihilated, Ryu.'

Because if she was focusing on the game, she couldn't be squeaking over him.

Foodgasm? *Blakegasm*, more like!

* * *

'You two looked pretty cosy when I got home.'

Aiden leaned back against the kitchen counter while Blake cleared away the last of the dishes.

'Cosy?' Not how Blake saw it. With her bare legs tucked beneath her, lip caught between her teeth, and eyes locked on the screen, she had him thinking every *non*-cosy thought. 'Hardly. She was whooping my ass on *Street Fighter*.'

His brother laughed. 'Never thought I'd see that day.'

'You and me both. I'm the king of that game.'

'And now you have your queen.'

Blake's own laugh cracked. His brother was teasing. He got the joke. But the way it knocked about inside him was anything but funny. He liked her. Liked her a lot. And that was a problem. A great big 'get the fuck out of town' problem.

Vulnerable. That's what she'd said about him. And that's how she had him feeling. And the way she'd trusted him with her own vulnerability, too... *hell*, it made him feel good. It made him feel worthy. It made him think he could be the guy that people looked up to. That he could step out of his brother's shadow and take control of his life. That he could trust himself with it.

'You had a good time then?'

'Yeah.' He took up his forgotten beer, surprised to find it three quarters full. 'She's easy to be around.'

'When she's not firing a thousand questions at you, right?'

He smiled as he poured the beer down the sink, but didn't admit the truth. Because even then, he'd happily take a thousand more to have her stick around.

'Since when do you throw good beer away?'

He shrugged. 'I forgot it was there.' He also knew he didn't need it. 'Coach okay?'

'Coach?'

'Yeah.' Blake looked at him. 'Tonight, when you went to see him?'

'Oh right, yeah, that. Yeah, all good.' Aiden pushed away from the counter and turned away. 'I'm going to hit the sack, big game tomorrow, make sure you get your beauty sleep, bro.'

He watched his brother leave, sensing his quick exit had more to do with cutting the conversation dead than a desperate need to sleep. And if that was the case, why? What had he been up to that he didn't want Blake to know about? Was he back to protecting his ass again?

Now he wished he hadn't poured the beer away.

His phone buzzed in his pocket, and he pulled it out.

ASTRID

Thank you for a great night. When you're ready for a rematch let me know x

And just like that he was smiling again...

BLAKE

Any time, anywhere, Twinkle Toes x

16

PMDD hit and it hit hard.

Which served Astrid right after the way she'd behaved. Getting all cosy with Blake when she should have left with Aiden. Offering up a rematch, too – gah!

How could she have been so duplicitous?

Only she hadn't *meant* to be duplicitous.

She'd sent a text to each twin. One to Aiden saying thank you along with praise for his cooking. And the other to his brother, also saying thank you but wanting to say so much more, because she'd been overflowing with... with so much *feeling* towards him... and the rematch had rolled from her fingers.

She was useless.

PMDD-ridden useless. And so she'd spent the rest of the week in hiding. Keeping up to speed with her girlfriends via message, keeping her distance from the twins, and carrying out research for her article while trying to track down their father too.

But she'd known come game day, she'd have to do something

to try and take the edge off. Something to exorcise every Blake-induced craving from her body *before* she saw him on the ice.

Something that would exhaust her body so much it wouldn't dare get all perky for him. And exhaust her mind so much that it would quit the negative spiral of PMDD gloom.

So that afternoon, she'd dragged Bella to NYC's most extreme hot yoga class...

Bella, who could help Astrid get out of her own head.

Bella, who could refocus her on the plan and boost her with an update on Chase.

Bella, who couldn't know the truth about her feelings for Blake – *hell*, Astrid didn't want to know about those – but could be told enough to sympathise with her.

And now here Astrid was, at the game, sore in places that hadn't existed before today, head still ranting, body too...

'Good evening, New York!' A roar rippled through the crowd as the announcer cut through the music and Astrid's head shot up, her heart too. 'Welcome to what promises to be an electrifying matchup here at Empire State Ice.'

The noise around her built, reverberating through her limbs as she stood with the crowd and cheered the teams onto the ice. The Knights came first, unperturbed by enemy ice as they swooshed around, sticks and fists pumping the air.

'And now, it's time to welcome your Titans...'

She turned to watch the players launch onto the rink, her eyes eagerly taking in every jersey, waiting and waiting until...

Blake appeared, his eyes finding her as though they were connected by some invisible thread, his grin making her perkier than perky! And in that moment, she didn't care.

'Good luck,' she mouthed.

His gaze swept over her, not that she could see his eyes clearly through his visor, but she could sense their approval as he took in her Titans jersey. It had been a last-minute purchase on her way in, not so much an attempt at blending in with the masses but *being* one of the masses. A few weeks living and breathing the hockey world and she was as caught up in the team and the game as the next fan.

Didn't think to catch Aiden's eye though, did you?

Oh God, she really was useless! She hunted him out now, caught the back of his 88 jersey...

'Both teams are hungry for this win,' the announcer was saying. 'The Titans want to maintain their lead, the Knights want to steal it, so buckle up, fans!'

Aiden turned, throwing her a grin as he settled into position. *Bullseye!*

She gave him a double thumbs up and then gripped her fists beneath her chin as the ref prepared to drop the puck...

* * *

Astrid was going to need a fresh manicure. Hockey was savage. It was fast. And it was giving her acid reflux. How could they *stand* it? The players, the fans, the poor refs caught in the middle...

Her gaze zipped up and down the ice with the puck, barely blinking as the closing minutes were upon them. The crowd around her buzzed as the Titans headed for a shutout. Their first against the Knights in a decade and perfect fodder for her article.

The twins were incredible. Seeing in the flesh what she'd only ever seen on screen and read about – the connection, the ability to know where the other was, where they were going to be, what they needed. It was evident in every play.

And Blake had escaped the penalty box – something the fans near her were all passing comment on. Questioning it. Judging it.

She didn't care. She was just glad he was in one piece. The way they hit the boards... she was gonna crack a tooth! But she hadn't dwelled on her PMDD. Not once. Who knew hockey could be another coping mechanism!

The ref called time, and she roared with the rest, the Titans' celebratory lap rousing the crowd further as the Knights left the rink and she stood there mesmerised. She'd never been big on spectator sport, never had the time or the inclination, but she was hooked now.

'Come on, Foxy, it's time to celebrate!' Harry hollered from the benches. 'Get yourself down to the locker rooms, stat.'

The woman beside her gave her a wide-eyed grin. 'He talking to you?'

'Yeah, he's talking to me.'

'Wow!'

'Right.' Lips pursed over a giggle, she fought her way through the crowds to the private tunnel, flashing her pass as she went and feeling every bit the VIP. The noise emanating from their locker room reached her long before she reached it. And then she was being tugged into the madness by one rookie as another thrust a beer into her hand.

'Is it always this crazy?' she laughed out. There were half naked bodies everywhere, bottles of booze being sprayed, noise, so much noise.

'Depends on the win!' Harry said. 'Against the Knights, always!'

And then Blake appeared in the throng, his grin making her own quiver... along with her nether regions.

She licked her lips as he approached, her feet rooted to the spot.

'Hey, you enjoy the game?'

'You bet she did, Fury,' Harry said, 'just look at her.'

'Why? How do I look?'

He came up close, his body towering over her, his protective gear making him feel twice the size. 'You look good. Especially in this...'

He tugged the sleeve of her jersey.

'Do you think it's my colour?'

'Everything's your colour, Twinkle Toes.'

She gave a tight laugh, his sincerity burning her up from the inside.

'You going to come celebrate with us?'

'I...' She wanted to say yes! High on the win, high on him, but she knew where that would lead. Could see it in his gaze as readily as she felt it in her own. 'I best not, I've got a busy day tomorrow.'

'You sure?'

'Yup.'

'But it's early, Foxy!' Harry piped in again. 'Come join us, we don't smell that bad surely.'

'You need to quit it with the Foxy, Harry,' Blake warned, flicking the lad a look that had zero effect whatsoever. They were all too high on endorphins. 'He's right though.'

'About the smell?' She wrinkled her nose. 'Because now you mention it... there is a certain aroma.'

His grin twisted to the side. 'You're—'

'Hey Astrid.' Aiden came striding up, swinging his arm around Blake's shoulders. 'Enjoy the game?'

She gave him the dazzles. 'It was immense.'

'You joining us for a drink?'

She flicked a look at his brother. 'I need to be getting home.'

'It's still early.'

'It's almost midnight, Aiden.'

He checked the clock on the wall. 'So it is, but we're hours from sleep.'

She laughed. 'You guys might be, but this little lady needs her beauty sleep.'

And to recharge her resolve and her ability to get done what needed to be done.

'Come on, stay,' Blake pressed softly.

Both twins were now giving her puppy-dog eyes and my God, she needed to get out of there and douse her body in ice.

'I need to go.'

She passed Blake the drink she'd been given and he immediately passed it on.

'So you keep saying.'

'And I mean it.'

He cocked a brow. 'And yet you're still standing there.'

She shook her head with a laugh and twirled on the spot. 'Congrats, boys! Have a great night!'

She got as far as the door when she felt a hand on her shoulder. Her traitorous heart soared as she turned, expecting Blake and getting Aiden.

'Is everything okay?' she asked as her heart took a dive.

'I just wanted to say thank you.'

She frowned. 'What for?'

'Whatever you've said to Blake, whatever magic you've imparted, thank you.'

'I haven't done anything.'

'That's not how I see it. Something's changed since you came along. He's different.'

'In a good way?'

'In the best way.'

He pulled her in, squishing her to his chest, and it reminded her of the overzealous hug she'd once given him. Only this time, she was the one stunned still. Her eyes found Blake's. He was back in the thick of the celebrations, but his eyes were on her, watching her, watching them. Her heart returned to her throat.

'So, thank you!' Aiden released her. 'Sleep well.'

'And you,' she said on autopilot, forcing her body to do her bidding and leave while her head and heart floundered on it all.

Aiden. His gratitude. The karma. And Blake. *Always* Blake.

* * *

'What was that all about?'

Blake frowned at his brother who looked even smugger post Astrid hug.

'Nothing.'

'It didn't look like nothing.'

Aiden gave him the side eye as he took a swig of beer. 'Jealous?'

He grunted and his brother laughed. 'Lighten up, bro, we've got a win to celebrate.'

And then he disappeared into the foray, his cheer drawing the team all around into a chant loud enough for the entire arena to hear. Blake looked back to the exit. To where she'd been stood... feeling her presence even though she was gone. Feeling the effect of that embrace too. His brother didn't give affection easily. Yet, there he'd been, hugging the life out of her.

'Come on, Pretty Boy!' Larsson punched him in the arm. 'You're lagging!'

He gave a choked laugh. 'Alright, alright, take it easy, Big Man!'

With one last look at the exit, he raked a hand through his hair and turned back to the throng. 'Chuck us a beer, Harry.'

He caught it mid-air, twisted off the cap and knocked it back though it failed to hit the spot. He had a feeling nothing would hit the spot. Nothing but a certain brunette with honey-gold eyes and a body that rocked the Titans' jersey.

He eyed the bottle and realised how much he hadn't missed it last night. Astrid's suggestion that he lose his negativity in the virtual world had worked.

Though if he was honest, his focus had only half been on *Street Fighter*, the rest had been on her and the questions she had raised over his life, the way he chose to live it, and the way he should be proud enough to stand apart from his bro. And the more he thought about it, the more he knew she was right.

He'd also woken that morning with a clearer head and an extra kick in his veins... a kick that had more to do with her attending the game, than the game itself.

And what was that about? The game was his life, Astrid was... he had no clue, but it was big, and it ran deep. Too deep to be ignored.

As for his brother... if she had the power to make Blake feel this way about her, did she have the power to make the Ice King feel the same? And if so, what the hell did he do now?

17

The Titans weren't the only ones on a winning streak, a week later Bella joined the ranks of the victorious. Chase Miller had got his comeuppance. Astrid had been avenged and in spectacular fashion too!

Last night, the girls had celebrated. Drank champagne and talked until their voices grew hoarse. But as happy as Astrid had been, post-PMDD and high on payback, she'd also been forced to come clean about her own failings. At least where Aiden was concerned... not Blake.

They couldn't know about Blake. Astrid didn't *want* to know about Blake. He made her feel too much. Want too much.

They'd been kind and understanding – more than she deserved – and immediately set about creating a fallback plan. Dedicating a chunk of the call to the many and varied ways in which she could mess with the Ice King... each idea more fanciful than the last.

And today was the day of the photoshoot. The perfect opportunity to do *something*...

But what?

As she hurried along the sidewalk to the twins' apartment, her mind buzzed with their suggestions and then it struck her, flashing before her eyes in vivid technicolour. The same billboard she'd passed that very first day walking home with Blake – Aiden grinning with his preferred brand of tan.

To be fair to the guy, if it weren't for a New York winter and the amount of time he spent on the ice, it could be considered *au naturel*. But there were other brands... brands with shades that shouldn't exist unless you intended to look like a pumpkin.

Now *this* she could mess with...

And checking her watch, she pivoted to the nearest department store.

* * *

Blake hated having his photo taken.

Even his professional profile pic had been taken under duress, and did he smile? Did he fuck.

Fin, the camera guy, was setting up in the living room. Astrid was supposed to be on her way over but running late. Stella was clucking about and Aiden, he had no fucking idea where Aiden was. The guy had become a law unto himself.

Was he the only one ready for this damn thing? Ready with a headache too. Not to mention the fact that his face felt weird. *And* he smelt of a goddamn biscuit.

Why he'd listened to Stella when she'd suggested he shave, he had no idea. As for the tan, that was all Aiden's doing – *the camera loves a tan, buddy.* Blake did not.

But he was determined to play ball. Do as he was told in the hope that the whole thing would be over as quickly and as painlessly as possible.

Though now Aiden was AWOL and he felt... he ran a hand

over his smooth jaw and grimaced, his skin prickling with mounting unease. This wasn't him.

Fin had taken some test shots earlier and Blake had struggled to recognise himself. Maybe he ought to change the clothing Stella had chosen too. White tee, stonewashed jeans. *So not him.*

About the only thing that was truly 'Fury at Home' were his bare feet. And Astrid had said she wanted this to be genuine, a true representation of their life...

So why did you listen to Stella?

Perhaps because Astrid wasn't here to tell him otherwise, and he was so far out of his comfort zone he'd take instruction from anyone who looked like they knew what they were doing.

Why hadn't Astrid rocked up with Fin? Was she the reason Aiden wasn't here either? Were they both off together doing God knew what?

He clenched his jaw and fired off another text to the man himself.

'Mr Carter?'

The voice accompanied a knock on his bedroom door, and he blinked through the darkness. 'Yes?'

It cracked open a slit and Fin's pixie-haired apprentice peeped in... what was her name... Betty? Betsy? Becky? 'What is it?'

'Fin's asking if we're okay to move the coffee table out of the living area?'

Did he want to move Blake out of the apartment while he was at it?

'No problem.'

'And can we take the—'

'Fin can do whatever the hell he likes so long as he gets this over with as quick as possible.'

'Great!' Though she sounded terrified now and he gripped his temples.

'Sorry, headache, my bad.'

'Can I get you something for it?'

'No-no, it's fine. Just do what you need to do.'

She hurried off and he dropped back on his bed, threw an arm over his head and closed his eyes. It was going to be a long morning...

*　*　*

'Everything going okay, Fin?'

Astrid? Blake's eyes eased open; he must have fallen asleep. Just the sound of her voice carrying down the hall had a smile working its way through him, the thumping in his head easing.

'Aye, all set. We're a man down but Stella reckons he'll be here in a wee bit. Thanks for the coffee.'

'No worries. I—' She broke off, her tone taking a turn. 'Sorry, Fin, I just have to make a call and then I'll be back.'

'Nae bother, take your time.'

Blake pushed himself to sitting and ran a hand over his hair – time to get this party started.

He hit the bathroom, freshened up and headed out, surprised to find Astrid coming down the hall at a lick, head down, ponytail swinging, thumbs working furiously over her phone. Why the sudden hurry? And why did she always look so goddamn sexy?

She'd skipped the glasses again today, but the waistcoat was back. Her white shirt lay open just enough to tease at the sweet spot between her breasts, while her jeans clung to her legs in a way that made his fingers itch to—

'Morning!' he blurted, eager to cut the thought dead... not, as it happened, scare the bejesus out of her.

She jumped, and her phone flew, hitting the floor and skidding past him, straight into his room.

'Shit!' She dived to rescue it as he did, hurling herself in front of him and catching the doorframe as she went. She ricocheted from it to him and back again, going down like a pinball, ping ping ping.

He lunged to catch her, but she dragged him off balance and they went down together. One moment, she was beneath him, his hands braced on her hips. The next, she was on top, clutching the phone tightly between them.

Wide, glittering eyes blinked down at him in the dark; her soft breath swept over his cheeks...

'Hey.'

Hell, was that his voice? All gruff and winded and weak. Though with her body pressed to every inch of his, her thighs straddling his hips and all the heat rushing south, it was lucky he could speak at all.

'Hey.'

She was just as breathless, just as startled...

She shifted over him, the friction firing through his groin. Shit. He needed to move before— too late. She knew. She felt it. Eyes widening and then closing as she dropped forward and before he knew what she was about, she kissed him. Hard. Insistent. Going all in. And he was so here for it. The passion, the fire – holy fuck this woman could kiss!

He buried his hand in her ponytail, tugged her head back as he rolled her under him, his groan as wild as he now felt. Oh yes, *this* was worth getting all preened for...

'Blake!'

They froze. *Aiden.* For fuck's sake. The king of bad timing had returned and was hollering from somewhere down the hall...

Blake lifted his head, gave her a lopsided grin. 'That was some good morning, Twinkle Toes.'

Now she scrambled. Hurrying out from underneath him, her hand quivering over her lips as she squinted up at him.

'Blake?' she whispered, her voice raw.

'Yeah, who else would it—' His gut shrivelled and rolled. 'You've got to be kidding me...'

But it was there, in her horrified gaze.

'You thought I was him, didn't you? That's why you...' He choked on his own words. 'Fuck. Of course you did.'

'But your face... your stubble... your *tan*...'

'Un-*fucking*-believable!' He launched to his feet. He wanted to puke. Fuck, he wanted to get the hell out of there and not come back.

'I'm sorry, I didn't – it's not... It was dark and you—'

Her phone started to ring in her hand, and she glanced at the screen, her pallor deepening. 'I'm really sorry, I need to take this.'

'So long as you take it elsewhere, Foxy, I couldn't care less.'

She stared at him, eyes rolling with emotion that he had no interest in responding to. The phone was still ringing, its lilt grating on his nerves. 'Just go, Astrid. And while you're at it, find your *fucking* glasses.'

She got to her feet, wobbling as she straightened. But he didn't care. He *didn't*.

She teetered to the door, gripped its frame and looked back – a moment's glance full of... regret? Pity? Guilt? And then she was gone and his gut bottomed out.

This was why he didn't let people in.

This was why he should remember who he was.

This was why he refused to feel anything for a woman.

Because it hurt. Hurt like *fuck* when they let him down. Or worse, chose his brother over him.

Well, more fool him for caring.

And more fool her for getting it so wrong.

And damn Stella and his bro for suggesting he make some changes. Though he only had himself to blame for listening. To Stella, to Aiden, to Astrid... and his own body that had wanted so much more from her and dared to believe it was possible.

* * *

No-no-no-no-no-no-no...

It rambled through her mind, past her lips as Astrid raced into the elevator and slammed the button for 'Ground', the lurch to her stomach nothing to do with the speed of the lift and everything to do with Blake and Bella. Bella and Blake.

How could she have thought Blake was Aiden?

And what the hell was wrong with Bella?

Everything had been rosy on their call. Champagne central all night!

She glanced at the screen, Bella's initial 'Code Red' message had been followed by two more:

JUST DESSERTS WHATSAPP GROUP. 10.39 EST.

BELLA

Code red.

Code RED.

HELP! NOW!

And now Bella was ringing them all.

Her head raced with what it could be while her heart raced over that kiss.

She'd been so caught up in the sudden karmic opportunity and utterly convinced that the AWOL twin would be Blake. That good boy Aiden would be prompt and ready with his trademark grin. And her quick glimpse in the hall had delivered everything she would have expected – freshly shaved jaw, golden tan, white tee, pale jeans – *all* Aiden.

Only it *wasn't!*

She squeezed her eyes shut, pushing out the guilt, the heat, the wrong man!

If only she hadn't been so determined to take advantage of a fresh opportunity. If only she hadn't been so fixated on her phone. If only she'd clocked him properly *before* she'd sent her phone flying. *Before* the panic had taken over that he would spy something incriminating on the lit-up screen. *Before* they'd become entangled in the dark and his need had been so evident that she'd been high on her own triumph.

Then she might have seen the slight nuances. The lack of a scar to his cheek, the extra line to his left dimple, the way Blake always made her shiver with a thrill... fuck fuck *fuck*.

And now... now what?

She'd *kissed* Blake!

His body, *his* need, *his* kiss – the realisation that it had been him all along... the desperation to rewrite the moment entirely and not knowing which way to go. To know it was Blake and to revel in it. Or to have avoided the catastrophe altogether.

The latter! the phone persistently ringing in her hand told her. *The bloody latter!*

She hopped from one foot to the other as she waited for the lift to arrive at ground level, and as soon as the doors parted enough to let her out, she was gone. Racing through the foyer and bursting into the frigid New York air as she swiped the video call to answer and promptly froze. Bella was sobbing!

'Oh my God, love, what's wrong?'

* * *

A little while later Astrid hung up the phone, but she couldn't move from the alcove she'd found herself in. She was a quivering mess. The news from Bella beggared belief.

Chase wasn't the unfaithful bastard she'd believed him to be. And Astrid wasn't the homewrecking mistress she'd branded herself as either. There had been so much more to that sorry scene in the hotel room all those months ago... and if Chase had only taken the time to explain things to her back then, this never would have happened. None of this.

Astrid wouldn't have embarked on a crazy karma plan that saw her smacking one on the wrong guy. And Bella wouldn't have played an innocent man for a fool... no, that wasn't quite fair. Because Chase *wasn't* entirely innocent. He'd left her to think the worst.

But he was hardly the devil.

And he certainly hadn't deserved what he'd got.

Half of Operation Just Desserts was imploding, and she was the common denominator. A total liability.

She wanted to race around the corner and help Bella.

She wanted to race back upstairs and fix Blake.

Neither were an option without the truth spilling free and the domino effect of that... no, just no. It was a nightmare.

It also meant she couldn't oversee the photoshoot. The last thing Blake needed was her on the other side of the camera. Fin would never get a decent shot.

Lifting her phone, she forced out a message to Stella and Fin making her excuses. And then she messaged the twins in their group chat to say she hoped it went well, that she'd review the photos with Fin later. Then she messaged Blake privately...

> ASTRID
>
> I'm so sorry.

It sat on delivered.

She stared at it, willing him to read it, willing him to respond...

* * *

Several hours later, the message remained delivered and unread. And no amount of checking was gonna change it.

Fin sat at her uncle's dining table running through the photos on his laptop, a beer and a bowl of nibbles on the go, while Astrid cooked them dinner.

They always reviewed the photos together, but today she needed Fin more for his company than his expertise, his warm Scottish brogue and down-to-earth nature a welcome distraction from the noise in her head.

She'd half expected Blake to walk out after she'd left. Half expected a message from one of the others saying the shoot was a no-go. But he hadn't. He'd stuck it out. How? Why? Who knew, but the look on Blake's face when she'd—

'Earth to Astrid?'

She blinked away the torment in Blake's blue eyes, zoning in on the pot of Bolognese she was stirring. 'Sorry' – she looked up – 'what did I miss?'

Fin gave her a bemused smile, flicking his red mop out of his face. 'Quite a lot today, I'd say.'

'Sorry, I didn't mean to bail on you.'

'I'm not talking about the shoot. I'm talking about the last hour. You've been somewhere else the entire time. What happened to ordering in pizza and having you sit on my shoulder while I run through the shots?'

It's what they'd usually do. But not this time. This time she'd been too afraid of what she'd see. What she'd feel.

'I'm almost done cooking.'

'I'm almost done too.'

'You are?'

He nodded. 'I've done a sweep and created a shortlist, but that Blake... he's the real deal, eh?'

'Huh?'

'All that attitude. I'm glad I got some pre shots. You might want to use one of them because the second he changed his clothes, everything changed.'

'He got changed?'

'Aye, he came out all in black and his mood with it.'

Oh God.

'That bad?'

'Depends what you're going for – the family maker or the heartbreaker.'

She gave an awkward laugh. 'Neither! We want the boys-next-door-done-good look.'

'Yeah, thought so.' He leaned back over his laptop, finger scrolling. 'There might be something we can do to take the edge off the twin shots.'

Take the *edge* off?

That didn't sound good. She released the spoon and hurried on over, took one look at the photo grid and swallowed. Hard.

Aiden was all charm, his well-versed grin on display, his stance relaxed. While Blake... Blake looked ready to commit fratricide. Arms folded, jaw clenched, he glared at Aiden to his right, but that mouth... she lifted her fingers to her own that thrummed with the echo of his.

'I reckon we can play around with the shadows, do something with it.'

She nodded.

'And failing that, we can overlay one of the earlier shots.'

Pre-her. Pre-kiss. Pre-epic-fuckup.

She started to walk away, her heart in her mouth, her guilt with it.

'There's also the shots with the wee lad Aiden brought back. I don't know whether they'd be any—?'

'*Kid*?' She halted. Turned. 'What kid?'

'Some lad called Leo. Aiden brought him home.'

'Aiden brought a random kid to a *photoshoot*?'

Fin chuckled. 'Not random at all. The twins knew them – Leo and his mum Chantelle. She was there too. They all seemed quite chummy.'

'How do they know each other?'

He shrugged. 'Beats me. But it got Blake smiling again. Enough to get some great shots. I just don't know whether they're what you want.'

She walked back over, glanced at the new photo spread. 'Oh my!'

'Good, right?'

Good was one word for it. Magic was another. Seeing Blake interacting with a lad of about seven – talking, laughing, tickling, fist bumping... the warmth, the charisma, the affection.

Who *was* this boy?

'And his mum was happy for him to be photographed?'

'More than.'

'They're... they're perfect.'

But the question remained, who was he?

And more importantly, could they use them? Could she write about them?

She picked up her mobile and messaged Aiden.

ASTRID

Great photos! Who's the kid?

AIDEN

You'll have to ask Blake.

She frowned. Reopened her message with Blake. Kinda hard to ask if he wasn't even reading what she'd sent…

'Keep it in the shortlist and I'll do some extra digging.'

'Will do, boss.'

18

'You going to tell me what's got into you?'

Blake sent his brother a look that said it all.

'Come on, buddy, ever since the photoshoot yesterday you've been crankier than Coach on a losing streak.'

Blake adjusted his earphones and leaned back into the airplane seat, closing his eyes and praying his brother would get the message. It was only ten in the morning but if he wanted to sleep, he'd bloody well sleep.

'I thought you'd be happy to see Chantelle and Leo.'

'You should've checked with me first.'

'I told you, I didn't plan it, I bumped into them and—'

'So you keep saying...'

And he didn't believe it. Chantelle didn't just 'hang out' in their neck of the woods. His brother had orchestrated the whole thing.

'Why is it so bad that they were there?'

He peeled open one eye. 'Because you *knew* I wouldn't want them involved.'

'Why not?'

He pressed back in his seat and closed his eye. *Let it go, bro.*

'It's just a photo, Blake.'

'Like hell it is.'

'Have you explained who they are to Astrid?'

He clenched his jaw; just her name alone turned his stomach.

'I'd have to speak to Astrid to explain.'

'What's that supposed to mean?'

'Just what I said.'

'Look buddy, don't be mad at her, this is all on me.'

'I know,' he bit out. 'I'm just not speaking to her right now.'

'What the hell's going on?'

He ground his teeth, fighting the urge to call the flight attendant over for a beer or something stronger. But he didn't *need* a drink. What he needed was to forget all about Astrid. Astrid *and* her hots for his bro.

'Blake?'

'We've fallen out!' he shot back, eyes open and glaring now. 'You *happy*?'

And now he felt like a petulant bloody child.

'Happy?' His brother looked affronted. 'Why would I be happy? That girl's the best thing to happen to you in a long time.'

Now Blake laughed and laughed and laughed, because my God, he'd thought so too.

And look how wrong he'd called it.

'Why do you think I got Coach to call me that night at ours? Why do you think I've been doing all I can to bring the two of you together?'

'Because she's saving my bloody ass, remember!'

'It's about more than that, Blake,' his brother said. 'There's something between you both, something—'

He scoffed. 'Got you fooled too, hey?'

'Fooled? What are you talking about?'

He shook his head. All this time he'd been driving himself half crazy over his brother and Astrid, and his brother had been playing at his own matchmaking game.

'Just let it go.'

'Not a chance. You guys have got something, something that's managed to put the right kind of spark in your eye and set you on a decent path too. If you've had some kind of argument, grow some balls and talk it out, don't give her the silent treatment.'

'Wow. You're telling me not to give a girl the silent treatment.'

His brother stiffened. 'That was ten years ago, Blake.'

'Yeah, well, doesn't mean I don't remember the constant calls and your stubborn refusal to pick up. Seemed to serve you alright, so excuse me while I do the same.'

'That was different.'

'Yeah, you're right, *you* were in love.'

His brother blanched and Blake cursed. 'Sorry, bro.' He raked a hand through his hair, took a breath. 'I shouldn't have said that.'

'No. You shouldn't have.'

Aiden shifted back in his seat and Blake searched for something to say, something to fix it, but nothing could. Not when he'd been the one to force his brother's hand. To make him leave not just their home, but his teenage sweetheart too.

And his brother had never met another woman capable of touching him in the same way. Blake had ruined that for him... perhaps even ruined it for good.

'Instead of throwing Sienna back in my face,' his brother said quietly, 'maybe you ought to realise that what I went through with her makes me the person to listen to now when I tell you, don't do it. Whatever's going on between you both, it's something worth exploring not walking away from.'

He gave a choked scoff, wanting to dismiss it, wanting to tell his brother he didn't have a clue because *he* was the reason there was nothing to explore. Astrid had made it clear which of them she wanted.

But then his brother wasn't just referring to Astrid's feelings, he was referring to Blake's and as much as Blake wanted to say he was wrong there too, he knew he wasn't.

And wanting a woman who wanted someone else – someone more deserving and someone he'd willingly lay down his life for – that wasn't just a reason to walk away.

It was a reason to run.

* * *

Astrid stared at the words on her screen, the opening to the article that she had rewritten several times now and still didn't *feel*. She was getting nowhere.

How could she possibly write about the twins when one refused to speak to her and the other was blissfully unaware of everything? It was killing her mojo. Guilt for Blake. Guilt for Chase. Guilt for continuing to fail Sissi.

She checked the time in the top corner of her screen. The Titans should be landing in Dallas any moment now, their game against the Stars taking them away for a couple of days and giving Blake ever more reason to avoid her.

Her phone buzzed beside her laptop, and she snapped it up, praying for Blake and seeing Aiden.

AIDEN

You free for a lesson early hours Saturday, before the arena opens to the public?

She gave a weak smile as she typed:

ASTRID

I'd love to. Thank you.

AIDEN

Great. See you 7 a.m. sharp.

ASTRID

7 a.m.?!

AIDEN

Told you it was early 😉

ASTRID

OK 🙄

She hit send then toyed with asking how Blake was. But asking Aiden would make it known that something was up – if he didn't know already – and she wasn't about to kick that hornet's nest. Especially when they had a game to play tomorrow.

But Blake's radio silence was driving her as crazy as the guilt. She hated that she'd hurt him, and that kiss... she kept reliving it over and over.

Maybe he'd message after the game. Maybe he'd message when they were back in New York. And if he didn't, she could ask Aiden in person on Saturday. As for the photographs and the unknown child... she glanced at the pic on her mood board.

Who was he? Or more specifically, who was he to Blake? And why couldn't Aiden just tell her?

Her research had drawn a blank; she still couldn't find their father and she was no closer to getting Aiden to at least admit Sienna had existed!

Some reporter she was turning out to be... muzzled by her own mess.

And speaking of her mess... Bella was heading back into the

gallery today, kicking off a new plan to 'save' Chase. Fingers crossed it worked. For his sake as much as Bella's, and her own.

She texted Bella to wish her luck, fired off another to Mum, then went back to her article.

> When you first meet these NHL giants, it's hard to imagine them as boys, lacing up borrowed skates, playing on frozen ponds...
>
> Now towering over opponents on the ice, the Titan Twins command attention with their skill and sheer presence, but behind the fierce intensity and celebrated success lies a story of resilience, a journey that began far from the bright lights of professional hockey...

The cursor flashed back at her... words refusing to come.

All she could see was the hurt in Blake's face, all she could feel was the intensity of that kiss. With a groan, she pushed away from her laptop, grabbed her trainers, and hit the streets, hoping a run would help and knowing in her heart that it wouldn't. Nothing would.

Because the one thing she wanted to do – come clean – was the one thing she couldn't work out how to do.

Not without making everything so much worse and dragging Sissi through it with her. And that girl had suffered enough.

But then, so had the twins...

Her watch buzzed with a message, and she peeled back her thermal top to check the screen.

> AIDEN
>
> PS Dinner Sunday at Mom's, 1 p.m.? We'll pick you up...

Her stride faltered. Shit, she'd forgotten about dinner.

Another reporter fail! But dinner with Mother Carter, Aiden, *and* Blake?

She could hardly say no...

AIDEN

She's looking forward to meeting you.

Great. But what about Blake?

19

Saturday morning, Astrid arrived at the rink just before seven and Joey, the security guard, let her in. He was a sweetheart, always ready with an eye-crinkling smile.

'Good morning, Ms Sinclair. Ready for your lesson?'

It didn't surprise her that he already knew; Aiden would have added her to the visitors' list.

'My head is. My body not so much.'

'Ah, you'll get there, give it time.'

She smiled. 'I appreciate the vote of confidence, Joey. Am I okay to go on down?'

'Sure are, he's already down there.'

'He *is*?'

She shouldn't be surprised at that either. Aiden was nothing if not punctual... save for the photoshoot morning when she really could've done with him sticking to form.

'He's been here an hour already; you're his second lesson of the morning.'

'I am? I didn't realise he made a habit of it...'

'Sure. He's been bringing little Leo here for a couple of years now. The kid's a huge fan.'

Leo? The kid in the photo? Aiden was teaching him too!

And if that was the case, why hadn't he just said that to her when she'd asked?

Unless... was there more to the connection? More than a simple case of tutoring a local kid... And why put it on Blake to explain?

'Thanks, Joey!'

She hurried off, yanking open the heavy doors to the rink and diving in...

'I did it, Mom!' a kid's shout echoed through the empty arena. 'I did it, Blake!'

Astrid froze mid-step. *Blake?*

The door swung shut, smacking her on the arse and propelling her forth. Ouch!

'Did you see?' the kid said.

Astrid could see nothing yet, they were hidden by the seats, but she heard a man chuckle. Awareness pulsed, warm and fuzzy, through her veins. Blake.

'I saw,' she heard him say over the gentle hiss of their skates. 'You aced it, buddy.'

She edged closer, eyes following the cones laid on the ice until the people weaving between them came into view. The blond kid from the photos and Blake. Her heart erupted with a thousand flutters – nerves and something else at work. She tugged her sleeves into her fists and wrapped her arms around her body.

Yes, she had watched the game against the Dallas Stars that week. Yes, she had devoured the postgame press conference he must have been coerced into attending after he'd delivered a record-scoring match. But *nothing* could beat seeing him in the flesh.

He wore his trademark black. From his jeans to the woollen beanie on his head to the same aviator jacket he'd wrapped around her just a few weeks ago. His cheeks were pink, and his stubble was back. God, how she'd missed him!

'That was amazing, Leo!'

Astrid followed the female voice to see a young blonde woman spectating off to the left, her red bobble hat as bright as her smile. She clapped her hands, her red mitts muffling the sound as the kid skated up to her and hopped out of the rink, straight into her arms.

'I'm so proud of you.'

'I'm getting good, ain't I, Mom?'

She was his mum. Either she looked amazing for her age or she'd been incredibly young when she'd had him. Not that Astrid was judging her. No, she was now battling the waterworks that wanted to spring at the sight of Blake teaching this child and the obvious connection they shared – to witness in the flesh what Fin had caught on camera...

'You really are.' Then his mum grinned up at Blake. 'Thanks to you.'

'Nah, this is all on him for putting in the work. He'll be a Titan one of these days, you mark my words.'

'You really think so, Blake?'

'I know so, buddy.' He ruffled the lad's blond hair and Astrid pressed a palm to her chest. Her heart felt fit to burst, her own smile watery as the girl suddenly spied her watching. She nudged Blake and Astrid sucked in a breath. Held it as he turned.

Her bubble of a heart gave a painful pop as his eyes found hers. Hot. Hard. *Angry.*

She tried to smile, raised a hand to wave but he'd already turned his back to her. He spoke to his companions, his words too low for her to hear. The girl sent Astrid a smile-cum-nod and led the lad away, while Blake... Blake watched them go.

Was he about to follow them out? Ignore her altogether?

Please, God, no...

She took a tentative step forward, freezing when he spun to face her, his blisteringly blue gaze pinning her in place as he crossed the ice at speed.

'What are you doing here?'

He stopped just short, spraying her in ice and she hugged her middle, wincing against the chill that was all him.

'I' – she swallowed the wedge in her throat – 'I was supposed to have a lesson with Aiden.'

She gestured to the skates hanging over her shoulder.

His frown deepened. 'This morning?'

'Now.'

'*Fuck* me.' He shook his head, his eyes drifting away in disbelief.

'What is it?'

He dragged his gaze back to her, his chin jutting with annoyance. 'Aiden ain't coming.'

'He is,' she insisted. 'He said 7 a.m. sharp.'

He was shaking his head again.

'I don't understand... Why would he organise a lesson if he wasn't—'

'Because I'm here.'

'But...' And then it clicked into place, her eyes widening with realisation. 'Oh!'

'Yes. Oh.'

'He knows we've fallen out?'

Blake nodded.

'And he's forcing us to talk?'

He hesitated, eyes breaking away from hers. 'He's doing a lot more than that.'

Her heart fluttered. 'Like?'

'Like forcing me to explain Leo to you.'

'Why would he have to force you to explain Leo?'

'Because he knows I wouldn't tell you about him.'

'Why?'

'Because it's personal and private and he's just a kid! Will you quit with the questions!'

Astrid flinched. 'I'm sorry.'

'No, I'm... I'm sorry. I'm just...' He fell silent, his jaw twitching for several strained seconds until, 'He's a fan, okay?'

'A fan you've been teaching to skate?'

'Yes.'

'And his mother?'

'Also a fan. Why?' He searched her gaze, the intensity of his blue eyes making her lean back as her body urged her to do the opposite. 'Did you think she was something more?'

'Huh?' she practically squeaked.

'Did you think she was an ex?'

She coloured. 'I didn't know what to think.'

'Of course you did. Bad Boy Blake. Bound to have left a trail of kids in his wake?' The bitterness in his voice was laced with something else. A sadness. A self-loathing. A wish for something different, while *she* wished she'd kept her suspicions better hidden.

He moved to lean back against the boards, his head turned away, his sigh heavy and weighing her down with it.

'Blake, I'm sorry. I didn't...'

'I met Chantelle at a homeless shelter two years ago,' he said quietly, surprising her with the soft admission. 'When Leo was five. I recognised her from the occasional game. She was in a bad way after her parents had kicked her out. Her father was much like mine. Her mother wasn't much better than him. And I wanted to help.'

Astrid eased closer, hooked on all he was telling her.

'I wanted to do something more than the usual – clothing, food, a roof over their head. I wanted to give them something to truly smile about. And they loved the game. But time on the ice doesn't come cheap and I thought... I thought if I can make him into a player, I'd give him the drive and the determination to make something of himself and then one day he could help his mother too.'

'Just like you and your brother helped your mum?'

He flicked her the briefest look. 'Yeah.'

'So you started to bring him here on your own time?'

He nodded. 'It's tough during the season but I try to get him here once a week. And I know it's just one kid among millions but...'

She blinked back tears. 'I think it's amazing.'

'*He's* amazing. He works hard and he deserves to get there.'

'And *you* deserve to be praised for it, Blake. Don't you see that?' She padded onto the ice so she could face him. 'This is why your brother brought Leo to the photoshoot, isn't it?'

'Aiden claims he just ran into them.'

'But you don't believe him?'

'No.'

'He saw an opportunity and he took it, knowing I wouldn't be happy about it, but doing it anyway... the story of my life.'

'Leo looked happy though. Fin said he was buzzing and the photos he captured... they truly are special.'

'Yeah, well.' He edged away. 'They're not getting used.'

'Why?'

'Because what I'm doing, I'm doing for Leo. For him and his mom, not for me.'

His words came back to her. *In my experience, people only care when there's something in it for them.*

He didn't want people thinking he'd done it to gain from it. That the world, or worse, Leo and his mother, would think it a selfish deed when it had been anything but...

My God. Could she adore this man more?

'What you chose to do that came from here...' She dared to place her palm over his heart. 'Just because the world learns of it, doesn't mean it suddenly becomes all about you, for you. It doesn't change what you did, what you *are* doing.'

He lifted her hand away, the gesture as cutting as any verbal attack.

'It changes it for me.'

'It shouldn't, and you should let them decide. Leo and Chantelle. Because if I were them, I'd want to do this for you. I'd want to give something back. I'd want to give the world an insight into the real you, not the media's sensationalised version, but you. Good, kind, *you*.'

He fell silent, eyes tumultuous but softening.

'Just think about it, Blake. Please.'

Silence, then, 'I'm not making any promises, and I'd need to talk to them first.'

'Works for me,' she said gently, grateful to have him consider it, grateful all the more to sense him thawing towards her. 'And FYI, you must be a great teacher because that kid... if I had a smidge of what he has, I'd be in my element.'

He gave her a hint of his lopsided grin. 'It helps to have a student who listens and follows instruction.'

'Are you suggesting that's not me?' she teased, pouncing on the opportunity to lighten the mood.

The smile crept into his eyes, their sparkle everything in that moment.

'Ask me again after our hour is up.'

She did a double take, expecting something cheeky and getting something so much better. '*You're* going to teach me?'

'That's why you're here isn't it?'

'But do you not want to give Aiden hell for setting you up?'

'I can do that later. Right now, you're due a lesson and I'm more than capable of giving it to you. Unless you think I'm not up to the task.'

'I *know* you're more than capable, I've just told you as much.'

'So, what's the problem?'

She couldn't believe he was offering. After everything she'd done, after everything he'd just divulged against his will too.

Was this an olive branch? His way of saying let bygones be bygones...

And if it is, what are you doing debating it?

Get your bloody skates on!

'Is it because I'm not Aiden?'

* * *

Blake stared at a flabbergasted Astrid and wanted to give himself a smack upside the head.

He'd been making amends. Trying to show her that he wanted to move forward. That he didn't care that she liked his brother. That the kiss they'd shared *hadn't* imprinted on him. That it *hadn't* kept him awake at night and stolen his concentration by day.

How the hell he'd managed a record-scoring game that week he had no idea, but he'd suspected she'd be watching, and he'd wanted to outshine the rest, be the best.

But to what end?

She liked Aiden and he needed to make peace with that.

Because looking into Astrid's eyes and seeing the compassion and understanding glistening back at him, to know that regardless of who she wanted in the bedroom, she cared about him... that it wasn't just about her article, it was about his wellbeing.

So why in the hell had he asked *that*?

'Get your skates on and forget I said anything. I'll go clear the cones off the ice.'

He pushed off and she reached out. 'Wait.'

Slowly he did a one-eighty, eyes narrowing on her frown, the way she chewed over her lip...

'I'm... I'm really sorry for what happened,' she said eventually. 'For what I did.'

His jaw pulsed as his body fired with the memory of just *that*... 'You should've been straight with me from the beginning.'

'Straight with you?'

'About liking my brother,' he said tightly. 'I wouldn't have liked it, but I wouldn't have got in your way.'

'You weren't in my way. It wasn't... it's not like that.'

He swallowed the noise in his head, in his heart, and focused on her and the potential hurt she was walking into. Because he could care about her too.

'Well, whatever it's like, just watch yourself. My brother's a good guy, he has a good heart, but he gave it to a girl a long time ago, and I don't think he ever got it back again.'

Her eyes widened, her chin lifting, voice weak. 'He did?'

'He hasn't mentioned her...?'

Of course Aiden hadn't. The man was trying to outrun his past, like the rest of them.

'No. How long ago are we talking?'

He hesitated, the shimmering emotion in her eyes giving him pause.

'Are we talking a few years? More?'

'They were childhood sweethearts.'

She gave a nervous chuckle, her false bravado destroying him. 'Long enough ago not to leave an impact now, surely?'

'Aiden would like the world to think so. But for a man who thinks he's an expert on how our exit from Ashbury Falls affected me and Mom, he's pretty clueless when it comes to himself.'

She wrapped her arms around her middle. 'Why are you telling me?'

'Because as much as I love him, I'm not sure he's the guy for you. And I'm not saying this because I like you...' *You sure about that?* 'I'm saying it to protect you.'

A weighted pause and then, 'Thank you.' She took a breath. 'I appreciate it.'

Did she? Or was she just saying that to make him feel better?

'You still want to do this?' He gestured to the ice.

'*Want* is questionable with these toes, but yes, let's do this.'

And then he swept away before he said anything else, did anything else to land him in further trouble. His brother was going to kill him for mentioning Sienna, but hell, the entire situation was killing him already.

He snuck a look her way as he gathered up the cones, relieved to see she hadn't bolted with his revelation. She'd taken a seat and was pulling on her skates. Her ponytail had fallen over one shoulder, that one stray curl falling from the rim of her black beanie to her thigh... and there went his fingers, tingling with the tease again.

Dammit all.

When he'd first seen her across the ice, he'd been mad. Mad

at himself for his own impossible reaction to her. Her warm honey eyes and a smile that got to him whatever level it sat at. Her body clad in skintight black, the layers doing nothing to detract from her femininity. Hell, she'd been a sight for sore eyes, and he shouldn't have wanted her still. Not after everything...

But he did. And what kind of an idiot did that make him?

The kind who's falling in love for the first time, perhaps?

'Ready?' He launched across the rink, pushing the answer away with every fierce stroke of his skates.

'All yours,' she said, slapping her thighs and giving him a grin.

Damn, he wished.

She launched to her feet and promptly fell back with a yelp.

'Alright, Twinkle Toes, you wanna try that again?'

He hopped off the ice and took her by the hand, ignoring the warmth that worked its way beneath their gloves as he tugged her up.

'I warn you,' she murmured, her voice as unsteady and apprehensive as her step. 'I'm not very good at this.'

'Don't worry, I've got you.'

Her lashes flickered, her eyes locking onto his. Warm and... trusting.

'We'll do this together, okay?'

She nodded and he eased her onto the ice, every inch of him attuned to her. Every breath, every wobble, every nervous giggle...

He moved around to face her, taking both hands in his. 'Okay? Now push off with the foot that feels more natural, and I'll match you... that's it, now glide.'

She followed his instruction, her gaze drifting to their feet...

'Uh-uh. Keep looking up.'

Her eyes came back to him and his heart pulsed with his smile.

'That's it. Now push... and glide. Push... and glide.'

He matched his rhythm to hers, kept up the instruction, losing himself in it and her, their bodies working in tandem, the soft whoosh of their skates filling the air. He let go of the pent-up tension, the questions, the unresolved feelings... though the urge to have her glide that bit closer, to catch her in his arms and spin away with her...

She laughed softly. 'I can't believe I'm doing it.'

'I can.'

Her smile was full of wonder. 'You really are good.'

'You might want to save the praise for when I have you going it alone.'

He eased out from her front, releasing one hand and felt her fingers tighten around his other. 'Just relax and keep doing what you're doing. I've got you.'

She gave a shaky nod, her jaw unclenching as she did so. Her trust in him danced along his veins, teased at his heart. 'You've got this.'

They did a few loops of the rink, her posture improving with her confidence. 'You ready to try it alone?'

She sent him a panicked look.

'Don't worry, I'll be right beside you.'

They took a few more strokes connected and then he peeled his fingers from hers. She wobbled, her tongue peeking out of the corner of her mouth as she fought to find her balance and her rhythm once more. 'I've got it, I've got—'

She started to go, her body rocking forward, arms flailing... He swept to her side, catching her around the waist as her skates went out from beneath her.

'Got you!' He launched her into his arms, a thousand volts

shooting through him as she pressed up against him, her soft yelp muffled by his chest.

He turned his head away as her scent tried to burrow its way in, everything about this moment taking him back to that kiss. *Fuck*, that kiss.

She'd tasted of heaven, felt like silk, her scent more intoxicating than any drink...

'You okay?'

He held her steady, his hands firm around her waist as she lifted her hands to his shoulders and regained her feet. She shook her head, her hat tickling at his chin.

'I warned you, didn't I?'

'It takes practice. You think I didn't fall on my ass several times over when I started out?'

Hell, he sounded gruff. Raw. Had she noticed? Of course she'd noticed. This was Astrid; the woman noticed everything.

'But you're teaching the unteachable Twinkle Toes here.'

He lifted one hand to her chin and forced her to look up at him. 'I promise, I'll get you there.'

His intent had been to make her believe him, to make her believe in herself, but as her eyes met his, the rink fell away... *there* was that look. A simmering heat beneath the vulnerability. Want. Desire. Only she didn't. And it hit like a sucker punch to his gut.

'You ready to try again?'

She took a breath that shuddered through her and into him. 'Okay.'

'Good.' It was abrupt, and everything he needed to be to snuff out the fire, grateful that he'd been able to see sense. Not so grateful to be right.

20

The next day Astrid was bobbing in her trainers on the pavement, waiting for the twins to pick her up. She felt like a huge weight had been lifted. She and Blake were in a better place. She'd learned that he believed his brother had left his heart in Ashbury Falls, which could only mean one thing: Sienna. And today she would meet their mum, one of the last two sources on her list.

She was this close to getting all she needed for her article.

And this close to a serious twist in her karma tale, too.

Her phone buzzed.

SISSI
Hope dinner goes well! X

She gave a small smile.

ASTRID
Me too, honey! X

More than you yet know...

She heard the roar of Blake's 4x4 before she saw it rounding the corner, her smile impossible to contain as she waved.

'Hey!' she said, pulling open the passenger door and clocking the empty rear. 'Where's your brother?'

'He's... dealing with a situation.'

She cocked a brow. 'A situation?'

'You'll see, but if you could avoid staring at him, that would be great.'

'Staring?' She gave a bemused smile as she slid into the seat, closed the door and buckled up. 'You're gonna have to explain...'

He gave a low chuckle. 'And spoil the surprise? Hell no.'

Surprise? What on earth...

He pulled out into the traffic as her eager gaze drank him in. From his jeans to his charcoal tee, to the stubble-covered jaw and lips – lips she could taste and feel now if she were to put her mind to it.

'So...' she blurted, pressing her palms into her thighs and willing her body and mind to chill. Getting horny wasn't part of today's deal, today was about work and if she was extra lucky, more Sissi intel. 'Is there anything I should know before I meet your mum?'

He cocked his head, the hum he gave vibrating through her overexcited core. 'Good question...'

'Like, I know I'm not to ask questions,' she hurried to say, looking out the window to take in the bustling streets of New York – far safer, far less evocative – but his scent was still there. A spicy thrill she couldn't ignore. 'And that's cool.' She ran a finger through the neck of her red sweater, trying to ease her rapidly rising temp. 'But I assume she knows who I am and what I'm working on?'

'She knows. Aiden explained the deal to her. She might be a

little wary at first but just be yourself and she'll soon warm to you like we have.'

Guilt warred with pleasure at his praise, the heat within the car now stifling even though the dash read a comfortable sixty-eight degrees Fahrenheit.

'Thanks for coming to get me,' she said, keen to talk over her hyperactive brain and body. 'And for yesterday. I really did enjoy our lesson.'

His mouth twitched up. 'I did too.'

'You mean that?'

'Yes, Twinkle Toes. You should know by now that I don't say anything I don't mean. I like your company... when you're not mistaking me for my bro that is.'

He shot her a look, his teasing smile firing straight to her clit. *Shit.*

'And there's that squeak again,' he said with a chuckle.

'I don't squeak.'

'Yes, you do. And when Mom brings out her infamous apple pie, I expect we'll hear it again and again.'

If she was watching him devour it, it was a guaranteed cert. But in front of his family... oh no no no, that could *not* happen.

'Apple pie, you say?'

'Apple pie and homemade custard. You'll be in food heaven.'

Food *squeaking* heaven, she groaned. *Blakegasms,* galore!

* * *

'Astrid, it's so wonderful to meet you!'

His mom was opening the door before they'd even reached the top step. Her blue eyes twinkling, her dark hair smoothed back into a bun, an apron protecting her woollen dress from cooking spills. She opened her arms wide and pulled Astrid in for a hug. So much for being wary...

'It's a pleasure to meet you too, Mrs Carter,' Astrid said, returning her embrace and Blake's heart gave a little jump at seeing these two women together. The two most important... *and quit that thought!*

'Call me Cynthia, please.'

'Cynthia,' Astrid beamed back. 'These are for you.' She reached into her bag and pulled out a box of chocolates. 'Aiden said they were your favourite.'

'Oh, how lovely! Thank you, dear. Though I hope you've got a pair of sunglasses in that bag of yours.'

'Sunglasses?' Blake said as he leaned in to give his mother a peck on the cheek.

'Your brother's hurting my eyes,' she said as she closed the front door and ushered them through. 'Why he does this to himself I have no idea.'

Blake pursed his lips – oh, this was too funny.

Astrid sent him a questioning look and he just shrugged.

'I told you, it's for the sponsors, Mom,' came his brother's grumbled response a second before he appeared, a blazing orange beacon amidst the muted colours of the hallway. *Too* funny!

'Just say whatever you're thinking and get it over with,' Aiden said to a frozen Astrid. 'Blake certainly had no qualms speaking his mind.'

Blake checked out Astrid's face. 'I told you not to stare.'

Her eyes were watering too.

'It beats what you did,' his brother said.

'Why, what did he do?' Mom pressed.

'*He* asked if I'd spent the morning bathing in Cheetos.'

Astrid erupted, the smallest of laughs before she pressed her fist to her lips. 'I'm so sorry.'

'Sorry?' Blake said. 'Why are you sorry? He's the one who went OTT on the tan.'

'For the millionth time, I didn't! There's something wrong with the stuff. It's never done this before.'

'I thought you were getting a remover?'

'Turns out they don't work instantly.'

Astrid squeaked; his mum did too.

'It better bloody fade before the game tomorrow, or I'm going to get roasted alive.'

'Ah don't worry, bro, you can blind the opposition for us.'

They all erupted, Astrid howling as she clutched her middle, his mother too.

'Funny, Blake,' his brother muttered. 'Very funny.'

'Hey, just be grateful you don't whiff of cheese too, bro.' He gave Aiden's shoulder a squeeze. 'But speaking of aromas, something smells delicious, Mom...'

* * *

Blake should have quit while he was ahead.

Over the next couple of hours, he joined his brother in the dying corner, wishing the ground would open up and swallow him while his mother regaled Astrid with tales of their childhood... *wholly unnecessary* tales.

No one, and he meant *no one*, needed to know he sucked his thumb until he was four.

'I get that Astrid needs a handle on our childhood, Mom, but can we steer away from shit like – sorry, *stuff* like...?' He waved a hand, unwilling to repeat it.

And she beamed at him, looking younger than her years. 'Nonsense. The embarrassing stuff is always the best.'

'For you maybe.'

'Your mum's right,' Astrid said, very much in her element and loving every word.

'If you two are going to stick with this road, I'm going to clear the table for dessert.'

'I'll help!' Astrid quickly volunteered.

'Oh no, darling, you're a guest,' his mom said.

'But I'd like to help. You've been so kind to welcome me into your home and the meal was delicious. It's the least I can do...'

His mother reached out to rest her hand on Astrid's arm. 'You're doing plenty already, my dear.'

He spied Astrid's throat bob, a look passing between the two women that didn't need words. 'I hope so.'

Jesus. He was choked up. He didn't get choked up. But knowing they were talking about him, looking out for him...

'You're gonna catch a bug, bro.'

He turned to find Aiden watching him and promptly snapped his mouth shut. But his brother had seen enough. Blake had *felt* enough. And that was a problem. A great big head-screwing problem.

And you honestly think it's your head getting screwed?

Fuck, yes. No girl had found their way into his heart before, and he wasn't about to let one now. Especially when she didn't want him in return.

* * *

Astrid watched Blake leave, wondering what Aiden had said to make him dart off. She looked to the man in question, but he was giving nothing away. Other than a smugness.

Though a smugness in all that orange – oh my God, she couldn't wait for the girls to see this. She'd forgotten about the switcheroo with his tan, her memory of that morning dominated by that kiss. But now she was seeing, and she was remembering, and she felt the smallest hit of triumph for Sissi. And maybe just a smidge of guilt.

But it had given everyone a hoot.

Everyone save for Aiden.

'I'd best go and finish off the custard,' Cynthia said, getting to her feet.

'It's okay, Mom, I can sort it.'

'You think I'm going to entrust my special custard to you? You'll add some weird *je ne sais quoi* to it.'

'Would I dare?'

'Yes!'

She was gone before Aiden could say another thing and as he turned that smug smile back on Astrid, she couldn't hold the question in, 'What did you say to Blake?'

He considered her for a long, tummy-squirming moment.

'I don't think it's what I said, more what he was thinking all by himself.'

'And what do—'

'Telling tales, bro?'

Astrid coloured as Blake returned to take up more of the dishes, and Aiden shot to his feet to help. She followed suit, hoping he wouldn't call her out on it. And it gave her something to do that wasn't listening to the nervous flutter in her tummy.

'Would I dare?' Aiden said, using the same response he'd thrown at his mum and catching Astrid's eye with a smirk.

Oh, the guy was a tease. An absolute tease. He deserved to be florescent!

They all piled into the kitchen and Blake loaded the dishwasher while Aiden scooped coffee into a cafetière.

The kitchen was a homely delight. Cream walls, warm wood, the scent of vanilla and apple on the air. A colourful array of flowers sat in the window, where she got a glimpse of the small backyard beyond, lovingly tended. Much like the cork board against one wall which housed various pictures of the boys and a dozen press articles. Forever the proud mum and homemaker...

'Could you pass me the jug for the custard, Astrid?' Cynthia asked, gesturing to a floral ceramic boat on the wooden sideboard.

She carried it over, her eyes drifting back to the board. 'You must be so proud of them.'

Cynthia followed her gaze. 'There isn't a board big enough to house everything they've achieved over the years, so I have to be very particular about what I pin up.'

'Bet my thumb sucking isn't on there,' Blake grumbled to much laughter.

'You just want people to believe you're a great big tough guy,' his mother said as she poured the custard into the boat. 'When really, you're as soft as you were back then. The shell is hard but the inside... the inside is as sweet and loving as ever, you just need to be given a chance to show it... Right, we're good to eat.'

Whether she knew it or not, her words had changed the dynamic of the room. Or at least, they'd changed where Astrid's head was at.

Because it was exactly how she felt about Blake. And though she'd told him it before, the desire to tell him again and have him hear it, to have him see it and accept it and know it didn't make him weak...

'I'll take the pie through,' Cynthia said, donning her oven mitts.

'And I'll take the bowls,' Aiden said, pulling them out of the sideboard.

Blake didn't speak. Probably because he was feeling his mother's words and wondering how it had gone from thumb sucking to something so deep.

'You okay to bring the custard, Astrid?' Cynthia asked as she followed Aiden out.

'Of course,' she said, forcing a smile.

'And bring the coffee, bro!' Aiden called back.

Blake closed the dishwasher and raked a hand through his unruly hair, looking ever more the foppish boy than the hard-ass man.

'You okay?' she asked.

'Yeah, I'm good.'

'She's right you know, your mum...'

He plucked the mugs off the side and reached for the coffee. 'So you've said before.'

'She got one thing wrong though.'

He paused, his brow furrowing. 'She did?'

'When you look close enough' – she stepped towards him – 'you realise the outside is just as soft too.'

His head flicked up, his eyes showing the full roll of his emotions. Surprise. Confusion. A flash of vulnerability before leaping to the safest of all – amusement. 'Let's be clear, we're not talking about my body per se, right? Because these muscles...'

He was teasing but she was in no mood to bite.

'It's all in your eyes, Blake. Your eyes and your smile, when you choose to give it.'

He'd said the same to her once, a long time ago, and she'd felt every word. She only hoped he felt it in return.

She paused before him, dragging her teeth over her bottom lip as she struggled to breathe this close to him. She wanted to kiss him. Kiss him until all she saw looking back at her was confidence, desire, the same need that burned through her.

'Fuck, Twinkle Toes, what I wouldn't give to know what's going through your head right now.'

What she wouldn't give to show him...

'Come on, you two!' Aiden swept in, grabbed the mugs from Blake's immobile hands, and swept back out again. 'Mom's pie is getting cold!'

Blake gave a tight laugh while Astrid's cheeks blazed. She'd been so close to jumping him. Right here in his mother's kitchen. And Aiden would have born witness to the lot.

'We'd best go.' She hurried to leave, her only thought to escape the danger zone, but her sweater caught on the door handle, throwing her back. She came up against his body hard, the jug lurching with her. Hot custard sloshed over the top, down her hand, her front – *ouch!* She yelped. He yelped. The jug fell.

With a mortifying crack it hit the ground, and her hands soared to her mouth, catching the plunger in the cafetière Blake held and sending it skidding across the floor, hot coffee splashing over his tee.

'Shit, Twinkle Toes!' he hissed, pulling the fabric away from his chest.

'I'm so sorry, I'm so sorry.' She flapped at his top, her only thought to ease the heat against his skin even as her own skin tingled and protested its scorching vanilla assault.

'It's okay,' he said over her, placing the cafetière down so that he could strip his tee. 'Are *you* okay?'

He was eyeing her sweater, but she only had eyes for his naked chest. His naked chest and oh my God, the mess, the custard, his mum's jug!

'Oh my goodness!' Cynthia appeared with Aiden close behind. 'What on earth happened?'

'I did. I'm so sorry, it was an accident. I'll clean it up straight away. I'm so sorry about your jug, I hope it wasn't sentimental.' She was rambling but she couldn't stop. 'I'll buy you a new one. I'll get—'

'Hush hush!' Cynthia clutched her hand to silence her. 'No, you won't. You get yourself upstairs and out of those clothes. Blake will find you something to wear while Aiden gets this cleaned up, and I'll make us some more custard.'

'I really am so sorry.'

'Come on, Twinkle Toes.' Blake took her hand, dragging her away, but she couldn't take her eyes off the broken china and the coffee-splattered gloop. She was always worse when she was nervous, stressed, or flustered. And she'd been all of those things.

'I can't believe I did that.'

'Don't worry about it. Mom's right, we need to get you out of those clothes...'

'And make sure you bathe those burns, Blake!' his mother called after them. 'Get some cream on them too.'

He gave Astrid a smile, his eye roll gently teasing. 'On it, Mum.'

He led her into a bedroom on the first floor, drew the curtains and turned on the bedside lamp, all semi-naked action while she was struggling to keep her mouth shut, her thoughts clean, and her mortified heart steady. Being around fully clothed Blake was hard enough. But in a bedroom, mostly naked? He was temptation personified.

And you'd do well to quit looking!

She lowered her lashes as he disappeared into the en suite. She could hear him going through cupboards, her ears refusing to tune him out as she peeled off her damp layers and took in the room around her.

It was masculine but cosy. Everything in a varying shade of grey. From the carpet to the curtains, to the walls and the painted furniture.

Was this a room the twins used when they stayed here? Or was this Blake's alone? The king-size bed already made up for when he might stay, the grey throw across the bottom a welcoming touch, the added cushions too.

'There's a dressing gown on the...'

He froze on the threshold, his eyes dipping over her semi-naked state, sweater and T-shirt clutched in her hands, custard-splashed socks discarded on the floor. His cheeks slashed red. His throat bobbed.

'I was going to say feel free to use the gown while I dig something out for you.'

There was only one thing she wanted to dig out in that moment, and it wasn't clothing.

'Do you want to run some cold water over...' His eyes traced the redness on her skin to the waistband of her jeans and she shook her head.

'Do you want some antiseptic cream...?'

He lifted the tube out to the side, his exposed muscles flexing and firing the heat within her as she shook her head again.

'What about my brother, Astrid?' His eyes flashed. 'Do you want him?'

She swallowed and didn't care if she squeaked. 'No.'

Her breasts heaved in the confines of her bra, the air too thick to breathe.

'Then tell me...' He threw the tube onto the bed and took a step forward. 'What do you want?'

No hesitation. 'I want you.'

21

'Then why the hell aren't we doing this already?'

Blake launched across the room and she met him halfway, an explosive coming together of mouths, lips, teeth, tongues. Their hands were buried in each other's hair, her sweater and tee tossed to the floor, bodies pressed so close there was no room for air.

It was hasty, desperate, ugly, fierce, but there was no time for slow. A fear that it would suddenly stop, that there would be another unwelcome interruption, a misplaced thought, and he had no care for either. Wild horses couldn't drag him off her now.

'It was always you,' she rasped against his lips. 'I always wanted you.'

He didn't doubt it, not in this moment, not for a second. The burn was in her eyes, her husky voice, her taut nipples that caressed his chest through her bra...

'You should have told me sooner.' He dragged his lips along her jaw, tasting, teasing, caught her earlobe in his teeth. 'We could have been doing this for days.'

She shuddered. 'Just imagine.'

'I am imagining,' he said into her ear, cupping her breast. 'I'm imaging every wild thing I want to do to you.' He rolled his thumb over her nipple and her body jerked, her cry making his cock weep and his voice hoarse. 'Every wild thing I want to do *with* you.'

'Yes, *God*, yes.'

Her nails bit into his shoulders as he slipped inside the lace, his thumb forcing her bra strap down as he filled his palm with her.

'You feel so good,' he groaned as she tried to climb him, tried to get him where she needed him to be. He came to her aid, lifting her off the ground and wrapping her jean-clad thighs around him. 'Taste so good too.'

'Blake!' came his brother's shout. 'Astrid!'

Their heads shot to the door.

'Fresh custard is served!'

'I'd rather be tasting you,' he growled under his breath, cursing his brother and his timing as ever.

She squeaked and hiccupped in one, her glazed eyes coming back to him. 'Me too. But we'd best...'

'Yes, we'd best...'

But she already looked thoroughly fucked. Her eyes, her hair, her mouth all swollen and begging for him to – *fuck it!*

He kissed her. Didn't stop kissing her until she was up against the door and moaning, her legs locked tight around his hips as she pressed him to her clit.

Damn, they needed to leave but he was too busy giving her what *she* needed. What *he* needed, the grinding pressure driving them both to the edge. If they carried on, he'd be changing his jeans too.

'Fuck, Blake. I need you.' She clawed at his back, his ass, gripped him tight against her.

He tore his mouth away to look into her eyes, worshipping the rising heat in her cheeks, her panting breaths telling him she was close. So close. He hadn't indulged in a crazed dry-humping session since his teens and now he wondered why the hell not. It was hot as fuck.

He pressed a palm into the door above her head, supported her rolling ass with his other and rocked his hips. 'Take what you need, baby... that's it. Come for me.'

Her eyes flared on his command, her head hitting the door as she arched back and bit her lip, trapping the whimpers that were driving him to the edge.

'Oh my God!' she blurted. 'Oh my God!'

He swallowed her cries with a kiss, smothered them as her orgasm claimed her. She shook and shuddered and his cock strained, the rush of his release coming. He held her gaze—

'Blake! Come on, bro!'

He froze. She froze.

Two footsteps on the stairs...

'The custard's gaining a skin!'

'Just a minute!' he called out.

'Oh God!' she exclaimed in horror now. 'I can't ruin another pot.'

He grinned down at her, his smile all for her but his shout for Aiden. 'We're on our way!'

'But you can't go. Not...' She eyed his erection jutting between them and covered her mouth.

'As much as I'd love to take care of it right now...' He eased back, setting her carefully on her feet. 'We have custard to eat.'

'You can't walk in there like *that*.'

He strode across the room and pulled open the middle

drawer on the dresser, tugged out a sweater. 'I always knew this festive monstrosity would come in handy.'

'Monstrosity?'

He pulled it over his head and turned.

'Oh my,' she murmured, righting her bra. 'Why is it...?'

'Why is it so big?'

She nodded, her eyes watering with laughter as the garish wool settled somewhere just above his knees.

'Mom got the dimensions on the reindeer wrong and insisted on making sure his legs were in proportion with the rest of him.'

He pulled another sweater from the drawer and tossed it to her.

'And his nose?'

'Damned if I know. Best not ask her though, she's a bit sensitive about her knitting disasters.'

She pulled the sweater on. 'Won't she think it's strange you're wearing it now?'

'She'll put it down to me being too caught up in you to care.'

She stilled as his words settled in the air between them, the sweater halfway down her body. She wet her lips, a mask steadily slipping into place with the clothing.

'It's what Aiden already thinks I am.' She could mask her feelings all she liked, he was done hiding from his. 'So why not her too?'

'And are you?'

'What do you think?'

'Blake!' came his brother again.

'Coming!'

He only wished he was for real...

* * *

Getting through pudding with Blake sat across from her, his Christmas sweater as bright as her post-orgasmic glow, was a challenge like no other. Didn't matter that he was wearing what could only be described as a festive tent, she'd never wanted a man more.

Every time he caught her eye, the look they shared was enough to torch the table and she was pretty sure his brother and mother knew something had happened upstairs. Which only made her cheeks glow more.

Talk turned to their last few games and the world's view on Blake 'reining in the aggression' and 'lacking the trademark fire of Fury'. The guy couldn't win. Either he was too unhinged, a blemish on the game, or he wasn't playing hard enough.

But what did it matter so long as he was still scoring high? Scoring high and enjoying it? Which he seemed to be...

'I scored a new record so all the doubters can go fuck themselves as far as I'm concerned.'

'Blake!'

'Sorry, Mom.'

'I'm just glad you're not getting in as many scrapes.'

'We all are,' Aiden said, turning his smile on Astrid. Did he really think it was all down to her?

'So you have the Massachusetts Penguins later this week?' Cynthia was saying. 'Back on your old ice. How are you feeling about it?'

'Like we always feel,' Blake said. 'Like we're gonna win.'

'We'll wipe the ice with them for sure.'

The twins exuded confidence, and so they should. They'd played the Penguins enough over the years. But it had to add an extra emotional punch to the game, skating in the arena they'd used as a haven to escape their father, to study and to train, to turn their lives around.

A phone started to ring from somewhere in the house and Blake looked to the hallway. 'That's gonna be me. Sorry Mom, can you excuse me a sec?'

'Of course,' she said, watching him go.

Aiden pushed his bowl aside. 'That pie was as tasty as ever, Mom.'

'Hand on heart, it's the best I've ever had,' Astrid added.

'I'm so glad you enjoyed it.' Cynthia beamed. 'Can I get you any more?'

'I'd love to have room for it but I'm so full.' She pressed a hand to her overstuffed tummy. It was no lie. She shouldn't have had that second helping.

'In that case' – Aiden got to his feet – 'I'll clear the dishes and sort the kitchen.'

'I'll help.' Astrid stood with him, feeling quite emotional about the whole affair. The way they'd welcomed her into their family tradition of a Sunday roast, the way they'd made her feel like a part of the family rather than an outsider. The way Blake had laid himself bare to her...

'Nonsense, let the boys do it,' Cynthia said, her blue eyes suddenly sharp and astute as she took Astrid's hand. 'It'll give us time to talk. Just the two of us.'

Yelp!

* * *

Blake hung up the phone and followed the sound of music to the kitchen.

Aiden was at the sink, shimmying away to Amy Winehouse and he chuckled.

'All these years we've lived together, and I'll never get used to you shaking that ass to Winehouse.'

'You're just jealous I've got better moves than you.'

'You wish.' Blake raked a hand through his hair and joined him at the sink. 'You okay getting Astrid home if I head out?'

His brother froze mid-shake. 'You're leaving?'

'That was the realtor; a property's come up and it looks the business, but it won't hang around for long.'

Aiden straightened. 'So you're serious about this?'

'Moving out? Yeah...' He'd only mentioned it in passing while they were in LA, and he'd figured his brother would think it a knee-jerk response to everything else he had going on. With Astrid. Leo. The pressure he was under with the Titans. But it wasn't. 'It's time, bro. Jesus, we're twenty-eight. And don't tell me you won't be happy not to have to clear up after me any more.'

'We have cleaners that do that.'

'No, we have cleaners who clean but you do the tidying.'

'To be fair, you've been a lot better of late.'

'I've been better at a lot of things.'

Aiden's gaze drifted to the wall, to where Mom and Astrid were on other side. 'Yeah, yeah, I know. She's a good influence.'

'She really is... so are things... you know... going some-where?' He lifted his brows and Blake choked on a laugh.

'Somewhere sounds about right.'

'Good. I'm glad. But I gotta say, bro, I'll be sad to see your stuff go. I'll be sad to see you go.'

'I'll only be around the corner, we can grab a beer – or a coffee, any time. And hell, we've always got the ice.'

'Too true.'

'So, you're good to take Astrid back for me?'

'Yeah, no worries.'

'Thanks buddy, I owe you.'

He turned away.

'Though, Blake...'

'Yeah?'

'You might want to change your sweater before you unleash that sight on the world.'

* * *

Astrid perched herself on Cynthia's sofa while the woman herself settled back in the armchair by the fire she had just expertly lit. The room was a reader's paradise. Shelves stuffed with books, paintings that oozed romance, cushions galore and a window seat to sit and watch the world go by.

Astrid admired it even as her heart went pit-a-pat with the conversation to come. 'You have a lovely home.'

'I'm very lucky, I know.'

'That's not what I—'

'Oh, I know that's not what you meant, dear, but it's how I feel. I don't deserve it. And I wouldn't have it, if not for them. They're—'

The door opened and Blake poked his head in. 'Everything okay in here?'

They both smiled, though she sensed hers was tighter than his mother's. 'Of course, darling. Astrid and I are enjoying a private catch up, woman to woman. Aren't we?'

Cynthia sent her a conspiratorial wink that instantly calmed her. So, she hadn't fucked up... not yet anyway.

'Everything okay with your call?' Astrid asked.

'Everything's great, but I'm going to have to go.'

'What?'

'You are?' Cynthia said, clearly disappointed but nowhere near as disappointed as Astrid felt.

'Afraid so. I have an appointment.'

'On a Sunday afternoon?' his mother asked.

Astrid's thoughts exactly.

'A property's come up that I want to take a look at and I'm away most of this week.' He looked to Astrid. 'Aiden's lined up to run you home.'

'That's not necessary.'

'We insist.'

But a property? Was he moving out? Had she pushed him into that with her whole co-dependency talk? Oh, God, maybe she should have kept her mouth shut. There was change and then there was a complete upheaval!

Could she really be the spark behind something so huge? She'd only been here a few weeks. And hell, she wasn't even going to be around come next month.

She tried to smile as he strode into the room. He'd swapped the garish sweater for his trademark black and though it fitted his muscular frame to perfection, she found she missed the light-hearted reindeer.

'I'll see you soon, Mom. Thanks for a lovely dinner as always.' He kissed her cheek, straightened back up and then hesitated. She could almost sense his silent 'fuck it' as he came up to her.

'I'll see *you* later.'

Her heart leapt and she nodded, accepting his peck to her cheek with all good grace and watching him go like an addict, wondering when her next fix would come and wanting it now.

The door clicked shut and his mother gave a soft laugh. 'Well, well, well, I never thought I'd see the day.'

Astrid pulsed out a high-pitched, 'Hmm?'

She wished her coffee was something stronger. Much, much stronger.

'When Aiden told me you'd been good for Blake, I didn't believe it. That boy has been the same since he was knee-high to a grasshopper, but his brother is right, you've got him growing into the man he was always supposed to be.'

She gripped her coffee cup in both hands to keep it steady. 'I think only Blake could truly do that for himself.'

Cynthia smiled, her intense blue gaze so like her sons'.

'Perhaps. Though there's no denying the shift in his behaviour since you came on the scene. He's out of the penalty box more and more, he's calmer, he's drinking less.'

Astrid smiled. 'It's lovely that you think I had a hand in it, but it was all him.'

'You shouldn't be so modest, especially when it's clear that my son likes you. A lot. And I'm hoping the feeling might be mutual?'

Oh hell, what was this? She was supposed to be doing the drilling, not his mother.

'I'm sorry, darling. I don't mean to put you on the spot, but those boys, they are my everything and to see them happy and settled, it would mean the world to me. Especially after all that came before.'

Her eyes glistened in the flickering light from the fire and Astrid felt her own eyes well up. She didn't want to say the wrong thing, give false assurances or say something that she'd promised the twins she wouldn't say, so she said nothing.

'I know they've told you about their father, and thanks to the press over the years, that stuff is public knowledge anyway. But... living through it. No one can know what that's like unless they've lived it too.'

'Of course,' Astrid whispered, wanting her to know that she got it. 'I'm no hack, Cynthia. I'll handle the truth with sensitivity and do my best by them. I promise you that.'

'I believe you. I only wish they believed in themselves more. I know they fear being like their father and no matter what I say, or what they do, they struggle to break free of him.'

The woman really did know her boys...

'If only I'd been stronger. If only I'd got away when they were young, and innocent, and they hadn't witnessed all they had. To know that I couldn't save them, that they had to save me.' Her voice trailed away as she looked to the fire, shook her head. 'It's not right.'

'But it wasn't your fault,' Astrid said, her heart aching in the face of a mother's guilt. 'What happened was done to you as much as to them, you were just as innocent in it all.'

She gave a slow nod. 'Did they tell you what happened the night we left town?'

'Blake did.'

Cynthia's throat bobbed, her hand shaking as she stroked it over her hair. 'If I'd had dinner ready, if I hadn't gone home at all and kept on driving, if I'd done anything but what I did...' She took an unsteady breath. 'You how many times I've replayed it? Anything to avoid seeing the horror on Blake's face when he realised what he'd done. To see Aiden shut down and take control. They became different overnight. Still my boys, who I adore and love, but something broke inside of them... I'd like to think that one day they'll find someone to help them heal.' Her tear-filled eyes lifted to Astrid. 'Someone who'll make them realise that they're worth loving and that it's safe to give it in return.'

Astrid's throat closed over, her heart breaking in two. Did she think that was *her*?

'Blake is a good man,' his mother stressed softly.

'I know.'

'What happened that night, it wasn't his fault. He was just

desperate to make it stop. Desperate to protect me when I should have been protecting him.'

'I know, Cynthia. I know.'

'If only I'd never met their father, but then I'd never have them.' She gave a tremulous laugh. 'How impossible is that?'

'But look at all you have now. A decade later and you have an amazing life, an amazing relationship with your boys who clearly adore you.'

She gave stiff nod. 'I'd like to think the sacrifice was worth it. That in giving up their lives, their friends, their girls, they found so much more.' She gave a soft huff. 'Not that Blake ever had a girl that I knew of but...'

'But Aiden did?' It was out before Astrid could stop it, her need to find out more for Sissi overriding her promise not to press. But then Blake had already mentioned it and his mother had raised it first. Surely, it didn't count.

'Oh yes. Her name was Sienna. Such a pretty name for a pretty girl.'

And there it was, her proof. She didn't need Aiden to spill his past, his brother and mother had confirmed it. And she trusted them more than Aiden himself. Because they had no reason to quash it, whereas Aiden... his silence *had* to be because it still hurt.

'I never saw them together all that much,' his mother was saying. 'Aiden rarely brought her to the house, and I couldn't blame him. It wasn't an environment for friends let alone a girlfriend. But I saw the effect she had on him. He had a glow about him, an extra sparkle that even the game couldn't bring... to see that in him again.'

'Do you think he loved her?'

She gave a sad smile. 'Yes, as much as a boy can. They were young, kids really... but there's never been anyone since. For either of them. Twenty-eight and no girl let alone a grandbaby on the horizon... until they brought you here today.'

Her eyes shone as she smiled at her and Astrid squirmed.

Oh, to genuinely be Blake's girl...

But she'd never wanted to be anyone's girl. She didn't *want* to be someone's girl now. Did she?

'That makes you special.'

'I think your sons thought it would be nice that I meet you because I'm writing about their life,' Astrid softly evaded, 'and you're the most important person in it.'

Cynthia's smile widened. 'You can tell yourself that, but I see the two of you, so does Aiden, and he knows his brother better than anyone. Better than Blake does himself at times. There's something special there, you mark my words. I may not know a lot about healthy love, but I know love, the early flutterings and the joy they bring. Now I just need to see it with Aiden again.'

'See what?' Aiden said, making a timely return. 'If you're talking about my Christmas sweater, it isn't happening, not now, not ever.'

'Spoilsport,' Astrid forced out as Cynthia gave her another one of those winks.

* * *

'Did you have a good time?' Aiden asked when he drove her home later that evening.

'I did, thank you again for inviting me.'

'You're welcome. I was also thinking, if you're free this week, why don't you come to Massachusetts with us? You've seen us with Mom, you should probably see us on our old ice, too. We can show you around.'

'Really?'

If she went, she'd be close enough to visit Sienna. She could speak to her in person. Tell her what Blake had told her, what his mother had also confirmed. That kind of closure had to be better than any kind of karma any day of the week.

'Why not? There's room on the private plane, the GM has already cleared you on the expenses front, and you're great for the team's morale.'

The team's morale or your brother's? she wanted to ask but daren't, not after custard-gate.

'Seriously, Astrid, the testosterone in the locker room when you walk through it is enough to fuel a shutout.'

'A shutout?' She laughed. 'I'm glad I'm good for something.'

'You're good for a lot,' he said, suddenly serious. 'My brother especially. So, will you come?'

She gave a shaky breath, surprised by his honesty and the way her heart bloomed out of her control. 'I'd love to.'

* * *

As she got ready for bed that night, Astrid fired off a message to the girls.

JUST DESSERTS WHATSAPP GROUP. 22.15 EST.

ASTRID

Dinner went better than I ever could've hoped! Sissi you MUST watch the game tomorrow night! No spoilers! 😶

Paige, I hope you're doing okay 🫶

B, hope things are coming together nicely at your end 🤍

She waited to see if anyone picked up and when they didn't, she fired off a private text to Sissi.

> Need to speak you honey! I'm coming to town!!
> Call me!! Xx

Then she climbed into bed and checked her phone again. No messages.

And she knew she wasn't checking for the girls this time, she was checking for Blake because... well *because*... holy fuck, she'd come so hard and so fast. The memory alone was enough to make her blood race, and her clit throb, and Delia's book wasn't going to cut it tonight. Tonight, she wanted him.

Wanted him so much that she feared she'd go on wanting Blake long after the article was done. No matter her intentions, her plans to return to the UK, to get her life back on an even keel... post-karma, post-Aiden, post-Blake.

Because life without Blake was unimaginable right now.

She didn't *want* to imagine it. And so, she wouldn't.

Her phone vibrated and she snatched it up.

BLAKE

> You still up?

Her entire body pulsed.

ASTRID

> Yes

BLAKE

> I can't get you out of my head

Her heart thudded against her ribs.

ASTRID

> I can't get you out of mine

BLAKE

Want me to swing by?

She shot up in bed.

ASTRID

Now?

BLAKE

I'm right outside... all you need to do is buzz me in...

Ohmigod!

She slammed on her bedside lamp, sending Delia's book skidding across the floor as she did so. Stared at her stunned reflection in the wall of mirrors. Devoid of makeup, her hair everywhere, and in her Metallica tee and shorts, she wasn't fit to be seen!

Her phone buzzed again and she buzzed with it.

BLAKE

Or not. No pressure. I was just passing.

22

Blake hadn't *meant* to call by Astrid's. He hadn't *meant* to text her. In fact, he'd done all he could to refrain from contact because he didn't do the whole needy pursuit thing. He never chased a girl. They came to him.

And his brother had messaged to say she was coming to Massachusetts that week. It was perfect. Two nights in the same hotel. So much opportunity.

But driving past her building, knowing she was there, not knowing if she was feeling the same. Wanting to ask her. Wanting to see her. Wanting her.

He looked at his phone, at the three dots rolling. Maybe he should—

The latch on the door released, his phone buzzing with it:

ASTRID

Apartment 807

He was through the door and across the foyer in a heartbeat, nodding to the concierge as he called the elevator. The doors slid open and he stepped in, barely sparing a glance for the shiny geometric panelling as he pressed the button for her floor. His phone buzzed.

AIDEN

You moved out already?

He suppressed a smile.

BLAKE

It was nice but not that nice.

He'd liked it though. And his first thought had been Astrid. What would she make of it? Not Aiden. His brother who'd led every decision Blake had made since leaving Ashbury Falls behind.

AIDEN

So where are you?

BLAKE

Visiting a friend. Don't wait up ;-)

AIDEN

We have a game tomorrow...

BLAKE

And?

AIDEN

Is this a mutual friend?

BLAKE

What do you think?

AIDEN

You're seeing her Tuesday!

Not soon enough, bro.

He pocketed his phone and bobbed on his feet. Come on

come on come on...

The second the doors opened, he stepped through and there she was. In the doorway to her apartment. Cropped tee, mini shorts, hair wild and eyes bright. A contemporary pop against the art deco hallway. And everything he'd needed since he'd left her that afternoon.

'Hey.' He paused before her, ran his fingers through his hair when all he wanted was to rake them through hers. Kiss her like he had not ten hours ago.

'Hey.' Those honeyed eyes lifted to his as she tugged at the hem of her tee. 'Excuse the mess.'

'If this is a mess, it's my kind of mess.'

Her eyes sparkled, her mouth curved up, her nipples beading beneath her tee – *fuck*, was she not wearing a bra?

'I was in bed.'

He let go of a gruff laugh. 'Then it's me who should apologise.'

She took a little breath, her tongue snaking out to wet her lips as she backed up. 'You can help me back in it if you like.'

He swung the door shut and swept her into his arms, her delightful giggle-cum-squeal cut short by their kiss.

God, she felt good. Smelled good. Sounded good. Her moans matched his as he cupped her against him.

'I've been fantasising about this all afternoon,' he murmured.

'Even with your realtor?'

'Even with him.'

She shoved his jacket to the floor. 'Poor guy.'

'Not so poor when I take up the lease,' he said, breaking away just long enough for her to shove his sweater and tee over his head.

'Are you going to?' She hooked her fingers into the waistband of his jeans, yanked him back to her.

'Possibly. Probably. I'd like you to come see it.'

Her head jerked back, her startled gaze meeting his. 'Me?'

'I'd like a second opinion.'

'And you want *mine*?'

Play it down, buddy. You're freaking her out.

'Doesn't hurt to get a female perspective on that elusive thing you call home.'

Her mouth hung open, her body teasing at his groin even as she kept her lips from his. He stroked his hands beneath her tee, from her waist to her bare breasts, felt her skin prickle, watched her eyes glaze, and her body start to arch. Better...

'So, you up for it?'

He rolled his thumbs over each tightened peak...

'You're playing dirty again,' she gasped.

'I warned you I could play dirtier, baby.'

'What if I can play dirtier still?'

* * *

Astrid popped the button on his jeans, her only thought to end the emotional connection and build on the sexual. Because the sexual felt safe. The other... she had no idea how to handle that. No experience either.

And she needed him. With every fibre of her being she needed him. And *this*, she knew. *This* she understood. *This* was right.

She kissed him deep as she tugged his zipper down.

'You want to take this to the bedroom?' he said.

'I want to take you right here...' She trailed her hands down his front, marvelling at every line of ink, every ridge. 'Right now.'

'Your—'

The word became a groan as she slipped inside his briefs.

'Easy, Twinkle Toes' – he grabbed her hand to stall her – 'I don't know how much of this I can take, not after this afternoon.'

'Let's find out, shall we?'

She dropped to her knees and his hands flew to her hair. '*Astrid...*'

He sounded pained, every exposed muscle taut as he fought for control. But she didn't want his control, she wanted him, as raw and undone as she had been.

She licked her lips as she drew him out to her awaiting mouth, her core clenching over his sheer size, the depth of his need evident in every straining inch. 'I owe you.'

'You don't—'

She flicked her tongue over the tip and he rocked back into the wall with a hiss.

'Shh...' she whispered, her lips caressing the velvety skin as she held his gaze, cherishing the heat and the wonder in his, his obedience too.

She stroked down his length, holding him firm. Then slowly, she parted her lips and took him in, devouring him with her eyes as much as her mouth.

'*Fuuuucck...*' His thighs trembled and his hips rocked, his teetering control fuelling her own. The thrill of having this great big hulk of a man at her mercy, to claim him so completely... it was exhilarating, mind-blowing, orgasm-inducing. She slid her hand inside her shorts, feeding her ache as she took him ever deeper and his eyes flared wider. '*Jesus H Christ*, are you...?'

She moaned around him in answer and his eyes rolled back with his head. 'You're fucking killing me.'

If she didn't expire first...

She found her rhythm with his, meeting him groan for groan as he wrapped her hair around his fist and thrust harder, faster... the salty taste of his impending orgasm hitting her throat—

'*Astrid!*' He yanked her back, sucking in a breath as he held her still. 'Bedroom. Now.'

She contemplated refusing but he was too quick, tugging up his jeans and lifting her into his arms like she weighed nothing.

'Which way?' he growled, his strength, his eyes, his fierce command, a turn on like none other.

She pointed and he followed. Kicking off his trainers, toeing off his socks, he threw her onto the bed. No finesse, no gentleness.

He tugged his wallet from his pocket and tossed it onto the bedside table before joining her, his knees forcing her thighs apart. 'You know what our problem is?'

She shook her head and he stripped her tee, his hungry gaze dipping to her breasts. Heat rushed beneath her skin, her nipples tingling against the cool air of the room, and then his tongue was there... laving over one taut peak and making her squeak.

'We both value our control.'

He wasn't wrong.

'So I vote we lose it together.'

Oh God, the way his cock was pressing between her legs, the way he was scraping his teeth around her nipple... she was losing it right now.

'What do you say?'

'I say...' She was panting, the pinch of his teeth shooting sparks to her clit while his cock kept up the pressure over her clothes. 'This isn't losing it together.'

She flicked him onto his back with a sudden surge of strength, his chuckle more growl than laugh. 'I was enjoying that.'

She swept a kiss over his lips. 'Not as much as me.' And easing his jeans down his legs, her mouth travelled south...

'Oh no, you don't.'

He had her on her back in an instant, arms pinned above her head. 'You're too fucking sexy.'

He glanced to the left, to the mirrored wall. 'Look at you.'

She turned her head and wanted to shy away from what she saw. 'Oh no you don't.' He shifted to her side, curved her back against his front so they faced it together. 'You're too beautiful to hide.'

Holding her wrists in one hand, he trailed the other down her body, along the curve of her breast, circling her nipple as she arched into his touch, into him... She dragged in a breath, her cheeks flooding with colour as she watched her wanton body demand more, her thighs falling open as he dipped lower still.

'Do you see what I see?' he murmured, fingertips teasing along the band of her shorts. 'Do you see how beautiful you are?'

She shuddered with a whimper.

'Do you?'

She nodded into his eyes as he slipped inside, one skilful stroke between her folds and she spasmed, her hips rolling for more.

'Was that a yes?'

She couldn't form a word. She was going to come apart and he wasn't even close.

'Watch yourself come, Astrid, see what I see.'

Fuck, she was watching, and she was going, and there was nothing capable of stopping it, not her control, not her will, nothing.

'That's it, baby, I'm with you.'

His breaths shortened with hers, his eyes hooded as they watched her in the mirror. She'd never been so turned on, never felt so desired... she wanted to grip him, tip him over the edge with her but he had her wrists held fast.

'Please...' she managed to pant. 'I want you.'

He gave a low growl. 'I want you too.'

'Then take me...'

She pushed back and he released her, freeing her to strip her bottoms as he stripped his.

'Please tell me you have a condom in that wallet?' she hurried out, rolling him onto his back and straddling his thighs.

He reached for it as she did. 'Oh no, you don't, I've got this.'

She snatched it up and he lay back, his blue eyes glittering with amusement, want... *adoration*? Her heart flickered to life and she ignored it. Focused on the heat, the task at hand. She found the packet and tore it open.

'Now lie still while I get this right...'

'Yes, boss,' he ground out, eyes glinting as his cock bucked within her grasp and she slid the condom down, keeping him pinned there as she lifted her body over him.

'Now you watch,' she whispered, turning his head to the mirror.

Then she took him in inch by inch, cherishing his groan, the colour in his cheeks, the way the muscles in his neck corded as he gripped her thighs.

'Do you see what I see?' she said, lowering her mouth to his ear, her eyes meeting his in the mirror. 'How beautiful, how sexy, how incredible you are?'

He shuddered, dark lashes flickering as his vulnerability threatened to surface.

'You're so fucking incredible,' she stressed, moving over him until his eyes were blazing anew, his cheeks hot, mouth slack. 'And it's time you realised it.'

He gave a guttural groan and threw her under him, one powerful thrust taking him straight to that sweet spot within. But she knew she'd touched a spot within him too. A spot that needed hitting, that needed telling, that needed loving...

No, *not* loving. This wasn't love. She squeezed her eyes shut against it and focused on the pleasure tightening through her core. Every hit against her G-spot taking her to the edge. To the all-consuming high that only sex could bring. A safe high. A temporary high. A—

'Blake!' She came so hard, so fast, her body gripping and shattering around him as he growled his release into the crook of her neck.

His entire body shuddered over her as he fought to keep his weight on his hands. But she didn't want his careful considera-tion. She wanted him to fall. Wanted to feel him top to toe, pressing into her, consuming her... wanted this connection for as long as she could keep it. And sweeping her arms up, she tugged his own down, forcing him into her embrace and holding him tight.

'Can you stay the night?' she whispered.

'Just you try and move me...'

* * *

They'd made love three times already and still he wasn't satisfied.

She lay on his chest as the first rays of dawn seeped into the room, not quite asleep but not quite awake either.

It was impossible to sleep with all this racing inside him.

He wanted more. From her, from this, but what was more? An actual relationship. Hell, he'd never had one of those. Not of the serious kind. Sex, sure. But commitment, no.

And that was what he wanted. Exclusivity. The whole of her. No half measures. But how to broach that when he knew her stance on relationships, knew it as well as he knew his own. But if he could change...

'What's wrong?' She lifted her head to look at him and he forced himself to relax as he traced circles on her shoulder.

'Nothing. Not really.'

'You're a rubbish liar, you know that?'

He gave a tight chuckle. 'I might have heard that once or twice before, yeah.'

'So out with it...'

He couldn't just say what he was thinking. Hell, he wasn't even sure he *trusted* what he was thinking. And maybe this was the norm for her, getting close to people she worked with, creating a bond that led to...

'Am I the first... what are we – subjects? The first subject you've slept with?'

Her face froze over, the panic in her eyes telling him to leave it alone. But too late, he'd asked. And he wanted to know. Even as the green-eyed monster reared its ugly head.

'Astrid?'

'No,' she whispered, tucking her head into his chest. He didn't know what pained him more, the confirmation or the fact she couldn't look at him as she said it. 'You're the second.'

'Who was the first?'

He felt her swallow. Was she protecting the guy's identity? Or protecting herself from something that still hurt? And if it was the latter – fuck, that *did* hurt.

'You don't need to tell me.' What came before him was her business, not his. He had no right, but... 'I just—'

'He was an artist.'

'An artist...?' Another creator like herself. Someone who would've inspired her as much as she did him. A perfect fit. 'How long ago?'

She wriggled even closer. 'We broke up six months ago.'

Broke up? That suggested an *actual* relationship... from the woman who claimed love and marriage weren't in her future.

'How long were you together?' He couldn't help himself now. He had to know it all.

'A few months.'

'Monogamous?'

Nothing.

'Astrid?'

'I was.'

Oh fuck.

'He was married,' she whispered.

'*What*?' Of all the things he'd expected... 'Did you know?'

She came alive, pushing up off his chest to glare at him. 'How can you ask me that?'

'Babe, I—'

'After *everything* I told you about my father. Who he was? What he did?' She turned away, dragging her knees to her chest as her shoulders quivered and he came up behind her, his hand gentle on her shoulder.

'I'm so sorry, I didn't think. I just—'

'I *swore* I would never do that to someone. I would never be the other woman. I would never... *never*... I hated my father for what he did to my mother, I hated what it did to her, and she hated herself for it. How could you...?'

'I fucked up, I didn't think.' Damn, he felt like the scum of the earth. 'Hey baby, I'm sorry.' He stroked her hair over her shoulder, kissed the soft skin of her neck. 'Please come back to me. Please.'

Slowly she turned, but her eyes were downcast, her body folding into him as he wrapped his arms around her.

'I trusted him,' she whispered.

'Did you love him?'

She shook her head. 'I cared for him. I thought what we had was special. Sex but a connection too. And then one day, his wife rocked up and I... I just ran.'

'I hope you gave him hell first.'

She swallowed a sob and his heart cracked open.

'It wasn't your fault, baby, surely you know that. It was his place to tell you, it's not on you.'

He eased her onto her back. Her eyes were clamped shut, the tears seeping from each corner tearing him apart.

'You did nothing wrong.'

He kissed each eyelid, traced each damp trail, and then kissed her trembling lips until she softened beneath him, her arms and legs wrapping around him.

It made so much sense now, the walls she had up. She wasn't just a woman who couldn't trust a man to stick around through the worst, she was the woman who had let a man in only to have it crush her. Turning her into her worst nightmare.

That was what he was up against.

At least he knew the score, and just like in the game, to know what you were up against was half the battle won... though he had a feeling that the stakes with Astrid ran so much higher than anything that had come before.

But she was worth it, and she'd made him feel worthy of it. That whole trick with the mirror, turning the act on him... he'd felt it. Every word she'd said, he'd felt it in his bones.

Of all the people in the world, she knew the worst of him and still she wanted him. That had to mean something deeper, something more, something worth exploring just as his brother had said... if only he could open her eyes to it.

'I'm crazy about you.'

It was out before he could stop it and she shook her head.

'Don't. You don't need to make me feel better. I don't deserve—'

'Hey, I'm not saying it to make you feel better. I'm saying it because it's true.'

She gave a tearful laugh. 'Well, you won't be saying that when my PMDD drops in to say hello next week.'

Next week? The team's bye week. No ice for five days. So many ideas filled his mind on how he could distract her, how he could work with her own coping mechanisms and convince her he was in it for the long haul.

'Consider it a date.'

'Blake!' She thrust her hips, the motion making his lower half perk up. If she'd thought to chide him, she'd be seriously disappointed.

'I'm not kidding around, Astrid.' He caught her chin in his fingers, lifting her face to his. 'I'll be here for you because I'm crazy about you.'

Her honeyed eyes widened. Was that fear, panic, mistrust? Whatever it was, he wanted it gone.

'You don't know what you're saying, what you're promising...'

* * *

Oh God, Astrid couldn't breathe. Not with that look in his eyes, the words flowing from his lips teasing at her heart...

She lowered her gaze. 'Until you live through it you can't know.'

And now she sounded like his mother using the same line about their past, but Astrid was using it in relation to her PMDD which was wholly within her. No one else's fault but her own.

'But I will soon.' He lifted her chin again, brought his mouth close to hers, those piercing blues too. 'And I have so many ideas on how to help.'

'And like I told you before,' she said softly. 'I'm better off on my own when I'm like that.'

'You just haven't met the right person to share that side of you with.'

She gave a sad smile, his sincerity chipping through her resolve. 'Maybe.'

Though she knew it sounded hollow because there was so much more at play here than he knew. So much more she had to tell him because any conversation over what they were to one another had to be built on the truth.

And she wanted to tell him everything. About Chase. About the girls. About the karma pact.

But she couldn't do that without speaking to Sissi first. And maybe, just maybe, telling Sienna all that she knew, telling her that she believed Aiden had loved her, that he still bore the mark of that love… well, it could change everything.

And telling Blake… *if* he forgave her, *then* the future was worth a discussion, but until then…

'Astrid?'

'Hmm?'

'Anyone ever tell you you're an over thinker?'

And then he kissed her, stripping away her ability to think as he travelled down her body, hitting on every erogenous zone until he reached his final destination, and her fingers and toes curled into the mattress with her cry.

'To hell with maybe,' he murmured between her legs, his eyes burning up into hers and choking up her throat. 'I say, definitely.'

23

Astrid's nose twitched in her sleep, her senses becoming aware of the glorious scent of caffeine before her brain had kicked in.

The glorious scent of coffee and... Blake!

Her eyes shot open as her body shot up.

'Morning, sleepyhead.'

She tugged the blanket up her naked chest and raked her mop out of her face, blinking wildly at his mostly naked, exceptionally hot, freshly showered, and towel-wrapped bod stood at the end of the bed.

'I think it's a little late for modesty, don't you?'

She swallowed and yup, there was her trademark squeak. Followed by his trademark smirk... he knew *exactly* what he did to her.

'Is that coffee I can smell?'

Because if she was drinking coffee, she couldn't be drinking him in again so soon. How could she still want him so bad?

'Sure is.' He gestured to the bedside table behind her.

'You brought me coffee!' She dived for it, addiction overriding modesty now as she sat back up and took a soul-satisfying sip. 'You're an angel, thank you!'

He chuckled. 'Now *that* I haven't heard before... but I'll take it. You might want to check your phone too. It's been flashing like a strobe.'

'It has?' She glanced its way.

'Good job too else I would've slept in.'

She wrestled one-handed with the tangled sheets to get to it, and he came to her aid, lifting it off the charging station and slotting it into her hand. 'Your friend Sissi seems desperate to talk to you.'

She almost dropped both it and the coffee. '*Sissi*?'

Heart in mouth, she checked the screen. Three missed calls and a text.

'She's an early riser, ringing you at that time,' he said, towelling off his hair, his rippling biceps threatening to disengage her panic from her brain as she gawped at him.

'She'll be on her way to work.'

'Which is where I should be, though I hate to eat and run.'

He strode across the room, losing the towel as he went. No worries over modesty there. Though with an arse like that, she couldn't blame him. Tight as—

Eat and run, wait!

'Have you eaten? Have I slept through all of that?'

He tugged his jeans on, zipped and buttoned them as he came back to the bed. Planting his fists into the mattress either side of her, he grinned into her eyes, their devilish glint and his proximity stealing her breath.

'I was talking about feasting on you.'

'Oh!'

'Yes, oh...' And then he caught her lips in his for the softest, sweetest, most tantalising of kisses. 'But now I have to go before Aiden and Coach send out a search party.'

He straightened up and her body instantly protested the loss of his.

'See you later, pre-game?'

'I... I'm not sure. I have stuff to do, calls to make, packing to sort.'

An article to write, friends to call, a conscience to revive... or batter into submission.

'Okay, Twinkle Toes, do what you need to do and call me if you change your mind. Else I'll see you tomorrow.'

'Tomorrow.' She nodded as her phone started to ring again.

'Say hi to Sissi from me...'

He gave her a wink and walked out, his parting words making her gut writhe and her cheeks bloom. Guilty as...

'Shit!'

'Woah, that's some greeting...'

Oops. Butterfingers had answered the call and now Sissi was looking right at her, naked boobs an' all.

'...I almost crashed the car.'

Sissi's blue eyes narrowed as they flicked from Astrid to the road and back again.

'Honey, are you—'

'Yes!' She tilted the phone, her cheeks burning deeper. 'I slept in.'

'God, I'm so jelly. I can't remember the last time I had a lie-in.' She looked over her shoulder as she shifted the indicator stick – *tick tock tick tock.* 'Oh yes, it was probably Christmas Day and even then, it took a dive when I got called into work.'

'Sorry Sissi, not trying to rub it in.'

'I know, ignore me, I'm just tired. I pulled a night shift and now I'm on early too.'

'And yet you look amazing on it.' Astrid smiled at her friend who truly did look incredible. Tired, always. But incredible, nonetheless. Sienna just had this quality about her that made one think of Hallmark movies and happy lives... even if the truth was far from it.

'Yeah, right!' She snorted. 'So, come on, spill! Why do I need to watch the game tonight, and what do you mean you're coming to town?'

'The former you'll have to wait and see...' Though Astrid couldn't suppress her grin.

'That smile tells me you've done something.'

'Just watch out for your heartbreaker on the ice.'

She screwed her face up. 'If I must. And the latter?'

'You busy Wednesday?'

Sissi cocked a brow. 'You're asking *me* that?'

'Sorry, stupid question, what I should have said is, can you spare a couple of hours if a bouncy brunette happened to rock up on your doorstep?'

'Are you for real? You're coming here?'

'Yup. The twins are playing the Penguins, and they've invited me along for the ride, all expenses paid. We fly in tomorrow.'

'Oh, honey!' Her eyes lit up, her grin taking the edge off the shadows under her eyes. 'That would be amazing; you can fill me in properly, we can talk, eat cake, drink that wine you sent me – thank you by the way!'

'You're welcome.' She'd forgotten she'd sent it, but the timing was perfect!

'So, when are you thinking?'

'Wednesday afternoon, while the team are busy with pre-game prep?'

'Amazing! I have a seminar, but I can skip it. It'll be so good to see you in person. I only wish it could be for longer. And even more that it could be all of us together.'

'Yeah, I know, I miss having us—' Her phone buzzed as a message dropped onto the screen, momentarily blotting Sienna's face. *Paige?*

'Hang on, babe... did you just get a WhatsApp from Paige?'

'Yeah.'

She clicked the message to open:

> PAIGE CREATED GROUP 'SOS!!!'
> PAIGE ADDED YOU.
> PAIGE ADDED SISSI.
>
> PAIGE
>
> I fucked up! Are you guys free for a call??

'Shit,' they both said in unison.

'I'm just gonna grab some clothes and I'll be right on it...' Because there was no way Astrid could go into an SOS call butt naked. Especially when the cause of her nakedness was something she couldn't talk about just yet. 'You?'

'I'll pull over and do the same.'

Astrid cut the call and smacked her coffee down on the side. Flying off the bed, she threw the quilt up as she sought out her clothing. She found her tee wedged between the bed and the table, plucked it out and pulled it on, all the while hunting out her shorts. Where were the damn things? They couldn't just vanish!

> SISSI
>
> I can jump on a call.

'I'm coming, I'm coming, I'm coming!' she muttered in desperation.

Not like you were last night... or this morning.

Not helping! She looked to the heavens with an eye roll and that was when she saw them – her shorts, hanging on the corner of the TV. She snatched them down and thrust them on, dropping onto her bed with a flustered 'oof!'

ASTRID

Me too!

Almost immediately the video call came in from Paige and she swiped to accept it, her friend's avatar being replaced by her IRL. She looked pale, her hazel eyes like panicked fish bowls.

'What's happened?' she blurted. 'Are you okay?'

Paige shook her head, her red curls dancing with the move. 'I did a bad, bad thing.'

Oh God...

* * *

'Where have you been?' Coach asked as Blake launched himself onto the ice.

'Sorry, Coach, slept in!'

With a swoosh he joined the line of players already in the full swing of drills, his grin impossible to dampen.

'Ooh, somebody got some last night,' V goaded as he swept past.

'Shut up, V!'

But it was too late, jeers rippled through the team like a Mexican wave.

Aiden came up beside him in a spray of ice. 'He's not wrong though, is he?'

'A gentleman doesn't kiss and tell, bro.'

'Since when have you been a gentleman?'

'Since I met a pretty lady who inspired me to become one.'

* * *

Astrid hung up the video call, Paige's news rolling through her, as surprising as it was nerve provoking. Paige had caught feelings for Olly. The man who had jilted Bella and broken her heart...

It was a mess. A great big mess. But they'd tried to reassure her, encouraging her to come clean to Bella, too... But all the while Astrid had felt sick, because there she was telling Paige to be honest, when she herself had been far from it.

Though she could hardly come out with her own messy situation when Paige was in tears divulging hers... and tonight, Bella would learn of it too. So much for all these men getting their just desserts. It seemed the only ones paying the price were her girls. Bella for Chase and now Paige with Olly.

Meanwhile, in Astrid-land, she had her cake and was eating too. Four orgasms and counting. She was bad, bad, bad. Not Paige.

And as the day came to an end, her guilt and her worry increased tenfold. Because Bella was now incommunicado. Paige had told her the news and Bella wasn't speaking to any of them.

Astrid had called her, but she hadn't picked up. She'd messaged and no reply.

And now she was fighting the urge to hightail it to her place with a mountain of red velvet cupcakes, threatening to set up camp until her friend let her in. But Chase lived right across the hall so that wouldn't do.

If the guy saw her, Bella would have more than just Paige's feelings for Olly to worry over, she'd have to explain away Astrid's presence too.

So here she was, throwing random shit at her suitcase and praying her friend was okay – Friends plural! – when her phone buzzed.

SISSI

OMG! You did it! I can't believe you broke the
Ice King!

Huh...? Astrid stared at the text. Broke him? How?

Oh, God, the game! Grabbing the TV remote, she launched the streaming service playing the Titans game.

'Not even the glare of the ice can tone that down,' came the commentator's voice over the noise within the arena. 'Do you think it's a new strategy from the Ice King?'

'Ice King?' the fellow commentator replied. 'Lion King more like, just look at that orange glow and the attitude, he's taking some serious stick for it tonight.'

Astrid covered her mouth. 'Oh, God.'

SISSI

Did you hear what the commentator just said?
Lion King!! 😂 💀 Priceless 😂

She glanced back up at the TV, her face scrunching over the sight of Aiden slamming the opposition into the boards, taking out another on the rebound too. The ref blew his whistle, ordering him into the box and Blake skated up behind, shook his head at his brother.

'We can all take a guess at what Fury is saying to his brother now...'

'To be fair, I'm surprised Ice hasn't gone into the box sooner.'

'I don't know, Bob, seems the twins have had something of a personality swap. Blake without his Fury. Aiden losing his cool...'

SISSI

You are a genius! Karma Queen! 😈

Karma Queen? Astrid felt a little sick. But this was what

she'd come for, or thereabouts, and Sissi was getting what she'd been promised... a slice of payback.

ASTRID

I try

SISSI

How did you come up with this?

ASTRID

I figured it was time for Prince Charming to turn into the pumpkin...

Though she'd never anticipated feeling this conflicted over it.

SISSI

Haha! Brilliant   God, I love you

ASTRID

Love you too, babe xx

She only hoped her friend still felt that way when she told her everything come Wednesday...

* * *

As she climbed into bed that night, having watched the Titans win their game and packed her case to leave, she checked her phone for news from Bella. Still nothing. She was about to set it aside when—

BLAKE

Missed you today x

Her smile rose up from deep within her, impossible to suppress.

ASTRID

Don't worry, I'll grill you twice over tomorrow to make up for it

BLAKE

Is 'grill' a euphemism? 😈

She laughed out loud.

ASTRID

Congrats on the win!

BLAKE

Winning feels so much better when you're in the seats with your Titans jersey. Don't forget to pack it. There are things I want to do to you wearing that, and only that, Twinkle Toes 😏

Her heart lurched as her clit pulsed. What was it about this guy that he could lift her spirits with barely a word said? Dire straits over Bella to the female equivalent of a horndog in a few texts. What was that? A horn*cat*?

ASTRID

Consider it packed. Night night xx

BLAKE

Night xx

24

'Are you having a good time?'

Astrid jumped. She'd been so absorbed in her chat with the girls and her relief that Bella was finally communicating again, that she hadn't heard Preston approach. But now the GM was standing over her, his overly potent aftershave making her nose wrinkle.

'The best.'

Which was the truth. Flying to Massachusetts with the team, checking into their swanky hotel in Springfield, and being swept straight back out again by the twins for a tour of their old haunts had been equal parts fun and fascinating. Not to mention Blake, *all* the Blake.

And news from Bella had been the cherry on top!

She just knew in her gut that Paige and Bella would be okay... whether Paige and Olly would be, that was another question entirely.

'I'm glad to hear it. The management team are heading out for dinner this evening since we don't have to suffer the same constraints as this lot' – he gestured to some of the team members milling about in the grand marble foyer – 'you're welcome to join us. It's an exclusive restaurant run by...'

Preston was still talking but she was no longer listening. Across the way, through the flurry of guests, she'd locked eyes with Blake by the lift. He flashed his room key...

'I'm actually quite full after today's tour of the sights.' She was already on her feet, pulling her handbag over her shoulder and slotting her phone inside. 'And I have some work I need to be getting on with. Thank you though.'

She gave him the dazzles for good measure.

'Of course. Right. Yes. Well, if you change your mind...'

Not likely. 'I'll let you know.'

'I thought you needed rescuing,' Blake murmured as he ushered her into the lift with several other passengers and she smiled up at him. They'd spent most of the day in each other's orbit but never alone, and not being able to touch him, to kiss him... torture!

'This is us,' he said as the lift came to a stop and he urged her out.

It wasn't 'us', it was 'him', because her room was on an entirely different floor, two levels up. She'd been in it to freshen up on arrival and not seen it since.

He took her hand as soon as the lift doors closed behind them. 'I've been dying to do that all day.'

She scanned the sleek and modern hallway. 'Surely there are cameras...'

'I'm talking about holding your hand, Twinkle Toes, nothing X-rated.'

She laughed as he unlocked his door and pushed it open.

'Though now you mention it...' He tugged her inside and kissed her, his mouth hot and urgent as his tongue swept against hers and her knees gave out. Thank God he had her pressed up against the back of the door!

'I've wanted to do *all* of this from the second I saw you get on the coach this morn.'

She gave a breathless laugh as he tugged her shirt from her jeans and swept his hands beneath, his palms rough and tantalising against her skin.

'I think the entire coach would have had something to say about that.'

'Let them talk, I don't care.'

But she cared. If news broke before she had the chance to tell Sissi, the girls...

'Don't you think we should keep this on the down-low for now?'

'Whatever you say, baby,' he rasped beside her ear, his hot breath shooting a shiver up her spine. 'So long as I get to do this...'

He pulled her top over her head, his head dropping to her breasts, his teeth surrounding one puckered nipple through the lace and she bit into her lip to stop from crying out, her hands burying into his hair.

'You're like an addiction, Twinkle Toes.'

Funny how that godawful pet name felt so very different from his lips.

'I just can't get enough.'

He dragged his sweater over his head, his T-shirt too, and her eyes dipped over him.

One day her pulse wouldn't spike the second she laid eyes on his tattooed chest, his glorious pecs, the V-shaped abs that disappeared into the low-slung jeans...

One day, lust would hit its expiry date.

But that day was not today.

'If you bite any harder' – he tugged her bottom lip from her teeth with his thumb – 'you'll draw blood.'

'You know you're the perfect male specimen?' She dragged her gaze back up his chest, her hands smoothing down it, goose-bumps prickling in the wake of her touch until she covered his need with her palm.

He hissed through his teeth. 'You make me sound like a science project.'

'A very... sexy... science... project.' With each syllable she pulsed her grip around him. 'I'm not kidding though. I'm struggling to accept that this is real, that you are real.'

He gave a gruff laugh, his cock thickening against her. 'Oh, this is real, baby. Let me show you.'

He slid the straps of her bra down, her breasts springing free. *Fuck*, they ached. Her nipples, painfully pert as they pleaded for his attention.

'Are you just going to stand there?'

He gave her that cocky grin she was coming to adore. 'Just returning the favour, baby.'

He reached around her and unfastened the clasp, letting it drop to the floor, everything about his gaze lighting her up inside. The fire, the tease, the... *emotion?*

What *was* that?

He trailed his hands down the side of her body, lightly sweeping her curves and she sucked in a breath... the question burning with her rising need.

'But I know what you mean, about the whole real thing...'

He cupped her breasts, his thumbs stroking her nipples as his eyes stayed fixed in hers. The heat of his hands nothing on the heat of his eyes... that *look*. She hadn't seen it before. She hadn't felt it before. But she was feeling it now and she... *no*, she couldn't go there.

'Too slow,' she breathed, forking her hands into his hair and pushing it all out with a tongue-tangling kiss, urging him back towards the bed where she sent him down with a bounce.

He gave a tight chuckle. 'And I thought it was just me who was desperate.'

'Are you complaining?' she demanded as she mounted him, claiming his lips once more. Fear driving her as much as need now. Fear of what he was feeling, of what she was feeling, of what this was, and what it couldn't be. Or could it?

'I wouldn't dare.'

* * *

Astrid wouldn't stay still long enough for him to worship her body like he wanted to. Every time he tried, she took over once more. And this wasn't like before, where they'd both been wrestling for control, this was on another level. Fierce. Fast. Feral even.

Though he wasn't complaining. After twenty-four hours of abstinence, he wasn't just happy to be inside her again, he was relieved. And he let her take what she needed. What he needed too. Her body tightening around him, the pulse of her climax milking his own. He threw his head back into the pillows with a groan, uncaring of their neighbours as he lost himself to it. To her.

She sank down over him, slick with sweat and he gave a tight chuckle.

'What's so funny?'

'As much as I loved you whooping my ass on *Street Fighter*, I think this beats it.'

'Me riding you is the equivalent of *Street Fighter*?'

'I was referring to your ability to sort out my pre-game jitters, but now you mention it...'

She dug him in the ribs. 'Oi!'

'Just saying it how it is.'

He grabbed a tissue to dispose of the condom and she started to roll away. 'Oh no you don't,' he said, tossing the tissue-wrapped rubber with precision into the bin and pulling her back into his side. 'I'm not done with you yet.'

'Won't your team wonder where you are if you don't head down soon?'

'Nah, most of us hit the sack for a nap in the afternoon.'

'It's hardly the afternoon any more.'

'And I missed my nap, so I'm catching up.'

'*This* isn't napping.'

'Give me a minute and I will be...'

She nestled into his side once more and his heart settled with her. He wasn't ready to let her go. Everything felt right when she was just there. The world seemed to calm, the noise in his head seemed to hush. For the first time in his life, he felt at peace.

So at peace it took him a while to register a buzzing. A phone. He peeked through one lid. 'Is that you or me?'

She looked at her bag abandoned next to the door and grimaced. 'Sorry, I think it's me.'

'It's okay.' He stretched out with a yawn – he hadn't been kidding about the nap. 'Get it if you need to.'

'Nah, they can leave a message.'

But no sooner had it rung off than it started again.

'Okay, I'll get it else you'll get no sleep.'

He highly doubted that and tried to murmur as much to her, the murmur becoming a sleepy grumble as she eased away, and his body protested the cold that replaced her.

She'd be back he told himself, rolling over and taking the pillow with him.

* * *

OMG.

The bad boy really was a freaking pussycat, hugging the pillow in her place, making her wish it was still her...

She stared at him, her bag in her arms, her body immobilised with the desire to return... until her phone started to ring again. She hurried to pull it out. What on earth could be so urgent that—

Sissi?

She frowned at the flashing blonde avatar with huge baby blues. Why would Sissi be calling her numerous times over when they were getting together tomorrow? Unless... Bella and Paige... *shit*.

She swiped the call to answer and dived into the bathroom, pulling the door closed with a gentle click.

'Honey, what is it? Are you okay? Are the girls okay?'

'Yeah, yeah, everything's good,' came her friend's hushed lilt over the bustle of the diner in which she worked. 'Well, as far as I know. But you're not gonna believe who's just rocked up in the bar across the street?'

Astrid frowned, her post-orgasm brain slow to piece anything meaningful together.

'*He's* here.'

'Who's here?'

'Rick. Their *father!*'

Astrid straightened like a meerkat. 'You're kidding?'

'No, he's just rolled into town, acting like he's never been away. I have no idea how long he'll stick around for, or what he's doing here, but if you want to see him, now's your chance. I doubt he'll be leaving that bar any time soon.'

'If he's only just appeared, surely he'll stick around a bit?'

'No idea, but I don't fancy swinging by to ask him his plans for the next twenty-four hours.'

'No, no, of course not. I wouldn't expect you to.'

'He might be rolling through to the city for the game but I'm not sure that's the setting you want for this conversation. Or if you'll even spot him in the crowd.'

Her friend was right. She'd dug up enough pictures of him to know what he looked like, but there would be almost 20,000 hockey fans milling about come tomorrow. He'd be a needle in a haystack.

She eased the door ajar and looked at Blake. Could she go?

Leave a note saying she had to work, and she'd see him tomorrow.

Should she wake him up and tell him?

And risk him talking you out of it?

Which he would do. She was sure of it.

Or worse, he'd insist on accompanying her and that was the last thing he needed. To come face to face with his father the night before a game.

No, she couldn't let that happen either.

This was work. And Blake was... she didn't want to think about what Blake was just yet. She was still reeling from what she'd glimpsed in his face, what she'd felt.

She closed her eyes like it could somehow shut it all out and took a sanitising breath.

Getting their father's side to the past was important. There were many sides to a story, a rule she worked by and one she should have stuck to in her personal life, too. Before raining hell on Chase. Before launching an attack on Aiden.

The twins' father, however... the personal tried to overrule the professional and this time she wasn't letting it.

'I'm on my way.'

* * *

Waking up to a note didn't fit with Blake's plans...

Plans that centred around room service and Astrid. Not necessarily in that order.

He checked the note again as he called for the elevator.

Need to work, I'll see you tomorrow,
 Sweet dreams, pussycat ;-)

Pussycat! Who did she think she was calling 'pussycat'? And what did she mean tomorrow? Surely, she was staying with him, or vice versa. He didn't care which room so long as she was in it.

The elevator pinged open on her floor and he stepped out, shoving the note in his jeans pocket as he went.

'Hey Blake.' Harry came out of the room across the hall. 'If you're looking for Astrid, you just missed her.'

Blake paused mid-rap on her door. 'I did?'

'Yeah, she was hurrying into a cab when I got back from my run.' Harry pulled a hoody over his head, mumbling against the fabric. 'I figured you twins had scared her off.'

A cab? What kind of work involved getting a cab? They'd already taken her around their old haunts. The only thing left was Ashbury Falls and it would be a cold day in hell before they ventured there.

'I was only joking!' Harry blurted when he clocked Blake's expression. 'Well, about you scaring her off, not the rushing, she was definitely rushing.'

'Do you know where she was heading?'

'Beats me, but V was chatting up one of the women on the concierge desk the entire time I was out. He might have heard something.'

'Thanks, buddy.'

He started to move off and Harry called after him. 'V was still in the lobby last I checked.'

'Great.' He hit the stairs; no elevator was worth waiting for, not now. He had a bad feeling about this. A bad, bad feeling.

'V!' he hollered when he saw him at the bar across the lobby, sneaking a shot. The guy tensed, choking it up until he saw who it was.

'Blake, *dude*, thank God it's you.' He gave him a lazy grin as he leaned back against the polished surface. 'You joining me for one?'

'Do you know where Astrid went?'

'Well hello to you too.'

'I'm serious, V. Harry says she got in a cab.'

'Yeah, she got the concierge to sort her one, said she was in a hurry, money no object. Poor move if you ask me.' He crooked a finger at the bar staff for another drink. 'Bound to get ripped off.'

'And?'

'And what?'

'Did you hear where she was heading?'

He shrugged. 'Might have done.'

'*Might* have done?'

'I was distracted.'

'Think, buddy, *think*!'

He screwed his face up. 'Something Falls? Ashton, Ash—'

Blake's gut rolled. 'Ashbury?'

'Yeah, that's the one.' He nodded, all smug now. 'Ashbury Falls.'

Fuck! Why would Astrid go there without telling him? Why not mention it that day when they were out together? What possible reason could she have to keep it a secret? Unless...

Dad.

No-no-no-no-no-no. He needed a car and he needed one now.

'You coming to dinner with us? Larsson's chosen some—'

Blake was already racing away.

'I guess that'll be a no, then,' V muttered into his fresh drink. 'Bloody women, they're more trouble than they're worth.'

This one wasn't... and he didn't want her within a mile of that man without him there to protect her.

25

Thank the lord for credit cards!

Astrid winced as she swiped to pay her cab driver. Either the guy had taken the concierge team at their word when they'd said money was no object, or cabs were genuinely expensive in this part of the world.

'You sure this is the right place?' he said to her, leaning over the steering wheel to eye the fizzing neon sign over the rundown joint. Crow Bar. How lovely.

Astrid checked the address Sissi had sent.

'Yup, this is the one. Thanks.'

'Want me to wait for you?'

At those prices?!

Then again, how would she get back? The town was in the middle of nowhere. Chances of her getting another ride back to civilisation that night were zero. Though worst-case scenario she could crash at Sissi's and get a ride in the morning.

'I'm good, thanks.'

She stepped out into the freezing night air and the cab pulled away, its tyres crunching over the gravel as the thrum of rock music reverberated through the windowless walls before her. Her kind of tunes. That was something at least...

She looked this way and that; it really was one street, the residential homes blending with the local amenities – a small playground, a tiny school, a grocery store, and a gas station. Before her, the one bar, with its rough no-nonsense exterior, and behind her, Sissi's diner. A typical American joint with its candy colours, chrome exterior and great big windows. What a contrast. Heaven and hell facing off against one another and she stepped towards her fellow avenging angel on instinct.

To see Sissi, to sneak a confidence-boosting hug...

But the diner looked busy which meant her friend was busy and she'd already done enough phoning Astrid in. She didn't need to be involved in this as well as everything else.

She jumped as the door to the bar slammed open.

'Sorry sweetheart, didn't mean to spook ya!' A grey-haired rocker rolled out, his smile friendly enough, the biker badge on his back as he swung his leg over his Harley, less so. Was he seriously going to ride that in *this* weather? With those fumes coming off him?

'You lost?'

She shook her head and he gave a laugh, revving his engine and making her startle.

'If I was you, I'd carry on walking; they'll eat you alive in there.'

Great. Just what her jiggly nerves needed to hear.

'I'll keep that in mind, thanks.'

He held her gaze as he backed his bike out, curiosity rather than concern creasing up his brow and then he was off, his words hanging heavy in the petrol infused air.

Don't listen to him, Sinclair.

This was small town Massachusetts. What was the worst that could happen?

You're the one about to confront the man who terrorised his family for almost two decades...

But she had witnesses, plenty of witnesses judging by the noise, and since when had she been too afraid to get the story? Never.

Tightening her cashmere coat, she reached for the door and—

'Astrid!'

Sissi...?

She spun on her heel to find her friend running down the steps of the diner, tugging a jacket over her pink checkered uniform. 'Wait up!'

'Honey, what are you doing?' she hollered over a passing truck. 'You're supposed to be working!'

'This is more important,' she said, racing across the road, straight into Astrid's arms and they hugged each other tight.

'It's so good to see you, Sissi.'

'And you, but if you think I'm letting you go in there without me, you've got another thing coming. They'll take one look at you in this utterly fabulous coat and eat you alive.'

'But Sissi—'

'No buts, you'll need me to translate your fancy accent.'

'My fancy—'

'Just kidding, come on.' She looped her arm through Astrid's and tugged her inside.

The second the door swung closed, every head turned their way. From the men at the bar, to those mid-game at the pool table, to those sitting in the booths against the walls. *Shit.*

Her nose wrinkled. What was that smell? Beer, sweat and

something indescribable. Age-old tobacco? And *not* the kind you'd stick in your reed diffuser.

She blinked, her eyes adjusting from the dark outside to the neon tinge within as she plastered on a smile. 'Bloody hell, Sissi,' she said under her breath, 'this place is—'

'A whole 'nother level, I know.'

The place wasn't small but the sticker-clad walls and low lighting made it feel tiny. Not to mention the narrowed gazes making her want to shrink into the floor.

Sienna strode towards the bar where three lone individuals sat, seasoned regulars judging by the way they seemed to blend into the wood.

'Hey Boots!' Sienna called out, seemingly to no one, and a guy appeared from the back. Grey hair, fuzzy beard, twinkling eyes.

'Sienna, doll, to what do we owe this pleasure?'

She gave him an easy smile that took the edge off Astrid's nerves, particularly as one of the seasoned regulars was currently giving her a snarl... or was that supposed to be a smile?

'I was looking for—'

'Well well well, look what the cat dragged in...'

A man rose up from a darkened booth, his black hair slicked back, its sheen making it hard to tell if it was grey at the temples or blue from the glowing Coors sign overhead. He was tall, broad, with a jaw as chiselled as his boys, and cheekbones just as high. Of course he would be handsome.

Take James Bond, stick him in biker gear and age him by thirty years and this man was him. Though most of that ageing came from the bottom of a beer bottle, she'd warrant.

'Take a wrong turn, Miss Prim?'

'Save the sarcasm for someone who cares, Rick,' Sissi threw back. 'My friend here wants to talk to you.'

He came a step closer, his glassy blue eyes narrowing into suspicious slits as he turned them on Astrid and gave her a thorough once-over that made her shiver.

'Well, why didn't you say so?' His dark brows twitched up and he ran his tongue over his lips. 'Walk this way, baby doll. I've always got time to talk to a pretty face.'

Oh, fuck. She felt the tension in Sissi ripple through her arm. They stepped forward as one and he rocked his beer bottle at them. 'Ah-ah, not you, Miss Prim, you can sort a round of drinks.'

'Carter, I don't want no trouble,' Boots said, his voice low in warning.

'Trouble?' Rick gave him a grin, his hands raised. 'Who said anything about trouble? Sounds like we're going to have a nice chat and a drink, right, baby doll? Gotta say, I'm curious to hear what about though.'

Astrid gave Sissi a nod. She had this. In fact, the more unsavoury he was, the better she felt. Because finding a broken man and making him relive the horror he'd inflicted would've have sucked. This guy however...

'What can I get you?' Sissi asked her.

'I'll have a Johnnie Walker neat.' More to warm herself up than to balance the nerves.

'A *real* drink.' He arched a brow. 'I like this one. I'll have the same, now hurry along little miss...'

Sissi fired her a subtle eye roll and walked off.

'Mick, Tommy, shift it!' Rick blurted with a flick of the wrist. 'I've got company.'

Two guys eased out of the booth and slunk off to the juke box in the corner as Astrid shrugged off her coat and took their place, careful to use up the whole bench so Rick would have to sit opposite her.

'So, what can a stunner like you need from me?' He pressed

his bottle into the table as he leaned back in his seat, eyes glittering. 'Because I have ideas, sweetheart...'

'I'm a journalist.'

He drew his mouth back to one side. 'That figures.' He gave her another one of those invasive once-overs that left her skin crawling. 'And how can I help?'

She entwined her fingers on the tabletop, leaned forward just enough to show no fear.

'I'm working on an article about the Titan Twins.'

He barely batted an eyelid, it was his jaw that gave him away, pulsing with the clench of his teeth. He raised his beer to his lips, took a swig.

'Of course you are.'

Sissi arrived with the drinks, her cautious gaze sweeping between them as she placed them down.

'Thanks, love.'

'Yeah, thanks love,' he mimicked, a lewd look in his eyes as they flicked up to Sissi and back to her again.

'And what exactly do you want from me?'

She swallowed the distaste in her mouth, waited for Sissi to take a seat far enough away that her friend wouldn't have to endure any more of his 'charm' then threw her drink back in one. Her eyes fixed in his as she slammed her glass down and stated very clearly, 'No bullshit that's for sure.'

'Then you've come to the right place.' Respect glinted in his gaze as he raised his whisky in salute and downed it with a satisfied hiss. 'Ah, that is good.'

'You're a whisky man?'

'I'm an any-kind-of-drink man, but I guess you've probably heard that already.'

She tilted her head. 'I have.'

'What else have you heard?'

'I'm not interested in repeating back hearsay, Mr Carter, I want to hear your side of things. I want to hear what it was like bringing kids up in Ashbury Falls. I want to hear about your family life, before you all parted ways. I want to hear how it affected you.'

He gave a derisive laugh. 'Oh, you're good. Very good. You really wanna hear my side?'

Something in his eyes set her teeth on edge.

'That's what I said,' she forced out, trying to ignore the wriggle in her gut that said maybe, just maybe, he was a source too far for her article.

He leaned into the table, his hands too close for comfort as he planted them in fists before hers. 'Pull the other one, sugar; you want to condemn me like the rest of them and I'm gonna be honest with you, I couldn't give a fuck.'

She winced.

'Not what you were expecting? You think you're the first person to hunt me down and ask me shit?'

'I want to hear about your life, your family, *you*. Your story, no judgement.'

'There's one problem with that, sweetheart.'

'And what's that?'

'I remember jack shit from those days.'

'Because you choose not to remember or—'

He leaned into her space and Sissi on her periphery leaned with him. 'Because I'm a drunk. Once a drunk, always a drunk, like my father before me and his father before him; you wanna put that in your goddam article, be my guest.'

'People can change, if they choose to. People can—'

'And now you sound like my ex-wife. How is Cynthia? Still running her mouth off while running around after them boys like they're the only people in her world?'

He was jealous, he was fucking jealous of his own children. Not only that, he was playing the victim, all hard done by. She gritted her teeth. Losing her shit was never the way to go, but this man, he got under her skin. And she knew why.

For the first time in her life, she'd let her personal feelings get in the way of her job. Because she wasn't sat here as a journalist getting the story now, she was sat here as Blake's girl.

And while that truth bomb detonated inside her, she forced her focus on the man before her, the man who'd given his son his looks, but sod all else.

'You know what, Mr Carter—'

The door to the bar flew open, an icy gust invading with it. Awareness prickled through Astrid's body, silencing her words and firing up her skin.

She didn't need to look to know who'd just walked in.

The mood in the bar turned brittle, the hum of voices lowering as heads turned, everyone sensing what she did – trouble.

Oh God.

* * *

Blake's laser-sharp gaze cut through the bar, landing squarely on Astrid and his father. He didn't know whether to sweep her into his arms or tear a strip off her for being so bloody stupid. Both. *Definitely* both.

His father blinked, blinked again. '*Blake?*'

He hadn't seen his dad in person since the day he'd left him on the floor. Aiden had though. Multiple times over the years. And only when the scumbag had wanted something. Money. Contacts. Fame. Ugh.

Seeing him now, seeing what the years had done to him,

seeing him *this* close to the woman he'd come to care for more than life itself...

His fingers curled into his palms. Anger. Hurt. Hatred. Disgust. It all rolled through him as Ugly Kid Joe's 'Cats in the Cradle' spilled into the heavy silence – someone up there had a sick sense of humour. Or not, as he spied the familiar faces at the juke box.

'Blake?'

It was Astrid this time and he followed the sweet sound of her voice, met her gaze with a ragged breath. 'Are you done here?'

'All these years and you're not even going to say hello?' his father sneered.

'Astrid?' he prompted, not even glancing his way.

She licked her lips, her honeyed eyes wide, her vulnerability screaming at him to get her out. 'I—'

'Well fuck me, you see this, *this* is my boy. Not seen him for a decade and he doesn't even have the decency to say hello to his old man. And you wonder what drove me to drink, what drove me to—'

'What, Dad? Beat the shit out of us all?'

His father laughed, the sound as evil as he looked. 'So you do still have that mouth on you.'

'Blake, please...' Astrid got to her feet, easing her body between him and his father. He knew what she was doing, she was talking him down, urging him to ignore the man behind her.

'Yes, Blake, *please*, why not take a seat? We can tell Astrid just how much a chip off the old block you are. It'll make for a great twist in her article. What do you say, doll? You like the sound of that, because believe you me, you think I'm bad? This guy left me for dead.'

Blake's gut iced over. 'That's not true.'

'No? Think you'll find the paramedics thought otherwise.'

'Blake, don't listen to him. Come on.' She shrugged on her coat. 'I shouldn't have come. I'm sorry. Please. Let's go.'

She'd got one thing right. She shouldn't have. But now his feet were rooted into the wooden boards, his eyes planted on his father's sneer.

'They wouldn't have even got to you if I hadn't called them.'

'Bet you wished you hadn't bothered.'

She pulled on his arm, but he wasn't done.

'It would make you feel better for me to say "yes", wouldn't it? To paint me as bad as you. But I'm not. I've spent the last ten years fighting you. And I'm done with it. I'm not you. I'm nothing like you. And for the first time in my life, I can truly see that.'

His father flinched, Blake's words landing harder than his fist ever could, and then he turned away. Wrapping his arm around Astrid's waist, he led her to the door.

'See you in another ten years, son.'

'Not if I can help it,' he murmured under his breath.

Getting the last word should have made him feel better. It didn't. As he pushed out into the cold night air and unlocked the truck, his relief at seeing her waned in the face of what could have gone wrong.

They were in the middle of nowhere for fuck's sake. Anything could have happened, and she knew no one. Had no support. No protection. No nothing.

And it would've been his fault too.

'Get in the truck, Astrid.'

Blake ground the command out through his teeth; he couldn't look at her now without feeling like he might puke. He rounded the vehicle and pulled open the driver's door. But she hadn't moved.

'Astrid—'

'I had to see him, Blake.'

'*Had* to?' he shot back at her. 'Not enough that you got all the gory details from us, you just *had* to see the man himself.'

'Yes.' She met his gaze head on.

He gave a harsh scoff, steam wafting up into the freezing air. 'What was it? Morbid curiosity? Didn't believe he could be as bad as all that? Or do you just like to scare the shit out of me by putting yourself in harm's way?'

* * *

'I—'

Astrid's words stole away as she realised it wasn't fury that she saw blazing back at her, but fear. Fear over her.

'I'm a journalist, Blake, this is what I do.'

'Putting yourself in harm's way isn't work, it's reckless and it's stupid!'

She gave a tremulous smile. 'You put yourself in harm's way on the ice all the time.'

'Don't make light of this.'

'I'm not. But this is my job, and like it or not, he is a part of your story.'

He swung the door closed and strode up to her, the intensity in his gaze leaving her breathless. 'Then *why* didn't you tell me you were coming here?'

'Because I knew you wouldn't like it.'

'Hell, I would have brought you!' He raked an unsteady hand through his hair. 'If it was what you really wanted to do, *I* would have brought you.'

She shook her head. 'You hate it here.'

'I don't hate it here, I hate him, it's different.'

'You know I've been trying to track him down, you knew it was a possibility.'

'And you should have fucking told me.'

'What difference would it have made?'

'It would've made all the difference!' He slammed his chest with his fist. '*I* would have been here to protect you.'

'*Protect* me?'

'Yes!'

'I don't need you to protect me.'

'Yes, you fucking do.'

Steel shot through Astrid's spine. 'I've been doing this job for years; you think your father is the worst I've encountered? I look out for myself, Blake. I don't need a man to hold my hand. Not now. Not ever.'

Something flickered in his eyes, pain, like she'd lanced him with her words. But it was true. It had always been that way, and it would continue to be that way, and she'd been pretty bloody clear about it up until now. Until him!

'Yeah, and what if you'd pressed the same buttons we did as kids, what if you'd made him snap, you never saw what I saw...' He choked on his own words. 'And the thought that you... out here, where you know no one...'

No one. Only she did. She knew Sissi. Had felt safe because of Sissi. Her friend's knowledge of the town and the people. But he couldn't know that because he didn't know about Sissi. And that was on her, 100 per cent, her.

'It didn't come to that,' she whispered, her deceit rolling through her, stealing her strength, her rigidity...

'But what if it *had*?' He reached out and gripped her arms. '*Christ*, Astrid, if something happened to you, I—'

'Let her go!' Sienna launched herself out of the bar, door swinging, eyes wild as she took in Blake's fierce grip.

'Sissi, it's okay,' Astrid hurried out.

'Sissi?' Blake's grasp weakened, his head turning as Astrid stiffened, realising her mistake to late. '*Sienna?*'

'If you want to be angry with anyone, Blake, be angry with me,' her friend implored. 'I was the one who told her he was here.'

'*You?*'

26

'*You're* Sissi?'

Blake couldn't believe it. The blonde woman before him with the big blue eyes giving a nervous nod was none other than Sienna Mastrangelo, his brother's ex. The same woman Astrid had been speaking to from the very first day they'd met. The same woman Astrid had claimed was a *friend*.

'Sissi knew I wanted to speak to him,' Astrid said, trying to tug his focus back to her, but hell, he didn't give a shit about his father now. How could these two know each other? How could they be *friends*?

'Does she know? Do you know?' he said, spinning back to Astrid. '*Who* she is? Her connection to my brother?'

Astrid's gaze flicked to Sienna behind him. 'I'm so sorry, Sissi.'

'What are you apologising to her for?' He was gonna freaking puke, his gut rebelling as he tightened his hold on her, feeling her slip from his grasp even though she was very much still there. 'What the fuck is going on, Astrid? You gave me the impression you hadn't been here before, that you hadn't met anyone here, and suddenly your friend rocks up and she's my brother's ex!'

But her gaze didn't shift from Sissi. 'I have to tell him the truth.'

'What *truth*?' he blurted.

She swept her tongue over her lips, her nerves putting him further on edge as her eyes finally came back to his.

'Did you come here before you met us? Did you dish the dirt with the locals, meet Sienna and...'

His voice trailed off at the shake of her head.

'Then *what*?'

'Hey Mastrangelo!' The door to the diner across the way opened and a dude leaned out. 'Hurry up and say goodbye to that friend of yours, I've got customers waiting to be served.'

The door swung closed and Astrid's stricken gaze went back to Sissi. *For crying out loud*, he was the one needing answers.

'It's okay, Sissi, I've got this.'

'Are you sure?'

He turned to look at the girl he hadn't seen in years... not since the night he'd kept her company after he'd found her father drunk and messed up in this exact same spot. Taken him home and stayed with her until he could be sure she was safe because he didn't trust dads at the best of times. Drunk dads even more so. But none of that explained why she was looking at Astrid like she would dive between them at any moment and separate them. With force if she had to.

'I'm not going to hurt her if that's what you're thinking?'

Sienna met his gaze, her own glistening in the neon glow coming off the bar. 'This isn't her fault, okay. It's mine. And I'm sorry you got caught up in it.'

How the hell could it be her fault? It was Astrid's article. His story.

Then she looked back to Astrid. 'You know where I am.'

Astrid nodded and with one last hesitant glance, Sienna dashed across the road, disappearing into the diner as the air fell silent once more, the music from the bar and the occasional vehicle the only sound. Until her teeth started to chatter and his nerves shattered with it. 'Get in the truck.'

'You can't drive like this.'

'I'm not suggesting driving anywhere. I want answers but not while we're both freezing to death out here.'

He headed to the driver's door and looked back at her unmoving form. 'Or do you want to stay here?'

She moved without meeting his gaze, joining him inside the cabin as he started the engine and set the heaters to high.

'Where did you get the truck?' She was staring at the dash as she said it, her hands twisting in her lap.

'A guy staying at the hotel loaned it to me.'

'Really? That takes some trust.'

'Money, more like.'

Her eyes shot to his.

'What did you expect, Astrid? You leave me while I'm sleeping, the next thing I know V tells me you're heading to Ashbury Falls and I knew it was to see him. *Dad.* I had no idea you knew anyone else here. So that either makes me naïve, or you dishonest, which one is it to be?'

'You're not naïve...'

'Then why didn't you say you'd been here before, that you'd met people—'

'I haven't been here before.'

'But you know Sienna?'

'Yes,' she whispered. 'I met Sissi, Sienna, before Christmas. In Chicago. Our flights were grounded, and we got talking.'

His chest tightened. 'Quite the coincidence.'

'It's not a coincidence.'

Though he already knew it wasn't... he just didn't know how to connect the dots. And Astrid looked so pale. Fragile and pale. He could only imagine the worst and even then, it made no sense.

'So why don't you explain what it's like before I go out of my mind trying to figure it out?'

* * *

Telling Blake the story of Chicago was the hardest tale Astrid had ever told. The judgement in his gaze, the shock and the... she swallowed... disgust.

Numerous times she had to stop and gather her thoughts, trying to find the right words to justify their actions, but they never seemed enough.

'You have to understand, we were hurting.'

'And you think that makes it okay?'

She flinched. 'No.'

'You didn't even *love* Chase.'

'I trusted him though. I thought I knew all there was to know. But a wife...'

'You just told me he was getting divorced, that Bella says his wife rocked up and purposefully used you to get to him. You let her manipulate you.'

'I know. But he didn't come after me, he didn't even try to explain... he let me think the worst of myself for months. I'd wake with the vision of his wife still locked in my head and want to be sick. It was like everything I hated about my past creeping into my present. I wasn't just angry at Chase, I was angry at my father. The two of them just merged into this one hateful being. And I couldn't get revenge on my father, not without dragging my mother through the hell of her past, and so...'

His eyes raked over her face. 'You did the next best thing.'

'Yes.' Her shoulders eased from around her ears, the idea that he might get it on some level, that he might not like it, but he might understand and not hate her for it giving her hope. 'Meeting them in that airport, talking about our experiences, sharing the pain and wanting to fix it for each other. It felt like a way to gain some closure over the past. Nothing too sinister, or serious, just a little messing—'

'You fucked with Chase's career, Astrid.'

She flinched again. 'I know. I know. But Bella is doing everything she can to fix it. And she will. I know she will.'

'And her ex in Cornwall with his houseguest Paige, that's seriously twisted. Having feelings for the guy she's been...' He shook his head, staring blindly through the windscreen.

'Paige is dealing with it.'

'While her ex... what's he getting?'

Fire licked through her, fortifying her defences. 'There can be *no* justification for what Paige's ex did to her. I'm only sorry we don't have the stomach to carry out tit for tat. The man deserves to have his dignity stripped entirely for what he did to her.'

'I take it Sienna's still working on him?'

She nodded as silence fell between them, the only sound the truck's motor turning over...

'So,' he said quietly. 'What was I, Astrid? Collateral damage?'

'No, Blake! No! That wasn't...'

His tormented gaze sealed up her throat.

'You wanted to give him a taste of his own medicine. He broke Sienna's heart, so you came to break his. That explains the kiss, the clothes...' His chilling smile sent ice through her veins.

'It was all for him, wasn't it? You were trying to get your hooks into him so you could be the one to walk away?'

Her mouth opened and closed. Because she couldn't lie to him. And she couldn't admit the truth.

He gave a soft scoff. 'And when you realised he wasn't falling for it, you what, tried to use me to make him jealous? Only he wasn't, was he? He was pushing us together.' He laughed, the sound cutting right through her. 'That must have really put a spanner in the works.'

'No, it didn't, it wasn't – wasn't like that.'

'Of course it fucking was. But to sleep with me several times over...' his voice cracked. 'You even had me *believing* all this stuff, you made feel good enough, worthy of... I'm such a fucking idiot.'

'Don't say that!' She reached out and he reared back.

'Don't. Don't touch me. Tell me you weren't trying to lure Aiden in. Tell me you weren't trying to break him like he broke Sienna.'

She couldn't. It hurt like hell, but she refused to lie to him.

And then his head snapped up, eyes wide. 'You messed with his tan, didn't you? That was no accident or misapplication, you fucked with it. Just like your friends fucked with...' He shook his head as her face gave her guilt away. 'You could have cost us the game!'

'I didn't know it would go to his head as bad as all that, that he'd...'

'Freak out?'

'You were laughing and goading him just as much as all the rest...'

'Fuck, I was.' He gave a cold laugh. 'You must have loved that. A dim-witted accomplice yet again.'

'No, it really wasn't like that. You have—'

'It was *exactly* like that, and more fool me for falling for it.' He punched the steering wheel, angry at himself now too. 'Get out of the truck.'

'Blake, *please*, let me explain. It's how it all started out, yes, but it's—'

'I'm done with your stories, Astrid. You can keep your fabricated article, too.'

'The article is real, I'm not lying about it.'

'No, you just lied about everything else.'

'I didn't, Blake. Everything I've told you since the day I met you is the truth. I just...'

'You just?'

'I just never told you about this. But I was going to. I just needed to speak to Sissi. I needed her to understand what I was doing first. I wanted to tell her about you, about us. I wanted to tell her that Aiden was a good man, that leaving her wasn't his fault, th—'

'No,' he scoffed. 'It was mine.'

'It wasn't your fault either.'

'Save the act, Astrid.' He leaned across her, his arm hot against her front as he shoved open her door. 'We're done here.'

'Blake, *please*...'

'You can tell Sienna that you got what you came for. She wanted to break the man responsible for her heartbreak. Well, she got him. Aiden left because of me. Sienna was hurt because of me. Karma complete. Now get out of the truck before I have to lift you out.'

Karma complete? What was he saying? She couldn't break his heart, because to break his heart he'd have to...

'If you're worried about your flight home, don't be. Just keep your distance and we'll be fine. But tonight, I don't want to breathe the same air as you.'

Pain tore through her. No, he didn't love her, he loathed her. Just like she'd loathed Chase, only worse. So much worse.

'Your partner in crime can put you up and make sure you get back to the hotel safe. I want nothing more to do with you.'

'Blake, please...' It was inaudible, her body lacking the strength for sound. It hurt to think, to breathe, to move—

'Go, Astrid.'

She gave him one last pleading look, but his eyes were pinned straight ahead, his jaw set like steel. He wasn't listening any more, he was shutting her out. Behaving like the man she'd met that very first day, playing offence and defence, fighting for his career. Bitter. Angry.

Only this time, she was the one who'd fired the shots, and she couldn't hate herself more.

For an award-winning journalist, an expert in words, she was lost for them now. The one thing she wanted to say, she didn't trust herself to admit. Nor did she trust him enough to hear it and not laugh in her face. So she stepped out into the cold, numb to everything but him.

'I'm sorry.'

Her words were snatched away by the bitter wind, the slam of the truck door punctuating the finality of it all. And hunching her shoulders against the cold inside and out, she did what he'd told her to do, she ran to Sissi, needing her friends now more than ever. She felt his eyes on her the whole way though, because of course Blake wouldn't leave until he knew she was safe.

He hated her but he was still protecting her.

And she deserved none of it.

Sissi launched across the diner as Astrid pushed through the doors, her arms wrapping around her as Astrid listened to the truck screeching away and then she crumbled, sinking into Sissi with a sob.

'It's okay, honey,' Sissi murmured. 'It's okay...'

'No, nothing's okay,' she cried. 'I don't think anything will be okay again.'

Because she knew in that moment Blake wasn't alone.

She was broken. She had torn her own heart in two. And she had no idea how to piece it back together again. Not without the man to whom she had given it to...

And what kind of karma was that?

Gorging on her own Just Desserts, that's what.

* * *

'You're going to have to tell him how you feel,' Sissi said, topping up her wine glass.

They'd been talking for hours. Ever since Sissi's shift had ended and they'd rolled home to her tiny two-up two-down, Astrid had been spilling her heart out. Her messed-up feelings for Blake. Her conflict over Aiden. The sex. *All* the sex. And the karma.

'He's never gonna let me anywhere near him.'

'You're one of the most resourceful women I know, you'll find a way.'

'I barely trust myself to feel it let alone tell him it.'

'Just because you've never fallen in love before, it doesn't mean you don't know it when you feel it. I *know* it. And I see it in you.'

'I really do love him, don't I?' Astrid buried her head in her hands. 'How could I have been so stupid, so careless...'

'Love has a will of its own.'

'But Blake, of *all* people? He's supposed to be like me; he doesn't do relationships, he doesn't fall in love...'

'It's probably why you were so drawn to him in the first place... he could never let you down like your father did your mother because he'd never lie to you about the future in the first place.'

Astrid lifted her head. 'I can't believe you remember all that stuff.'

'Of course I remember, I'm your friend, one of your best. I listen. We all knew it was a risk with Blake; you like a bad boy because on the face of it, they're nothing like your dad.'

It was true. Her father was so clean cut, so perfect on the outside, quick to make friends and influence people, quick to tell his mother what she wanted to hear and snatch it away when it suited him. 'Christ, I'm a psychologist's wet dream.'

Sienna chugged on her wine. 'Welcome to the club.'

She squinted at her. 'You too?'

'Not the bad boys, but definitely the daddy issues. My father was so flaky after Mom died, he just stopped showing up, and then along came Aiden. So good, so kind, so dependable... until he wasn't.'

Astrid opened her mouth to bat for him anew, but Sissi cut her off. 'Don't, Astrid. I know what you're saying. I hear it. But that man, he doesn't know, he *can't* know, because he never let me tell him.' She covered her stomach with her palm, the action as telling as the unshed tears in her eyes. 'And I can't forgive him for that.'

'But he cared, Sissi, and I'm convinced he still does, and if I could tell you what happened that night to drive him away I would, but I swore I wouldn't tell a soul.'

'It wouldn't make any difference.'

'But Blake feels responsible, love. He believes he gave Aiden no choice but to flee, to choose his family over...'

'Me?'

'Yes. But if you could speak to him, if you could hear it from him, you would see—'

She choked on her wine. 'Absolutely not. It's hard enough seeing him everywhere I go. But you, you have a chance to tell Blake how you feel. If I'd had the means to hunt Aiden down and make him listen to me about our baby, I'd have done it.'

Astrid didn't doubt it and she reached out and squeezed her hand. 'I know.'

'Blake wouldn't be this hurt if he didn't care about you.'

'You didn't see his face, Sissi. He hates me.'

'Love and hate, there's a reason why they call it a fine line. Take it from someone who knows.'

'He isn't a bad boy either.'

'If he was, you wouldn't have fallen so hard for him. If he was, I'd be urging you to run the other way. But he's not, honey, and he deserves to know how you truly feel. If he knows you're not faking it, then maybe there's a chance you can put all this behind you and look to the future.'

'I think it's too late for that.'

'Shouldn't you let him be the judge?'

Astrid blinked at her friend. Was she right? Could she lay her heart on the line? For the first time in her life, could she tell a man she loved them and risk having it thrown back in her face?

'What if he rejects me all over again?'

'Would it hurt any more than it does now?'

She shook her head. She couldn't imagine anything hurting more than this.

27

'Blake?'

Aiden caught him up in the tunnel as the distant roar of the crowd rose into a deafening crescendo. The Penguins had hit the ice...

'What is it?' he ground out, his sights fixed on the rear of Larsson's helmet before him. He'd done a damn good job avoiding any kind of conversation since his return to the hotel the night before. The last thing he wanted was to shoot the breeze with his brother now. Not when he was this close to oblivion.

And not when he knew she was here somewhere, too close to breathe easy, let alone speak straight.

'Rumour has it Zorro is after you, so watch your back out there, yeah?'

'I always watch my back.'

'I know you do, but ever since that illegal check last—'

'He made it illegal, not me.'

'Not what he cares about.'

'Not what I care about right now either. He can talk smack all he likes, I'm ready for him.'

Blake ducked around Larsson, using the giant Swede as a buffer.

Get the message, bro.

He just wanted to play hockey. Once he got on the ice, he could quit thinking. He could quit feeling. He could just be. Because everything would be about the game. Just as it always had been. Just as it should be.

'Blake?' His brother came up alongside him again, his concerned gaze boring through their visors. 'What's going on?'

'Nothing's going on. Just let me get out there and give me some peace.'

He launched ahead of him onto the ice, thrusting his stick into the air and relishing the chants and the cheers as he swept around like a coiled spring unleashed. This was where he was at home. Not some swanky flat in the city and not in the arms of some broad who he'd been fool enough to let get close.

V chuckled as he swept past him. 'God help Zorro is all I can say.'

Blake grunted. *Too right.*

Zorro clocked him, their gazes colliding across the ice, the guy's sneer like striking a match over gasoline.

Bring it on, buddy.

Bring. It. On.

* * *

Astrid's fingers hovered near her lips as the opening minutes unfolded at breakneck speed. The slash of skates on the ice and rattle of the boards charged the erratic thud of her heart.

She'd seen them play multiple times over, but never like this.

Blake had *never* been like this. He wasn't just out to win the game. He was out for blood. And the opposition knew it.

Her eyes stung as she stayed glued to him, each near miss and crushing hit making her wince, her body pulsing with empathic pain.

'Fury's back,' Harry muttered under his breath from his seat on the bench before her.

'Zorro's goading him,' Jake, the rookie beside him, said.

'Zorro?'

They both turned to look at her.

'Number 21,' Harry explained. 'He's an enforcer for the opposition.'

'I thought enforcers were no longer a thing.'

'Once an enforcer, always an enforcer...'

'Especially when they've got unfinished beef,' Jake added.

'Unfinished beef?' she repeated, fear stealing her voice as her eyes found the other guy on the ice and her heart sank into her toes, her stomach with it. 'He's...' She swallowed. 'Huge.'

'Don't worry, Foxy, Fury knows what he's about.'

She nodded and eased back into hiding, using their heavily padded bodies as a shield. She knew Blake didn't want to see her and she was doing her best to remain 'unseen', all the while willing the team to victory, and willing Blake to stay safe.

He *looked* like he knew exactly what he was doing, his skill and determination making Zorro's attempts to throw him off seem more desperate by the second. But with the game moving at this speed, things could change in a nanosecond. And her straining eyes knew it. Her beating heart too.

Two periods sped past, the pace of the game sending her dizzy as she struggled to catch her breath. The players were here there and everywhere, the puck flying at lightning speed. They were locked in a brutal stalemate, the rivalry on the ice reaching fever pitch. The rivalry between Blake and Zorro even more so. Checks turned sharper, glances grew more venomous, and the crowd could feel the confrontation building.

Every pass he made, every hit, every sharp turn pulled her further and further forward. *Please be safe, please be safe.* Hell, she didn't even care if they won any more, she just wanted him to be okay.

Blake had the puck, Zorro was bearing down, the speed and ferocity making her sick. She edged forward, her hand lifting to her mouth and then time seemed to slow as Blake's gaze lifted, collided with hers – *crack!*

One second, he was there, looking right at her. The next he was gone. Taken out by another player. The sickening impact of his body hitting the boards echoed through the arena as the crowd gasped and he went down hard. *No, God, no!*

Astrid shot to her feet, her blood running cold as the ref's whistle pierced the air. Coach cursed, their trainer launched onto the ice, his teammates circled as shouts ran out. He was bleeding. There was blood. She could see it seeping into the ice.

'He'll be alright,' Harry told her. 'He'll tape an aspirin to it and be back out there in no time.'

'Or not,' Jake piped up as Blake failed to move. 'Shit.'

All the players on the bench rose, some breaking onto the ice and heading straight for the player who'd blindsided Blake. Others headed for Blake. Her heart slammed painfully in her chest. She couldn't see him for the team now crowding around as the ref escorted the offensive player off to the box, saving him from a beating as much as penalising him.

Please be okay, please be okay, please be okay.

Eyes straining, heart too, she watched as a stretcher appeared and she couldn't take it any more, she clambered over the bench, heading for the ice when at last, the team parted. A cheer rippled through the crowd, and she stilled. He was moving. Blood marred his cheek, but he was moving – refusing the stretcher as Aiden and Larsson each took an arm. Together, they hauled him to his feet and helped him off the ice. Head bent, every step slow, deliberate, stiff with pain...

This was all her fault. She'd done this. She'd thrown his attention and now...

'Go after him, Foxy.' Harry appeared at her side. 'He'd sure as shit prefer to see you over anyone else right now.'

He wouldn't, but how could she not...?

* * *

'Get the hell off me, doc. I'm good.'

'You're not fucking good.' His brother pushed him back on the bed. 'And you're not going back out there like this.'

He was taped up, glued up, dosed up – he could play. The longer he had off the ice, the sooner he'd seize up and then he'd be fucked. But right now...

'It's not happening, Blake,' Coach piped up from the doorway, arms folded across his chest. 'The ice is cleared, Aiden. It's time to get back in the game.'

'For fuck's sake,' Blake growled. 'This is bullshit, I—'

'Blake!'

That voice, *that* woman... Tension shot through his frame, pain with it, and he clutched an ice pack to his battered ribs, fully aware of what hurt more.

'For the love of God, keep her away from—'

Astrid flew into the room, a security guard hot on her tail. 'She says she's with you?'

Aiden gave a lopsided grin. 'She sure is.' He turned back to

Blake. 'Maybe she can make you do as you're told. Watch him like a hawk, Astrid, and take no shit.'

No shit? She was the fucking reason he'd... He ground his teeth as everyone else filtered out of the room. He dragged his gaze back to her and wished he hadn't. Every fibre of his being came alive, pain be damned.

'What the hell are you doing here, Sinclair?'

She hugged her middle, her eyes shining bright in the harsh overhead lights. 'I had to come and see you for myself. I had to make sure you're okay.'

'I'm just peachy,' he said through his teeth. 'You can go.'

Please fucking go because all he wanted to do was cross the room and kiss the concern off her swollen damn lips. Had she been chewing them the entire game? And what the fuck was he doing looking at her *lips*?

They'd lied to him. Played him for a fool.

Hell, she was the reason he was stuck in here, missing the rest of the game.

Coach had told him he'd been unpredictable, reckless...

Too fucking right, he was. He'd been playing like he had something to prove. To Zorro. To himself. To *her*. That he was the hard *effing* bastard they all thought he was... until he'd become aware of her peering through the guys on the bench, his eyes finding hers of their own cursed accord and he'd realised he was fooling no one. Least of all himself.

'You're not fine...' Her voice croaked as her eyes swept over him – the glued up slit to his temple, the ice pack on his naked chest, the bruises that were already starting to shine...

'It's nothing.'

And it was nothing. Any other game, any other player they'd be back out there. But reckless wasn't in the Titans rulebook, not any more. And he'd been reckless to a fault, too pumped up wanting to forget that he'd been pushing for a fight. But he hadn't seen it coming, hadn't been prepared... all because of her.

'It doesn't look like nothing. This is all my fault.'

'Don't flatter yourself, honey.' He refused to give her the satisfaction of knowing it. 'This is Teddy's handiwork.'

'Teddy?' she spluttered.

'The guy who boarded me.'

'Teddy! He looked like a freaking grizzly!'

His mouth twisted. 'Exactly that.'

She shook her head. 'You players and your crazy names.' She took a tentative step forward. 'Does it hurt?'

'Which bit?' He pushed up off the bed, tossing the ice pack away as he stalked towards her, anger firing in his bloodstream as her concern broke through his walls, teased at his heart. He didn't *need* to feel it beat for her. What he needed was to fight. Get her to go. 'My body, my face, or what you did to me?'

'Blake, please... I didn't want to hurt you.'

'No, you wanted to hurt my brother, and you think that makes it better. That man turned his life upside down for me.'

'I know. I know what he did. And I know he's a good man. And I've tried to tell Sissi that too, but he hurt her, she's *still* hurting.'

'She isn't the only one.'

His eyes dipped to her parted lips; it had been an epic mistake coming this close to her. Her familiar scent – sugar and spice and all things nice – swirled through his senses. Her honeyed eyes clawed their way into his very soul while his groin thickened and pulsed, his need for her heightened by the adrenaline still pumping through his veins. High on the game, the impact, the fight, and her... *fuck* her.

* * *

'Blake?'

It was part gasp, part plea, because his eyes, they were telling her something else. He was angry, it was there, but more than anger, there was need. His ravaged cheek, nothing on the ravaged look in his eyes. The faint smell of menthol and male teased at her senses, the heat radiating off his half naked body, too, the power rippling beneath every muscle as he held himself still.

She only had to take a step and...

With a growl he claimed her mouth, his lips hard and punishing and everything she craved. He forced her back against the door, plundered her mouth with his tongue, stripped her of her coat, her sweater, her tee... His hands were rough upon her breasts, his mouth rougher still, but she wanted more. So much more.

'Why do I still want you so bad?' he growled, grinding his hips against her sweet spot, her leggings and his base layers doing nothing to hinder the rhythmic drill. Need driving against need as their breaths quickened and their bodies quaked.

'I don't know.' She couldn't understand it. Not after all she had done. 'But I know I want you too.'

He spun her around, backed her up against the bed as he tugged her bra straps down, freeing her breasts to the nip of his teeth.

'The door?' she blurted on a cry.

'Locked.'

He must have done it when he'd held her up against it, and *oh God*, how she wanted this. How she *needed* this.

He threw her on the bed as she kicked off her trainers, wriggling free of her leggings before pulling him back to her. His clothed need strained against her throbbing clit and then his fingers were there, slipping inside the lace – *fuck!*

Her core clenched, his deft caress making her legs fall open and her body arch back, pleasure tightening every limb as she planted her hands into the bed and begged him for more.

'*Fuck, Astrid,* you're killing me.'

Hell, he was killing her too. She didn't recognise herself in the woman she had become. A woman so utterly consumed by a man. By him.

'Please,' she cried, hooking her feet into his pants and thrusting them down his thighs, freeing his erection to the air, to her... 'I want you.'

He rolled her clit until her thighs trembled and her pants were as loud as her cries. He covered her mouth with his hand, stifling her sounds, sending her dizzy and desperate and willing him for more.

'Fuck, Astrid!' His cock bucked between them. 'I need you.'

She nodded, clawing his bruised behind and making him hiss.

'Sorry did I hurt—'

'*This* hurt I can deal with.'

He stole her breath with his fevered kiss, his cock sliding over her slick heat and she shifted position, getting him where she needed him the most and as he bucked, she sunk him in deep.

'Baby...' He gave a pained groan. 'You feel so fucking good.'

Baby. Oh, how she wanted to be his baby again. Her nails clawed into his shoulders, desperate to have him stay. Desperate to have him lose his all. Lose it all to her.

It was mindless. Uninhibited. Raw. She came around him, her body clenching him to her, her eyes shooting open to see his head rock back, his neck cording, his torso tighten as he came with a guttural cry. It was beautiful. *He* was beautiful.

He rocked forward, his shoulders undulating with his breaths that gradually steadied out with hers...

'We shouldn't have done that.'

She stiffened. They weren't the words she wanted to hear. Not the words she expected either. She stroked her hands up his sweat-slickened chest, over the goosebumps now rife across his skin and he tensed. Backed up.

'You should get cleaned up.' He tugged on his trousers and stepped away, eyes averted, hand raking through his hair.

'Blake?' She couldn't move for fear now. 'I thought...'

'You thought what? That we'd fuck and everything would be like it was before?'

She licked her lips, the sickness in her stomach making her wilt as she closed her legs and righted her bra. Yes. Yes, she had thought that. Or near enough. Not before, but in the middle. Of course she had.

'Blake, please...'

'If you're worried I'm going to tell Aiden about your sordid little scheme, you needn't. I have no intention of raking up all that shit again and hurting him in the process.'

'I wasn't thinking about that.'

'No? I don't believe you.'

She dropped to the floor and gathered up her clothing, getting dressed on autopilot as her entire focus remained on him. 'I was only thinking about you, about us...'

He gave a harsh laugh. 'There isn't an us. How can there be when it was all based on a lie?'

'It wasn't a lie. Everything I told you about me was true. I've told you more than I've ever told anyone. I've shared stuff with you I've never shared with anyone.'

She'd shared her heart...

And what about having sex without protection – you idiot!

Her eyes caught on the bed. It was hard to believe what

they'd been doing just minutes ago. The connection they'd shared, how right it had seemed.

'I'm clean if that's what you're worried about.'

Her eyes snapped to his. 'What?'

'The sex, Astrid.'

She swallowed the rising sickness. 'And me.'

She didn't think to tell him she wasn't on the pill. She'd deal with it. There had to be a twenty-four-hour pharmacy nearby and she sure as hell could do with the walk. If she missed the coach to the airport, all the better.

'Good.'

Good? Nothing was good!

She picked her coat up off the floor and shrugged it on, picked up her bag and unlocked the door.

'Astrid?'

Her heart lifted, hope soaring out of her control. 'Yes?'

'Was it worth it? All this betrayal and secrecy, just so you could get your own back.'

'I told you...'

'I know what you told me, but I don't understand how someone like you, or at least, the person I thought you were, could get caught up in a scheme like this.'

'I guess you had to be there to truly understand how it was between us. They're my girls, the sisters I never had, and I love them.'

'*Sisters?* You've known them what, two or three months?'

She held his gaze. 'I've known you for a lot less and I still...'

He stiffened, his jaw clenching shut. How could she tell him now? Open up her heart in the face of his hate. But then, how could she not when this was what she'd come here to do? What Sissi had urged her to do? To take the opportunity her friend had never had and speak the truth.

She owed it to Sissi. She owed it to herself. And more than that, she owed it to the man before her.

Taking a deep breath, she wet her lips and let it go. 'I still fell in love with you.'

He didn't blink, he didn't breathe, he said nothing.

And perhaps that was all she deserved for everything she'd done.

Absolutely nothing.

'Goodbye, Blake.'

The coach, the hotel, the flight home – they all flashed before her eyes and she couldn't do it. She couldn't be in the same space with him and not break down.

'Tell Preston I got caught up with a friend. I'll find my own way back to New York.'

She walked and then she ran, desperate to be free of his world before her own came crashing in.

Stupid, stupid girl. Loving a bad boy. Letting them in.

Only Blake wasn't a bad boy. He was good. He was kind. And she'd broken him.

She deserved to be broken in return.

Karma – it truly was a bitch.

28

'Have you read it yet?'

Aiden came striding into the living room, eyes glued to his phone as he interrupted Blake's date with the TV and New York's finest cheesecake.

'Read what?'

Blake forked up a mouthful and went back to his movie.

'Astrid's article, she sent it over this morning for us to review.'

'Oh yeah, that.' He forced the wedge of cheesecake down. 'No.'

'Why not?'

'Been busy.'

'Busy eating contraband and watching... what in the *hell* is this?'

He shrugged. 'A movie.'

Aiden clicked on the remote and choked out a laugh. 'I've seen it all now.'

'I haven't so if you don't mind...' He snatched the remote back and turned it up. Kate Hudson was doing a splendid job of lying through her teeth... though in all fairness, the lead guy was giving as good as he got. It was funny too. Much easier to laugh when it wasn't real, and it wasn't yours truly getting played.

'This has to stop.'

'I don't know what you're talking about.'

Aiden strode up to the TV and turned it off at the wall. The sudden silence was deafening. Silence meant thinking. Silence meant remembering. Silence meant reliving and his gut rolled with a pained honey gaze that looked all too genuine. Too crushed. Too...

'It's our bye week, Blake.'

He slid the half-eaten cheesecake onto the coffee table and hunched forward. 'Tell me something I don't know.'

'Usually you're lining up a party, kicking back with the team and the beers. Instead, you're in here, watching a sappy movie, and eating cheesecake. It's fucked up, man.'

It was. He was. And all because of a pretty little journo and her pretty little lies. He didn't want to read her article because he didn't want to read any more of *that*.

'Something's been off with you ever since Massachusetts and—'

'I saw Dad.'

'You *what*?' His brother stiffened. '*When*?'

'When Astrid snuck off to see him.'

'She never...' He sunk into the sofa beside him. '*Fuck*.'

'It's where I was when I missed dinner the night before the game.'

'In Ashbury Falls?'

He nodded.

'Why didn't you say anything?'

'Because I handled it.'

'Bloody hell.' His brother shook his head. 'What was he like? Dad?'

'Oh, you know...' Blake took a slug of his water, trying to wash down the distaste. 'The same class act, bottle in one hand, fist in the other...'

'He *didn't*...?'

'He wouldn't dare.'

'And you?'

'Give me some credit, bro.' Though he'd come close. But he hadn't. Because of her. She'd handled him. Made him believe he was better than his father, better than how the entire world saw him, too. And he'd lapped it up. Desperate to be better. Desperate to be the kind of man that could deserve someone like her. And it had all been an act, a ploy... 'I wouldn't give him the satisfaction.'

'I did wonder whether she'd got to him somehow.'

He glanced at his brother. 'Dad? Why?'

'The way she talks about him in the article, the way she phrases it. Much better than anything I could have said.'

He swallowed. 'How so?'

'You need to read it for yourself.'

He went back to the TV, the black screen as haunting as the noise within him. 'No.'

He sensed his brother's frown, his growing confusion. 'You *have* to read it. She wants our sign off.'

'I trust your judgement. You sign it off.'

'Blake—'

'I'm not going to read it, okay! I don't want to read what she has to say about us, about me...'

It was hard enough reliving what she'd said aloud.

'I still fell in love with you.'

His stomach twisted, the cheesecake threatening to make a return over her biggest lie. What had she been hoping for? Some kind of absolution so she could move on guilt-free? Did she honestly think he'd believe her?

'She told me she loves me.'

It came out choked and for a second, he wondered whether he'd admitted it at all and then his brother spoke. 'Astrid?'

'Who else?' he threw at him, pained, frustrated, angry, but Aiden didn't even flinch.

'Well, that explains the rest.'

'The rest of what?'

'Your mood, the article, the last couple of months.'

'It explains nothing because it's all a lie.' Not that his brother would understand. For that he'd have to tell him the full truth. Though there was only one truth that mattered in that moment. 'She can't love me.'

'Why in the hell not?'

'Because I'm a fucking mess.'

'No, you *were* a mess. Then she came along and untangled all the messy parts to you, helped you understand them, to face them, and you changed. Granted you were asking for it with the Penguins, with Zorro, but seeing Dad would have done that to the both of us.'

'It had nothing to do with Dad and everything to do with her. I couldn't get her out of my head.' He couldn't get her out of his heart either and that was the problem. Didn't matter what he knew, he still wanted her. He still... 'She isn't all you think she is, you know. She has her secrets.'

'We all have secrets, Blake.'

'Hers ain't pretty.'

Though everything she'd done, she'd done for her friends. For love and for loyalty. And she'd owned her mistakes. Much like she'd helped him to own his. Own them and move on.

'Neither are ours, but the way she handles our story, the way she handles Dad even... She's a good person and she's good for you. I think you know that deep down and it scares the life out of you. You're running the other way because accepting her love will force you to accept your own feelings for her in return.'

Was his brother right? Was he so determined to paint her in a bad light to protect himself from what he already knew?

'Read the article, Blake. Read that and tell me she doesn't mean every word she says.'

'She's a journalist, this is what she does.'

'Just read it.'

* * *

Astrid had lost track of the days. She'd allowed herself a day of wallowing in Massachusetts and then flown home and thrown herself into work. Sissi had messaged for an update, and she'd played it vague, skipping over the emergency trip to the pharmacy and playing down the emotional fallout.

There was so much going on in the world of her friends that she didn't want to offload her mess on them too and she knew that was her all over. Never showing people the worst of her for fear of losing them, but it wasn't so much a fear of losing them as it was feeling guilty for the part she had played in everyone else's problems.

Bella for Chase.

Sienna for Aiden.

Blake for her betrayal.

And Paige for not sharing her own epic blunders and making her friend feel a little better about her own. But she couldn't tell Paige without Bella, and she wasn't burdening Bella when Bella already had enough going on with Chase. It was an impossible circle she hoped to break come Friday when all her karma girls would be in the same room again, attending the pre-opening party for Chase's gallery and showing their support to Bella.

She had her disguise picked out already to avoid catching Chase's eye and she'd hopefully find the right moment to confess all face to face. Then she could move on from this whole damn mess.

Her heart though, she had a feeling that was going to take so much longer to heal...

As for the hurt she'd inflicted on Blake... she could only hope her article would go some way to helping him heal.

She'd sent it twenty-four hours ago and heard nothing. Not that she'd expected an instant response, but maybe just an acknowledgement of receipt. From Aiden at least.

She refreshed her email again, triple checking she'd sent it. Triple checking the contact details too. Refresh.

No email.

She couldn't relax until she knew. Couldn't move on to her next job either. Her life felt like it was stuck in some post-Blake limbo. Is this what Sissi had felt like after Aiden had left?

Lost. Disheartened. Alone.

Christ, she was used to being alone. But it had never felt as vacuous as this. As depressing.

She looked outside at the sleet and shivered. It was definitely time to get out of New York. She'd do the gallery visit and then she'd fly home.

Not that the weather would be much better in the UK... but Blake wouldn't be around the corner and that had to be better than this – hoping and praying he'd come knocking. He'd made his feelings clear almost a week ago and every day without him since only hammered that message home.

Her phone buzzed in her hand, a bubble with Mum

appearing for a video call. She shook off the melancholy and forced a smile.

'Hey Mum.' Tears pricked as her mum's familiar face filled the screen, her eyes so like Astrid's, sparkling with warmth as she smoothed her dark hair out of her face and peered closer at the screen.

'Oh my gosh, darling, what's wrong?'

So much for shaking off the melancholy.

'I'm okay, just that crappy time of the month.'

Which wasn't a lie. Though she had a feeling the over-whelming depression had little to do with her PMDD and every-thing to do with Blake.

'Oh darling, I wish you were here so I could give you the biggest hug and feed you sticky toffee pud.'

She gave a choked laugh. 'That does sound great.'

'Do you think you'll come home soon? John would love to spend some time with you properly. Christmas was all a bit of a blur and I miss you, love.'

'I miss you too. Things with John still good?'

'Better than good. And stop avoiding my question.'

'I wasn't, I was just—'

'Just marvelling at how long I've kept this man for...'

Her mouth twitched. 'Something like that.'

'Darling, I'm telling you, this is the one. It may have taken several wrong turns and a good few years to find him, but when you know, you know.'

She smiled. 'I'll take your word for it, Mum.'

'One day you won't have to take my word for it, you'll find it too.'

That was just it, Astrid was pretty convinced she already had, and she'd ruined it before it even had a chance.

'Oh love, I didn't mean to make you feel worse, I was only trying to say—'

'It's fine, Mum, honest. And I'll be home soon. I have a party Friday for my friend Bella and then I'll wrap things up here and fly back.'

'Oh, that would be great! I'll make sure I'm stocked up on black treacle.'

'You mean you're going to make sticky toffee with a fresh tin, rather than one from last century? I really am being spoilt.'

'That only happened once, darling, and it tasted fine.'

'Reckon we'll all be eating stuff like that come the apocalypse.'

'It'll make the cockroaches taste better.' John appeared on the call, his smile warm and engaged. 'How's the work going, Astrid?'

'It's all good, thanks.'

'Glad to hear it.'

Astrid looked at her mother and John together with fresh eyes; they really did look good together. At Christmas she'd been too busy avoiding the relationship drill and putting a smile on her doubts about them, but now...

'I'll send you my flight info when it's all—'

She broke off as the doorbell rang through the apartment. A sound she rarely heard without a warning from the doorman first.

'Sorry Mum, I need to go, someone's at the door.'

'No problem, darling. Keep your chin up and we'll see you in a couple of weeks.'

'Will do. Love you.'

'Love you too.'

She blew a kiss down the phone and hung up, pushed up off the bed and combed her fingers through her mop of hair. It was time she tried to get back to business as usual, to shake off the PMDD, Blake, *this*, and get with the real world again.

She pulled open the door to find no one there. Frowning up and down the empty hallway, she was about to close it again when she saw the bow-adorned box on the ground. *Huh*. It wasn't just any box either, it was an Xbox box...

What on earth?

She crouched down to lift it up, plucking the note off the top.

I hope this helps x

'I owe you a date and a rematch.'

Her heart leaped into her throat as Blake appeared from around the corner, a game in one hand, a shopping bag in the other, and she blinked, blinked again. Was this real? That face, those eyes...

'I have ice cream, chocolates, sweets, wine... I tried to think of everything you might need for Mr PMDD, but if I've forgotten anything, you only have to say the word and I'll get it.'

The *word*? She felt incapable of saying anything. Everything within her had turned to mush. Save for her heart, that was galloping at a million miles an hour and taking great leaps as he started to walk towards her.

'I also owe you an apology.'

'An a-apology?' she stuttered out, tightening her grip on the box when it threatened to slip from her grasp.

His nod was slow, deliberate. 'You poured your heart out to me, and I refused to listen.'

'I... I did.'

It was a statement, not a question, and as he paused before her, she felt her heart swell with the same three words: *I love you.*

'Can I come in?'

*   *   *

He feared for a moment she'd say no and tell him to go to hell. It was what he deserved for what he'd done.

And seeing her in her oversized sweats, looking so goddamn cute and vulnerable... all he wanted to do was wrap her up in his arms. Apologise until she forgave him. Start over with his own heart laid bare. But first...

She backed away from the door, her action telling him he was welcome, even if she wasn't saying it.

He walked inside and she closed the door, her eyes on the games console as she slid it onto the side table.

'I took a guess at Xbox, but if a PlayStation is more your vibe, I can get one here stat.'

Her mouth quivered into an almost smile, her voice quiet with disbelief. 'You remembered...?'

'I remember everything, Astrid. Every second, every word, every feeling.'

Everything they'd done in this hallway too when he'd been none the wiser and...

Her eyes glistened up at him, silencing his head with her pain and her sadness and fuck, he'd done that to her. 'I'm so sorry.'

'I still don't understand why you're sorry.'

'I didn't believe you. You said it, but I didn't believe you.' He tightened his grip around the items in his hands. 'I didn't dare let myself believe you.'

'I don't blame you after everything I did.'

'That's just it, it wasn't about your pact with your friends, I could blame it, but it wasn't. It was about me. I never thought someone could love me in that way. I never thought I was worthy of it. But from the very first day I met you, you tried to convince me otherwise. You *had* convinced me otherwise. I started to believe... and then when you told me the truth, it gave me an out. A reason to go back to being the man I was. Untouchable. Safe. Because believing the worst about myself, about you, meant I could avoid accepting the cold hard truth.'

'What truth?'

'That I love you, Astrid.'

Her lashes flickered over eyes that shone with his confession, but he wasn't done...

'I loved you before Massachusetts and I love you still.'

She gave a teary laugh. 'That sounds like a lyric...'

'I guess it does.'

'For a cold hard truth, that isn't cold at all...'

'No, but it is equally chilling and terrifying and exhilarating and surprising.'

'I know.'

'Because' – hope flared to life, warm within his chest – 'you feel it too?'

She nodded. 'You were my worst nightmare, my kryptonite.'

He raised a brow. 'Kryptonite?'

'A bad boy with a heart of gold. To fall in love with you knowing it could have no future... but a friend once told me that love has a will of its own and she was right.'

'Sissi?'

'Yes. And she would know.'

Because her friend still suffered now, ten years down the line. He didn't doubt it. Before Astrid he might have. But now... he couldn't imagine a day passing without thinking of the woman opposite him. Thinking of her, wanting her, loving her.

'Yeah, she would know.' He held her gaze, every fibre of his being firing with the urge to reach for her, but... 'I saw my mother this morning, I wanted to show her the article.'

'Oh…' She looked almost fearful as she crossed her arms over her front. 'What did she say?'

'She said what I said.'

'What's that?'

'That it's beautiful.'

Her eyes glistened all the more, her mouth pursing to the side. '*You* said it was *beautiful*?'

'In a more manly way, of course.'

She smiled softly. 'Of course.'

'My brother loves it too. I think my father will even appreciate the truth in it.'

'He has his demons, Blake. They're not excuses but they do exist.'

'And we all make mistakes. It's how we choose to move on from them that matters. You helped me to see that.'

'But it was all you… *You* broke the cycle, father to son.'

'Fuck, I hope so.'

'I know so,' she whispered, and he took a breath that shuddered right through him, hope blazing stronger than ever as he took a tentative step forward.

'My mother said love can go one of two ways, it can destroy you, or it can make you stronger. I want the latter, Astrid, and I want it with you. For the rest of my life, I want to be at peace with you.'

'Blake…' It came out in a rush as she met him halfway and he emptied his hands to fill them with her. Her warm body, warm lips, warm soul the balm to his own.

'I love you,' she brushed against his mouth.

'I love you too.'

'Always.'

'Forever.'

EPILOGUE
TWO MONTHS LATER…

Astrid twisted the diamond ring on her finger and held her breath. She wasn't sure when she'd been more nervous. The day she'd told Blake they were pregnant, that the emergency pill she'd taken in Springfield hadn't worked. The day they'd waited with bated breath for the baby's heartbeat to appear. Or today, waiting for her ride-or-die besties to respond to the news that she, Astrid Sinclair, was pregnant!

They'd all come together in her uncle's NYC pad to celebrate her engagement to Blake. Only Sissi knew the bonus news. Astrid had been careful to tell her alone, knowing the painful secret of her friend's miscarriage, she'd wanted to handle the news with all the love and care Sissi deserved. Bad enough that someday soon Sissi would have to come face to face with Aiden at their wedding, but to do so with her friend pregnant too... it was a lot. A lot, a lot.

But as Sissi took her hand now, her smile was all warmth and encouragement.

'I *knew* it!' Paige declared, slapping down her untouched glass of champagne. 'It's a freaking shotgun wedding!'

Astrid gave a choked laugh. 'It's really not.'

'No?'

'Sounds like a shotgun wedding to me,' Bella agreed. 'You know, you don't *need* to get married just because you're having a baby.'

'It is the twenty-first century,' Paige stressed, 'you do have a choice.'

'I know that, my loves, I do.'

'And you're sure about this?' Bella pressed.

She couldn't blame her friend for being overly cautious. After being jilted at the altar the idea of walking up it again had to fill Bella with the heebie-jeebies and not even Chase's love and Olly's reasoning could rid her of *that* horror.

'None of us can know for sure what the future holds,' Astrid said calmly. 'But I know what I want right now, and that is to be married to the man I love.'

'I'll drink to that,' said Sissi.

'But three months?' Paige murmured, her VA head doing the math. 'That means...'

Astrid nodded. 'Karma days.'

'Oh my God, love, why didn't you tell us sooner?' Bella asked, her brow creasing with concern. 'You must have been going out of your mind? You kept Blake to yourself long enough but this... I thought we'd made it clear that we're here for you. No matter what's going on in our world, you can tell us anything.'

'I know I can. I just wanted to wait for the scans and for us to be sure, and then I wanted to do it in person. And I know how it looks, believe me. The idea that I've trapped him into marriage. The press will have a field day over the headlines. The Hoe of a Hack has a particularly good ring to it.'

'Don't!' Sissi squeezed her hand. 'It's pointless thinking about any of that, they'll soon find something else to talk about.'

'True enough. Blake and his PR crew met with *Sports Illustrated* this morning to look at how best to manage the news.'

'Shouldn't you have gone?' Bella said. 'It's your area so to speak.'

'Blake thinks it would only incense me further and he's not wrong. He's taking this whole protective father, protective husband role to a whole other level. Besides, he has it handled. He's become something of a media pro with his revamped image.'

'Something he has you to thank for.'

She smiled. 'I only told the world the truth.'

'And you do look so very happy,' Sissi said softly.

'I am. Truly. Blake is too. I'm not gonna lie, the day I took the pregnancy test, I was all over the place, but the second Blake walked in the door, I knew it was going to be okay. That whatever we decided, we'd be okay, because we were in it together.'

Sissi's hand flexed around hers and Astrid bit her cheek, knowing her friend was thinking how different it had been for her. How Aiden had abandoned her. She hated that her happiness could bring her friend the opposite. 'Sissi...'

'I'm *happy* for you,' she stressed, knowing exactly where Astrid's head had gone.

And Astrid knew she meant it, but...

'I really am, honey. Now let us toast to your happiness!'

They all clinked glasses and Astrid grabbed the OJ she'd set aside so as not to hint at the baby surprise. 'You know—'

Her phone interjected with a buzz and she glanced at the screen.

BLAKE

Do I need to wear my jockstrap? 😊 🥢 🍪

She laughed into her drink.

'What's so funny?' Paige said.

'Blake's asking if he's safe?'

'Safe?' Bella asked.

'He's scared of what you might do to him for getting me pregnant.'

'Well, it takes two to tango,' Paige murmured.

'That's what I said you'd say and for the record, it's what I said too.'

'Oh my God, he really is a pussycat!' Bella laughed out.

'He is and he's all mine – well, *ours*...' She touched a hand to her invisible bump. 'And in a few months, he'll be my husband, which brings me to my next bit of news.'

'Is it *twins*?' Paige asked.

'No! But I'd really appreciate triplets' – three sets of eyes bugged out – 'in the maid of honour sense.'

'Now you're talking!' Paige said.

'*Three* maids of honour, is that even legal?' Bella said.

'It's my wedding, I can have three if I want three.'

The girls squealed with excitement, all save for Sissi who took a calming sip of champagne, then, 'Is *he* going to be best man?'

And Astrid had to dampen the mischief in her smile... because though Sissi wouldn't like her answer now, Astrid hoped with every fibre of her being that come her honeymoon, her friend would be thanking her for more than just the pretty frock.

She'd be heading for her own sparkly rock...

* * *

'You told them then?' Blake said, sweeping her into his arms when she returned home to their house in Brooklyn later that evening.

'Yup.'

He pressed a kiss to her lips. 'About the baby?'

She nodded.

'And the wedding plans? The island location, the wedding party, Aiden...?'

'Mm-hmm.'

'And Sienna?' he said, leaning back so that he could search her gaze. 'She knows she'll have to play nice?'

'I think play nice is a bit extreme. Civil, if he's lucky.'

He gave a low chuckle. 'Aiden's gonna kill me.'

'Sissi didn't kill me.'

'That's because she's had a hand in this from the start, he doesn't even know you two know each other yet...'

'Speaking of which, don't you think it's time you had that conversation?'

'About how my fiancée tried to—'

'No, Blake! We can never tell him that!'

'Just teasing, babe.' He kissed her mortified lips closed. 'But yeah, I know it's time. Though finding the right moment and the right words to tell him his sister-in-law-to-be is best buds with his ex, ain't easy.'

'Better now than on our wedding day.'

'For sure.'

'And once they're stuck on an island together for a whole week, they'll have no choice but to talk and then who knows what might happen.'

'Alright, Little Miss Matchmaker, don't get ahead of yourself. I'm still not convinced we should be using our wedding venue as a neutral battleground for them to sort their shit out.'

'I think it's genius.'

'It could backfire spectacularly.'

'Well if your brother had picked up the bloody phone all those years ago, we wouldn't be in this situation.'

'I might never have met you then.'

She grinned. 'Hell of a Catch-22.'

'But Astrid...?'

'Yeah.'

'We're not going to spend our wedding taking sides, are we?'

'That depends.'

'On what?'

'Whether you choose the right side...'

'I'm starting to wish we'd eloped to Vegas, Twinkle Toes.'

'And miss the opportunity of throwing the best man and maid of honour together... I don't think so.'

'What's a wedding without fireworks, hey?'

'My sentiments exactly.'

* * *

MORE FROM THE KARMA CLUB

Another book in the Karma Club Series, *How to Get Even*, is available to order now here:

https://mybook.to/HowtoBackAd

ACKNOWLEDGEMENTS

Just like the gleaming empty table in snowbound O'Hare airport, projects like these are the stuff of pink magic. You get to collaborate with kindred spirits, soak up the warm and fuzzies at every turn, and feel luckier than a leprechaun on a Just Desserts sugar high. That's me!

And while *The Karma Club* may be fiction, the sisterhood that formed between Amy, Pippa, Clare, and me is as real as it gets. For that, I'll be forever grateful. I adore you, ladies, now bring on the next one!

Of course, no book comes to life without an incredible team behind the scenes. A huge shoutout to Boldwood Books for wholeheartedly embracing something outside their usual wheelhouse – a cross-author series – and doing so with such unwavering passion and commitment. To the team of editors who have helped make this story the best it can be, and to the marketeers for creating a launch plan that zings with Boldwood's famed enthusiasm. I salute you!

Also, special thanks to our commissioning editor, the fabulous Megan Haslam for believing in our vision and paving the way for it to become a reality. We are beyond grateful that you took a chance on us and our girls!

To our amazing readers and reviewers – thank you for picking up everything we put down and for sharing your love of these stories with the world. We couldn't do this without you, and I truly hope this series delivers on your every romance-reader wish. I can't wait to hear what you think!

And last but certainly not least – to my kids, for enduring my endless ice hockey chatter, and to my husband, for always being there. For lifting me up when I feel stuck, letting me ramble through my icky plot points, and generally keeping me sane – I couldn't do this without you. I love you all so very much! xxx

ABOUT THE AUTHOR

Rachael Stewart is a bestselling romance author, writing billionaire romance for Boldwood.

Sign up to Rachel Stewart's mailing list for news, competitions and updates on future books.

Visit Rachael's website: www.rachaelstewartauthor.com

Follow Rachael on social media here:

facebook.com/rachaelstewartauthor
x.com/rach_b52
instagram.com/rachaelstewart3

ALSO BY RACHAEL STEWART

The Karma Club Series

The Payback Plan by Amy Andrews

How to Get Even by Pippa Roscoe

The Puck Stops Here by Rachael Stewart

Settling the Score by Clare Connelly

Boldwood
EVER AFTER

xoxo

JOIN BOLDWOOD'S
ROMANCE
COMMUNITY
FOR SWEET AND
SPICY BOOK RECS
WITH ALL YOUR
FAVOURITE
TROPES!

SIGN UP TO OUR
NEWSLETTER

HTTPS://BIT.LY/BOLDWOODEVERAFTER

Boldw**oo**d